Claire Zorn is the multi-award-winning author of four books for young adults and the author/illustrator of one picture book. She lives on the south coast of New South Wales with her husband and two sons. Her first young adult novel, *The Sky So Heavy,* was a 2014 Children's Book Council of Australia Honour Book for Older Readers, shortlisted in the 2013 Aurealis Awards—Best Young Adult Novel and shortlisted in the 2014 Inky Awards. Her second young adult novel, *The Protected,* was the winner of four awards: the 2015 Prime Minister's Literary Award for Young Adult Fiction; the 2015 Victorian Premier's Literary Awards—Young Adult Fiction Prize; the 2015 Children's Book Council of Australia Book of the Year for Older Readers; and the 2016 Western Australian Premier's Book Awards—Young Adult. It was also shortlisted in the 2015 Inky Awards. Her third book for young adults, *One Would Think the Deep* was awarded the 2017 Children's Book Council of Australia Book of the Year for Older Readers. *When We Are Invisible* is her latest novel for young adults, and the sequel to *The Sky So Heavy*. *Better Days* is Claire's first novel for adults.

Claire Zorn is the multi-award-winning author of four books for young adults and the author-illustrator of two picture books. She lives on the South Coast of New South Wales with her husband and two sons. Her first YA novel, The Sky So Heavy, was a 2014 [illegible]

BETTER DAYS

Claire Zorn

Atlantic Books
Australia

This is a work of fiction. Names, characters, places and incidents are products of the author's imagination or are used fictitiously. Any resemblance to actual events, locales or persons, living or dead, is entirely coincidental.

First published in 2025

Atlantic Books Australia
Cammeraygal Country
83 Alexander Street
Crows Nest NSW 2065
Australia
Phone: (61 2) 8425 0100
Email: info@allenandunwin.com
Web: www.allenandunwin.com

Atlantic Books Australia acknowledges the Traditional Owners of the Country on which we live and work. We pay our respects to all Aboriginal and Torres Strait Islander Elders, past and present.

NATIONAL LIBRARY OF AUSTRALIA
A catalogue record for this book is available from the National Library of Australia

ISBN 978 1 92292 807 8

Typeset in 13/17 pt Adobe Jenson Pro by Bookhouse, Sydney
Printed and bound in Australia by the Opus Group

10 9 8 7 6 5 4 3 2 1

FSC www.fsc.org MIX Paper | Supporting responsible forestry FSC® C001695

The paper in this book is FSC® certified. FSC® promotes environmentally responsible, socially beneficial and economically viable management of the world's forests.

For all the Dorothys who have gone before us, shine on you cut-throat diamonds

'Anything could happen and it usually does.'

AMY WINEHOUSE

PROLOGUE

2013

FROM THE FORTY-SEVENTH FLOOR GRACE COULD ALMOST SEE THE whole of the city. She could perhaps even see her own house. Maybe. She wasn't great with direction—only Grace could get lost in the city she lived in, Ed said. On the writing desk by the window, next to the hotel stationery, Grace's phone pinged again with the eighteenth unread text message from Ed. How she wished he would stop. Turning the phone off wouldn't be enough; the messages would just keep rolling in. Grace briefly considered throwing the phone from the window, but the proprietors of the hotel did not want the guests to access the street via the window and had sealed it shut. Probably a good thing, given the circumstances. Besides, if she were to throw the phone out the window it might hit someone and kill them. Why bring even more misery into this situation?

He was trying to call her now. Again. Oh, Ed. Grace went into the lovely bathroom (freestanding tub for two!) and threw the phone as hard as she could against the tiled wall. She didn't have a very strong arm. The phone clattered to the floor in a rather pathetic fashion.

Next, Grace took a fluffy white bath sheet (sheet!) from the stack under the marble sink, buried her face in it and screamed.

Pretty soon after that her boobs started leaking.

PART ONE

A Crying Bloody Shame for Someone that Fit to Go Up in Flames

1
GRACE

2000

'I CAN'T FEEL SORRY FOR RICH PEOPLE,' NISH SAID. 'IT DOESN'T MATTER what happens to them. I can't feel sympathy.'

Grace was sitting beside Nish in what the university called a garden but was in fact a hundred square metres of half-dead grass between the car park and the engineering building. Nish was dating an engineering PhD student from India. She said Ravi was the dullest guy she'd ever met, but he was obsessed with weightlifting; this, Nish said, meant that he was 'well ripped' and had magical abilities in bed. He could hold Nish above him one-handed while horizontal, apparently. Grace didn't really understand why this was a good thing. She didn't ask. Nish told her anyway—in detail.

Now, Nish was watching a young man with a business haircut approach a gleaming BMW, its lights blinking as he drew near. 'Like, if that bloke got into his Beemer and the whole thing went BOOM, up in smoke,' she said, 'I'd have a hard time feeling sorry for him.' Nish took a swig from a little plastic cup of something the colour of lagoon slime.

'I don't believe you,' said Grace. 'And what is that?'

'Wheatgrass. Flushes toxins. A lot of people aren't even aware that their body is full of toxins—numpties heading for their graves. But for real, if that guy in the suit—that's polyester by the way, that shit never decomposes. Evil. Anyway, if he got into that Beemer and it exploded, I'd struggle to feel sympathy.'

'Why would it explode?'

'That's irrelevant. It's like you're determined not to hear my point.'

'You've got me interested in his backstory.'

'How's this for a backstory: that guy has probably consumed more wealthy-type shit this week than most people do in a year.'

'Wealthy-type shit?'

'Gone yachting, eaten lobster. Do you know lobsters live for, like, a hundred and fifty years? Or they would, if rich tossers like him didn't eat them.'

'I'm just not sure how rich he is if he's wearing a polyester suit. And it's not like he's driving a Lamborghini.'

'If he was driving a Lamborghini I'd put a bloody bomb under it meself.'

'There's something wrong with you.'

'*Me?* He's the one destroying the planet. He's on his P-plates, for fuck's sake, and he drives a BMW. Like, a new one. Look at the shine on it.'

'It's gorgeous. He might be a really nice guy.'

'A nice guy whose priorities are fucked.'

Nish talked a lot about priorities. Priorities, toxins and globalisation. Her plan after uni was to work for a large charity and 'tidy it the fuck up' so they could make some proper money.

Grace had no plan after uni. She was hoping one would occur to her along the way.

When Grace was slaving away for her final high school exams, she hadn't planned on attending a second-rate (perhaps third-) university in a part of Sydney that was formerly a dumping ground for hazardous chemicals. According to Nish, they'd dug a hole for all the deadly shit, put some prefab buildings on top along with a car park and a million-dollar hockey field (a million was a lot of money back then) and baptised it Australia's youngest university. Grace believed what Nish said about all the deadly shit, assuming that because Nish was four years older and had lived in various places across the globe, she possessed a worldly wisdom as yet unearned by Grace.

Nish's family was from India via London, specifically East London—a place Grace knew mostly from her parents' excessive consumption of British police procedural dramas. Grace found Nish's quirks of language exotic and endearing, especially the way Nish inserted the word 'well' before descriptors: well pleased, well chuffed, well ripped, well hot. Nish used a lot (seriously, a lot) of language which would make Grace's mother boil with disapproval, but in Nish's London accent it was somehow forgivable. In 1995, when Nish was eighteen, her father had dragged his family from London to the outer suburbs of Western Sydney so he could take a job at Australia's Youngest University. 'Imagine going from London to Emu fucking Plains,' Nish said. 'Bit of a disappointment that was. And me mum—and I'm not taking the piss—wouldn't leave the house for three months 'cause she thought she was going to get attacked by a fucking emu. Not to mention the bloke next door, complaining any chance he gets that he can smell curry wafting from our house. Honestly, I don't know how

I've survived this long. Me mum, mind you, now complains that she's lived in Emu Plains five years and is yet to see an emu.'

Grace had met Nish's mum several times. She was small and shouty and seemed to enjoy hitting Nish with a tea towel, or newspaper, or whatever was in reach. Nish found this hilarious. 'Her name is Anishka,' Nish's mum told Grace. 'She calls herself this Nish because it is a boy's name and she knows it upsets me. Don't be her friend. She is very silly.'

Grace considered her own life to be quite boring compared to Nish's. She'd lived with her parents in the same house in the Blue Mountains her entire life and at nineteen had never even been out of the country, let alone 'lived abroad', as Nish put it. (Grace loved that phrase—it made her think of big white trans-atlantic ships.) Many people considered the Blue Mountains to be an oasis of scenic bushwalks, clear skies and breathtaking views. Grace had liked it as a child, but by the time she was in her late teens the appeal of pristine wilderness was diminished by the overabundance of fire-stick twirling, *Lord of the Rings* devotees and shops selling incense, cheesecloth clothing and crystals. Her schoolfriends enjoyed getting high in the nature reserve behind the supermarket, while Grace enjoyed discussing the evolution of folk rock and the enduring influence of the Canyon artists. The two seemed to overlap less and less. (Something that would no doubt surprise the Canyon artists.)

Grace had always envisioned herself at Sydney Uni or New South; it didn't matter as long as there were lots of places to see music and not all the guys had posters of Middle Earth on their walls or, worse, Elvish tattoos. Grace imagined living in a share house where she could have interesting conversations about the origins of trip hop, try reading *Ulysses* again (and this time really get it) and maybe even have a tryst with a Spanish philosophy student. (Why Spanish? Nish would ask her. Grace could only guess that it had something to do with Mandy Patinkin in *The Princess Bride*.) She'd wear op shop clothes and spend hours wandering museums and galleries. Or so she'd thought.

After her final exams Grace enrolled as an English major at Sydney Uni and moved out of home into a dilapidated Glebe terrace with rising damp and a neighbour who often mistook her front door for his own (a story Grace believed for a shamefully long time). The sad reality was that in 2000—the festive glory of the Olympics notwithstanding—Sydney lacked the requisite number of museums and galleries to facilitate endless wandering (two hours could cover it), she hated James Joyce and the people who pretended to like him, she failed to meet any Spanish philosophers, and her job at the 7-Eleven on King Street brought far more sexual harassment and vomit clean-up than she'd anticipated. Grace had spent her senior high school years counting down the days until she could leave behind her dull Blue Mountains life, but now the promise of no rent to pay, regular catering, a well-stocked fridge and laundry service had a definite appeal. Besides, she could easily avoid her mother by spending as much time as possible on campus. So, despite all her previous vows never to again live in the mountains, Grace dropped out of Sydney Uni after one semester and enrolled in the Youngest University instead.

Grace met Nish on the first day of second semester, when Nish—wearing a fur coat, mesh miniskirt and Chloé sunglasses, a far cry from the usual Western Sydney attire—took the seat next to her for a twentieth-century music history lecture (a subject Grace had slotted into her vague humanities degree). Because Grace had made no friends as yet, she smiled at Nish, pleased that this cool-looking person had chosen a seat beside her.

'You going to talk during the lecture?' Nish asked. ''Cause I'm here to learn, like. I don't want distractions.'

'I'm not planning on talking during the lecture,' Grace said.

'A lot of people seem to think that this is like a pub. You notice that? It's a disgrace. And do you have a pen I can borrow?'

Grace rummaged through her pencil case and gave Nish a blue pen.

'Do you have black? Sorry, I just fucking hate blue pens. They look amateur.'

'Sure.'

'Look at you with your little pencil case. And you got post-its too. I like that.' Nish eyed Grace's book of class readings. 'May I?'

'Sure.'

'Mate, you got things highlighted. Very nice.'

'Thank you. Have you done the reading?'

'Nah. I'm doing economics, like.'

'With music history?' Grace asked.

'Nah. I'm here to check out the talent, if you follow.'

'Talented musicians?'

'The fellas. I'm here to check out the fellas. Absolutely no talent in my lectures. Zero. Very sad state of affairs.'

'Is that why you enrolled in this subject?'

'I'm not enrolled. A lot of people don't realise this, but you can walk into any lecture and listen in. You won't believe the shit I've been learning. Went to a class on the Roman Republic of third-century BC the other day. Fascinating. I wish I could go to another one but it clashes with my corporate finance tute.'

◎

Two months later in the appalling excuse for a university common space/garden, Nish had finished her rant about not pissing on rich people if they were on fire and was rolling a cigarette. The wheatgrass, she claimed, was just one component in her war against bodily toxins. Nish had devoted herself to a clean lifestyle bar two vital elements: alcohol and tobacco. She theorised, that if she eliminated all other chemicals from her diet, eating only organic produce and shunning genetically modified anything, she could balance out the detrimental effects of those two indulgences.

While Nish rolled her cigarette (organic tobacco), Grace observed as the guy in the suit continued on his path through the car park, beyond the BMW, to a white hatchback with a ding in the rear bumper. 'The suit guy drives a Ford Laser,' Grace said. 'You owe him an apology.'

'Then whose is the Beemer?'

Nish and Grace turned. The only other person visible had shaggy hair and was wearing the baggy style of jeans that were de rigueur in the early years of the twentieth century, the waist-band so low that the band of his Calvin Kleins was visible. (A non-negotiable sartorial style for anyone who refused to work for The Man.)

'*That* guy?' said Nish in disbelief.

'Appears so.'

'Bloody hell. Get a load of him.'

'He's in my music history tutorial.'

'He's well fit. I thought I'd seen all the musos. A very disappointing bunch. There is one who looks like Jeff Buckley, if you sort of squint from a distance. Voice like an eight-year-old girl, though. Or David Beckham in that Pepsi ad.' Nish took off her sunglasses to better assess the owner of the Beemer. 'Get an eyeful of that. How did I miss him?'

'He's not here much. Only been to three classes.'

'You mates?'

'Sometimes we smile at each other.'

'For fuck's sake, you need to make a move.'

'So you'd piss on him if he was on fire?'

'It'd be a crying bloody shame for someone that fit to go up in flames. That said, you need to put a firecracker under Dorothy's arse and he might just be the firecracker.'

'Please don't make this about my mother.'

'Love, everything with you's about your mother. Anyway, he's too young for me.'

'Plus you're with Ravi.'

'Go say hi,' Nish said. 'He's getting closer.'

'I can't just strike up a random conversation.'

'Look at you! You're gorgeous, what with your legs and your hair and all that. He should be so fucking lucky!' Nish stubbed out her cigarette and stood up.

'No,' said Grace. 'Please.'

'Leave it with me,' Nish said.

Grace watched in horror as she approached him.

'Oi,' said Nish to the guy. 'Cobain, tell me that's not your car.'

The hot guy stopped walking.

'My mate over there said that if it exploded she wouldn't feel sorry for you. She's anti-capitalist.'

Hot Guy looked appropriately startled until he saw Grace.

She stood up and brushed dead grass from her skirt. Grace didn't usually wear skirts so short, but she'd been trying to annoy her mother that morning and she'd thought a short skirt would be guaranteed to do so. (Dorothy had been strangely silent in response.)

'Is my car going to explode?' he asked Grace.

'Is there someone who wants you dead?'

He frowned in mock concentration. 'Not today. And if you're anti-capitalist, doesn't that make you a communist?'

'I don't think so.'

'Bollocks,' said Nish. 'You think Che Guevara is hot.'

'Is it me or the car you have a problem with?' he asked.

'I never said I wanted it to explode. I like your car. Six-cylinder, right?'

'I don't . . . It's my dad's, so . . .'

'Grace has a pathetic admiration of auto engineering and flagrant disregard for the future of humanity,' said Nish. 'Other than that, she's excellent company.'

'I don't doubt it.' He grinned at Grace. 'Good to properly meet you, Grace. Strange but good. Please don't put a bomb under my car.'

'She'll reconsider,' said Nish.

They watched as he turned and walked away.

'Nish, you're a complicated person to be around,' Grace said.

'I just did you an enormous bloody favour.'

◎

The following day Grace was taking her seat in the lecture theatre when she spotted the hot guy across the room. He seemed to notice her at the same time. It was truly a magical moment. He smiled at her like she was an old friend. The lecture began and still he kept smiling until Grace giggled like an idiot and the lecturer paused, annoyed by the interruption.

After class, the hot guy waited for Grace by the door.

'I'm done for the day,' he said. 'Do you have another class?'

'No.' This was a lie; Grace had another lecture in forty-five minutes, followed by a commerce tute (commerce being a subject Grace's mother had insisted she study).

'Do you need a lift to the train station?'

And that was how Grace ended up in the passenger seat of Hot Guy's father's BMW, exiting the car park at the very same moment as her lecture began.

'It sounds amazing,' Grace said.

He gave her a puzzled look.

'The car,' she clarified.

'Thanks?'

Grace eyed his admirable forearms. His hands were perfect too: finely sculpted without being dainty. Grace knew she could never love a man with dainty hands.

'Where do you live?' he asked, shifting the BMW into third. It made a low growl as he accelerated out of the corner.

'Bullaburra. It's an hour—'

'I'm just up the road. Katoomba.' He didn't look like he was from Katoomba—no ratty dreadlocks or hemp fisherman pants. 'I can drive you,' he said.

'Are you sure?'

'Of course!'

Grace imagined sliding her palm up his forearm, slipping her fingers under the edge of his t-shirt sleeve. It was a white t-shirt, screen-printed with the words *Grotty Maverick* in brown.

'What's Grotty Maverick?'

'Oh.'

'What is it?'

'It's just . . . you know . . .'

'No, I don't.'

'It's a band. I'm in it.'

'What do you play?'

'Guitar and vocals. To be honest, I think it's a bit of wank to wear a t-shirt with your own band name on it. But we have a gig coming up on the twenty-fifth of September and we need to promote it. Baz—he's in the band—says we should wear the t-shirts. I also have to put up those.' The guy flicked his head in the direction of the back seat, where an open cardboard box revealed a stack of poorly designed flyers. 'Baz made them. But he forgot to put the date on, so first I have to add that to a hundred posters.'

'He should do it.'

'Baz has crap handwriting. It would be illegible. Anyway, I can stick a bunch up in Bullaburra when I drop you off.'

'I'm not sure it's worth it. Only about five people live there, and I'm the only one in your demographic.'

He laughed and, keeping one hand on the wheel, he twisted his lovely torso around and reached into the back seat for a poster, his hand brushing Grace's hair in the process.

It was an awful poster: an illustration of cartoon worms wriggling out of a wheelie bin.

'I'll be sure to write the date on it,' Grace said.

'Ha. Good. That just leaves me with ninety-nine.'

'How long have you been in the band?'

'Six months. Baz started it. He plays guitar and he used to sing, but . . . oh, man, I shouldn't say.'

'Now you kind of have to.'

He glanced at Grace. Nish had called him Kurt Cobain, but she was wrong. He was a definite James Dean type. Grace had never seen a James Dean movie but she had seen a picture of him in one of her mum's magazines a few years ago. It was an article about hot men who were tragically dead. Grace's fifteen-year-old self had agreed that, yes, it was very much a shame that James Dean was dead. (But then again, as Nish later pointed out in a conversation about hot guys who were tragically dead, Dean would have been sixty-nine by then, so less likely to be hot at that stage.)

This hot guy took a corner at a frustratingly slow pace, but the tendons in his forearms looked fantastic as he shifted gear.

'Baz's a great guitarist,' he said.

'I'm sure he is. But?'

'Man, he cannot sing for shit. I think he thought he sounded like the guy from Joy Division . . .'

'Ian Curtis?'

'Yeah. Him. But. The band recorded a couple of songs and Baz listened to them and I guess he had a moment of, like, deep introspection and realised maybe he wasn't Ian Curtis. Maybe he was just . . .'

'Bad?'

'Yeah. So anyway, we were mucking around in our composition class and I sung a bit and he asked me if I wanted to join the band. So that's how that happened.'

'Do you write the lyrics?'

'Yeah.'

'Have you played many gigs?'

'Um.' He grinned, glanced at her again. 'Three or four. There aren't that many venues up here. And there's a bit of an organisation issue—as in there's not much organisation. But we've got that gig happening at the uni bar.'

'On the twenty-fifth.'

'Exactly . . . You should come.'

◎

An hour of thoroughly enjoyable conversation passed before Hot Guy pulled up in front of Grace's house. Although the front garden was just lawn and pruned roses, it was neat beyond what should be possible. All the roses were white, which created a more uniform look, according to Dorothy. 'The impression one gives on the outside says so much about what's on the inside,' she said to Grace. Many times.

'I thought you weren't supposed to judge a book by its cover,' Grace had responded.

'Darling, that's about the appearances one can't change, not ones you have full control over. And people do judge, so it's best to be on the front foot.'

Now, Grace looked at the perfectly bland garden and wondered what it was telling the hot guy about her family. Her mother's car—a sensible Camry—was parked in the drive. Dorothy would have already looked out the window and seen her daughter arrive home with some mysterious guy. Grace didn't want Dorothy to be on the front foot.

'Do you want some help with writing the dates on the posters and sticking them up?' Grace asked. 'I have nothing else to do.'

Another lie; Grace had three essays to write.

'It's kind of a big job,' Hot Guy warned.

The venetian blinds in the kitchen window twitched.

'I'll do it if you give me a drive of the Beemer. Deal?'

'Hell yeah.'

2

APRIL 2022

GRACE HAD THOUGHT OF NISH AS SHE STOOD IN THE DEALERSHIP GAZING at the Lamborghini. (Would Nish want to put a bomb under it?) The glass-walled dealership was like a patisserie for wealthy people—so many opportunities for decadent consumption. Grace was determined not to feel guilty for what she was about to do. Besides, she would cancel out this indulgence by giving the same amount to charity. Some people squandered their wealth on five cars and a temperature-controlled garage to keep them in, but Grace had never done that; Ed wouldn't have let her, even if she had wanted to. She'd waited years to buy a car like this, and she wouldn't keep it long anyway. She'd set it on fire and push it into a pond or something.

Ed didn't appreciate cars. He wasn't that kind of guy. But to Grace, driving a well-designed car was like being inside a song—it was sublime to experience something so perfectly formed; a creation of genius, of a mind which operated on a plane most people didn't have access to. Grace didn't possess any kind of genius, but she was good at identifying it in others and had built her career on that very specific skill.

It had been a long time since she'd owned a car like this.

She'd made do for years with a little Volkswagen thing because she didn't need to drive much except around the city. The family car had always been a Land Rover of some variety, sourced by Ed second-hand. They were great for the kids and all their gear. You could just chuck everything in the back and be on your way, Ed said. Only it was never like that. He was so fastidious about packing for holidays that everything had to be put on the driveway and arranged to Ed's specifications by Ed. He would stand back and assess everything visually before he began the game of Tetris, contemplating it with the same expression he wore when he looked at his paintings.

They never went anywhere luxurious on holiday. People in Grace's tax bracket usually went to the Greek islands, or the French Riviera, or the Maldives. But Ed preferred camping or, at his most indulgent, a little cabin somewhere in the bush. And Grace didn't care; she spent enough time in hotels as it was. Besides, as soon as Ed pitched a tent his face would fill with the kind of joy that made Grace's chest crack wide open. The kids loved it too; he would fish with them and build campfires, take them out on the water in kayaks.

Grace didn't do any of those things. Grace made the money that bought the kayaks and the Land Rover to carry them on.

Actually that wasn't entirely fair—Ed's paintings were selling for a decent amount of money now, although he never said that out loud. He couldn't seem to spend any of it. Once a starving artist, always a starving artist, she'd told him. They'd been on holidays at the time—standing by a lake, drinking wine, swatting mosquitoes. Normally he would have bristled at that kind of comment, but instead he'd just laughed.

Grace had wandered into the luxury car dealership this afternoon after a lunch meeting in which she hadn't paid attention to a single thing that was said. She had sat there in the elegant restaurant with the beautiful food and watched as grey clouds rolled through the blue sky towards the harbour, all the while feeling as though her mind was a gong that had been struck with a mallet, reverberations from the blow thrumming in her skull. Grace had excused herself after the main course (she'd been tempted by the lobster but couldn't bring herself to order it), claiming a family emergency. It was true in the sense that her family, the perfect unit she and Ed had formed, was in a state of unprecedented calamity. So.

After escaping the restaurant she could have ordered an Uber to take her home, but the house that used to feel like home was now only a collection of silent and often-empty rooms. Instead Grace wandered. Which was how she came to find herself gazing at the car. When she went in to have a closer look, the sales guy waltzed over, no doubt thinking he knew all about her: some bored socialite whose hubby liked fast cars.

His name was Terry and he had the kind of neck that reminded her of vacuum-packed dog meat. 'This one is a real motoring enthusiast's car,' he said. 'A Lamborghini Huracán.'

'And sadly only two seats,' Grace observed.

Terry laughed. 'If you're looking for a family car you might like the Urus—soul of a Lamborghini in the body of an SUV.'

'I don't want an SUV. What about the Lotus?' It was a lovely little thing by the window; Grace hadn't seen it at first.

'Ah! A Lotus. Very rare to get that sort of drive in a four-seater. Can be a touch tricky to handle. I do find that a lot of ladies like the Porsche 911.'

'It's important that the ladies don't take too much on.'

'I only meant that—'

'I'll take the Lotus.'

'Of course! You are very welcome to do so.'

'I'd like to take it with me now.'

Doubt gathered on Terry's broad pink face. He was wearing a wedding ring; somebody loved that broad pink face. He was probably a lovely guy who had made an unfortunate sexist remark.

'I'm quite serious,' Grace told him. 'I would like to take it now. I don't need a test drive. This is a good day for you, Terry.'

Even though she was being nice, Terry clearly still thought Grace might be a madwoman, and he wanted to faff about with finances and bank approvals and delivery times. Grace made a call and had the money transferred instantly. She asked for the keys and Terry gazed at her like she was made of pure gold.

And yet when she'd taken the Lotus for a little detour onto the motorway, just to see what it could do, the thrill she had expected failed to materialise.

◎

Two weeks later, Grace was yet to park the car in her own garage. Probably because she didn't want to have to explain her one-hundred-and-fifty-thousand-dollar impulse buy to her children. This evening, Grace had driven home after a late meeting and parked the Lotus where she always did, twenty metres down the street from her house. It was a lovely street, lined with Moreton Bay figs, which didn't drive the real estate prices up themselves but were definitely an added bonus. Like a free dessert in a combo deal for the affluent. As Grace pulled into the kerb a big drop of bird poo splatted onto the windshield. Oh well.

And now rain. The Lotus did not care for rain. It emitted a small beep and the wipers started swishing, smearing the poo across the glass in a big arc. Grace watched the arch of poo grow bigger and bigger as the wipers swished. The rain wasn't heavy enough to wash it off. This was like London rain, and Grace spent a while reflecting on that, only to be jolted back into reality by her phone. She expected her nanny's number to show on the screen. It did not.

'Hi, Mum.' Grace hoped Dorothy didn't hear the sigh in her greeting.

'Tell me, are you still coming to visit tomorrow?'

'I am.'

'And you're bringing the children?'

'I've decided they are too young to fend for themselves at home.'

'How are their school holidays going? I do hope they haven't had to spend the whole week with that Lotte person.'

'The Lotte person's name is Lotte. You can just call her that.'

'I'm making lamb for lunch. They will eat that, won't they?'

'Henry probably. May won't.'

Dorothy tutted. 'I don't think that's the right attitude. I was reading about strategies for dealing with picky eaters, and you must go in with a positive mindset.'

'I'll summon a more positive mindset if you have some chicken nuggets for her.'

'You know there's not any chicken meat in those; it's all processed garbage.'

'She seems to still be alive. Can you provide them, or do I need to bring some myself?'

'I wish you wouldn't make jokes like that. And of course you don't need to bring them.'

'I have to go. I'll see you—'

'I do wish you could stay for more than one night.'

'Ed wants to take them camping. We'll drive up tomorrow, have a lovely lunch, stay the night and Ed will pick them up on Sunday. We've talked about this.'

'Yes, but—'

'I have to go.'

'Of course you do.'

The rain was heavier now. It might have been fun if the car had given a little shake to get the water off, like a dog. It wasn't the kind of vehicle to be left out in the elements. Poor thing. Across the street a man in a tight polo shirt was waiting while his small dog did a wee on the trunk of a Moreton Bay fig. He failed to notice when the dog finished its wee—too busy looking at the Lotus. When Grace got out of the car the man gave her a nod. 'Nice car.'

'Thank you.'

Grace locked it and walked in the direction of her house.

'You're not going to leave it out here, are you?' he called after her.

◎

The side gate didn't squeak when Grace pushed it open; she made sure the hinges were kept oiled, so the dog wouldn't start barking and alert the kids to her presence. She removed her shoes and tiptoed along the cobblestone path down the side of the house and into the backyard. She crept past the patio and the pool and into the pool house, where she collected Ed's jumper. She continued on beyond the cubby house and the studio (where, in a haze of grief and thinking it might help, Grace had let herself in and first found the jumper; she had been unable to set foot in there again) all the way to the back corner of the garden, out of sight of the kids if they happened to look out the window. Which they wouldn't, as they would be glued to the television; it was *Survivor* night and there was a strong chance cancer survivor and life coach Mitch would be voted off.

Survivor wasn't always ideal family viewing for a nine- and five-year-old, but at night Grace needed something to dull her mind and all the kids' programs were excruciating except for *Pingu* and, honestly, there were only so many times you could watch a penguin ruin someone's day. May loved *Pingu*; loved anything involving animals. Even the huntsman that took up residence in the laundry was granted amnesty thanks to *Charlotte's Web*. Grace was forbidden from killing anything, no matter how many legs. It was unlikely a bikini-clad marketing graduate from Coolangatta was ever going to need to be ejected from their home, so *Survivor* provided suitable family entertainment in that respect at least.

If Grace hadn't been so late she would have had time for a lie-down outside before *Survivor*, and May would now be snuggling in her flannelette pyjamas on Grace's lap, smelling of strawberry shampoo and occasional farts. Henry would be nestled beside Grace, providing commentary on every *Survivor* challenge.

Grace pulled on Ed's hairy brown jumper and lay down on the grass. Damp seeped through her silk dress. Down low like that, the wind was hardly noticeable. Grace pulled the cuffs of the jumper over her knuckles, breathing in Ed's scent. The wiry hairs bristled on the skin of her neck the way Ed's beard had. She put her earbuds in and looked up into the clouds while she listened to the music and the sky sprinkled small, cold drops of rain on her face. If she'd had hours to spare Grace could have lost them lying there, bathed in sound and colour. But her phone started to ring.

She let it go to voicemail.

It rang again.

Grace reached over and felt for it in the wet grass. *Lotte.* Bugger.

'Grace? I thought you'd be home by now. Mitch got voted off and May is beside herself . . . Grace, are you there?'

Lotte the Belgian Nanny had begun working for Ed and Grace back when Henry was small. Most people would have moved on from nannying by the time they were twenty-eight, but Grace paid Lotte more than any other nanny in the country (she guessed), and because Lotte was attempting a career as a playwright there were few other options for her to ever again earn that kind of money. She was sweet, organised, understood *Minecraft* and the kids ate everything she cooked. Their pyjamas were always washed with fabric softener and Grace never ran out of milk. Lotte was wonderful like that. Wonderful and annoying. Ed used to say that Grace was too hard on her and it wasn't her fault she looked like an elf.

Only a few months ago, during a turbulent flight to Rome when Grace was sure she was going to die, she calculated the ratio of hugs her children received between herself, Ed and Lotte. No matter how Grace did the maths, she would always be at the bottom. She just didn't have the face-to-face hours required to remedy seventy percent of the innocuous injuries sustained by small people over the course of a day. Later, years after her imagined plummet into the sea, Grace's children might put flowers on her grave occasionally, but she feared it would be Lotte they remembered most fondly from their childhood. (Grace had been so busy contemplating this that she hadn't noticed the seatbelt light go off, and was still gripping the armrests when the flight attendant came to offer her a glass of wine.)

What would Ed think of if he were plummeting into the sea? Would it be her? Would it be the kids? Or something like, 'Shit, I haven't paid the school fees, and Grace doesn't know the login for the Parental Portal.'

Then again, Ed would know not to worry about Grace's ignorance. Lotte knew the login.

◎

Inside, Grace dropped her shoes on the floor of the entry hall next to the two pairs of small muddy sneakers. Beside the shoe rack. Which was empty. She dumped her bag on the bench seat that no one ever sat on and pulled the hairy jumper over her head, balled it up and stuffed it in the cupboard under the stairs where Henry used to leave sandwiches for Harry Potter.

Henry didn't do that anymore.

May's wailing could probably be heard from two blocks away; she was like a siren and had nailed the exact pitch that filled Grace's head with white static, like an old TV without an antenna.

The strategy with the tantrums was to ignore them. Don't react. Continue on as if the episode wasn't occurring, Dr Rosie said. She always referred to the tantrums as 'episodes'. It was never 'when May has a tantrum' or 'when May loses her shit' but, rather, 'when an episode occurs', as if May's behaviour was a weather phenomenon: a high-pressure front combined with a blood sugar low that resulted in the occurrence of a tantrum.

But it was difficult to ignore the wailing, like trying to have a conversation while a security alarm was going off. (The acoustics in the house were fantastic.) Grace would quite like to lock

Dr Rosie in a room with May during an episode and see just how long the child psychologist could last without reacting.

May was planted in front of *Survivor*'s closing credits; wet-cheeked, fists balled at her sides. Slinky the dachshund was sitting at May's feet barking. Camilla the Barbie was face down on the polished concrete floor, nude, head on backwards, her shiny torso smeared with bolognaise sauce. Not a good sign. A dirty Camilla was never tolerated.

Adhering to Dr Rosie's instruction of ignorance, Lotte was flitting around in the kitchen, clattering pots and pans and inadvertently adding to the cacophony.

'Look who's here, May!' Lotte exclaimed—pointlessly, because May couldn't have heard her over the screaming and barking. Henry was sitting at the head of the dining table—a position he'd assumed since Ed's departure—and shovelling spaghetti into his mouth, determined not to be interrupted by his sister. Grace kissed the top of his head and then approached her daughter like one would a zoo escapee: quiet, careful, reluctant to have her limbs torn off.

'May? I'm home.' Grace touched her daughter's arm, only to be smacked away. 'Can you lower your voice, please?'

'No!'

'There'll be no bedtime story if this continues,' trilled Lotte.

This pissed Grace off. She did the bedtime story—it wasn't Lotte's to take away. Also, Dr Rosie said that no threats were allowed.

'You should put her outside with Slinky,' Henry said.

May increased the pitch of her shrieking to the point where Grace was sure the lights would start flickering.

'If you don't stop,' Grace said, 'we can't go to Granny and Granddad's.'

What was a threat and what was a consequence? The line was blurred. And it didn't matter because now the wailing had stopped. Cop that, Dr Rosie. Grace couldn't wait to tell her.

May looked up at Grace. She was a tiny little thing, tall for a five-year-old but with spindly arms and legs. Grace fretted a lot over May's lack of weight, as if she might be taken away by a light breeze.

'You don't unnerstand.' This was May's new catchphrase.

'I do understand. It's very upsetting that Mitch is gone. But he's returned home to his family. He's not hungry anymore, and now he has nice warm clothes.'

May frowned at the rolling credits. One deep breath. Two. Then she nodded in grim agreement.

Grace sat at the table beside Henry. He looked at her with suspicion while he ate.

'Why do you have grass in your hair?' He reached over and plucked a long green blade from the back of Grace's head. 'And why are you all wet?'

Henry possessed a level of intensity and seriousness that Grace worried was unnatural for a nine-year-old. He was a prepubescent barrister. A diminutive detective.

'I didn't have an umbrella.'

Henry gave no indication that this was a satisfactory answer.

'It's very windy,' said Grace. 'I think the grass must have . . .'

'Blown into your head.'

'Yes.'

It was a trap. He was setting a trap for her. *We propose that the defendant is lying, Your Honour.*

'I saw you,' Henry said.

'What?'

'Lying on the grass. In the rain. In Dad's jumper.'

'No, you didn't.'

Henry appeared disappointed by the feebleness of her defence. 'What were you doing?'

'Nothing. Relaxing. Thinking.'

'Dad's been looking for that jumper.'

'Henry, if you leave me alone you can have ice cream.'

Bribery or incentive? Again, the line was blurred.

Lotte placed a plate of spaghetti in front of Grace. 'I called the kennel to confirm Slinky's booking,' she said. 'I booked her for the rest of the school holidays. Do you want me to drop her off in the morning?'

Henry's frown intensified. 'We're not taking Slinky to Granny's?'

May, who had again been absorbed into the television screen, snapped to attention. 'Why aren't we taking Slinky?!'

'I thought we were taking her,' said Henry.

'She'll be lonely!'

'She'll make friends at the kennel,' Lotte assured her.

'She won't make friends!' said May. 'She hates dogs!'

'Granny hates Slinky, and Slinky hates the car. A two-hour drive is difficult enough,' Grace said.

May did not think a two-hour drive was difficult enough. She picked up greasy Camilla and launched her, javelin-style, at Grace's head.

'May!' Lotte skipped over and pointed at the doll on the floor. 'Pick Camilla up and apologise!'

This would be the time Ed would have made a joke. *Apologise to Camilla or Grace?*

Nobody made a joke.

May ran screaming from the room.

3

GRACE STOOD IN THE GARAGE AND ASSESSED THE SIZE OF THE LOTUS compared to the amount of luggage waiting to be packed into it. The packing had been complicated; not only did the kids need clothes for a night at Dorothy's but also for a week of camping afterwards. She didn't notice Henry's stealthy arrival.

'Whoa!' he said. He was looking at the Lotus, now slotted in the space Ed's hardy, practical four-wheel drive used to occupy. (Grace had decided it was not a good idea to leave the Lotus abandoned on the street.)

'For real? Is it ours? We have to drive it to Granny's, Mum. We have to. *Whoa!*'

'It's not going to fit everything. And I'm probably going to return it anyway.'

'No, Mum. *Please.*'

'Can you find May?'

Henry gazed at the car for a few more moments and then went in search of his sister.

He soon returned with May, who was attempting to cradle a squirming Slinky in her arms—the dachshund rejecting the plastic baby bottle May was thrusting towards its mouth.

'Slinky is very unsettled,' May observed.

'I don't blame her,' said Grace.

After much arranging and rearranging, Grace managed to strap the kids into the Lotus, with one suitcase on the front passenger seat and another crushed between Henry and May in the back, a backpack on Henry's lap and Slinky on May's. Grace hadn't informed her mother of the unfortunate fact that Dorothy's least-favourite family member would be joining them.

The car wasn't even out of the automatic gates before Slinky began her incessant protest, yapping and yapping directly into Grace's ear—such were the cramped dimensions of the Lotus. Unlike the Lotus, Slinky wasn't Grace's idea. She was Henry's. When Grace had expressed hesitation, Ed said, 'It's not like you'll be the one looking after her most of the time.' Which was true of course, and thus Grace's voting rights were rescinded.

On the freeway now and stalled in Friday afternoon gridlock. Yap, yap, yap. Both children were oblivious in their noise-cancelling headphones. Grace fought the urge to toss the dachshund out the window. Instead she turned the music up. Rage Against the Machine began to boom at a volume that stunned the dog into silence. The car-full of teenage boys beside Grace stared at the deranged woman screaming about the LA police.

Soon enough May was pounding on the back of Grace's seat with her ferocious little feet.

'You forgot Charles!'

'What?'

'Turn down the music! You forgot Charles!'

'May, it is your responsibility to remember your toys.'

'We have to go back!'

'We are definitely not going back.'

'We have to go back!'

The dog took this as her cue to recommence barking.

Grace passed her handbag to Henry. 'There's a bottle of tablets in there. Give Slinky two.'

'What are they?' Henry asked.

'Sedatives from the vet.'

Henry found the small orange bottle in her bag. 'The label says they're for when she's anxious.'

'She's anxious!'

'No, she's not. She's just loud.'

'Henry, give the dog the tablets.'

Henry fixed her with a stern gaze.

'Do it,' Grace ordered. 'Please.'

'No.'

'I want Charles!' screamed May.

And the traffic inched forward.

◎

'I'm hungry,' said Henry.

May and Slinky had screamed and barked themselves into a deep sleep. The traffic had cleared a little and they were finally moving, although this wasn't enough to satisfy Henry.

'Have a banana,' Grace said.

'I don't like bananas.'

This should have been a benign statement. Ed knew Henry didn't like bananas. Lotte knew Henry didn't like bananas. Grace knew that she had come up short. Yet again.

'Have an apple.'

'You didn't pack apples. Can I have chocolate?'

'No. The chocolate is for Granny's.'

'Are we having chocolate?' May asked, woken by her radar detection of the word.

'No one is having chocolate. There are crackers.'

'We ate them.'

'When?'

'Before,' said Henry, a brief note of condolence in his voice. 'Can we have McDonald's?'

'McDonald's! McDonald's!' chanted May.

'No. We're not stopping. If we do, the traffic will get worse and worse.'

The silence of parental victory followed. Until . . .

'I need to do a wee,' said May.

It was no coincidence that May needed to do a wee at almost the exact point in the journey when they were approaching the only McDonald's in the Blue Mountains, a line of cars snaking out of its parking lot.

'Why don't I just pull over, you can do your wee and we'll keep going,' said Grace.

'Do a wee where?!'

'In the bushes.'

'Girls can't wee in the bushes,' said Henry, as if it were a national decree.

'They can. You can, May.'

'I don't want to wee in the bushes!'

'What about food?' asked Henry.

'We can't go into McDonald's with Slinky. We'll get drive-through and I'll pull over a little further so May can go to the toilet.'

'But there's no bushes, there's just people's gardens. She can't wee in someone's front garden.'

'It's fine, she's a little girl.'

'I don't want to wee in the garden!'

'She can't do that, Mum.'

'So what do you propose I do, Henry?'

'It's a toilet emergency now!' screamed May.

'Oh, for frig's sake.'

'Don't swear!'

'Frig is not a swearword, May.'

'Lotte says it is,' said Henry.

'Lotte is not the mum. I am the mum, and I say—'

'I'm going to wee!'

'Don't wee, May. Please.'

Grace did a terrible, terrible thing: she zipped the Lotus into the McDonald's parking lot through the exit lane, bypassing the queue of cars. People honked and shook their fists. She was a self-entitled cow who thought she was above the law because she drove a luxury vehicle. Yes, but she was also a self-entitled cow with a five-year-old on the verge of weeing all over the tan leather upholstery. Grace swung the car into a spot that a retiree was dithering over. The bespectacled man wound down his window and shouted at Grace. At least he was too polite to swear or call her names.

'We can't leave Slinky in the car!' said May, refusing to get out.

'Dogs aren't allowed inside,' said Grace.

'They let assistant dogs in,' offered Henry.

'Slinky has never assisted in anything except chaos,' said Grace. 'She has to stay in the car. Leave the window down a little. She'll be fine.'

'She'll die!' shouted May.

'She won't even notice we're gone,' Grace said.

'Because she'll be dead,' said Henry.

'She won't die,' Grace insisted.

May was crying now. 'Don't make her die!'

'May, we will be very quick. Wee, food, out. We'll eat in the car.'

The crying stopped.

'If she dies can we have ice cream to make us feel better?'

'What? No!'

'Lotte gives me ice cream when I miss Daddy. She says it makes me feel better.'

◎

The line to the women's toilets was very long, and every time the automatic doors to the restaurant opened and closed Slinky could be heard barking from the car. May's lip wobbled and Grace squeezed her hand.

'She won't think we've done this to her,' Grace said. 'She doesn't have that logic. She'll just be glad when we rescue her.'

Animals were so convenient like that.

May was hopping from one foot to the other. Henry had gone quiet.

'Henry, do you need to go? There's no queue for the boys' toilets.'

Henry contemplated the treacherous solo journey.

'I'm not going in there alone.'

'Okay, you can come in with us.'

'But it's for girls.'

'No one will notice.'

The line moved along. Only one person stood between them and the door to the ladies. Henry glanced around.

'You'll be fine going into the men's on your own,' Grace said.

Would he? Her imagination was abuzz with child-abduction/assault headlines, some of them accompanied by Henry's recent school photo. (Such terrible hair, he hadn't even brushed it.) At least if he waited outside the toilets for her there would be a lot of witnesses, therefore a much-reduced chance of abduction. Grace wondered whether Henry could sense her doubt. His face indicated he could.

A woman came out of the toilets. It was now their turn.

'No one will mind if you come in with us,' said Grace.

Henry hovered, uncertain.

The woman standing behind them in line cleared her throat.

'I need to wee!' shouted May.

'Henry, we're going in. I'll meet you out here.'

Grace hustled May through the toilet door.

When they came out, Henry was waiting for them. No visible signs of trauma.

'Did you go to the men's?' Grace asked.

He shook his head.

'But if you need to—'

'We have to get food,' he said. 'Slinky is still barking.'

After five minutes of negotiation about soft drinks and ice cream, Grace ordered the food. She held on to the little ticket with the number on it while Henry and May clambered around on the play equipment and felt grateful for the glass separating herself and the other customers from May's joyous squealing. Grace's number was called and she approached the counter. There was a guy in front of her, telling the teenager behind the counter that the fries were missing from the bag. The skin on the back of his strong neck was smooth and tanned, and there was a curve of a bicep at the edge of his sleeve. Grace's longing for Ed's touch had morphed into a longing for anybody's touch. The undeniably hot man was being very patient with the staff.

Patient but firm. Grace wondered if he had witnessed her terrible behaviour with the Lotus.

The issue with the fries was resolved and the patient/firm guy picked up his brown paper bag and turned around. Grace looked away. She hadn't been admiring him at all.

'Grace?'

4

2000

'WHAT DO YOU WANT TO DO IF HIS BAND IS CRAP?' NISH ASKED. 'STAY and lie? You're a rubbish liar so I'm not loving that option.' She put the beers on the plastic table. Much like with the campus gardens, the university had been aspirational in its declaration that the venue—a low-ceilinged, poorly lit, characterless room with industrial carpet—constituted a bar.

'That was a long line to get in the door,' Grace said. 'They can't be that bad.'

'True,' said Nish. 'Terrible bloody name, though. Did you tell him that?'

'Surprisingly, I chose not to tell him his band had a crap name after he'd driven me to my door.'

'Well, twenty bucks is a bit steep. Can always ask for a refund, I suppose.'

'You can't ask for a refund after a gig.'

'You bloody can. I got one once after Liam Gallagher walked off stage. It was a disgrace. To be fair, those tickets were sixty quid.'

'A bit different then.'

'S'pose. Is that him?'

It was. He was walking across the tiny stage carrying a guitar and wearing a white t-shirt emblazoned with *The Clash*. When he crouched down to plug a lead into the amp his bum crack peeked above the low waistband of his pants.

'Oh dear,' said Nish. 'Maybe you should tell him we can see his arse.'

'I'm not doing that.'

Thankfully he stood up. He fiddled with his guitar. Tested a pedal.

'Hello, ladies.'

Grace turned to see Ravi the Engineering Student grinning in a button-up shirt and knitted vest. She tried to hide her surprise.

'What?' Nish said in her ear. 'Your bloke's here, why can't I bring mine?'

'He's not my bloke.'

'True, let's hear him first.'

'Pardon?' Ravi asked.

'Nothing,' they answered in unison.

Nish ordered Ravi to get them some drinks and he scurried away.

'Don't give me that look,' Nish said. 'He's all right. Patient, like. A good listener and all.'

'I didn't realise you were in it for the conversation.'

After the first song Nish declared that not only could Beemer actually sing, but the song was good.

Grace responded that most musicians could produce at least one good song. If not, then maybe a different profession was in order.

'You know,' Nish said, 'you're at risk of sounding like an arrogant twat.'

'Tautology. A twat is by definition arrogant.'

'Really edging towards full twatdom now.'

'They're taking a long time getting to the next song,' Grace said. 'Maybe they don't have one.' She considered his t-shirt. 'Do you think he really likes The Clash, or does he just have "London Calling" on a mix tape?'

'Would it be a dealbreaker?' Nish asked.

'I don't know.'

The next song was great. The third even better. After that, the person whom Grace guessed was Baz attempted some banter.

'Beemer should have a go at that,' Nish said. 'Can't be any worse than this bloke.'

The band started up again and that was when Beemer/Hot Guy finally peered at the audience. As soon as his eyes found Grace he looked away. Throughout the remainder of the set he never once glanced at the audience again. It was the back wall, the ceiling, his feet.

After the set Grace saw him trying to squeeze politely through the crowd, headed for the bar. He caught Grace's eye and she didn't know if she should smile or pretend she wasn't there. But he made a drinking motion, raised an eyebrow.

'Make it two, buddy!' shouted Nish.

When he arrived with the beers, Nish said, 'You're too kind.'

'So they say.'

'What's your favourite Clash song?' Nish asked him.

'Do you know The Clash well?' he said.

'Do you think 'cause I'm a woman I don't?'

'Um . . .'

Grace kicked Nish under the table.

'I like The Clash!' Ravi piped up. 'That song about London!'

The next band came on (terrible) and Beemer moved his seat closer to Grace.

'Do you know them?' Grace asked.

The music was so loud he had to lean in close to hear her, and when he answered he moved in even closer. Grace could smell his sweat and feel the heat of his body.

'Yeah,' he said. 'What do you think?'

She turned her attention back to the stage. He nudged her with his beautiful arm but she wouldn't look at him.

'Come on!'

'They're okay . . .'

'I can't hear you. Want to go outside?'

◎

It was raining and Grace knew that her hair would frizz as soon as she stepped outside—a shame because she'd spent forty-five minutes trying to straighten it like Joni Mitchell's. (Grace loved Joni; few of her friends had heard of her.) The bass thudded through the walls of the bar. There was nowhere under cover other than a little alcove along the wall where the skip bins were parked. Beemer shoved his hands in his pockets and grimaced.

'Don't you have access to some glamorous backstage area?' Grace joked.

'Yeah, that's it,' he said, nodding towards the skip bins. 'Do you want to go back inside? Or . . .'

'Or?'

'I have an umbrella in my car.'

'How big is it?'

'Not very. You can have it. I'll stand in the rain.'

'And they say chivalry is dead.'

'It is; I'm the only gentleman left.'

'Lucky me.'

He went through with the rigamarole of trying to locate the umbrella, leaning inside, trying to pull his t-shirt down over his crack while feeling for the umbrella under the passenger seat. 'I can't find it.'

'We could just sit in the car?' Grace said. 'My shoes are full of water.'

'Yeah. We can do that.'

He even opened the door for her.

The interior smelled damp and he apologised for it, muttering something vague about a broken seal. Grace pulled out the stack of CDs from the centre console.

'Good luck,' he said. 'They're mostly Dad's. I've got Green Day, though.'

She found Bruce Springsteen and slipped him into the CD player. 'Here we go.'

'You're kidding. *Born in the U.S.A.*?'

'Honestly, this is the best song to test your speakers with.' She cranked the volume and he winced. 'Close your eyes. Block out all the cheesy stuff that tried to imitate it and properly listen.'

He closed his eyes; he had the kind of eyelashes women paid for.

'Think about this song on its own,' Grace shouted over the music. 'It's wonderful'

'Riiiight. So you were saying, about my mate's band?' He still had his eyes closed.

'They're not very good.'

'Oh yeah? So what about my band?'

'You can't say the name.'

'What?' He looked at her then.

'You find it cringey. I've never heard you actually say it.'

'Baz came up with it.'

'It's a shame, because you're good.'

'Sure.'

'I'm not going to lie. I thought you were very good.' Grace continued her search through the CDs. 'Ooooh, look, Fleetwood Mac.'

'No.'

She put *Rumours* on and flicked to 'Go Your Own Way'.

'This is the worst,' he said. 'How can you like this?'

'The drums. You're not listening. Let the beat hit you.'

'Um . . .'

'You need to open up. That rhythm, it's genius.'

He laughed, self-conscious.

'I mean it. You've heard this song in the supermarket, or on the trashy radio stations, but I don't think you've listened.'

'You're very presumptuous.'

She restarted the song. 'Close your eyes.'

She put her hands on his cheeks because already she felt she could do that.

'Mick Fleetwood is an incredible drummer. Let the beat hit your body, let it go where it needs to go. Let it in.'

He listened, taking the assignment seriously.

'Do you get it now?'

He grinned. 'I get it.'

Grace let him go, settled back into her seat, switched to track seven, 'The Chain', and closed her own eyes. The sound danced in her rib cage and beat through the membranes of her skin. It was gold and white stripes thrumming. It was everything.

First she felt the warmth of his face close to hers, then his lips. She kissed him back.

Grace had little experience in this area. There had been a high school boyfriend briefly and a few random kisses at parties, but nothing more because she'd never wanted anything beyond that from those particular people. Grace surprised herself by attempting to climb onto his lap. The steering wheel got in the way. The horn blared. He laughed and tried to kiss her again. It sort of worked but the handbrake was digging into her thigh. Grace retreated back into her seat. The windows were all fogged up and she couldn't catch her breath.

Grace didn't want to leave the bubble of the music and this boy. She didn't know him at all but it was a moment she wanted to inhabit forever. With the rain on the window and the music and the smoothness of his skin under his t-shirt, the way she wanted to climb inside the song with him—this, she understood now, was life. And it was hers.

◎

The bubble was burst when Nish, under a polka-dot umbrella, rapped her knuckles on Beemer's window. He jolted with surprise, pulling back from Grace. When he saw Nish he looked scared.

'You should open the window,' Grace said.

'I don't know if I want to.'

Nish knocked again.

'She's not going to go away,' Grace said.

He wound down the window.

Nish ignored him altogether. 'Let's go,' she said to Grace.

'Where did you get the umbrella?' Grace asked.

'Found it at the door. Come on.'

'I can give her a ride,' Beemer said.

'No offence, love, but she doesn't know you and neither do I. This is all very fucking romantic, but time's up.'

He reached through the window and held out his hand for Nish to shake. 'I'm Trent.'

'That's lovely for you.'

'Nish, I'm fine,' said Grace.

Nish marched around to the other side of the car and opened Grace's door, hauled her out into the rain. 'Say your goodbyes, love. We're out of here.'

It was horrible to be dragged across a car park in the pouring rain when there was an extremely hot guy in a BMW who was intent on kissing Grace.

'You'll thank me later,' said Nish.

'Bullshit.'

'You had two beers, Grace. For someone who falls over after half a bloody Breezer that's a lot. I'm not leaving you in a car with some tosser you just met.'

Grace yanked her arm away. 'Hang on, he was your idea!' she said. 'You started this whole thing!'

Nish just scoffed and continued dragging her towards Ravi's Barina.

'Hi, Grace!' Ravi said from the driver's seat as Grace was unceremoniously shoved into the back.

'He's not a tosser,' said Grace.

'That guy thinks he is hot fucking shit,' Nish said.

'No, he doesn't. And he kind of is hot shit, anyway. They were really good. *Really* good. Ravi, help me out here. Did he seem like a tosser?'

'Well, I actually thought he was quite a nice guy.'

'You don't even know him!' shouted Nish.

'Sorry.'

'Grace, I'm looking after you. There's a process. Make him work a bit harder, yeah?'

◎

The next day Grace and Nish emerged from a lecture to find Trent sitting on a low brick wall outside of the lecture theatre, rolling a cigarette and looking generally cool.

'If he has that guitar with him because he has class and he needs it, you're welcome to keep him,' Nish said. 'But if it's a prop, you gotta return him to the RSPCA shelter because that is pathetic, that is.'

Grace never found out if Trent had actually needed his guitar that day or if it was in fact a prop. It didn't seem relevant.

5

GRACE'S MOTHER WAS ALWAYS DOROTHY, NEVER DOT. GRACE DELIGHTED in calling her Dotty, which made Dorothy seethe and Grace's father say, 'Don't upset your mother'—when upsetting her was, of course, the point. Dorothy had spent her working life as an Office Lady (the most terrifying of ladies) in various schools, where she exerted a level of power disproportionate to her title. Teachers and students alike were terrified of her, probably because of Dorothy's sceptical expression—a way of saying, 'That's what you think, is it?' without even opening her mouth. Those she bestowed it on would inevitably worry about what exactly had provoked Dorothy's scepticism. Clothing? Hairstyle? Life choices? Grace had tried to make peace with the fact that the answer was everything. It was difficult.

When Dorothy was eventually diagnosed with chronic anxiety, it was Grace's turn to be sceptical. Her mother made people nervous, not the other way around.

'It's all about control,' Grace's dad had attempted to explain. 'She's frightened that the world is going to fall apart if everything isn't done exactly to her standards.'

That was ridiculous. Dorothy had already been proved wrong: if the world was going to fall apart because her standards weren't met, it would have fallen apart a long time ago.

It was Dorothy—trim, neat, curated down to the taupe varnish of her manicured fingernails—who answered the doorbell on a Saturday afternoon to find Trent standing on the doorstep, car keys in hand. As was customary for Dorothy, her greeting wasn't a greeting but a question.

'Yes?'

'Is Grace home?'

'And who are you?'

From the kitchen, Grace heard this exchange and—anxious to prevent an interrogation—abandoned the extremely late breakfast she had been eating.

'Leave him alone,' Grace said, inserting her body between her mother and Trent as a barricade.

'I was simply asking—'

'Oh, hey.' Trent did a cute thing with his eyebrows and Grace felt her heart take flight. 'Where do you want to go?'

'Firstly,' began Dorothy, 'I would like to know—'

But Grace was out the door, closing it behind her. In Dorothy's face. Trent was already en route to the getaway car.

'Did you wash it?' Grace asked, admiring the Beemer. 'It looks shiny.'

'Yeah. Washed my hair too.'

'At the same time?'

'Of course.'

'Can I drive?'

Out on the highway Grace slalomed the BMW around the smooth curves.

'Please be careful,' Trent said.

'I know where all the speed traps are.'

'That's not what I meant.'

'Relax, I've done this at least twice before.'

'Where are we going?' Trent asked. 'I like that dress by the way.'

It was a five-dollar Salvos find, blush pink and, as Dorothy had pointed out, technically a petticoat.

'The most amazing place in the world. Or Sydney. You'll love it.' Grace reached one hand behind to the back seat, where she had flung her bag, while simultaneously navigating a sharp bend in the road.

'Can I?' He was watching both her and the road.

Upon retrieving the bag Grace told him to pull out the CD.

'What's this?' he asked.

'It's Pink fucking Floyd, you numpty.'

A two-hour drive: down the mountains, through the flat western suburbs and into the choked streets of the CBD. Grace had to go around the same block three times before she found the entry to the parking station, then it was a ten-minute walk via Chinatown, doubling back because she went the wrong way.

'Are you sure you know where you're going?' Trent asked. 'I'll happily follow you around, I'd just like to know if there's going to be food at some point.'

'Yes. No. I've been here with Nish. Be patient.'

It was a black door below an arrow with the word *Souper*, hand-painted and far too small. Down a narrow staircase to another doorway, this time manned by a bouncer in a fedora who demanded ID. He examined both drivers' licences before grunting approval.

The room beyond was all heat, colour and noise. No windows, walls covered in posters. The nine musicians crammed onto the stage were producing a racket that could be best described as experimental jazz. Whether the experiment would succeed was yet to be determined. Trent looked like he'd fallen through the looking glass into a peculiar world where steins of beer and bowls of soup were served through a hole in the kitchen wall by a grumpy woman with a mohawk. They found a spot to sit on one of the long shared tables, squashed beside a bunch of rowdy old guys in three-piece suits.

'Do you like jazz?' Trent asked.

'Not really. But I like it here. It feels like something's . . . happening. Do you ever feel like your world is too small?'

'It's only just occurred to me that it might be.'

◎

The I Want to Know Everything About You phase began at Souper and grew and grew until it consumed Grace entirely. There was so much to know and so little time, given that much of it was spent kissing in various states of undress. Most of that happened at Trent's house, which they had to themselves whenever Trent's father—a sweet, affable man, who always seemed pleasantly surprised whenever he saw Grace—was at work.

Trent's mother had passed away when he was five. He had few memories of her, the sharpest of which was in a store—it must have been the National Geographic shop, he said—where she bought him a small collection of beetles, preserved in perspex, treasured and now kept in a shoebox under his bed with other memorabilia from his childhood: bits of shell, interesting rocks, birthday cards from grandparents now gone. He showed Grace these things during an intense session of Getting to Really, Truly Know You, which was soundtracked by Massive Attack's album *Mezzanine*. The music had brought the precious shoebox to Trent's mind because of the stag beetle on the album cover.

'I should probably throw it all out,' he said.

But not as if he believed it; more looking for reassurance, Grace thought.

'That would be the worst thing you could do,' she said.

'What do you think I should do with it then?'

'Give the box to me. I'll look after it until you miss it and want it back again.'

They lay side by side on his bedroom floor, listening as 'Black Milk' played. The single bed being too narrow to accommodate them both, plus, Grace shared, lying on the ground, looking up at the ceiling or the sky was the perfect way to listen to music. The carpet in Trent's room had once been shagpile but was now flat with a polyester sheen. Bits of blu-tack, smooth and hard, were stuck in the fibres. Grace knew that when she sat up there would be bits of fluff and crap in her hair (Trent was a grub), but she didn't particularly care. Candlelight flickered on the walls; she liked that he'd lit them, even if it was a bit Hobbitty.

Trent turned to look at her. He took her hand, laced his fingers through hers. 'Gracie.'

'Yes?'

'I love you. I know that's intense and it's probably too much too soon, but I do. I love you.'

Dorothy and Warren didn't talk about love. Warren had spent hours quietly building Grace a cubby house without the requisite skills, splinters in his hands. Then there were all the nights he'd picked Grace up from her high-school restaurant job, from gigs, even buying her and her mates a six pack of Bacardi Breezers before he drove them to a party. *One each, that way I know what you're drinking and you won't break the law for it.* And Dorothy. Grace assumed her mother's persistent scrutiny was motivated by some variety of maternal bond. But Grace had no memory of her parents ever looking her in the eye and saying the words 'I love you'.

It felt good.

'Because I've realised,' Trent continued, 'that I can't be without you. You're my muse. You're the reason I make music. I woke up in the middle of the night and it came to me: I need Grace. I *need* you. Man. So intense, hey.'

He held her hand against his chest; she could feel his heart pounding.

'I love you too,' Grace said.

Trent held her hand a breath longer. Then he let it go and sat up. 'Whoa, it's late. We've been here for hours.'

Cool air touched the skin of Grace's hand where he had been holding it.

◎

The first time Grace stayed the night, Trent's room was tidier than she had ever seen it. He'd also bought a new set of sheets, later admitting that there might have been a bit of planning going on beforehand. Trent didn't know you were supposed to wash the sheets first and when Grace woke up in the morning her white t-shirt was covered in blue marks. They hadn't had sex. They'd tried but Grace hadn't been able to stand the discomfort. She'd apologised too much, was annoyed about how sorry she was. She worried there was something physically wrong with her and that's why it hurt. He reassured her that there wasn't and that he didn't mind. He promised that he wasn't disappointed. A part of her wanted him to be disappointed.

It took two more tries to get it right, and when they did Grace felt a bit underwhelmed by the whole experience. It wasn't as good as she'd hoped and felt a bit more like a procedure than something you would actually enjoy. She'd preferred the feeling of just lying beside him with her head on his bare chest.

Grace asked Nish if it got better and Nish had laughed. 'No need to get better—I loved it from the get-go. I think. Can't actually remember my first time. I was pretty pissed.'

Grace wished she could ask Dorothy.

Trent was always enthusiastic about sex and Grace started to feel like he thought it was a guaranteed event every time they were together. But it did get better. Or maybe she just learned to relax.

◎

Nish told Grace that it was typical of her to fall for a guy with a guitar and a sob story. 'Are you sure his mum is even dead?' she asked. They were in the beer garden (a rectangle of threadbare astroturf) of the uni bar, sitting at a picnic table that was impossible to get in and out of wearing a skirt without showing your undies. Grace would have liked to tell Nish to fuck off but she had never done that in an un-ironic way before and the prospect was scary. Even more so now when, at five past noon, Nish was on her third beer; Grace barely through her first.

'You need to calm down, you do,' said Nish. 'You've seen him every fucking day for six months.'

Grace's courage and general irritation with Nish had been brewing over the last few months as Nish continued to insist that Trent wasn't interested in Grace as a person, but rather as a subject he could write songs about. 'What should I do?' she asked. 'Treat Trent like crap but sleep with him every now and again? I would rather have an actual meaningful relationship.' She hadn't mentioned Ravi by name, but the implication was clear, she thought.

'If you think a twenty-year-old guy is looking for meaningful, I've got some news. And don't you dare judge me and Ravi. He's a good guy.'

'You treat him like crap!'

'And I apologised to him for that. Doesn't matter anyway. He finished his PhD and is going back to India.'

'Oh. I'm sorry. You never said.'

Nish stubbed a cigarette out on a soggy coaster. 'It doesn't matter.' She watched it smoulder and hiss, and when she looked up at Grace there was no humour in her eyes. 'I'm saying be careful.'

Grace used to think that Nish was wise, but now that Grace was in a mature, committed relationship she saw that Nish wasn't wise, just pessimistic. She could find the darkness in anything. Probably enjoyed it.

'He's an artsy musician type who clearly feels everything at a stratospheric level,' Nish continued. 'It cuts both ways. That kind of guy is a pendulum. He'll swing away from you as fast as he's swung towards.'

Nish and Grace had never had an actual disagreement—probably because Grace never contradicted the rubbish Nish spewed out.

Grace stood up (with difficulty due to the stupid picnic table). 'I need to go to the library.'

'I'm not trying to piss you off. Honest. I love you like a sister. More than, because my sister's a bitch. What can I say? I don't trust him.'

'You don't know him like I do. Good guys do exist. You don't have to ruin it.' Grace had to hold the front of her skirt down while she stepped over the seat.

'I'm not trying to ruin anything, but go ahead, do whatever you want.'

'Thank you. I will.'

◎

Nish was jealous. It was clear. She resented that Grace had found the kind of connection with a guy that she had obviously never experienced. She'd messed up her thing with Ravi and now he was gone. And the thing that really, truly pissed Grace off about this conversation was the way in which Nish's negativity disguised as care mirrored Dorothy's. Dorothy didn't even try to like Trent; it was as if she didn't trust anyone who wasn't opposed to everything Grace did, said or believed, just on principle. Grace was so preoccupied by her fury at Nish and by extension Dorothy that when she got to the library she couldn't concentrate on the essay she was supposed to be writing. So she messaged Trent and told him that she was available for the band meeting after all.

Baz and two other members of Grotty Maverick—Emma and Steve—lived in a share house in Katoomba. 'House' was a generous term for the collection of four small rooms (one of them passing as a kitchen due to the fact it had a lino floor, a sink and a stand-alone cooker) with no heating other than a wood burner complete with clogged chimney. Nobody knew how to light the thing anyway, Trent said. The bathroom was separate from the rest of the place, down a cracked concrete path in the backyard. It was just a loo with a shower head fixed to the wall and no mirror—which Grace felt explained a lot about why Baz looked the way he did. (Feral, Dorothy would have said.) Trent was keen to move in, which Grace found perplexing.

Despite the shambolic nature of the house, Grace liked being there when the band were jamming. She never watched, but would sit at the kitchen table and pretend to study while she listened. It felt like Trent was responsible for eighty percent of the music they made and the rest of them were along for the ride.

This afternoon Grace had been invited to join them for what they loosely called a meeting. She had spent a good portion of the previous week in conversation with managers at various bars in Sydney and had lined up three, possibly four gigs. The rest of the band just needed to be brought up to speed before dates were scheduled. Although, the way things were going it seemed like Baz and Trent were the only ones interested in what Grace had to offer. Emma and Steve, who were drinking beers and playing Xbox, only seemed to engage when Grace mentioned Sydney.

'You mean we have to drive all the way to the city?' asked Emma.

'These are good venues,' Grace said. 'If you want to move on from the uni bar or the bowling club you need to—'

'What if we're okay with the bowling club?' said Emma.

'We have a good following here,' said Steve. 'I'm fine with the bowling club.'

Exasperated, Grace looked to Trent, expecting him to be the voice of reason. For a moment it seemed like he might speak up. The moment passed.

'If you play these gigs you'll make more money.'

'If people come,' said Steve.

'It's a long way to go if no one shows up,' said Emma.

'If I can get you a Friday or Saturday night, that won't be an issue,' said Grace. 'People always show up.'

'But the venues will take a bigger cut.'

'The cover charge is higher. Once you make some money, we—you—can record some tracks and get some airplay. On the radio.' Again she looked to Trent for support but he didn't meet her eye.

'We know what airplay is,' said Emma.

'I just don't get why you're so interested,' said Baz.

'Because I think you have something. Honestly, if I didn't think you were any good I'd stay out of it. You could be big—but it takes work.'

Baz glanced at Trent, who just shrugged and cracked his beer open, but Grace caught the brief flicker of irritation that passed between them.

◎

Trent and Grace were sitting at a cafe reading the Saturday paper together (like a proper, sophisticated, adult couple) when Trent ripped a page from the travel section and slid it across the table to Grace. There was a sunset photograph of a piazza with a marble fountain and the sea in the distance.

'That's Trieste,' Trent said. 'That's where we'll go. We'll eat pizza and swim in the Adriatic Sea.'

'When?' Grace wasn't paying much attention—Trent had a habit of making ambitious, grandiose statements, knowing how ridiculous he sounded and not caring. Grace felt as though up until she met Trent she had been in the company of overly serious people. Even Nish. Especially Nish.

'June. We'll backpack.'

'I have uni,' Grace said. Trent had already dropped out of university. A degree would keep his dad happy, Trent had said, but maybe he needed to stop trying to keep his dad happy. Let that go.

'It's best to travel in their summer,' Trent argued. 'So many jobs. We don't have to go to Italy first. What about France? Do you want to go to France first, then Italy?'

'I have uni,' she repeated.

'So defer. Have a break. What are you even studying for anyway? You've already said you don't know what you're going to do with a degree. Come away. Think. Give yourself time.' He was watching her in that way he had. With a searing intensity. Like she was a wondrous creature he'd just discovered. 'You can finish uni whenever.'

'I'm supposed to be moving in with Nish. That flat in Enmore?'

'It's okay to change your mind. We'll go to France, Italy, Spain. Six months, maybe longer. Then we can come back and get a place together.'

◎

Grace chose to break the news to Nish when they were at Nish's favourite pub, the one beside Newtown station with black-and-white pictures of train crashes all over the walls.

Nish slammed her beer glass on the table. 'You're *what?*'

'I'm sorry, I—'

'I've already put in the rental application! The real estate guy said we're a sure thing. And now you're going off on the whim of some bloody Romeo?'

'I've always wanted to travel. This is perfect timing.'

'Perfect timing for his raging hard-on!'

'You'll find someone else, Nish.'

'I don't want to fucking find someone else. You agreed. You committed. And what? I'm just going to have kick them out when you saunter back into my life like the fucking sea breeze?'

'No.'

'What then?'

'When I get back, Trent and me, we're . . .'

'What?'

'Moving in together.'

'Oh, fuck off. That is well out of line, that is.'

'I'm sorry.'

Nish shook her head. 'I don't want to bloody hear it. *I'm* supposed to be moving in with you.' Her voice wavered. 'My best friend.'

'I'm sorry,' Grace whispered.

Nish downed the rest of her beer. She wiped her eyes and slung her bag over her shoulder, walking a wobbly line out of the pub.

During the last two months of semester, Nish was fine sometimes, but colder in other moments. Grace was sad about it, but not enough to put any real effort into mending their relationship. Their friendship was flimsy and shallow compared to what she had with Trent. She couldn't believe how long it had taken her to see it.

After their final exam Grace and Nish went out with a bunch of classmates to a bar in Sydney. Nish had some acid and she offered some to Grace, who declined. Later, on a heaving dance floor, Nish pulled Grace in close, wrapping her arms around Grace and slurring in her ear, 'I fucking love you, mate. You know that, right?'

Grace caught the two a.m. train home afterwards, reeking of cigarette smoke and her own sweat. The next day she awoke at midday to a voicemail from Nish: *'I'm getting on a plane to London.*

Need to go home. It won't be any fun here without you and Rav. My aunt has a flat I can live in. Didn't want to tell you, fucking hate goodbyes. If you're in Europe with Romeo, email me.'

Grace listened to the message three times to make sure she'd heard it correctly. Nish was gone.

6

APRIL 2022

TRENT WAS THE SAME: CHEEKBONES IN THE PERFECT PLACE, SMILING blue eyes, a level of scruffy that only seriously good-looking people can get away with. At first he seemed as shocked as she was. Then he caught up and produced a grin. Some people would say it was the shit-eating kind. Nish would have been one of those people.

'Grace.'

She wasn't doing the right thing with her face. She should smile and be friendly: *How are you? So good to see you!* But Grace didn't say anything. The glimmer in his eye faltered a touch. It would have been barely detectable to anyone who didn't know him like she did. The smallest crease formed between his eyebrows; a questioning look, like a dog expecting a treat and wondering why it hadn't arrived.

'Grace Harlow? It's me.' He searched her face.

The teenage McDonald's worker called Grace's number again.

'It's me,' Trent said again. 'It's Trent.'

Still, Grace failed to make any sort of sound or movement.

'Trent Keaton,' he said.

People in the queue around them were watching now.

Grace, regaining slight control of her nervous system, looked past him to the counter. 'Excuse me, I just need to . . .'

'Sure, sorry.'

He stepped out of her way. Grace collected the paper bag and drinks tray. It wasn't easy as the drinks were overfilled and the weight of the three cups unevenly distributed. Such was his nerve that he attempted to help her and she found herself jabbing him with her elbow to prevent it.

She could feel his eyes follow her as she walked away.

Cheeks ablaze and concerned she might have forgotten to put on deodorant, Grace was halfway across the pedestrian crossing when she realised what she *had* forgotten and stopped in the middle of the road. A horn blared and it shocked her back into life. Grace raced back through the sliding doors, drinks sloshing everywhere, and into the restaurant play area, where her offspring were oblivious to the fact that their mother had momentarily forgotten their existence. Trent was still standing at the bloody counter watching her.

Henry saw Grace, dutifully collected his sneakers and sat down to put them on.

'What's wrong?' Always his first question these days, because there was always something wrong, it was just a matter of what.

'Nothing. May!'

Grace's daughter was halfway down the slide. Halfway and not moving. Progress had stalled, whether voluntarily or involuntarily.

'May, we're going!'

'I'm stuck!'

There was no conceivable way the girl could be stuck unless she had been struck by some sort of Wonka-esque curse and transformed into a giant blueberry on account of her negative response to everything that was asked of her.

'Is she stuck?' Grace asked Henry.

He shook his head.

A sort of numbness had spread through Grace; she was unable to move on to the next step of her day, the step that involved extracting her five-year-old from McDonald's.

'If we don't go now Slinky will die!' shouted Henry.

That got everyone's attention, including May's. In an instant, she was running towards the exit, stopping only to pick up her yellow sandals. That was, until she noted that Grace was not carrying ice cream.

'You didn't get ice cream!'

'No. Put your sandals on.'

May didn't bother with second gear, she slipped straight into sixth, releasing a scream worthy of a Hitchcock film.

'Stop screaming,' Grace ordered. 'We're leaving.'

May threw her sandals at Grace. The other restaurant patrons were being treated to a good show—Trent among them, no doubt. Grace handed Henry the drinks tray and bag of food, and hoisted May up. She carried her squealing, squirming daughter under her arm across the car park.

By the time they reached the car May was silent. (Was this a win? Grace wasn't sure; no doubt Dr Rosie would tell her.) Slinky could again be heard scrambling and barking from within the Lotus. Grace put her daughter on the ground, took the food from Henry (the drinks now half empty) and put it all on the roof of the car. She fished around in her bag for her keys among the lucky dip of tissues, lip balm, hair elastics and band-aids. A few long moments passed when Grace was sure she'd lost her keys, until, yes, there they were. She wasn't completely useless after all. Grace unlocked the car and opened the door.

'Grace!'

She froze. Trent was jogging towards her.

Slinky did not freeze. Instead the dog jumped out of the car and took off across the asphalt.

'Fuck,' said Grace.

'Slinky!' screamed Henry.

'Fuck!' screamed May.

Trent, however, did not take note of the fleeing dachshund and continued his determined path towards Grace. 'Grace, I'm sorry, I can't just let you walk away—'

He saw it now, the dog galloping at full pelt on its ridiculous little legs.

'Oh.'

'Wait there with Trent,' Grace said to her children and took off after the dog.

'Who's Trent?' Henry called out after her.

But there was no time. Slinky had exited the car park via the IN lane.

And out onto the road.

And now here was a red Toyota Yaris zipping along.

Intercepting the dog.

◎

Grace gathered Slinky's little body into her arms. The driver of the Yaris—a woman in her sixties—was crying in a way Grace resented; it wasn't her dog, it was Grace who had the right to cry, but she didn't have time. Grace carried the animal to the side of the road and sat on the kerb, wrapping the little thing in her skirt as best as she could. (It wasn't working very well; the skirt was too short.) The dog's chest rose and fell, rose and fell. Don't you dare die, thought Grace. It would be the ultimate act of disobedience.

'I'm so sorry,' sobbed the woman. She was wearing activewear and ugg boots. Grace felt inexplicably annoyed by this. Who was this woman trying to kid? She wasn't going to the gym, she was going to McDonald's.

'It wasn't your fault,' Grace said. 'She ran out in front of you.'

'I'll do anything!' pleaded the woman, and Grace was still trying to work out what she meant (a deal with God?) when Trent appeared. He whipped off his t-shirt, revealing his well-ripped torso, an act which silenced the sobbing woman. (Did Trent go to the gym now? Grace had a clear recollection of him mocking the jocks who used the uni gym—something about them being motivated by vanity.)

Trent handed Grace his t-shirt. 'Here, wrap her up.'

'Where are the kids?' Grace asked.

'They're with Shaleah.'

'Who?'

'Please,' said the woman, 'what can I do to help?'

'Nothing, it's fine,' said Grace, even though there was nothing fine about the situation, what with the half-dead dog in her lap and her children in the care of a stranger.

'The vet on Rickard Street isn't there anymore.' Trent had his phone out, tapping away. 'There's one on . . . Nicholas Parade. What's your number? I'll send you a pin.'

Grace recited her number. A few more taps from Trent and her phone pinged.

'Or just let me drive you,' he said. 'I'll be careful with your fancy car.'

'What? No.'

'You're shaking.'

'I can drive. Please just go away now.'

Grace wrapped the dog up in the t-shirt and tried to get to her feet without showing every passing car her undies. Trent didn't go away; he held his arms out. Grace huffed and handed Slinky to Trent like a baby. He looked like something from a charity calendar: *Hot, Probably Unemployed Guys With Dogs*. Rapidly expiring dogs in this case. Trent was very gentle when, once Grace was on her feet, he passed Slinky back to her. It was impossible not to imagine him holding a newborn.

On the walk back to the car he kept glancing over at her, an annoying level of concern in his gentle eyes.

'I'm sorry. That was totally my fault.'

Grace was so overwhelmed by the number of things he could be referring to that she didn't reply.

Beside the car, a young woman in the kind of denim shorts easily confused with underwear was talking with Grace's children. May saw Grace with the dog and came running.

'Is she okay? Is she dead? Is she squashed?'

'She's not squashed, but she needs to go to the vet,' Trent said.

The girl in the shorts peered at the dog. 'Oh my god! I'm so glad she's okay!'

'She's not okay,' said Grace. 'Is this your daughter?' she asked Trent. She knew the answer.

'No, she's . . .' He trailed off. Shanilah or whatever her name was looked at him, waiting. But Trent didn't finish his sentence. Shanina's smile faded.

Grace opened the car door and May, whimpering, climbed through to her seat in the back, beside Henry who was already in, buckled and ready to go. If there had been a siren available he would have put it on. As Grace passed the bundle of dog to him she could see he was doing his very best not to cry. 'I think she might be okay,' Grace said. Henry nodded. Grace stroked his hair, then May's. 'Talk to Slinky. It will keep her calm. You're both doing really well.' As she spoke to them, Grace told herself that she could not, under any circumstances, cry. If she didn't panic, maybe they wouldn't either. And if Slinky didn't make it, Grace resolved to somehow find them a new puppy as soon as she could. Two puppies even. Three. Surely there was a dachshund breeder nearby.

She should at least thank Trent. She started the car and put the window down, but when he bent down to look at her she couldn't find any words so she just rolled the window back up again. He started signalling madly. She cranked the music and ignored him.

It wasn't until she'd backed out of the parking spot and was en route to the exit that she remembered the food had been on the roof.

'I'm not hungry anymore, anyway,' said Henry. 'But do you think the vet has a toilet?'

Grace generally resented vets, finding that they often treated a week's lapse in worming as a symptom of disinterest and therefore cruelty on the part of the owner. When Slinky got mange as a puppy and was prescribed twice-daily baths with medicated shampoo which cost fifty dollars a bottle, Grace had asked if it was absolutely necessary. The vet, who couldn't have been more than twenty-four and therefore, in Grace's opinion, didn't know the meaning of busy, looked at Grace in disbelief, as if it were an abomination that the dog was not the centre of Grace's universe. Now that Slinky was on her deathbed, Grace would have agreed to twice-daily medicated baths and aromatherapy if it meant the dog's survival. Yet this vet was what Grace's mother would have called cuddly (not in a complimentary way) and had kind eyes. The absolute worst type of person to be around when one was trying very hard not to fall apart.

'She's been hit by a . . . by a . . .' Grace couldn't get it out.

'She was hit by a car,' supplied Henry.

'And my brother is having a toilet emergency,' said May.

Henry thumped her on the arm, and May shrieked.

'Stop it,' said Grace and, surprisingly, May did.

'Yes,' said the vet. Her name was Julie. Grace couldn't imagine how anyone called Julie could ever be unkind; it was just that sort of name. 'Your partner called ahead. He said you were on your way.'

'He's not my partner,' said Grace. She rummaged through her stupidly large bag looking for tissues, which always seemed plentiful until they were needed.

'Her partner is Daddy,' said May. 'But he lives in an apartment now.'

'Oh, I'm sorry,' said Julie. 'He was very worried about you, anyway.'

◎

Once Slinky had been whisked away, Grace and the kids sat on the plastic chairs in the waiting room. It was ten minutes before Henry looked at Grace with a pained expression and confessed that he really did need to go to the toilet soon. Thankfully he too was whisked away by the receptionist.

Grace's phone buzzed. It was Dorothy, wondering how much longer they would be, as the roast was already resting and if they weren't there in twenty minutes it would certainly be cold. Grace's reply was short: *Dog hit by car. At vet. Start without us.* She knew that Dorothy would never begin a meal before the guests arrived, no matter what the temperature of the meat, but Grace wanted to point out that some people had real problems. When Dorothy texted back asking which vet, Grace presumed it was a ruse to check that they had actually left home.

Julie appeared then, beckoning Grace into an examination room.

'I'll just be talking to your mum a moment,' she said to the children. Never a good sign.

'Please, take a seat,' Julie said. She closed the door softly behind them. Julie smiled with compassion and began talking about internal injuries. Grace realised she was in fact in the bereavement room, not the treatment room. This was the quiet place people were taken to when they were to be told terrible news. Perhaps it was the smell of disinfectant that did it. Or maybe exhaustion and stress. Grace didn't really remember anything after that, just that the walls turned black and Julie's voice sounded very, very far away.

◎

Something soft had been placed under Grace's head. It was several more moments before she was able to piece together the series of events which had led to her being there, on a linoleum floor with a display of tiny pet urns on the wall. A toilet emergency. Trent. Yaris.

'There you are!' Julie said, her face popping into Grace's view. 'Lucky I caught you on your way down. You fainted, that's all. It's very upsetting when our loved ones are unwell, I know. Now, I don't think you should drive anywhere, so I've given your, er, friend a call and he's on his way.'

'My friend?'

'Yes. Trent. He'll be here any moment.'

'Oh no. And Slinky's dead?'

'No! I was just about to tell you that when you passed out. I think there might be some internal injuries but she's a good candidate for surgery. I do need to get moving, though, if we're going to go ahead. If you feel up to giving your consent we'll get started. And don't worry—we do have payment plans available.'

Grace guessed Julie hadn't seen the Lotus in the car park.

7

TRENT ARRIVED IN THE WAITING ROOM WITH TWO HAPPY MEALS, A BIG Mac and a salad. 'You lost your food, so . . . And I didn't know what you'd want.'

'I sure as hell don't want a salad.'

'I want a Happy Meal!' said May.

'We can have them, right?' asked Henry, looking at Grace.

'As long as you don't tell Granny,' Grace said. 'We can't have her meal upstaged. Trent, I don't need you to drive me anywhere. This is completely unnecessary.'

'It's only forty-five minutes. I'll take you and get an Uber back here to get my car. You staying at your parents'?'

'I'm fine to drive,' Grace insisted.

'Mum, you might pass out,' said Henry. He was already shoving fries in his mouth. 'And crash.'

'And we'll all die,' added May.

After much rearranging of luggage (it was lucky Slinky was staying at the vet, as there was no more room for her in the car),

Grace slid into the passenger seat beside Trent and tried not to think about the first time she was in a car with him.

'This is an amazing car,' he said.

'Still drive your dad's Beemer?' Grace asked.

He laughed. 'Nah. I crashed it, not long after . . .' He trailed off.

◎

Once they were on the highway again, Grace sent her mother a text with an updated ETA. The roast was now so well rested it would be dinner, not lunch. May and Henry had fallen asleep and Grace felt the silence between her and Trent, at first a small sensation, grow and grow, like motion sickness.

'I heard you're doing well,' he said eventually.

'From who?'

'Everyone knows. You're the big success story: moved to London . . . and now you drive a Lotus.'

'It wasn't quite that simple.'

'But you're not in London now.'

'No.'

Trent drove very slowly; Grace was aware of every single movement and function of her body. The road curved up through the mountain villages. There was nothing about this place, or the man sitting beside her, that was unfamiliar. He even had the same scent. How was that possible? It made her feel tight and wrong in her stomach and she wished that they could teleport the rest of the journey to make it stop.

'How are you feeling?' Trent ventured. So concerned for her wellbeing.

'So, Shalulah,' said Grace. 'What is she? An influencer?'

'That's a very unimaginative insult. No. She's a stylist.'

'Of course she is.'

'Oh, fuck off.' He was grinning. 'And her name is Shaleah.'

'How'd your date go?'

Silence, and then: 'It ended prematurely when a woman I used to know sustained a concussion,' he said.

'I don't have a concussion.'

'Sure you don't.'

'I think I'd know.'

'You have windmills in your eyes. They're swirling around. And you have tiny blue birds hovering around your head, like happens in cartoons.'

'So what do *you* do? I mean, when you're not on dates with twenty-two-year-olds.'

'She's thirty.'

'Bullshit.'

'Fine. Twenty-eight . . . I'm still a musician.' Trent flicked on the stereo. He turned it up loud, no doubt to avoid further questioning. 'Hey, who is this? It's cool.'

'Ada Black.' Grace stopped the track. 'That's a demo. If you hear any more you'll have to sign an NDA. I'm not joking.'

Trent started laughing in a slightly unhinged way. 'This is wild. This is like one of those dreams you have after you eat too much cheese. You're a record executive or whatever and you drive a convertible. It's like the ultimate revenge, you know that, right? Of course you know that.'

'Yeah. I designed my entire life to get at you. It's all about you, Trent.'

'That's not what I meant.'

◎

When the Lotus pulled into the driveway on Grevillea Close, Dorothy was standing on the porch, waiting. Who knew, perhaps she had been there since lunch. Grace opened her door and took a deep breath in preparation.

'Goodness me!' Dorothy said, trotting down the steps. 'What drama! You must be exhausted! Oh, have you brought a guest?'

Dorothy was trying to disguise her panic as excitement. *Would there be enough lamb?!*

And then Trent got out of the driver's seat and Dorothy turned a colour Grace hadn't seen since she was fifteen and had thought it would be fun to upset Dorothy by dying her hair purple. (It was.)

'Good god,' said Dorothy.

'Hey, Dorothy,' said Trent. He extended his hand. She didn't take it.

'Have you lost your mind?' Dorothy asked Grace.

'I passed out at the vet. Trent offered to drive me here. It was a coincidence, and I have no intention of ever seeing him again.'

'Good to know,' said Trent.

Dorothy stood for a moment with her mouth agape, seeming unsure how to react, until the children, awake now, emerged from the car. She instantly saw that May was barefoot. 'Where are her shoes?' she asked in a shrill voice that seemed to say, *Why the fuck is* he *here?* (Something she would never actually say aloud.)

Grace was off the hook as soon as May and Henry launched into a dramatic retelling of Slinky's near-death experience.

Trent gave Grace a sad smile, clearly contrived to elicit sympathy. 'I guess I'll be off. Uber's five minutes away. It was good to see you, even though you're not into it.'

'Thank you for the lift.'

'The pleasure's all mine.'

'Oh, shut up.'

◎

Inside, the house was as immaculate as ever. (For a brief time, Dorothy hired a cleaner but, according to Warren, she didn't meet Dorothy's standards and had to be let go. Warren said this in a tone which suggested the cleaner had finally been liberated.) The kitchen had been recently renovated but other than that the house was the same as it had been when Grace was growing up. A few years ago Grace had offered to buy them a new place, perhaps near the coast. Dorothy and Warren had toyed with the idea for approximately five minutes before declaring that no, they would like to stay put. They already knew the neighbours here, Dorothy explained, and the shops—as if other neighbours and shops were not to be trusted.

Dorothy gave the appearance of someone who had a team working behind her—stylist, dietitian, personal trainer, beautician, colourist—wherein reality she was across all of those things personally. Today she was wearing a crepe sheath dress the colour of a Tiffany gift box. She followed as Grace lugged the bags up the front steps, the kids trailing behind.

'Goodness, what on earth did you pack?' Dorothy asked.

'They're going camping.'

'Perhaps you could go camping too?'

'I don't think I'm invited.'

'And did you get a new car? It doesn't look very safe.'

'It is very safe.'

As they went inside, Dorothy said, 'Excuse the mess,' referring to the crumpled tea towel on the kitchen bench. 'Now, tell me what happened! Is it your blood pressure again? I told you; you need to—'

'Where's Dad?' Grace interrupted.

'The bottle shop. I realised I only had red wine, but now that the lamb's to be served cold I wondered if we should have white.'

Out the kitchen window, Grace could see Trent waiting by the letterbox for the Uber.

'He should be back any moment,' Dorothy said. 'Now, like I told you before, you must—'

Grace picked up her keys. 'I'll be back soon,' she said.

'Where are you going? You shouldn't be driving!'

But Grace was out the front door, down the steps and in the car.

She reversed out of the driveway and wound down the window.

'Get in,' she said.

Trent beamed at her and did what he was told.

'I'm not doing this as a favour, got it?'

'Sure. I would never think you would do me a favour. Where are we going?' He sounded delighted.

'I'm taking you back to the vet—where do you think?'

'Are you going to have me put down?'

'Can you stop taking the piss just for one moment? Please. I'm only doing this because my dad's on his way home and he said he was going to kill you.'

'Oh.'

'It might have been twenty years ago, but he doesn't tend to forget these things. He's a gentle man but you could be his tipping point.'

Grace was taking the scenic route down the mountain—less chance of traffic cops. The Lotus cornered the winding road with precision, and if she weren't so preoccupied by the person sitting beside her, she would have felt a thrill each time she slipped through the gears.

'It's good to see you,' Trent said.

Grace needed to feel something other than confusion. She wound down the window, inviting the ear-piercing shrill of cicadas into the car. Perhaps May was a cicada in a past life. (Nish had been into past lives; for a time she was convinced she had been a Victorian child chimney sweep and that's why she felt the plight of the underprivileged so deeply.)

'But, um, do you think you should maybe slow down?'

'What? You think I can't drive?' Grace pumped the accelerator down a straight.

'Fuck.' Trent was gripping his seatbelt. Grace flung the Lotus around a hard left into a cul-de-sac. 'FUCK!'

She yanked on the handbrake and the Lotus's divine derrière slid in a circle, emitting the sweet scent of burning rubber into the crisp mountain air. The car jolted to a halt.

Trent looked at her, wide-eyed.

'If you don't like it, you can get out,' Grace said.

He laughed. 'Who even are you?

Grace would have liked to say that she was the person she'd always wanted to be, but he would have known she was lying. She closed her eyes, her hands gripping the calfskin steering wheel. A calf had died for her steering wheel. There was a pressure behind her eyes.

'Hey, are you okay?'

Grace tried to focus on the air expanding and contracting her lungs.

'Grace?'

'Please stop.'

'Just take a sec. Breathe.' Trent put his hand on her back: warm, reassuring. Kind. He rubbed her back and Grace breathed. 'Do you want me to drive?'

'I'm fine.'

'You don't seem fine.'

'I am.' Grace opened her eyes.

Neither of them said another word until Grace pulled into the Furry Friends Animal Hospital car park.

'Which one's yours?' she asked.

Trent pointed to a van: old and white, the kind kidnappers were rumoured to drive in the eighties.

'Impressive.'

'It fits all my gear in it.'

'Oh. The band.'

'Don't say it like that. We're good, you should . . .' He thought better of it.

She pressed a button and his door swung open. Trent didn't get out.

'Are you sure you're okay?' he asked.

Henry had once tried to explain the space–time continuum to Grace. She hadn't got it. Now, as Trent looked at her and was able to read her as if twenty years hadn't passed, she understood.

'I'm fine.'

'Can I say something?' he asked.

'Can I stop you?'

'I've thought about this a lot. I've imagined running into you. It's weird that I haven't.'

'I can't believe you still live here.'

'I don't. I'm just visiting Dad for a few days. I live in Enmore.'

This would be an opportune time for her to take a stab at him, ask if he lived in a share house with twenty-year-old wannabes. Grace said nothing.

'I want you to know that I—'

'We were kids.'

'No, we weren't.'

'Yes. We were. I have to go.'

Trent hung his head in defeat.

'Now, Trent. I have to go.'

He got out of the car and was closing the door when he paused, ducked down to look at her. 'You have my number from when I sent the pin. Just in case you need to talk. Some people say I'm a good listener.'

'I don't need to talk to you.'

'Sure.'

As soon as Trent's door was closed Grace sped out of the car park.

Down the street and around the corner, she pulled over and sat in the quiet, unable to think, unable to pull everything in herself back to where it needed to be so that she could return to her children—presentable, normal—and be Grace in 2022 again.

PART TWO

Hardly a Spotless Track Record

8
DOROTHY

2002

DOROTHY DIDN'T LIKE THE IDEA OF GRACE TRAIPSING ACROSS EUROPE without proper accommodation (hostels were *not* accommodation), meeting god knows who, eating god knows what, all on a budget of next to nothing. The first stop was France apparently. Grace said the plan was to save money by eating mostly baguettes and cheese. The French didn't pasteurise their cheese, Dorothy had learned about it on a travel show: the host had visited various vineyards and cheesemakers, it all looked very picturesque, but what was the point of that if one was on the toilet the whole time?

Grace said the plan after France was 'loose', which as far as Dorothy could tell meant non-existent. It was all very well to stay in hostels to save money, but how far ahead did one have to book? What if they arrived somewhere and couldn't find a place to sleep? Then what? And just how clean were hostels? What if the mattress was crawling with lice? Were these hostels for homeless people as well as backpackers? According to Grace, Trent knew how it all worked as he'd spent the summer break before university in Italy. Although Dorothy had overheard Trent joke that he'd had to sleep under a bridge one night because he got lost and couldn't find the hostel. Hardly a spotless track record. Dorothy resented the influence Trent seemed to have over her daughter. He had dropped out of his degree halfway through, a decision Grace had gone to great lengths to justify. And now, no doubt at the cad's suggestion, Grace was deferring her own degree. The stress had made Dorothy want to vomit when she found out. Warren said not to make a fuss. 'Grace has a good head on her shoulders.' But that was the problem, wasn't it?

Underlying all of Dorothy's fears was the lurking dread that Grace might end up marrying this Trent person. *That* was something Dorothy couldn't stomach. Warren agreed. Neither of them were fond of Trent. He was so intense with Grace, always touching her, stroking her arm like she was a pet. He might have been trying to make up for an emotional deficiency—a wayward heart perhaps. A wayward something else, more likely. He hadn't had a haircut in a very long time and didn't mind that the hem of his flared jeans was all tattered. (In fairness, his mother had passed away. It was the one concession Dorothy was able to offer him.) The youth of today thought they were so original with their flares and long hair, as if they'd never heard of the sixties.

Back in the sixties, Dorothy had long hair, all the way down to her bottom. She'd never gone in for flares much, though—she didn't care for the sloppy, hippie style. Dorothy had thought of herself as more of a mod and had lusted after the Mary Quant dresses she saw in *Vogue*. She'd been quite the seamstress back then, buying similar patterns and making her own shifts and A-lines. At one point they'd been very short! Although her father wouldn't let her leave the house in a hem above her fingertips.

Dorothy remembered standing before her father, drawing her shoulders up in an attempt to make her arms shorter and pass his test. He'd driven her mad with it, but now she knew he was just doing his job. 'If a nice boy can ogle you, so can a filthy old man,' he would say. He was right and Dorothy was reminded of it every time Grace left the house.

There had been a time when Dorothy made nearly all of Grace's clothes. Gorgeous Liberty print rompers, smart corduroy pinafores. And hair scrunchies to match, which Grace adored. Not anymore. Grace didn't go in for short skirts very much, which was a relief. Instead she antagonised Dorothy by wearing underwear as if it were outerwear. A petticoat wasn't a dress, not even if it was tie-dyed. (In the bathroom sink! Dorothy had a conniption when she came home from work and found Grace trying to scrub the purple marks out of the basin.) Big boots, like she was off to war. Fishnet stockings in all manner of colours. 'There's only one kind of woman who wears fishnets,' Dorothy had told her. 'And it's not the kind you want to be.'

Not to mention the unfortunate period of purple hair when she was fifteen. This time done in the laundry sink—at least she'd learned one lesson. Grace, who had a glorious head of hair the colour of spun gold (a wonderful phrase), had squandered it in the space of forty-five minutes. Dorothy had to suffer the humiliation of a letter from the school. There was nothing to be done except dye the whole lot black. Dorothy knew brown would have done the trick, but of course Grace had relished undermining her on that as well. It was a small mercy that Grace didn't have dreadlocks like some of her friends; Dorothy had no end of sympathy for *their* parents. Nothing to do about dreadlocks except shave them off, and even that seemed to have an appeal for girls these days.

When Grace's blonde hair began to grow back it looked a fright but there was no way Dorothy was going to let Grace keep dying the roots, so she'd taken her off to Janet at Hair and There who had given Grace a lovely pixie cut. Dorothy would be a hypocrite to object to that; Quant had sent many a pixie cut down the runway and Dorothy herself would have gone full Twiggy if her father hadn't threatened to toss her out of the house. (He would never have done that, but Dorothy hated to displease him. Why couldn't Grace have the same amount of respect for *her?*) The short style showed off Grace's lovely slender neck and Dorothy felt they'd turned a corner as far as sartorial harmony was concerned. Until Grace came home one day with a nose piercing. Another letter from the school.

Now, as Dorothy rummaged through the enormous backpack (almost as big as Grace herself!), she saw that Grace had packed only one cardigan (which Grace had allowed Dorothy to knit for her, a small victory) and no waterproof jacket. No hat either. ('There's no UV there, Mum. You can't get sunburned.' Bollocks. Grace would be sorry if she got crow's-feet at twenty-five.)

Dorothy heard the front door open but didn't manage to flee the scene of the crime before Grace found her.

'Why are you going through my stuff?'

As if she didn't know.

'You don't even have a jacket,' Dorothy said. 'By the time September comes it will be very cold there.'

'It'll only be autumn!'

'Pamela said that when she was in Austria it was very cold in autumn.'

'I'm not going to Austria.'

'You don't know where you're going!'

'If it's cold, I'll buy something when I get there.'

'They'll all be full price. That will be your budget for bread and cheese gone.'

Grace rolled her eyes.

Dorothy took her to David Jones and bought her an excellent parka on sale. Grace even managed a small thank you. That alone was worth a hundred dollars.

◎

Dorothy remembered when Warren had first been referred to as 'her man'. It was at a party, someone's engagement: Pamela had given her a glass of punch and asked where 'her man' was. Gosh, Dorothy loved how that felt. It gave her a little frisson (excellent word) of satisfaction. She finally felt like a grown-up. Now, she knew Warren hadn't been a man at all; he was a boy, only twenty-one. And she barely twenty! They were both children playing pretend. But even children are capable of making good decisions. And it had been wonderful fun for the first few years. Dorothy loved being married, she loved saying, 'That's my husband,' when he walked into the room at a social gathering. It always drew admiration, comments about how well she'd done.

Dorothy knew that deciding who to give her heart to was one of the most important decisions of all. It was this which caused her the most worry for Grace. Her daughter made decisions *with* her heart, not *about* it. Even though Dorothy knew Warren would never find her as fascinating as the Battle of Britain, he loved her and looked after her. Always choose someone who will look after you, she told Grace. (Another roll of the eyes.)

Naturally, the novelty of being Warren's wife wore off, as well it should; marriage wasn't supposed to be novel! And of course there were times he drove her mad. But it wasn't supposed to be fun, was it? That wasn't the goal. She'd been to a wedding ceremony where 'having fun and adventure together' had been in the vows. Talk about setting yourselves up for failure. Sickness and health was a tough ask. Good times and bad even more so. But promise to have fun and adventure? Didn't these people know that adventure wasn't always a good thing? And who on earth could promise to have fun?

But yes, those early years were fun. And Dorothy had almost forgotten about them until one day years ago she was in the supermarket and first heard that song 'Rooms on Fire' by Stevie Nicks. It had made her pause right as she was reaching for the fabric softener. She loved the song so much she bought the cassette for herself. She couldn't remember the last time she had listened to music she'd chosen; it was always Warren's records. Dorothy would sing along to the tape when she cleaned the bathroom or did the ironing. When Grace was around thirteen, Dorothy found the old cassette and played it for Grace, thinking perhaps she would like it the way she liked the music that Warren played her. Grace had again rolled her eyes. 'God, Mum, that is so eighties.' Of course, only a few years later Grace remarked that Stevie Nicks was one of the best female musicians of the twentieth century, as if she had been the one to discover her. When Dorothy reminded her of the time she'd felt otherwise Grace claimed not to remember.

One of the things Dorothy did have to admit frustration over was Warren's lack of ambition. Dorothy realised his deficit in this after they had been married for five years, during which time he'd made no noises about moving on from his position teaching chemistry at the Catholic boys school he'd been at ever since he'd graduated from university. It bothered her. Dorothy couldn't understand not wanting more, not wanting to develop, to progress. She didn't have the opportunity to grow or progress after having Grace. It didn't trouble her too much—she wasn't *supposed* to be ambitious; she had a child (and looking after Grace was the equivalent of two full-time jobs at least). But Warren could do anything, she was convinced of this. He was whip-smart; he should be teaching at a university or in research. Imagine doing that! Discovering something! Or finding a solution to a problem! He didn't have to cure cancer but he could at least . . . try.

She put it to him one evening (career development, not curing cancer) while she was making dinner. 'Are you thinking of staying at St Christopher's much longer?' she'd asked.

'What do you mean?'

This wasn't a good start; clearly he hadn't been thinking about it. That was another thing which made her wonder about Warren: sometimes he didn't seem to be thinking about anything at all. She'd catch him gazing out the window and say, 'What are you musing about?' And he'd give her an (even blanker) look and say, 'Nothing at all,' in a way which made her believe him entirely. Could there really be people out there who sometimes didn't think about anything in particular? Dorothy felt her mind was always whirring, always wondering, always reaching about for something to fiddle with.

'I mean, have you been thinking about what you might like to do next?' she asked him.

'Next?'

'If you're bored.'

'I'm not bored.'

'You could do some more study. Pamela said Stuart got some money from the university to do a PhD.'

'I don't want a PhD.'

'Or more teacher training, so you could go for deputy head when the opportunity comes up.'

'I'm fine as I am. Happy enough. That's the point, isn't it?'

Was it?

The thought of a man who could do pretty much whatever he wanted sitting around thinking about nothing in particular and just being happy was baffling to Dorothy. Her father had been a Methodist minister, and the biggest barrier for Dorothy as far as a Christian faith was concerned was the idea that Jesus had atoned for all her sins and there was nothing more she could do. She couldn't level up, couldn't impress God further by doing virtuous tasks. She was tempted to believe in reincarnation—at least it gave one something to work towards.

Unlike her two elder brothers, Dorothy had left school at fifteen; no point educating a woman who was going to be a mother soon enough, said her father. Dorothy's mother agreed, although she agreed with everything he said. She had been that kind of woman, 'agreeable'; the sort of housewife and mother who smoothed out every crease and bother on the home front so her husband could glide though his days without pause. Dorothy never heard her express an opinion, and by the time Dorothy was old enough to ask her mother anything of import she had passed away. She did so as quietly as she had lived; a stroke of some sort. The months after had been difficult. Some of the worst. Dorothy had been halfway through her typing course and she remembered being grateful for the distraction the monotonous typing drills provided. *The Quick Brown Fox Jumps Over the Lazy Dog.*

Dorothy herself was that quick fox, bounding over her classmates in speed and accuracy.

She went on to work at a real estate agent, where she was soon managing the office and then some. If she could have done anything at all she would have liked to become an author or (in her wildest dreams) a fashion designer. Although no one asked, so no one knew. Something Dorothy's mother *had* given her was sewing skills, and Dorothy made all her own clothes as well as frocks for friends. She read everything she could get her hands on and even kept a little notebook where she jotted things down from time to time: funny things she overheard, observations. But then along came Warren (so handsome!), followed by Grace.

There was simply no more time.

Dorothy often told herself that Grace was enough work on her own without adding another child to the mix. Everything happens for a reason! Four-year-old Grace had no interest in television beyond fifteen minutes of *Play School*. (And God help us all if Benita wasn't the host. The tantrums!) The child simply never stopped. That was until the day when Warren bought himself a Walkman and three new cassette tapes to go along with it: Led Zeppelin, Jimi Hendrix and Janice Joplin. Grace, of course, demanded a turn as soon as he took the thing out of its box. So Warren, ever accommodating, fitted the fuzzy little headphones over his daughter's ears. Grace's eyes nearly popped out of her tiny head when the opening notes of 'Purple Haze' tunnelled their way from Jimi Hendrix's guitar, through this miraculous contraption and into Grace's busy, busy brain. And, well, that was it, wasn't it? Grace gripped the shiny black Walkman and refused to give it back. Two minutes passed, five, ten, with Grace sitting quietly in her chair absorbed in the sound. It was the longest she'd ever sat still.

Dorothy worried about the volume and what it would do to Grace's developing eardrums. However, those moments when Grace was still—not climbing up the pantry cupboards or dropping her My Little Ponies from the upstairs balcony—were too precious to give away. Dorothy never had to put the harness on Grace and tie her to the Hills hoist again. (Dorothy's friends always laughed at that line. They thought she was joking.)

Warren bought himself another Walkman.

Long car trips were suddenly possible again.

Once Grace was older, Dorothy felt immensely proud of her in some ways. Grace was a striver. If she got an A in an assignment, she reached for an A+ the next time around. In any read-a-thon she had to read the most books, no matter how many hours of television she had to give up. Yet she'd never had any particular career goal, and Dorothy didn't want her ending up like her father, all that potential just going to waste.

In primary school Grace had been asked to make a poster about what she would like to be when she grew up. She told Dorothy she didn't know what she wanted to be other than herself. (She'd succeeded: Grace was always perfectly herself.) In the end she had written 'Racing car driver' above a picture of a sports car cut from one of Warren's magazines—something Warren, of course, found amusing. Dorothy told Grace that girls couldn't be racing car drivers and resented how Warren had developed into the fun parent while she was the one who had to lay down the law. When Grace was a little older, Warren was the star whenever he dusted off the old records. The Beatles, Neil Young, Supertramp, the Rolling Stones. Hardly appropriate, but by this point no one cared what Dorothy had to say about anything. Soon enough Grace started reading biographies about musicians, and Dorothy was left to fret over what she might learn from Keith Richards.

Things did seem more promising once Grace set off to Sydney to study literature. Perhaps she would become a writer! Unfortunately it became apparent that Grace had no real interest in the subject. She couldn't stand any of the books she was supposed to study. How anyone could reject *Anna Karenina*, Dorothy did not understand.

Warren had always encouraged Grace to do whatever she wanted—more 'fun parent' prerogative. Dorothy was relieved that in this instance his freewheeling advice meant Grace returned to the hygienic safety of home after the festering heap in Glebe. At least Grace had made friends with Anishka once she switched universities. Despite the salty language, Dorothy didn't mind Anishka; Grace actually listened to her friend when she offered sensible advice. Grace had arrived home from uni after a row with her one day—she was upset because Anishka had expressed reservations about that boy. Wise woman.

Letting Grace fly halfway across the globe with Trent was the most difficult thing Dorothy had ever had to do. By that time, Dorothy had gone from knowing every single thing her daughter experienced in a day to the scant scraps Grace deigned to relate to her. It felt like ever since that first day of kindergarten ('kinder garden', as little Grace had called it) her daughter had been drifting on a tide that took her further and further from Dorothy's shore until they would soon be on different continents altogether. Dorothy would be trying to wave to her daughter across a vast ocean, keeping watch for distress signals, even though if Grace sent up a flare, it wouldn't be to her. Dorothy would be the last to know about it.

9
GRACE

NISH MET GRACE AT HEATHROW AIRPORT. SHE'D TOLD GRACE TO WAIT outside Waterstones and so, struggling not to cry with heartbreak and delirium, Grace did what she was told. When she spotted Nish weaving through the swarming crowds Grace burst into actual tears of relief. Nish didn't even greet her, just marched over and picked up Grace's backpack.

'Fucking hell!' she said. 'What did you pack? Concrete?'

'Thank you for coming to get me.' Grace burst into tears again and Nish pulled her into a tight hug.

'Some poet broke your heart, yeah? Don't let it destroy you. Oh god, look at you. You look like rubbish. It'll be okay. Hoes before bros, yeah?'

'Yes. Okay.'

'Fucking hell.'

With Grace's sobbing assistance, Nish hoisted the backpack on, took Grace's hand and guided her down into an Underground station where she bought her a train ticket, a phone card and a giant iced coffee from a vending machine.

'Drink it—you need to stay awake.'

'I want to go to bed. I've been awake for thirty hours.'

'No. It's eight thirty in the morning.'

'Is it?'

'Change your bloody watch, that's the first step.'

Grace and Nish took the tube and then changed to an Overground train for the final leg to Dalston Kingsland. Grace watched London roll by the window, it was strange to be in a place that seemed familiar thanks to British television shows and yet entirely different. When they got off the train and emerged onto the street Grace took in the graffiti, the shuttered shopfronts, and windows either boarded over or coated in the grime of exhaust fumes. Grace followed Nish along the street, past a continental grocer, a tobacconist selling cigarettes and—inexplicably—boxes of zucchini, and a store with a faded sign advertising *Nothing over 89p*. Grace had never seen anything but Australian light, here it was mid-morning but there was still a gentleness to the sunshine. It wasn't Paris, where she'd dreamed of being, and yet the very contrast of it all to Grace's regular life had an appeal that, even among her feelings of disorientation, was instant. Ahead of her, Nish walked with confidence. Chin high and self assured. Fearless.

◎

Grace and Trent's flight was to leave at nine thirty in the morning. Trent was playing one last gig the night before. He would meet Grace at the airport at seven, at the cafe next to the newsagent.

So she waited. First leafing through a magazine. Then eating an eight-dollar stale croissant. It was an hour before the panic really hit, gushing through her, tingling down her spine, pooling in her chest. There'd been an accident. He was injured. In an ambulance. Or dead. Maybe he was dead. How could you find someone like that, so perfect, and then lose them? If he was late he would have called. She rang and rang his mobile. Fourteen times. Nothing. Grace imagined his phone inside a ziplock bag in a hospital. Beside his dead body.

The call to check in came over the PA. No, she was being silly. He'd missed the train and his phone was out of battery. He would come running, lugging his backpack with the five different padlocks. He'd be laughing. *Sorry, sorry, sorry! I'm here!* He'd kiss her and she'd laugh too, scrambling for the check-in counter.

It didn't happen.

Grace went to the counter.

A woman with excellent eyeliner smiled. 'Checking in?'

'I need to . . . I can't . . . I . . .'

The woman waited.

'I can't get the flight. He's not here. Can I change the ticket, or delay it?'

'I'd have to do it before boarding opens. That's in fifteen minutes.'

'Can I get a refund?'

'Yes, minus a cancellation fee. Which is considerable.'

Grace phoned Baz. Surely he would know what was going on.

No answer.

She left a message: 'I'm worried something's happened to Trent. Please call me.'

She tried again.

A third time.

This time Baz answered. 'Hey, Grace.' His tone was odd.

Trent was dead. She knew it in her skin, in her blood cells.

'Do you know—'

'He's okay. There hasn't been an accident.'

The relief came so fast she thought she would collapse. She was crying with it. The woman with the eyeliner watched her.

'He slept in, didn't he? I'll talk to the woman at the counter; she said she can put us on another flight. He's not answering his phone. Maybe he's on the train.'

'Grace.'

'What?'

Silence.

'What?'

'He's not coming.'

She heard Trent's voice, faint, in the background.

'He's changed his mind,' Baz said.

'About what? Baz, put him on the phone.'

'He doesn't . . .'

'What?'

'Fuck.' Baz was talking to Trent now. 'Why am I the one doing this?'

'Baz, what's going on?'

'He's sorry. It's not you. But he's not coming.'

'I don't understand.'

Nothing. Then the line went dead. And then she knew.

Grace was sweating, beads of it running down her back. And the shaking: it wouldn't stop. She'd never felt this distraught in a public place; people were looking. The airport felt like a cavern of noise and people and jarring unfamiliarity.

Dorothy answered the phone after two rings.

'Are you boarding?' she asked. 'How lovely of you to call.'

Grace tried to say the word 'Mum' but she couldn't.

'Are you there?' said Dorothy. 'I can't hear you.'

'He didn't come.' The words came in a staccato sob. 'He's not here. He's . . . I think he's dumped me.'

Grace waited for Dorothy to say that everything would be all right, that she would drive to the airport immediately and collect Grace.

'I told you he was no good,' Dorothy said. 'Honestly, I have to say I'm relieved. I know you don't want to hear that.'

'He's left me here and you're happy?'

'I'm not happy that you're upset. But I think this is the best thing that could happen to you.'

Dorothy said something more but Grace was too caught up in trying to process her mother's reaction. Dorothy was glad she had been humiliated. Dorothy was glad Grace felt as though her rib cage was being slowly crushed.

The woman behind the counter looked over to Grace and held up five fingers. Dorothy was still talking when Grace hung up the phone.

'Can you change it to London?' Grace asked the woman.

'I can get you on a flight to Heathrow leaving at eight o'clock tonight. What about the other ticket, your friend's? I can change that too.'

'No. It's just me. Will he lose his money?'

'I'm afraid so.'

'Good.'

The corner of the woman's mouth twitched. Almost a smile. 'Oh and look,' she said, clicking on her computer. 'There's a seat in business. Shall I upgrade you?'

'I can't really afford it.'

'An upgrade is complimentary.'

'Oh.'

The woman handed Grace her boarding pass and winked. 'You'll have fun in London.'

◎

Surely it shouldn't feel as bad as it did. It wasn't like they were married. They'd only been together a year or so. Yes, she'd lost her virginity to him, but people, normal people, could do that then break up and move on. Grace couldn't imagine moving on. She felt like she'd had a limb torn off and the rest of her had been thrown into a fire. What was he doing now, while she was choking on tears in Nish's tiny, damp Dalston flat? They had been deep in each other's worlds ever since their second date. She would never again know what he was doing. She would never again dial his number. The humiliation made her nauseous: she'd vomited twice on the plane; the flight attendant had thought she was a nervous flyer. In reality Grace wasn't sure that she would have minded if the plane had gone down in flames. 'God, you're dramatic,' Nish said.

It soon became clear that this wasn't the European Trip of a Lifetime. This was Grace sleeping on Nish's couch in a flat that made Baz's house in Katoomba look like a five-star resort.

'You're not going to like this, yeah?' Nish said to her one afternoon. 'But from where I'm stood, it looks like you're wallowing.'

'I'm not. And you sound like Dorothy.'

'You've been on the couch, hiding under a blanket for, like, nine days straight. Nothing's going to change until you get your arse into gear.'

'I don't know what to do.'

'Go see some sights. I'm not here to bloody entertain you. Go to the Tower of London. Actually that would suit you; you can go ponder your romantic choices.'

'I don't deserve to have my head chopped off.'

Nish unzipped Grace's backpack and began pulling things out. She tossed various garments at Grace.

'And have a bloody shower.'

'I had a shower on Tuesday. I just . . . Nish, I don't see the point of anything.'

'Right. Well, me razor's in the shower if you need it. Or there's rat poison under the sink. Take your fancy.'

'I cannot believe you just said that.'

'What do you want me to say? Your life is over? Fucking hell.'

Grace threw off the blanket and snatched up her clothes. 'Fine. I'll leave. I'll go home.'

'Like hell you will. What you're going to do is have some self-respect and not let that git destroy you. You're a smashing chick and I love you, but if you want to stay with me you've got to cheer the fuck up because right now you're doing my head in. Sub-par bloody company you are.'

◎

'And here,' bellowed the yeoman, 'is where Anne Boleyn, second wife of Henry the Eighth—Queen of England!—spent her final hours before being taken for execution! Follow me now as we retrace her last steps!'

The small sandstone room was packed with ten tourists and Grace. The white-gloved yeoman ushered everyone down the spiralling stone staircase.

'Imagine! These were Queen Anne's very last steps before her untimely, brutal death! Careful now, lest they be yours too!'

The tourists chuckled.

Back outside, the yeoman (or Sir John of Clapham, as he enjoyed being called) led the twittering group to a small paved area bordered with a low fence. Sir John stood beside a small wooden block.

'Here! The Tower Green! A jolly name for a place where many a sorry soul parted company with their heads.'

He had a poor grasp of grammar.

'I need a volunteer!'

The tourists giggled. At the urging of his wife, a beefy man raised his hand.

'No, no, you're not suitable. You, young lady there at the back—yes, I see you hiding away!'

'I didn't volunteer,' Grace objected.

'Let's have a round of applause for this lovely young lady!'

Grace tried to back away but John of Clapham grasped her arm and pulled her to the front of the group.

'Now, I would never normally ask a young lady her age. Not until afterwards!' He laughed and a few of the men joined in. 'But I dare say you're a touch younger than our Queen Anne. Although she was but two and nine! What's your name, my love?'

'Georgia. And I'm not your love.'

'Ho ho! We have a feisty one here, ladies and gentlemen! Well, Queen Georgia, kneel down here and rest your lovely neck over this here chopping block where I shall take your last confession before your young life is cut short.'

Grace turned around and walked away from John of Clapham and his chopping block.

'An escapee!' he called after her, struggling to maintain his jolly air. 'We have an escapee, ladies and gentlemen!'

◎

Grace sat at the hop-on-hop-off bus stop picking pastry from a danish she had bought at the Tower's cafe. She wished she could have bought two danishes, or a danish and an eclair, but that would have been beyond her budget. On her journey in there had been announcements on the tube about a heatwave. Passengers were advised to drink lots of water. It couldn't have been more than twenty-five degrees, but in the park across the road from where Grace stood, Londoners were stripping off layers to bask in the sun. Several women were in bikinis, as if they'd packed for a trip to the beach. They all looked so content, so thrilled to have the sun on their skin. A tear slid down Grace's cheek and she wished she had a napkin.

'I saw you escape execution,' said a voice. Accented, possibly Spanish.

Grace looked up, wiping at her cheek, and saw a bronzed guy with dark hair licking his collar, tank top revealing the subtle rippling of his biceps. The band of his Calvin Kleins peeked above his slow-slung jeans.

'I feel for you. Idiot tour guide, hey?' He extended a hand to Grace. 'Mateo. Georgia, yes? I am not following you. I saw you there, now I see you here. Excuse me for interrupting your . . . What do you have there? I don't know what that is called.'

'It's a danish.'

'Oh, very nice. Very nice. May I sit?' He held up his palms. 'Tell me to go away and I will. I don't want to interlude.'

'Intrude?'

'Yes. That one.'

'You can sit down.'

'Thank you. Otherwise I will go stand over there but that would be awkward now that we have spoken, yes?'

Grace laughed.

'Tell me, Georgia, where do you come from?'

'Australia.'

'That is a beautiful place.'

'Have you been?'

'No, I see the TV show. *Home and Away.*'

'Ah. Yeah, that's exactly what it's like.'

Mateo was from Spain. They talked about nothing, laughing at Londoners who thought it was a hot day and discussing whether the Queen was allowed to eat swans. The bus came and went and two hours later Grace and Mateo were in a pub, shouting to be heard over the music. Then there was dancing. And soon after that they were in a dorm room at a hostel, surrounded by sleeping backpackers. Mateo had a double sleeping bag, which indicated a level of premeditation. This was the kind of place Trent had booked. Perhaps the very same one. Maybe he was there somewhere.

It was over quickly. Mateo was snoring the moment he rolled off her. It was difficult to slip out of the sleeping bag without waking him but she managed.

At four a.m., when Grace came through the door of the flat, she found Nish sitting on the couch. Her head had lolled to the side and she was snoring. On the television a man was talking about the Battle of Britain and it made Grace think of her father. And by default, Dorothy, and about how they were both all the way over on the other side of the world.

She tried to close the door as quietly as she could, but Nish jolted awake, her expression slipping from confusion to fury very, very quickly.

'I thought you were dead!' she yelled.

'You told me to go out, so I went out. Met a guy from Spain. I thought you'd be proud.'

'I meant go to Top Shop, not find some homeless Spaniard to shag.'

'He's not homeless, he's a backpacker.'

'That's the definition of homeless. I was about to call the police!'

'He was pretty hot.'

'I had no idea where you were! One minute you're crying on the couch, next minute you've bloody vanished. And after me joking about rat poison!'

'I'm sorry.'

'By hot, like, how hot? No. It doesn't matter. I thought you'd chucked yourself in the river.'

It wasn't irritation in Nish's words. It was despair. 'I've work in the morning and look at me! Up all hours waiting for you! I'll be a wreck! You're so busy being the victim, you've forgotten about the person who actually gives a fuck. When was the last time you asked how I am?' Grace began to apologise, but Nish cut her off. 'Finding someone to mess around with isn't the answer, Grace. You can trust me on that.'

◎

Grace told herself that she was very young. She was young and inexperienced and maybe a bit dumb as far as guys went. It had been a wise decision to slip out of Mateo's bed without saying goodbye. It was wise to forget about him and be okay with her decision. This wisdom was something she would continue to cultivate, Grace vowed. She would cultivate it and ignore the spreading feeling of unease that made itself apparent whenever she thought about how she had slept with some random guy she met at a bus stop. She would wait for that unease to be replaced by the sense of empowerment that sexual liberation had promised. She thought about all of these things while she waited in line for a blood test to rule out pregnancy or STDs. Nish had lectured her about contraception, infuriated that Grace had trusted the

Spaniard to use an appropriate condom (*How long do you think it'd been in his backpack?!*) and told her it was worth the twenty quid for the tests rather than waiting two weeks to see if her period showed up. Nish was right, of course. The peace of mind Grace felt when the tests came back all clear was worth it and for the first time in four days she was able to sleep through the night.

◎

Grace had been in London for six weeks before Nish requested that she start contributing to the food she was taking from the fridge. By that time, Nish—true to the plan she had made at the very start of her degree—was working for a charity that provided training and work experience for underprivileged and migrant youth. She left the flat every morning full of purpose and returned full of complaints about the entrenched inequities of society. She was not satisfied with a diet of bread and cheese, and Grace's five-pound daily budget blew out quite quickly. Soon Grace had to call Warren and ask if he could send her a little bit more money, just to get her by until she came home. She would pay him back, she said. Warren agreed under the caveat that she was, under no circumstances, to tell Dorothy.

Within a month Grace was broke again.

'I'm going to have to go home,' she said to Nish.

'To Dorothy?' said Nish. 'No. I won't have it. I'll miss you so much I'll be sick. Who will cook for me? We'll get you a job.'

'I don't have a work permit. And even if I applied, they take ages.'

'We'll bend the rules.' Nish went to the kitchen and got a notepad out of the drawer. 'What are you good at? Wait. I'll just write "everything", shall I? Interests? CDs. Losers not worth your time. Skills? Being a top chick.'

Grace laughed.

'You're organised, what with all your folders at uni and pens and everything. I'll put that down. Ambitions: avoiding dickheads and homeless Spaniards. Interests: music. What other interests?'

Grace couldn't think of any.

'I'll just put music times a hundred.'

◎

Nish knew someone who knew someone who got Grace an interview for a receptionist job at a place called Eastlake Management. The address indicated a dingy office above a panel beater in Hackney, and Grace thought it was a mistake until she saw the business's name handwritten on a piece of paper that had been laminated and thumbtacked to the door. She pressed the buzzer three times before she accepted that it didn't work and knocked, again and again, with no response. It looked like a crappy place to work anyway, Grace consoled herself. But when she turned to walk away the door opened.

'You gotta post the CDs. Can't be showing up on the doorstep.'

The voice belonged to a stocky black man, possibly in his thirties, with close-cropped hair and beard, so it was all the one length around his head. He wore a well-cut suit with a white t-shirt. A shiny chrome watch glinted at the cuff of his jacket.

'I don't have CDs. I'm here about the—'

'Not a musician?'

'Er, no.'

'Well thank Christ for that. Enough of 'em in the world as it is.'

Grace told him she was there for a job interview and he looked puzzled. The cogs were attempting to turn.

'Danny's mate, is it? Receptionist?'

'I don't know Danny but, yep, the receptionist job.'

'Right, right. I'm Tony. Come on then. First rule, yeah? Don't let anyone just drop discs at the door. If they go on the website they'll see the postal address clear as day. They gotta post 'em.'

'Absolutely.'

Grace followed Tony into a tiny room with a chaotic desk in one corner and a plastic chair in the other. A window offered an uninterrupted view of a brick wall.

Tony pointed to the desk. 'That'll be you.' He pointed to a door. 'I'm in there.'

Tony shifted a pile of papers from the desk onto the plastic seat, revealing a phone. 'You take care of that. This is important, yeah? I am never available. Even if I'm just sat in me office. Never. Available. They gotta make a time, I will call 'em back. Or sometimes, if you feel like it, you can put 'em on hold for a bit, then tell 'em I'm unavailable. I don't care if it's the Queen—they gotta wait.'

'Which is the hold button?'

'I don't know! That's your job. You answer, you take a message, you make 'em wait. Easy as.'

'Sure.'

'Now. People who need me, my boys, they'll call the mobile. Never the landline. Don't you worry about that. Oh, and if a Michael Wester from Warner calls, I'm in a meeting at DMU. If Paul Teck from DMU calls, I'm in a meeting at Warner. That is very important, that is. Write that down.'

Grace spotted a stack of post-its on the desk and took a pen from a marmalade jar.

Tony looked at an unsteady shelf which, like the desk, was crammed with files and towers of CDs. He sighed. 'And you gotta sort all this, yeah? Bloody nightmare, that is.' He said it as if the shelf itself were responsible for the mess it was in and Tony was disappointed by its choices.

'Now. Cleaner comes in every Tuesday night. Cheryl or Shirley or some such. She don't want anything on the floor, so Tuesday afternoon you gotta pick up all the shit off the floor and put it on the desk or chair or fuck knows, I don't care. Just put it back on the floor Wednesday morning. Otherwise I don't know where anything is. Or maybe I'll give you some cash and you can go buy another shelf. That's a good idea. Write that down. Then you can just put all the shit on that. I wouldn't get a cleaner but I got allergies, yeah? Fucking nightmare.'

Tony proceeded to give detailed instructions about where to buy his lunch and the way he liked his tea; he gave her the key to the postbox and instructions as to how often it was to be emptied.

'So do I get the job?' Grace asked.

He looked at her like she was an idiot. 'Yeah. What you think this is?'

◎

Grace learned that Tony managed the careers and affairs of a small collection of recording artists: mostly hip hop, dub and electronica, all of whom believed themselves to be the next Roots Manuva or Massive Attack. Tony was good at spotting potential and guiding artists to find their own sound. Grace liked Tony, and Tony liked the way Grace didn't have a work permit so he was under no obligation to 'mess about with paperwork'. It was cash in hand, cash that Tony pulled out of his wallet and handed to her at the end of each week. The amount always varied and Grace suspected he couldn't remember how much he had agreed to pay her.

The soundtrack to Grace's workday was incessant hammering and the whine of angle grinders from the panel beater below, all accompanied by Tony's overly loud telephone voice. He believed that talking very loudly, very quickly, created an impression of success, as if he were fielding several million-dollar deals at once. (It later became apparent that this tactic worked.) One evening Nish met Grace at the office at the exact moment that Tony was going what was best described as ape shit at some sorry sod on the other end of the phone line. Standing in the crowded space between the leaning bookshelf and several precarious towers of CDs (Grace was yet to buy another shelf), with an expression of Dorothy-worthy scepticism on her face, Nish flinched visibly at Tony's booming voice.

'He always like this?'

'No. Yes. Sometimes.'

'To you?'

'No.'

'Like, I'm glad you got a job and all, but if you wanted something a bit more . . . normal . . .'

But Grace didn't want normal. This place, this room with the noise and the traffic outside and the fizzing energy Tony radiated, gave Grace the feeling she had had in Souper, the underground jazz bar back in Sydney—a feeling like the world was so much bigger than her small life in Australia. And here she felt as if she were becoming a part of it. Something which had been dormant within her since she arrived in London was beginning to awaken. It was helped by the way Tony had come to like her beyond just the convenience of her lack of work permit. He enjoyed telling people that she was Australian and he had plucked her from nowhere. 'Bloody priceless, she is,' he would say. He loved that Grace was actually interested in the music and the job and was always giving her CDs and tickets to gigs. He would constantly check that she'd eaten enough ('Don't waste away! I need you!')

and offered her a lot of advice about the music industry. 'It's all an act, everyone's got their part, me included.' It filled Grace with an inner glow she hadn't felt for a long time.

While the agency was doing well, it wasn't doing quite well enough to facilitate presentable headquarters so Tony always held meetings in restaurants, usually expensive ones. One morning he strode into the office, took a hundred-pound note from his wallet and dropped it on Grace's desk.

'You need to buy yourself something nice to wear. Something sharp, like. That's your budget, you gotta spend the lot. Shoes, the whole deal.'

Grace looked down at her jeans and tattered AC/DC t-shirt.

'We're going out. Dinner, label meeting. I need you.' From his pocket he pulled a bunch of crumpled receipts, all of them covered in his messy scrawl, and dropped them on Grace's desk. 'That's everythin' I remember from yesterday's meeting. I can't make head nor tail. Need someone else there to write this shit down. Phone numbers, figures, contacts, dates. Professional, like. I'm giving you a promotion, Gracie. Shit's coming together and we got to be ready. Got to look the part. That's a big part of this game, Grace.'

The meeting was with an executive from Warner Music and took place in a restaurant with panoramic views of Southbank and the Thames; it was unlike anywhere Grace had ever been, much less eaten. Boats and ferries adorned with twinkling lights meandered beneath the grand bridges. As the maître d' took their coats Tony pointed out a balding man who looked thoroughly bored by the view, as if he went to fancy restaurants every day. (It turned out he did.) The man shifted in his seat, took another sip from a glass of water that was almost empty. Checked his watch.

'Are we late?' Grace asked Tony.

'Nah, we is right on time.'

Grace had no experience taking notes. No experience of fancy restaurants with powerful people.

'Breathe, Gracie,' Tony said. 'You got me. I got you.' He patted her on the shoulder. 'Showtime.'

Grace followed as Tony waltzed up to the man's table like he was meeting an old friend. 'Mike! What's happening, bruv? Sorry we're late, had a meet at BMG. Went overtime. This my PA, Grace. She's gonna take my notes and whatnot.'

Tony opened his suit jacket, revealing the designer label, plucked a key from his pocket and dropped it on the table beside his phone. The key to a Ferrari that was not his, a Ferrari that didn't in fact exist. It was a replica key, he explained to her later. Gotta look the part to be the part.

Later, in the cab, Tony wheezed with laughter. 'You see that? Did you see that?' He clapped his hands. 'Mike Wester scramblin' for *my* boy, Grace.'

He was right: by the end of the meeting the guy had practically been begging to meet the young rapper Tony had pitched him. Grace felt the rush of it all, like they'd pulled a heist.

'You were *tight*, Gracie! Ice-cool.' Tony laughed and laughed and Grace felt it, a sensation that she didn't know she had always missed growing up with Dorothy: Tony was *proud* of her.

10
DOROTHY

2005

THE WORD DOROTHY FIRST HEARD WAS 'BOMB', AND THEN 'LONDON'.

She was in the kitchen trying to cook a risotto, Warren was in the living room and had been watching the ABC since the news at seven, as was his habit from the very first day of their marriage. It was almost eight o'clock and dinner was going to be terribly late. She'd already thrown one lot of risotto in the bin; this was the second attempt. Dorothy was so fixated on trying to prevent the rice from sticking to the bottom of the pan she hadn't even been listening to the television, but just as she had been attuned to Grace's faintest cry when her daughter was a baby, her ears seemed to pluck the words from the air and shoot them straight into her. Without even removing the spoon or turning off the stove, Dorothy rushed in to where Warren was standing in front of the television, the remote still in his hand. He looked at her and his face was whiter than she'd ever seen. The two of them stood side by side for a few moments, staring as Kerry O'Brien relayed the breaking news, but then Dorothy's legs started to feel very wobbly. She grasped Warren's hand and he guided her to the armchair.

Warren was on the phone after that, punching in Grace's number and standing silently as he listened and Dorothy looked from him to the TV and back again, over and over. On the TV, Kerry said something about trains at Russell Square, Aldgate and Edgeware Road. Dorothy repeated the words at Warren as if that information would somehow result in a more direct line to Grace.

'It's voicemail,' Warren said. 'It's voicemail.'

'Maybe she's trying to call us,' Dorothy said. 'That's why she's not picking up.'

But Warren kept on pressing redial.

'Hang up! Warren, hang up the phone! She's trying to get through!'

Dorothy knew that if the worst had happened, she would be at fault. The times, oh so many times, she had replayed the conversation she had when Grace called her from the airport. All Dorothy had needed to say was: 'I will come and get you right away.' That's it. If she had said that, instead of venting her anger about that good-for-nothing cad, Grace would be here. Home. Away from all the terrible things Dorothy worried about every day. Now the worst thing, the unimaginable. And all the times Dorothy could have apologised! Grace hadn't spoken to her for months after she left home; the first proper conversation had been when Grace called to ask Dorothy for her birth certificate so she could get a work permit. Stupid, stupid, stupid. If Dorothy had said, 'I'm sorry. I love you. Come home,' maybe Grace would have come back.

Now, Dorothy had her hand on Warren's arm as he pressed the phone to his ear. 'Hang up! She might be calling!'

But of course he ignored her, because he believed that he was the reasonable one in any situation. It was only then that Dorothy remembered the existence of Warren's mobile phone. She jumped up and ran to the bedroom where it sat on his bedside table. How she clutched at the thing, shaking, sweating, hoping the little screen would show Grace's number, or a message, anything.

Nothing.

For an hour they sat in front of the television waiting. The house phone rang, of course it did, over and over. Each time, Dorothy thought it would be Grace, only to find that no, it was another friend calling to check that Grace was okay. It was maddening. Down the bottom of the television screen was a little bar of information and soon there was a number that people could call. The embassy in London or Foreign Affairs or something, and so Dorothy tried to punch in that number but *now* Warren was carrying on about keeping the line clear.

An hour passed and then an update—just coming through now, the television said. Another god-awful explosion. Hackney. A bus on the way to Hackney. A sound came from within Dorothy; somehow she could picture the sound she was making but not hear it. It was a black whirl of despair, like those cosmic spirals of dark matter captured in space. Warren held on to Dorothy's shoulders. He was talking right into her face. 'Calm down,' he said, over and over.

Then the tinny, tinkling sound of Warren's mobile ringing on the coffee table, buzzing, crawling sideways. At first they both just watched it, neither reaching for it. Dorothy didn't recognise the number, only knew that it was international. It was going to be terrible news. She answered. 'Yes? Hello?'

'Mum?'

◎

Later, Warren would tell a psychiatrist that Dorothy was not quite the same after that. She was more 'on edge', and she said, 'Of course I was on edge, our daughter was almost killed.'

'She wasn't,' Warren said. As if he had been a picture of calm and reason. 'She wasn't even in the country; she was in Paris.'

'But I didn't know that,' Dorothy said. She hadn't even known what country her daughter was in, or why. And surely that was the most important thing. She should have known. It was her job to protect Grace, and although Grace would never acknowledge it, Dorothy had always done it very well.

◎

There was the time, years ago, when she had been running late for a doctor's appointment.

Dorothy despised being late; this was probably not unrelated to the fact that she despised lateness in others, which was often the result of chronic laziness or a shambolic lifestyle. Dorothy did not have a shambolic lifestyle, but that was what the doctor would think when she was late for the appointment. And she'd had to wait a week just to get one, even though she was sure it was urgent. She was only about seven weeks pregnant, but the abdominal pain just didn't feel right. Dorothy would have to make a point of explaining to the receptionist that her lateness was the fault of an inept shoe salesperson.

Grace had wide feet; they were positively triangular. 'Like a duck!' said the saleswoman. Dorothy resented her five-year-old being compared to poultry, so it's fair to say she and the saleswoman got off on the wrong foot, so to speak. When the woman finally stopped trying to win Grace's favour (Grace did not bestow her smiles lightly) by talking about ducks and flippers and some nonsense about swimming lessons, she found several pairs of shoes in Grace's size, but Grace refused to try any of them on. She had entered a phase of self-determination whereby she chose to exert her powers by responding with tyrannical fury to any wardrobe options offered to her. She had always been a mercurial child. (Mercurial was Dorothy's absolute favourite word; she was delighted to have found a way to use it in her everyday life.) Dorothy had then been forced to engage in complex negotiations with her daughter, which were derailed when the idiot saleswoman suggested a boys' style of shoe, which triggered a next-level tantrum. Dorothy had been forced into making a rushed decision under a frightful amount of pressure.

She was hurrying through the shopping centre car park, with shoes which her daughter would no doubt refuse to wear in one hand and hauling a screeching Grace along by the wrist with the other, when a car came flying around the corner, tyres squealing. Grace stopped dead (terrible choice of words, Dorothy told herself later), staring agape at the car. Somehow Dorothy managed to push her daughter ahead of her, out of the car's path, while Dorothy, in her fury, stood her ground as if her outrage would be enough to halt the car in its trajectory. Funnily enough, it worked. The boy—for that's what he was, although he no doubt fancied himself a man—slammed on the brakes, stopping inches away from Dorothy's legs. She marched to the driver's door and wrenched it open.

'You stupid, moronic, waste of space!' she hissed. 'You could have killed my daughter!'

The boy started blubbering something about being sorry.

'You would be sorry if you had hit her. Because I would definitely kill you in that instance. Appointment or not.'

Dorothy always found it irritating in movies, television shows or songs when people talked about 'believing' in love, as if it were a concept like pixies at the bottom of the garden, or sweet and wispy like pink fairy floss. The love inside Dorothy was not fairy floss: it was galvanised steel with strength enough to stop a speeding Commodore driven by an idiot. Much later on, Dorothy had been tempted to tell her daughter that she had willingly used her own body as a shield for her. It was during one of those arguments which always ended with Grace screeching that she didn't understand why Dorothy hated her so much. Dorothy wanted to say, 'I don't hate you—I love you so much I would die for you.' But Dorothy knew she wouldn't be able to bear it when, instead of saying, 'I love you too,' her daughter stayed silent.

11
GRACE

2006

WHEN GRACE THOUGHT OF THOSE FIRST FEW YEARS WORKING FOR TONY, she remembered the hunger to fill herself with something she could love. She put everything she had into becoming indispensable to Eastlake Management. And it worked. Tony appreciated that she not only had a brain for business, but also cared about the clients—a rare thing apparently. She could overhear most of his conversations, read all his emails (at his request) before forwarding on what genuinely required his attention, and was present at every one of his meetings. It didn't take long for Grace to realise that she could do everything he could, only with a lighter touch—an ability to talk a client out of taking a hit of cocaine before going on stage, or soothe a damaged ego in the wake of a bad album review.

Tony made some good judgement calls on a few young artists and got them sizeable deals, leading to more clients, and soon the business was moved out of the old Hackney place and into a shiny new Shoreditch office. (Tony even hired a receptionist so Grace could be his PA and not worry about the phones.) Grace was now able to supplement Nish's meagre income and they moved into a less-damp flat.

Grace accompanied Tony and his clients to festivals and met a lot of musicians. It was impossible to ignore how few of them had the amount of talent that she'd seen in Trent, impossible not to wonder what he was up to, if he was still making music, who he was professing his undying love to. A residue of pain remained longer than it should have—a raw ache like a fatal flaw in her structure. Grace was learning that time was stretchy, pulling and springing back: an elastic thing of colour and sound and smell. Some things faded into nothing, but that moment lying on the carpet with him, the music and the smoothness of his skin under his t-shirt, the way she wanted to climb inside the songs with him—that moment remained with her, potent. She hadn't listened to Massive Attack since. Once, while she was flicking through LPs at a thrift store, 'Black Milk' came floating through the speakers, and she'd had to leave, escaping outside into the frigid air, hoping it would cleanse her of a pain which she felt should have dissolved a long time ago.

Ashamed, she never talked to Nish about it. Her feelings for Trent seemed insignificant compared to the enduring saga that was Nish's relationship with Ravi. He had come to the UK to visit for what turned out to be a very intense and noisy (the walls in the flat were too thin) month. He wanted to marry Nish, arguing that it was the only way they would be able to live together without their respective parents losing their minds. Nish told Grace that she didn't buy his reasoning. 'I think he properly loves me,' she said. 'It's bloody terrifying.' Unable to get a straight answer out of her, Ravi had left again. Grace being maudlin about an old boyfriend couldn't compete with the fireworks that were Nish's love-life.

◎

Grace was walking to the tube after work one night when she passed a small club called Drop with a line outside that snaked all the way up the block and around a corner. A bouncer was counting people as they came in; Grace heard a disappointed groan from the unlucky punters when he announced the venue was at capacity and closed the line.

'Who's playing?' Grace asked him.

'Ada Black,' the guy told her. 'Always pulls a crowd. You're too late.'

Grace pulled out her business card and slipped him twenty quid courtesy of a fund Tony set aside for such purposes. The bouncer stepped aside and opened the door.

It was shoulder to shoulder inside, surely more people packed in than was legal. The walls were papered with layer upon layer of promo posters for various acts. Ada Black was to follow a dubtronica act called Colossal Fraud that was currently pumping the place with far too much bass. The whole room was pulsating with it. When they finally left the stage Grace took the opportunity to shuffle her way through the crowd and find a spot up front. She pressed her phone to her ear and pretended to be listening intently to an important call—the most effective way of avoiding conversation with anyone male. Roadies came onstage to set up the gear for Ada: keys, drums, double bass and a turntable.

When the house lights went down, the space around Grace filled and a cheer went up.

Four guys in black came onstage and took their places. A single golden light shone on the microphone. The music started and the mic stand remained vacant. A good few bars were played before a petite woman in a black fifties-style wiggle dress and pumps came out and joined the band, her shaggy blonde hair covering her face. The music continued for so long that Grace wondered if the woman was going to sing at all, or maybe just walk offstage. Someone whistled loudly and Ada took the mic from the stand, lowered her head, and opened her mouth.

The voice she released didn't sound like it could come from a woman scared of a microphone. She sounded somewhere between Etta James and Dusty Springfield, with a throatiness which, anytime her voice drifted towards sweet, cut through strong and raw. It was indigo and violet. Velvety midnight blue and sometimes, just a little, cold crimson. A gritty symphony of sensual pain that tapped at the fragile structure holding Grace's insides together so it began to tremble. She had no tissues in her bag, nothing to wipe her tears with but the back of her sleeve. Ada performed the entire set barely once looking up at the audience, and Grace noticed the times when her voice slid away from the music in a way which Grace doubted was intended, moments when it seemed she might stop altogether. But the band held her, filling gaps so she carried on through. Ada performed six songs which Grace guessed were her own and finished with a cover of Otis Redding's 'These Arms of Mine', by which time most of Grace's make-up had run off her face. Ada whispered her thanks into the microphone. The cheers swelled as she left the stage.

Grace rode the tube home, rattled and flickering like the fluorescent lights above her. The rest of the world was muted, the exterior noise and clamour stamped out; all she could think of was the small woman in the spotlight, her voice soaring. The music had washed straight through Grace, and she thought that if she let it, the music could flush away her old self. The old Grace had been naive, closeted from the world by her overly protective, meddling, controlling mother; the old Grace had stupidly thought she was loved by a man who was clearly a dick.

But now there could be London Grace. It was easy because so many everyday things in the UK were different to what they were back home. No, not home. Australia. Different shampoo brands, different power sockets, different varieties of bread, different labels on jam, different types of leaves on the ground (except for those from the Eucalyptus tree on the end of the street), different birds, front gardens full of plants which were considered weeds in Australia but in the UK were quite legit, different care labels on clothing, different clothing stores, squirrels, people who walked down Oxford Street looking like they had stepped off a runway or filmset, city farms, different radio stations, different news presenters, more cyclists, people of all colours from all corners of the world, red buses, different scented washing powder, old people playing chess in the park, big parks, lots of big parks.

London Grace would not be fooled by cute boys with guitars. She would not be naive. She would not dwell on what she had lost, because London Grace had not lost anything.

◎

When Grace went back to Drop a month later she didn't go inside to watch Ada perform; instead she gave the bouncer another twenty quid and he told her about the rear door, down a back alley. Ada never hung around after gigs, he said. Never came out and sat in the bar. So Grace waited for an hour in the cold alleyway, her back turned to the hostile wind, her numb hands stuffed under her armpits. Grace was usually only nervous before big meetings, when she was anxious on Tony's behalf. He would just wink at her and say, 'Showtime,' under his breath before they walked into some bigwig's boardroom. It's a part, Grace, she imagined him saying to her right now. It's a part and you gotta play it.

When the door opened it was the drummer who came out first, feeling around in his pockets, an unlit cigarette between his lips. Grace stepped up to him and held out a lighter she had bought for this very purpose, wishing her hand wasn't trembling; wishing she knew what the fuck she was doing or had at least talked to Tony about it first. The drummer eyed Grace, but he took the lighter.

'I need to talk to Ada,' Grace said.

He shook his head. 'You're not gonna.'

Grace held out her business card and the guy glanced at it. 'Congratulations. But you're not talking to her.'

'Isn't that for her to decide?'

'Yeah, and that's what she's decided. My job is to come out first and make sure everyone has fucked off so she can go home.'

'She hasn't met me.'

A cab pulled up.

'This would work for everyone, you know,' Grace said. 'The whole band. All she needs is someone to look after her.'

'We've got a manager.'

'Who? Because I'd never heard of Ada until I walked past here a few weeks ago. So they're not doing their job very well.'

The door opened and a man—fifties, greasy-looking in a black vinyl jacket—came out. He looked Grace over. 'Who the fuck are you?'

'Grace Harlow. Eastlake Management.'

'Oh yeah? We don't need anything from you.'

He was definitely the manager.

'Why's she still playing in tiny clubs?'

'Because that's what she likes.'

'How much does he take from your pocket?' Grace asked the drummer. 'Fifteen, twenty percent?'

'Oh, piss off,' said the manager.

Grace held her card out to the drummer. 'I'll only take five percent. Have a think. Talk to Ada.'

She walked away, regretting she hadn't said seven rather than five. Seven would have done it.

◎

The playground in Wanstead was as far from a posh Southbank restaurant as Grace could imagine. At first she couldn't see Ada among the gathered women and little kids, but a girl in a pink hoodie and trackpants stood up from a bench next to the swings and gave Grace a small wave. She was almost unrecognisable and younger than Grace had originally thought. When Grace introduced herself, Ada only nodded towards a little girl swooping back and forth on a swing at alarming speed.

'No, I'm not the nanny,' she said. 'Yes, she's mine, a teen pregnancy, and no, I'm not with her dad. He died. Accident at work, in a warehouse, not drink and drugs. So you can give up any ideas you got about me being your next big thing.'

'Thanks for meeting me anyway.'

Ada swept hair from her face. 'Well, Tom said you waited an hour in the cold. So.'

'What's her name?'

'Susie.' Ada pulled a drink bottle out of rainbow backpack and called her daughter.

'She's very . . .' Grace wasn't adept at kid talk. 'Cute?'

The girl slid off the swing and ran to her mother. She sniffed loudly and wiped her nose with the back of her hand.

'Oi! That's not how we do it, is it?' Ada wiped her daughter's nose with a tissue. 'Say 'allo to Grace.'

''Allo, Grace.'

Ada gave the girl her drink bottle and Susie took a long sip, eyes locked on Grace. When she was done she handed the drink back to Ada and ran off to a climbing frame.

'I looked at your website,' Ada said. 'What you want with me? I'm not really your cup of tea.'

'I saw you play and I think you're incredible.'

'Pfft.'

'Are you on the radio?'

'I've only recorded two tracks.'

'Why's that?'

'It's fucking expensive. Ronnie books the gigs, puts the money in my account. Not usually enough left over to hire a studio for more than half an hour.'

'Does he get you?'

'What's that supposed to mean?'

'Does he understand you, what you're doing? Does he see your potential?'

'Did you miss the bit about me being a single mum of a four-year-old?'

'Ada, if you could get a record deal—'

'My name's not Ada Black. It's Allison Brown.'

'Well, you wouldn't have to pay for a studio out of your own pocket. I'm a twenty-five-year-old woman with a corner office in a business that doesn't listen to twenty-five-year-old women. I've got a boss who is always on the lookout for people with real promise. I will look after you and I will make sure that you can do all the things you want to do: record, play gigs, all of it.'

'I'm unreliable. I get nervous. It's a wonder Ronnie can book me anywhere at all these days.'

'But there's always a line out the door.'

Ada shrugged. 'At Drop, sure. I don't play hardly anywhere else.'

'I can help you with that.'

'Babe, I vomit me guts up before every gig as it is. You think I'm gonna play Wembley for you one day?'

'I can help with the nerves.'

Ada watched Grace and said nothing. Susie ran over to her, wrapping herself around Ada's leg.

'Mummy, I need a poo.'

'I don't have time for any of it,' Ada said to Grace. 'As you can see.'

'I'll get you a nanny when you need one.'

The mention of a nanny made Ada pause.

'You're incredible,' Grace said. 'I've seen a lot of acts. A lot. But nothing like you.'

'I need to think.'

'Do you still have my card? There's a postal address on it. Think. Send me the tracks you recorded. Anything else you have too. Sing into a tape recorder. I don't care, just send me something. I can make this happen. You could be Ada all the time.'

As Grace rode the bus back to the office she wondered how Tony would feel about giving her a corner office.

◎

Grace set Tony's peppermint tea and a sticky bun on his desk beside the stack of financial spreadsheets she'd given him an hour earlier. He took a bite from the bun and kept his eyes on the numbers.

'This is fucked, this is. My whole life I wanted this job, now I'm sat here looking at fucking numbers the whole day.'

'Not the whole day. You have lunch with Flip.'

Flip Breezy was Tony's latest obsession—he was twenty-two and lived on an estate with his mum, who had been on welfare her whole life. Flip had a shimmering talent for lyricism. He was the real thing.

'Are the numbers okay?' Grace asked.

'The numbers are a pain in arse, but they are fine. Why you hovering like that?'

'I found someone.'

Tony took another bite and made a listening sound.

'Not hip hop, though. Not electronica. Not a rapper.'

'Oh yeah?' He picked up a sheet of paper and squinted at it. 'What then?'

'She's a singer, writes her own stuff. Unsigned. I can't think how to categorise her. It's a bit soul, a bit bluesy, but . . . different. I don't think there's anyone else like her out there.'

'You got a disc?'

Grace placed the CD Ada had sent her on top of the spreadsheets. 'I just gave you an excuse to take a break from the numbers.'

'Hmm.'

A little later Tony emerged from his office. He put his hands in his pockets and leaned on the doorframe. 'She's not like our guys,' he said.

'No.'

'She's not like anyone.'

'I know.'

'She your thing?'

'I think she's phenomenal.'

'Then you should bring her in.'

◎

When Grace had asked Tony to come with her to the meeting at Universal he'd laughed.

'Whadda you want me there for?' he said. 'She's your girl. You got this.'

But now that she and Ada were sitting in a plush meeting room in Kensington opposite someone called Jacky Sloane—who was chewing gum and looking at Ada like she was a menu item—Grace wondered if she really did have this.

'What you have to understand, ladies,' said Sloane, 'is that when I'm selling an act, I'm looking at the whole picture, yeah? The tracks are great. Love the tracks. Really top stuff. But what you gotta understand is that in order for you to make it in this industry, I've got to know where to put you. Say you're a vegetable, I've got to know where to put you in a supermarket, yeah? Are you a carrot? Are you a potato? Are you celery? So then I can say, yeah, Ada Black, she's—'

'I'm not a potato,' said Ada.

'It's an analogy, love.'

'It's not a good one.'

'Doesn't matter!' He laughed. 'What I'm saying is, I love the tracks, love them, but I've got to know where to put Ada Black in the supermarket, like. And to be honest, I just can't think of where I would put you at the moment.'

'Maybe it would help if you didn't think of me as a bloody potato,' Ada muttered.

Grace cleared her throat and tried to keep in mind Tony's technique of making authoritative statements rather than asking pleading questions. 'The thing that's exciting about Ada's sound—and I'm sure you'll agree—is that it's unique. She can't be pigeonholed.'

'Sure, sure, absolutely. I'm not saying I don't like it. I love it! What I'm hoping you are open to is developing that sound and—'

Ada's scowl intensified. 'Developing?'

'Take Holly Chase, for example. When we started working with Holly she was a bit jazz so we *developed* that and now she's top five on the charts.'

'You developed it into mindless pop shite,' said Ada.

'Okay,' said Grace. She placed a gentle hand on Ada's arm.

'Another thing you need to consider is the changing market demands. People ain't buying albums like they used to. It's all the internet this, internet that. Someone was telling me just the other day that CDs might be done away with completely. Everybody listening on their computers. So where's the money coming from? I'll tell you for free. Touring. Live shows. So the question I'm asking myself is, what's Ada Black like on a stage? Because I'll be square with you: I've heard some whispers and they ain't all complimentary.'

Ada pushed her chair back from the table.

'Now hold your horses,' Sloane said. 'We are willing to put a very attractive offer on the table. Very attractive. A game changer. If you're willing to work with us to reach your full potential.'

Grace's phone vibrated. She silenced it. Once more the screen lit up. Tony. He wouldn't normally interrupt a meeting.

'Excuse me, Mr Sloane. I have to take this.'

Grace pressed the phone to her ear.

'How's the meet?' Tony asked.

'I'm still in it.'

'Sloane there? Say to me: "Sure thing, Paul. She's looking forward to it too." Say it.'

'Sure thing, Paul. She's looking forward to it too.'

Sloane's eyes darted to Ada.

'Now,' said Tony, 'say goodbye, and when you hang up make big-time apologies, say a meeting has moved and you gotta run.'

'Okay then.' Grace glanced at her watch. 'No, we can get there. Thanks, Paul. Bye now.'

Grace ended the call and smiled at Sloane.

'Mr Sloane, this has been so great. Very exciting. Thank you for fitting us in, but I'm afraid I've just had a meeting shift and we have to dash.'

◎

'That true about touring?' Ada asked Grace in the elevator. 'And who is Paul?'

The doors slid open and Ada followed Grace out into the sleek atrium where huge photos of everyone from David Bowie to Lily Allen hung on walls which really were quite impressive in height.

'Paul Teck is at DMU,' Grace said.

'And we're meeting him now?'

'No. That was Tony on the phone.' Grace lowered her voice as they passed the reception desk. 'We want Sloane to think we have a meeting at DMU right now. We want Sloane to feel pressure. With the right pressure we can get what we want from him.'

Ada stopped walking and planted her five-pound Top Shop heels firmly on the marble floor. 'I don't want anything from him. He's a fucking tosser.'

A receptionist glanced at Ada.

'Well, he has a direct line to Michael Wester here at Universal. That means a lot of influence.'

'Fuck his influence. I'm not interested.'

'Ada . . .'

'I'm not doing this.'

The other receptionist was watching now. As were the three people sitting on the extremely comfortable lounges.

'Ada, we can control—'

'Nope,' repeated Ada. 'No, thank you very much. This is what I don't want. Fuck him.' She turned to the onlookers. 'Fuck the lot of you. Bloody tossers.' Ada slung her bag over her shoulder and strode away through the automatic doors at a pace that was impressive for someone in stilettos.

◎

For the three days following, Ada ignored Grace's phone calls. On the fourth day, when Grace took a chance as she was making toast, Ada finally answered.

'What?'

'I'm just checking in,' Grace said. 'You've been quite difficult to get a hold of.'

'Rubbish. You're not checking in; you're lining up your bloody cash cow.'

'You're not my cash cow, Ada.'

'I don't want any of it! I told you. I don't want to play fucking Wembley. I'm perfectly bloody happy the way I am. I don't want any of those tossers and their bloody deals. They're not turning me into another Holly Chase. I don't care how many houses she has.'

'Ada—'

'Nope. We are done, Grace. Don't call me again.'

The line went dead.

Grace bit into her toast. This was a spanner in the works.

It was days since Grace had spoken with Ada. Tony had been in the US but now he was back and looking for an update. He stuffed a sticky bun into his mouth, leaning back in his chair, feet on his desk. It was a habit he had developed following the record deal he had brokered with Warner for Flip Breezy's album; a habit befitting a mogul, Tony felt.

Grace was not feeling like a mogul, or indeed like anyone who had a future in the industry beyond sourcing sticky buns.

'So?' Tony's voice was muffled. 'Where we at with your girl Ada? You heard back from Sloane?'

'Well . . .'

'Well?'

'Well . . . Sloane called her a potato and wants to turn her into Holly Chase.'

Tony chuckled.

'That's how Ada sees it, anyway,' Grace said. 'Oh, and she thinks we think she's a cash cow. Specifically my cash cow.'

'And how do you see it?'

'I don't think of her as a cash cow; I genuinely want—'

''Course you don't. And it don't matter how she sees it. You gotta make her see what *you* see.'

'So . . .'

'Spit it out, girl. This ain't like you, backward in coming forward.'

'I had an idea.'

'Oh yeah?' Tony crammed the last bite of sticky bun into his mouth and licked his fingers.

Grace handed him a napkin. 'What if *we* recorded her?' she said. '*We* release it? Under our name. Your name. You could diversify. I've done the budget, and it will cost, yes, but you can take my pay, put that towards it. I know it won't be much but . . .'

'You want to give up your pay to record her?'

'Well, some of my pay. I'll still need to eat and stuff. She doesn't want to ever talk to me again, but she might if we're the ones recording her.'

Tony was watching her, wiping his hands.

'What do you think?' she asked him.

'If we record her, we become a label.'

'I guess.'

'And if you put in a few quid, you're a co-founder.'

'Is that okay with you?'

Tony laughed. 'Girl, it's cool with me. It's a fine idea.'

'Thank you.' Grace turned to leave his office.

'Gracie,' said Tony.

'Yes?'

'You got a good head on them shoulders.'

12

2008

THE RELEASE OF ADA'S ALBUM FLIPPED THE BUSINESS ON ITS HEAD AND blew it inside out.

The money they were making allowed them to record more artists and soon East Common Records was more than afloat, it was soaring. And Grace had a fifty percent share.

She bought a flat in Shoreditch, a nice one in a building that wasn't sinking into the ground, and insisted Nish move in with her. At first, Nish had baulked at the idea.

'You took me in and looked after me,' Grace said to her. 'Let me look after you for a bit.'

'Fine. But if you turn into some rich tosser who drops six hundred quid on, I don't know, a fucking paperweight, I'm moving out.'

Sometimes Grace took Nish to award ceremonies and parties as her plus one because Nish was always keen to take the piss out of everyone behind their backs, which was highly entertaining and helped pass the time when things were tedious. A lot of people assumed Nish and Grace were a couple, something Grace found immensely useful in that it prevented most guys from coming anywhere near her. (Most guys. It never ceased to amaze her how many men thought they were the gateway to heterosexuality.) Nish had bounced back and forth among a few guys, but none of her relationships stuck. She remained in contact with Ravi. They were friends, Nish insisted. Nothing more.

◎

Tonight, half an hour before Ada was supposed to take the stage in front of nearly five thousand people, she was in the dressing room, crouched in a corner, head in her hands and making a soft moaning sound. Grace should have been there much, much earlier.

The stage manager was unimpressed.

'What's she on?' he asked Grace as she came through the door. ''Cause she was fine for sound check.'

'Nothing. It's stage fright.'

'Sure,' he sneered. 'Of course it is. She needs to sort herself out.'

The Royal Albert Hall was sold out. It was bigger than any venue Ada had ever played. Grace had spent hours convincing her to do it. Most of the time it was wonderful to be so needed; Ada was like an extraordinary creature, mythical, luminous, and nobody could see her unless Grace was there to speak the magic words, breathe life into her. At other times it was really bloody stressful and Ada's dramatics felt inconvenient and unnecessary, especially when there was trackwork on the Piccadilly Line and Grace had worn the wrong shoes for rushing.

Ada's moan increased in volume, and Grace crouched down beside her.

'You're going on,' Grace told her. 'You always do: you go onstage, open your mouth and sing, and it works. Every time.'

'I thought you weren't coming.'

'I was. I am.'

'I can't do it without you.'

'You can. And I'm here now anyway.'

Ada took huge gulping breaths and Grace stroked her back like she was sick child.

To Grace, Ada's journey across the darkened stage to the microphone took an age. At each step, she looked as though she might topple, or turn and run. But she made it: she stood at the mic, smoothed her black dress over her hips and took a deep breath. Grace gave a nod to the stage director. A single spotlight illuminated Ada and the audience roared. She had no hair to hide behind; it had been teased into a glamorous platinum bouffant. Her diamond earrings twinkled but Ada didn't move.

She had once told Grace that she was never sure if the audience was happy or jeering with disappointment once they saw her in the flesh. It didn't matter how many times she did it, Ada said, in that moment, under the lights before she opened her mouth, she could never tell. And this time, as she stood before the microphone, she looked certain the crowd was yelling at her, not for her. Grace could tell Ada was trying to see the faces, trying to gauge their disappointment. The roar was thunderous now. Ada glanced over at Grace in the wings. Her expression was one of blind panic. She opened her mouth and nothing came out.

'Put the houselights up,' Grace said to the lighting director.

The auditorium flooded with light and Grace grinned at Ada. Saw her take in the thousands of people who were losing their minds with excitement. Saw her breathe.

''Allo, London, don't you look blooming gorgeous,' Ada said, like she was chatting to a neighbour over the fence. The wave of applause rolled over her, she closed her eyes, the houselights went out again, the music swelled and Ada opened her mouth.

Backstage afterwards, Ada flopped into an armchair, pulling pins from her hair.

'Can you believe that? Can you believe it?' she said over and over, eyes wide. 'They loved it. I never seen anything like that. My god. The Royal Albert Hall. Can you believe it?'

'I can. They love you.' Grace was exhausted. She needed to sit on her couch, put her feet in an ice bath and watch television. 'What do you want to do? Go home? Or do you need something to eat?'

'What time is it?'

'Ten thirty.'

'Oh shit. Shit, shit, shit. I missed Susie's bedtime. I was supposed to call Charlie before I went on. Oh shit!'

Charlie had started out as Ada's personal trainer, but Ada had a way of pulling people into her orbit. Charlie had developed first into her friend, then her partner and now husband. Grace was grateful for these promotions; it almost halved her workload.

'I called Charlie. He said Susie was fine; she went to bed no problem.'

Ada sighed. 'In that case I want to go down the pub.'

'Then that's what we'll do.'

◎

It was a pub in Soho, nice but not as nice as it could be. The air was thick with lager and whisky, laughter and talk. Scrubbed of make-up, in her jeans and t-shirt, Ada passed as just another girl at the bar.

She returned to the table and handed Grace a whisky sour. 'Cheers, babe.'

'You did a good job tonight.'

'Couldn't do it without you,' Ada said and launched into a detailed debrief. Grace desperately needed the loo, but she listened and nodded with understanding as Ada talked. When Ada paused to take a breath, Grace excused herself.

Three women were lined up waiting for the single cubicle and Grace had to lean on the door to keep it open. There wasn't enough room for them all in the tiny bathroom. A full five minutes passed. Grace was conscious of her very famous charge waiting in the upstairs bar; her famous charge who was no doubt harbouring the simultaneous longing for anonymity and craving for attention. The women in the queue were exchanging glances now.

'Do you think everything's okay in there?' Grace asked none of them in particular.

The girl at the front of the queue knocked on the cubicle door. 'You all right in there, love?'

'Give me a minute, for eff's sake!'

'You've had ten.'

'Feck off!'

The men's bathroom was empty, and even if it wasn't Grace would have challenged any man who tried to deny her right to a wee. The cubicle had one of those stupid locks where it was impossible to tell whether it was locked or unlocked, so just in case Grace leaned forward and held the door closed with one hand while trying to wee. It was awkward and she was terrified someone would push the door open. When she was done and attempted to open the door it became apparent that it had been locked—so effectively, in fact, that now she couldn't get it open.

She twisted the lock back and forth, pushed and pulled, to no avail. Ada was probably feeling quite abandoned by now. Grace looked in her bag for her phone and realised that she'd left it on the table. She rattled the lock and thumped on the door.

'You all right in there?' asked a man's voice. Australian accent. Grace wondered if he would be offended by her female presence in his designated bathroom.

'Um. No. Quite stuck actually. Door won't open.'

'Oh. Are you a woman?'

'I'm not stuck because I'm a woman.'

'I wasn't suggesting that. You just sound a bit like a woman. I didn't want to try and open the door if . . .'

'I'm fully clothed. Go for it.'

'Right.'

He was trying to unlock the door and having the same level of success as Grace.

'Are you Australian?' Grace asked.

'That's not why I can't open the door.'

'Ha. I'm Australian,' Grace said. 'Maybe that is the problem.'

'You don't sound Australian,' he said. The lock rattled.

'I'm not lying.'

'I wasn't suggesting you were.'

'You're not having much effect,' she said.

'No need to rub it in. I'll go and see if there's a key or something. Don't go anywhere.'

'I don't think there's a keyhole.'

'I could get a screwdriver and take the door off.'

'Do you reckon anyone in this place has a screwdriver?'

'Only one way to find out.'

'Actually, while you're at it, can you go up and find someone for me? She's tiny and blonde and wearing a grey hoodie. Sitting near the bar, probably freaking out. Can you tell her I'm okay, just stuck in the loo?'

'Sure. Screwdriver, tiny blonde woman.'

'Sorry. Thank you so much.'

'That's okay. I'm here for a stag thing and everyone's slaughtered already. It's nice to have something to do.'

A few moments later and Ada was knocking on the toilet door. 'Some bloke said you're stuck! He's looking for a screwdriver.'

'Go home. I'll be fine. Just get a cab. You don't look like Ada out of your make-up. There won't be an issue.'

'I don't feel right leaving you.'

But Grace could hear the slight lack of sincerity.

'You should go. You need sleep.'

'He's quite cute, you know.'

'Who?'

'The bloke who's trying to rescue you. He's got a bit of a lumberjack look to him. Oh, hang on, here he is. Love you.'

And Ada was gone.

'Bad news,' said the bloke. 'There're no screwdrivers to be found. I suggested various other ways of getting you out—breaking down the door and so forth—but they are very concerned about safety and insurance or something. So they've called the fire brigade.'

'I'm not on fire.'

'Then that's one less thing to worry about.'

'How long till they get here?'

'Depends how many fires they have to put out first, I guess.'

'Annoying for me, probably good for people dealing with fires, I suppose. Well, thanks for your help anyway.'

'No worries. Too easy.'

She'd missed that phrase. Grace unspooled a few metres of perilously thin toilet paper and made herself a little mat to sit on. She leaned her back against the tiled wall, closed her eyes and tried to settle in for the night.

'Hey, what's your friend's name?'

The voice startled her. 'I thought you'd gone!'

'Nope. Sorry, is that okay? I didn't want to leave you here for god knows how long.'

'What about the bucks' night?'

'I'd rather be in the toilets talking to a stranger. I could swear I've met your friend before. What's her name?'

'Allison.'

'I've got no idea how I know her.'

'Where are you from?' Grace asked him. 'In Australia, I mean.'

'Sydney.'

'How come you're in London?'

'Oh. Um. I got an artist's residency thing.'

'Are you an artist?'

'So they say.'

'You must be legit if you don't want to talk about it. The good ones never do. What sort of artist?'

After much encouragement he told her he was a painter, and that he wasn't sure how he felt about London but he knew it was a rare opportunity, 'and so on, and so on,' he said. Somehow, while they were talking, almost two hours passed and when the fire brigade turned up Grace was disappointed their conversation had to be cut short.

◎

Nish walked out of her bedroom and dumped a dozen pairs of earrings onto the kitchen table. She was wearing the kind of sequinned jumpsuit that would make most people look like a circus performer but made Nish look like a goddess. Grace was surprised at how well Nish had pulled herself together in order to accompany her to Ed's exhibition opening. (Although Nish was still referring to him as Loo Guy, an unhelpful nickname on a number of levels.) It was only a week ago that Grace had come home one evening and found Nish curled up on the couch with an empty bottle of tequila on the floor beside her.

'Ravi's engaged,' Nish had sobbed. 'The love of my life is marrying someone else.'

Grace did not point out that this was the first time Nish had referred to Ravi as the love of her life.

In the week that followed, Nish stumbled about in a haze of inebriated distress. She had always been able to put away a serious amount of alcohol, but this was worse. Grace was tempted to tell her she was being melodramatic and should take herself on a tour of the Tower of London to remind herself what true suffering was.

Yet tonight Nish was upright and looking smashing as she scrutinised Grace's pleated, seventies midi-dress. 'Is that what you're wearing?' she asked.

'What's wrong with this?' Grace sorted through the earrings; they were all very large.

'Can't see your legs, love. You should wear that black-and-silver mini.'

'I have a thing at eleven.'

'Who has a bloody meeting at eleven p.m.?'

'Flip has a gig. Tony has another thing he needs to be at, so I need to be at the gig.'

'I'm sure Flip Breezy will feel very well supported by a white chick dressed as Margaret Thatcher's secretary. This is about priorities. You need to take this seriously.'

'I take my job seriously.'

'We all fucking know that. But in this instance you should be prioritising lovely Loo Guy.'

'You haven't even met him.'

'He sat and talked with you for two hours without even seeing your face.'

'Then he should be fine without seeing my legs. And I told you he's not my type.'

'Love, if he's a brooding artist he's your type.'

'He's not brooding.'

'Then he mustn't be very good. Get changed.'

◎

An hour later, Grace—in a very short dress—was standing before a painting that took up almost an entire wall. From what she could tell it was of the sky and tree branches and something else in the middle distance—or what she thought might have been the middle distance—that she couldn't identify. Perhaps a moose. Or a rock. It didn't matter to Grace that she couldn't identify all the objects because the painting itself—the movement, the colour—was extraordinary. And she couldn't work out why. Perhaps that was its brilliance. The brochure said it was three thousand pounds and the artist's statement talked about a dialogue with the landscape, and something or other about the exterior and interior self.

Across the room Ed was standing among of knot of loud people, one of whom was delicately beautiful and appeared to be topless beneath her fur jacket. She had a shaved head and a tattoo of a lotus flower on the nape of her neck. She had been beside Ed most of the night. Now, she took Ed's hand and said something in his ear. The group erupted in laughter, all of them except Ed. He looked away and his eyes met Grace's. Ed slipped his hand out of the woman's grasp and joined Grace in front of the painting.

'Don't read that,' he said, nodding at the brochure in Grace's hand. 'It's all shite.'

'I don't know anything about art,' Grace said. 'It might help.'

'There's nothing to know; what I wanted to write was that I like trees and the sky. Also mountains. So that's why I paint them, only I don't care if they actually *look* like trees and mountains. I just want the painting to make people feel something.'

'It's beautiful.'

He grimaced and pointed to the bottom left corner. 'I'm not sure anymore. I don't like that bit.'

'Are you going around and pointing out the bits of the paintings you don't like?'

'Gustus expressly told me not to do that.'

'Well, you didn't get here in time—it looks like it's sold.'

'Means I can pay another month's rent.'

'That's good.'

'Yes, it is . . . Do you really like it or are you just being nice?'

'I'm not just being nice. If I didn't like it I wouldn't say anything at all.'

'Oh really?'

'Really. It's beautiful.'

'Thank you.'

Ed didn't say anything more, and Grace couldn't think of anything either. So they stood beside each other looking at the painting. She was aware that she didn't want him to go away. Men didn't make her nervous generally, and she wasn't even sure she was nervous now, she just couldn't find a way of keeping the conversation going, of stopping him from wandering off to find more faults with his paintings. But he didn't wander off. After a few more moments of silence he let out quite a loud sigh and said, 'That's my girlfriend over there. I don't like her very much. I've tried to break up with her, but she always argues me back into it.'

Ed didn't look at Grace while he spoke. He stood with his hands in his pockets, staring at the bottom left corner of the painting. He had a neat beard and thick brown less-neat hair; he wore jeans, boots and a chunky brown sweater—which itself was quite hairy. The week before, when Grace was released from the toilet cubicle, it felt like the big reveal from one of those old dating shows, where two contestants chatted for a bit while separated by a panel before—voila!—they finally they saw each other's face. In the moment when the two of them had looked at each other Grace hadn't found him breathtakingly attractive, but she had wondered if he was single.

'I'm thinking about running away and changing my identity so she can't find me,' he said now.

'That's quite extreme.'

'Would you go out to dinner with me? She's probably going to come over here and lick my neck or something in a minute. So I wanted to put that out there before she does.'

'Will she be at dinner too?'

'No. If we are going out for dinner it gives me a deadline. I absolutely one hundred percent have to break up with her before then.'

So he wasn't really asking her out, was he? No. It sounded more like she was part of a strategy.

'You're not part of my strategy,' he said before she could reply. 'Sorry, I should have pointed that out. I would actually like to have dinner with you. Is that still what people do? Man. I'm not great at this, am I?'

'I think it's still what people do. It's something I would like to do.'

He looked at her now, surprised. 'Really? Great. That's . . . yep. That's great.'

'Good.'

'Yes. Good.'

13

ED

THE TWO FIREMEN ENTERED THE TOILETS WITH A LEVEL OF NONCHALANCE Ed felt was inappropriate. He wondered if they had come as soon as they could or if they'd stopped for a kebab on the way. They didn't smell of smoke.

'Are you the manager?' one of them asked Ed.

He didn't know what to say. He wasn't the manager but he didn't want to bow out of the situation either. If he left now he might not meet her face to face. 'No, I'm her . . . mate.'

'Aw, thanks,' came the voice from behind the door.

She had a great voice. And Ed couldn't remember the last time he'd been in the company of a genuinely funny person. It felt like everyone he met was either conceited, pretentious or a dickhead who thought their dickheadish shenanigans were hilarious. She wasn't any of those things. She was a woman trapped in a bathroom stall and he wanted to spend more time with her.

Ed's girlfriend—or the woman he'd thought was his girlfriend—wasn't funny, but she was interesting. And very, very hot. Livia could spend a long time talking about art, and Ed very much appreciated this—it was a topic his mates back in Australia were less inclined to indulge in. Ed had been under the impression that they were a couple, but when Livia had introduced him to her art school mates (wankers) she said, 'This is Ed, we fuck a lot,' which Ed supposed was true but not exactly how he would define his relationship with her. He also wasn't sure how sustainable it was to have a relationship was with someone whose art he found . . . jarring. Performance wasn't really his thing. Recently Livia had acquired a small grant to stand on a plinth in Trafalgar Square all day wearing a nude bodystocking and moaning. (The moaning was difficult to sustain, and in the end she'd had to conceal an amp in the plinth so it could play a recording of the moan.) Livia's original plan was to be hoisted fifteen metres above the ground in a cherry picker and drop raw eggs to the ground while moaning, but the cherry picker hire really blew out the budget in her grant application. Plus the council were likely to throw in some Public Health and Safety bullshit to prevent her from dropping eggs. That fully conceived performance was something to work towards, she said. More an Established Artist's grant than an Emerging one. It worried Ed that Livia considered herself to still be in the process of emerging. The fully realised Livia had the potential to be truly terrifying.

'What's your girlfriend's name?' the fireman asked Ed, nodding in the direction of the toilet cubicle.

'Um . . .'

She laughed. 'Grace. My name's Grace.'

And when, after some work from the firemen, the door was removed from the cubicle, Ed could see that it suited her perfectly.

Now that his exhibition was opening, Ed felt the paintings were okay. An improvement on last week's fear that they were naive, insipid rubbish. Openings were weird: a bunch of people crowded into a white space, drinking wine from plastic cups, talking and laughing and barely looking at the actual art. There was so much bullshitting involved. A lot of 'Oh my god, it's amazing!' even though a lot of the time it wasn't amazing. He'd actually been talking to someone at an opening once, someone who was telling him how shit the works were, only to witness them turn around and gush to the artist's face about their evident genius. So you couldn't trust anyone's opinion, really. This was Ed's first solo show and he didn't want to go to the opening. He'd rather sit at home on his own, watch *QI* and go to bed at a reasonable hour. Let people come and look at the paintings, sure—just, please, not in his presence. That didn't fly with Gustus, though. (Ed was surrounded by people who were missing the first part of their name: Livia, Topher, Bastian etc.) Gustus said Ed's presence at his own opening wasn't negotiable. Nor was the delivery of a speech. 'I'll talk about how brilliant you are,' Gustus said, 'then you do your charming, self-deprecating schtick. They'll lap it up like thirsty kittens and buy all your shit.'

Until that point, Ed hadn't been aware he had a schtick. He was usually just trying to avoid sounding like a wanker. 'You'll never make it with that attitude, honey,' Gustus told him. Frequently.

It felt like no one was painting anymore. It was all installation, performance, video or sound. Nothing, Gustus said, that you could actually sell. 'Believe it or not, Eddie, people still live in houses with walls and they like putting pictures on them. People with money. That's where you come in.' Plus his work was important etc. etc. 'Trust me, the tide is turning,' Gustus assured him. 'And luckily for you, you're already a bloody good painter. All the other twats will have to learn how to hold a brush.'

There were more people here than Ed had anticipated. How many of them would actually want to put his paintings in their house, he didn't know. He leaned on the wall outside, sipped his beer and watched them arriving. No one noticed him. Surely he could just stick around for the speeches and then slip away.

Grace wouldn't come. He was certain of it. She was probably just being polite when she'd said she would. In fact, he had convinced himself that he hoped she wouldn't come. He'd rather her not show up than turn out to be a person who bullshitted about paintings.

Only here she was, walking towards him with a woman dressed as an acrobat. They were talking and Grace was laughing. She was wearing a short black dress and looked amazing. Better than amazing. He hadn't exaggerated it in his imagination since they first met. The other woman noticed him before Grace did. He gave a nod of greeting. Grace saw him then.

'Well, hello!'

'Hey! Thanks for coming!'

'How are you?' She kissed his cheek like she'd known him forever.

◎

By some miracle, Grace had agreed to have dinner with him a few days later. She was already there when Ed walked into the restaurant. He'd suggested a different place, somewhere closer to her work. He was stupidly old-fashioned with outdated ideas and concerns for women's safety (Livia's words) and didn't like the thought of her having to catch the tube and the bus *and* walk across a park at night just to meet him. But she insisted. She told him over the phone that Manjit's was better and, according to a friend of hers, the place he'd suggested was shithouse. He'd felt a bit ashamed for suggesting the apparently crap restaurant, but he also liked the way she used the word 'shithouse'.

This place didn't look better, it looked much worse: vinyl tiled floor, peeling wallpaper, plastic chairs. But it smelled good. Grace was reading a book with her chin resting on her hand, elbow on the table. Her golden hair was piled up in a knot, perfectly dishevelled, a stray lock curling at the nape of her elegant neck. He was already at the table before she noticed him.

'Am I late?' he asked.

'No—gosh no.' She seemed flustered, closing the book, reaching around for her bag to put it in. 'I was early,' she said. 'My meeting was cancelled.'

'Oh. Annoying.'

'It's fine. I got to read for a while. I never get enough time to read.'

'What are you reading?'

'Um. Patricia Cornwell. Murder mystery. I'm not very high-brow—I'm addicted to crime thrillers. The worst thing has already happened, you know? Everything's gone to shit and then a classy woman with a scalpel waltzes in and sorts it all out. I like that a lot.'

'She's killing people with a scalpel?'

'No, she's a forensic pathologist. Cuts dead people open. Solves crimes.'

'Ah. That makes more sense.' Ed sat down and tried to relax.

'I just can't enjoy the books I wish I could enjoy,' Grace said. 'I was going to study English lit but discovered that beyond Austen I don't like it very much. I prefer this stuff. I wish I was the kind of person who adored *Anna Karenina*. But, wow, so much farming. And I'm sure it's relevant, it's there for a reason, so if I don't read carefully I'll miss something important.'

'It's not that important. You can skip a lot of the farming stuff and still get the gist.'

'Oh, have you read it?'

Ed nodded.

She laughed. 'You love it, don't you?'

'Yep. I really do. Sorry.'

'Should I leave? I'm the girl who likes the trashy crime books now, aren't I.'

'I think people should read what they want to read. And . . .'

'Hm?'

'You could give it another go, try skipping the farming. Honestly. It's an incredible book. Made me cry.' Why did he have to tell her he cried? 'Did you end up studying something else? At uni, I mean. A degree isn't a prerequisite, by the way.'

'You'll still have dinner with me?'

'Yeah.' He probably sounded like a dickhead. This was all the wrong way around. She was the gorgeous one who could have as many prerequisites as she wanted.

'I dropped out halfway through. Studied economics with a lot of humanities that had nothing to do with economics. Too much music history and theory. There's not a lot of call for music historians it turns out.'

'Do you play anything?'

She smiled. 'I play a lot of records.'

14
GRACE

AFTER DINNER, GRACE CALLED NISH FROM THE BUS.

'And?' Nish said by way of a greeting.

'It was fine. He's nice.'

'Wow, you need to slow down, you do. Too much bloody excitement. Fine? Nice? What does that mean? Boring? Sounds boring.'

'No. It wasn't boring at all. He's lovely. I just . . .'

'Yeah?'

'Well, it's not . . . there's not instant sparks.'

'Instant bloody sparks? Is that you want? Ohhhh, you want it to be like it was with that tosser.'

'No, I don't.'

'You don't?'

'No.'

'Because you never want to love again, am I right? This is nothing to do with this Ed fella. This is about that fuckwit who broke your fucking heart.'

'It was seven years ago.'

'Don't matter how long ago it was, love. You're not match fit.'

'He is really nice. And he's funny. But . . .'

'Would you see him again?'

'I don't know. I'd like to be friends.'

'Oh, fuck that. You've got enough friends. And have some bloody respect; he doesn't want to be your friend. You know what's interesting to me? You're on the bus. You'll be home in a half-hour, plenty of time to talk to me then, but you've called me, haven't you. Which in my mind means you're contemplating something, and if you're contemplating something it means it was more than just bloody fine. Tell me: am I wrong?'

'Maybe.'

'Fuck me, you're hopeless. I'll pop the kettle on. See you soon.'

◎

A week later Grace and Ed met at a park bench on Southbank, outside the Tate Modern. Ed handed her a coffee and a danish in a paper bag and they sat down. The coffee was good. So was the danish. He had a bacon sandwich and he chewed it, looking at the river. Not in a hurry to say anything. And Grace didn't rush to fill the silence either, deciding instead to sit back and see how everything panned out.

'Is this the first thing you've done today?' he asked eventually.

'Well, I got up and got dressed.'

'What? No way. I thought you just went to bed all . . . all'—he waved his hand in her general direction—'fancy and woke up like that.'

'Fancy?'

'Maybe not fancy, just . . . you know.'

'I'm not fancy?'

'Well put together. You're well put together. That's a nice dress and your hair is nice and your face is very impressive.'

'I'm glad your impressed by my face.'

He shrugged. 'You get to hang around with a face like that all the time. Some of us only get to see one like yours every now and then. It's good of you to bring it out and let people look at it.'

'Thank you.'

'You're welcome.'

'Is this the first thing you've done today?' she asked him.

'Fuck no. I've been up since five. That's the one thing about this place I really can't get a handle on: in summer it's so bright so, so early.'

'So early.'

'And I got a sleep mask, but the thing always winds up twisted so it's covering my ear, or my forehead, but never my eyes. Anyway, so yes, been up for hours. I went down to the farm, actually.'

'The city farm?'

'Yeah. In Hackney. It opens early so I went and got some breakfast and had a look at the animals and that.'

'I've never been there.'

'What? That's outrageous. You should. There's a pig there, honestly it's the size of—I don't know: a boat. A rowboat.'

'Is that the official unit of measurement for pigs?'

'Yeah. This one was about one point five rowboats in size. If I was a pig and I saw this pig, well, I don't know. I'd end things, I think; there's no point even trying to be a pig when there's a pig like that in the world already.'

Grace was laughing so hard she couldn't drink her coffee, which was a shame, because she really needed it.

'So you've already had breakfast?' she asked.

'Yes! This is lunch. I'll turn in at about two this afternoon the way things are going.'

'Sounds wonderful.'

'That it does. But you can't because you are a very busy lady.'

'That I am.'

'Hm.' He had a face that seemed always ready to smile; a generous sort of face. And the way he looked at her brought a memory, clear, crisp, straight to the forefront of her mind; a memory of Trent. She sipped her coffee. It was cold.

'What?' he said. The smile shifted to something more uncertain. 'What did I say? Sorry, I'm not mocking you; I believe that you are a busy person.'

'No. Nothing. It's fine. I didn't think you were.'

'Okay.' He wiped his hands on a napkin and passed one to her.

'Thank you.'

'You're welcome. You have jam on your cheek.'

Grace wiped her cheek and found that yes, there had been a glob of blueberry jam on her face.

'How long has that been there?'

'Since you arrived. No! I'm joking. It appeared on your face about ten seconds ago, so I orchestrated the whole wiping-my-hands-on-a-napkin thing so that I could give you a napkin and you could just take care of it and things wouldn't get awkward.'

'It worked. Not awkward at all. Wait, did you really? Is that true?'

'I'm never telling you. So you said the other night that you work in HR?'

'Yes. In the record industry.'

'Oh cool.'

HR was neither cool, nor an accurate description of her job.

'And I am in constant awe of people who create for a living,' Grace continued. 'Or half a living, as is often the case.'

'Yeah, it's not as glamorous as people think.'

'Oh, believe me, I know.'

'Hey, do you want to go and look at some art?'

'Sure.'

'I like spending time looking at art with people who claim not to know anything about art.'

'I *don't* know anything.'

'There's nothing to know. That's the big lie: that there's a riddle you have to solve, an equation to balance. Anyone who claims to know about art, whatever that means, and then starts talking about art as if it's a riddle or an equation, well, they don't know anything about art because all you need is some feelings. If you are a person with feelings, then you know about art.'

'Because art is about feelings?'

'Yes. All of it. Anyone who says otherwise is full of shit and I'm willing to die on that hill or rock or whatever the saying is. Do you have feelings? Because they're all you need to understand art.'

Did she have feelings? Grace imagined her feelings now as drifting dusty motes, only glimpsed in narrow shafts of light.

'So the guy who did the big coloured rectangles . . .' she said.

'Rothko.'

'Yes. Him. He had feelings about coloured rectangles?'

'Yeah. Big feelings.'

Ed took her into the Tate and stood her in front of a Rothko. A huge slab of colour that at first looked only burgundy. Then, looking closer, Grace saw moments of midnight blue, moments of scarlet.

'I learned about him at uni,' Ed said, 'all the theory and history, but none of that matters when you stand in front of his painting and feel all swallowed up by the colour.'

The colour loomed in front of Grace. She couldn't look away; the pigment was enveloping.

'How often do you get the chance to look at a colour and think about how great it is, really marvel, really take the time. Rothko gives you a colour and says, "Take a look at this, motherfucker."'

It didn't seem a natural word to come out of his mouth, but his eyes were alight when he said it, looking at the painting.

'Do you see it?' he asked Grace.

Grace breathed in the colour. 'I know a song that looks like this.'

When Grace looked away from the painting, at Ed, she saw that he had caught what she had said.

He nodded. 'I get that.'

After that he took her to another painting, this one by a guy called Wayne Thiebaud. Much smaller than the Rothko, it was of a piece of lemon meringue pie. It was called *Lemon Meringue Pie*. 'Do you know a song that sounds like this?'

Grace laughed. 'No. It doesn't usually work like that. Normally I sort of attach colour to music. It becomes very clear in my head. That Rothko is the first time I've seen a painting that makes me think of a song. Although I haven't spent much time looking at paintings.'

'I love this one. It's on loan from another gallery, so I wanted to see it again before it goes home. People—art people, critics—they often say that this is about nostalgia, or a retort to the consumerism of the late fifties or, I don't know, melancholic desire—that's one critics like to throw around—but when Wayne was asked why he painted this, he said: "Because I like lemon meringue pie." That right there is all you need to know about art. Everything else is superfluous. I hate seeing those long dissertations some artists write now. Like, if you have to write five hundred words to explain what you're doing, you've failed, if you ask me. I get asked to write these things about my work and I'm, like, for eff's sake, I'm not a writer. I'm not a talker. If

I was I probably wouldn't spend so much time painting. All I'm trying to say is: Hey, check out this shade of blue or look at this nice wobbly line over here, or how great is the sky? Or I'm trying to express a complex emotion that I can't give a name to. I don't know if that makes sense.'

'It does.'

'Sometimes it feels like I'm being asked to retrofit some meaning to what I'm doing. If you don't get anything out of looking at it, go look at some other painting, I don't care.' Ed paused. 'Although of course I do care, and when someone doesn't like my work it makes me sad.' He grimaced. 'Sorry. I've been talking for a long time. I don't usually, if it helps.'

It was a dangerous place Grace found herself in, watching and listening to this man, glimpsing inside of him and wanting to see more.

Ed let out a long sigh and dropped his head, ploughed his hand through his hair. When he looked back at her his expression had changed.

'I woke up early because I'm a nervous person and this has made me nervous. I am not good at this.'

'I'm not either.'

'Yeah, I disagree. You are an impressive person. I like you very much. Even more than last time. Now I feel like I'm auditioning for something.'

'You're not . . .'

He shook his head and looked away. So she reached over and brushed his hand, linked her fingers through his. He looked at her, surprised.

'You're not auditioning,' she said. 'I'd like to see some more art, please.'

◎

A week later Grace accompanied Ed to the opening of his mate's exhibition. Standing in a cluster of guests, someone asked Ed what he was working on. Grace sensed how uncomfortable it made him and he brushed it off as well as he could.

'You don't like talking about what you're working on?' Grace asked him when they were alone.

'I don't want to sound like a wanker,' he said.

Grace felt that he was as far from that as anyone could possibly be. Unexpectedly, on their way to dinner, Ed offered to show her his studio.

The building reminded Grace of the place Tony used to rent in Hackney. The studio itself was a room with barely anything in it other than a large paint-covered table, a few easels, and a shelf crammed with paint tubes, empty jars, various spirits and tin cans stuffed with every shape and size of paintbrush imaginable. Grace asked how he coped with all the paint fumes and he just shrugged and said he opened a window. It was worse in winter, when it was too cold to have the window open for long and he had to work in a fume mask.

'What if it's poisoning you?' Grace asked.

'I guess we'll have to wait and see.' He said this with humour. Grace knew that if she continued to grow attached to him she would worry about it.

The most inconvenient aspect of the studio was that it wasn't intended to be an art studio at all. It was supposed to be an office. Ed definitely wouldn't get his bond back if he got paint on the carpet, so he had to cover it all with tarps. He said that in summer his feet would get sweaty and stick to the tarp. 'Sorry,' he said. 'I don't want you thinking about my sweaty feet.'

But she didn't mind him mentioning his sweaty feet. Nothing he had said in the short time she had known him rankled her.

The large painting he was working on was propped on two upturned milk crates and covered in an old floral bedsheet.

'Can I see?' she asked.

Ed hesitated, looking at the sheet like it was shrouding a horrible sight. 'I mean, you can, but I'll have to stand outside while you do. It's crap at the moment.'

'I doubt that.'

'Thanks, but I'll wait out in the corridor. I don't really want to talk about it at all. Just pretend you haven't seen it.'

'I don't have to look at it.'

'No, no, no, it's fine. Have a look.'

Ed waited outside while Grace lifted the edge of the sheet. She held it up as high as she could, so it was like a tent, and while she stood there and took in the ethereal shapes and milky light of the painting she felt very close to Ed, as if he were holding her. He hadn't done that yet, but that was what it felt like.

When he came back in, the grimace was still on his face. 'What do you think?' he asked. 'Is it okay?'

'You said not to talk about it. Is this a test?'

'No.' He was embarrassed then, she could tell.

'It's beautiful.'

'Okay. That's . . . thank you. Let's get dinner.'

Ed had suggested his favourite greasy spoon because Grace had been out to dinner almost every night that week and requested something comforting; please, no tiny stacks of radish on enormous plates.

'How did the break-up with Livia go?' Grace asked.

'She wasn't really open to it, as a concept. I didn't want to be cruel, but in the end I had to say, "I don't like you. At all."'

'Yikes.'

'She was the first friend I made in London,' Ed said. 'The fellowship I got, they connect you with different artists' collectives. I met her through that, and then I saw her again at a party and she was really friendly. Actually I never saw her act that friendly with anyone since. Including me. I wasn't expecting her to be into me the way she was.'

'She's very beautiful,' Grace said. 'Not that you're unworthy of it. I mean, it makes sense to me that she would be into you. It's just, that's the first thing I noticed about her.'

'No, she is beautiful-looking and I was stupidly flattered. But I was in a relationship with her before I realised that I didn't like her very much. She just has this way of, I don't know, pulling people in. And you feel really good about it at first, but then . . .'

'You don't.'

'Exactly.'

'Do you like her art?'

'It's performance stuff.'

'Ohhhh.'

He laughed.

'I can definitely see that in her,' Grace said.

'Yeah, well. Yeah. That's her thing.'

'And do you like it?'

'No. I do not.'

'That must have made things interesting.'

'Interesting is a good word for it. Sure as hell wasn't boring. She's quite . . . I don't know how to put this . . . aggressively sexual. Like, not that there's a problem with women who . . . I don't have a problem with . . .'

'I understand what you mean.'

'I just . . . She . . .' He was blushing then, really blushing. He focused on his chips. 'Being with her, aside from that, wasn't the best experience.'

Grace felt the space open up where it was probably appropriate for her to say something about past relationship experiences.

'Apologies,' he said. 'Too much information.'

He'd laid himself bare just now and the terrain felt unbalanced. It would be rude not to reciprocate.

'No, not at all,' said Grace. 'I understand. I had a bit of a bad experience before.'

'Oh. I'm sorry to hear that.'

She felt she'd misled him. Made it sound worse than any normal adult would think it was. It was a university boyfriend who had broken her heart. That's all. That's all. That's all.

'This food isn't a bad experience,' Grace said quickly.

He agreed, and they moved into easier territory, talking about how they'd grown to love weird British food.

Ed told Grace about his parents. Their names were Joan and Ian, and they lived on Sydney's Northern Beaches.

'It's not the kind of place I would choose to hang out in,' said Ed. 'Believe it or not, I didn't really fit in with the league fanatics or the surfers.' His brothers—he had three—did, though, and Ed knew his dad loved him but had never really understood him. 'Man, the amount of sports he tried to get me into: football, tennis, cricket. Cricket! I was shit at that. Terrible batter, worse fielder.' Ed mimicked his dad: '"Why are you always off with the bloody fairies?"' He laughed. 'I was looking at the trees. They had great trees at that oval, huge squiggly gums. I like soccer now, though, played it a bit in uni. Didn't tell Dad.'

Ed said his parents were baffled as to where his arty streak came from. That's what they called it. 'My grandfather was an architect, and they tried to push me in that direction for a bit because I liked drawing. I hoped that when they came to my grad show they would, I don't know, validate it. Understand. See that I wasn't wasting my time. You know, my dad used to tell people I studied graphic design. Never said I was an artist. But I won the fellowship and was given eighty grand to come study at Saint Martins, so that got their attention. Now Mum loves telling people I'm an artist in London. She's a good egg.'

'And your dad?'

He mimicked his father again. '"As long as you're happy and got a roof over your head." I don't know, I've never been able to get a good read on him. I do miss Mum a lot. I should go back and see them. It's been nearly twelve months. And Mum had breast cancer a few years ago . . .'

'That's awful.'

'It's okay, she's good now. I still feel weird being away for too long. Things feel more finite than they used to. Anyway . . . do you go back much?' he asked.

'No. Never.'

'Oh.' He went quiet, like perhaps he thought he had spooked her. 'Are your parents not around anymore?'

'They're around. I think my mother might turn out to be immortal. She's only in her early fifties but I suspect she's got a solid titanium core.'

'And your dad?'

'He's along for the ride.'

'Ha.'

'I just . . . it's a long way and work is really busy. So.'

Grace dipped the edge of a chip into the last puddle of gravy and focused on swirling it around rather than eating it. 'I haven't been entirely honest with you,' she said. 'It's okay, I don't have a secret husband or anything, it's more that my line of work . . . I'm not in HR.'

'Are you a spy?'

'I think the hours would be better if I were. Do you remember when we met?'

'Yep, I think so. Yep.'

Grace laughed. 'Okay. Well, the blonde girl I sent you to find, her name's actually Ada. That was Ada Black. I'm her manager.'

'You're having me on.'

'I'm not. I swear.'

He frowned. 'Wait. Shit. That *was* her.' He grinned and threw a chip crumb at her. 'You bloody liar! I trusted you!'

'Please don't say you want to be a musician. I can't help you. My books are full.'

'No. I don't want to be a musician.'

'Thank goodness.'

'Is that why you said HR?'

'Yes. If certain people find out what I actually do, they think I'm their ticket to fame and fortune.'

'Certain people who want to be like Ada Black?'

'Yes.'

'And you're assuming I don't want to be Ada Black?'

'You don't have the right hair for it.'

'Harsh but fair. So when you are too busy to have dinner with me it's because you're at the Grammy Awards or something?'

'Yes. Normally. Or I'm just at dinner with other people, but in a different context.'

'Not my context.'

'No.'

'What is my context? Just while we're on this topic.'

It had taken guts to ask her that, she could see it in his face while he waited on her answer. Bated breath.

'I definitely don't do this with anyone else,' she said.

◎

Grace knew a lot about musicians. She knew how the good ones, the really talented lyricists, noticed rhythms in speech. Patterns. Somehow they could take words and meld them into sound and beat. She firmly believed that the mark of true creative talent was the ability to write about more than romantic love. They were able to take a scalpel to their own psyche. They had to truly examine themselves, unflinchingly. When writing, Ada went into a mode of excavation within herself, trying to capture an internal world in an external sound. And every time she performed the songs she'd excavated her soul for, she had to open up the mine again, venture back into the cave, carving more and more out. On tour Ada could become erratic; one moment she was supremely sure of herself, the next paralysed by doubt or, worse, shame—she'd get caught in speculation about the way the stories she told in her songs might be interpreted. It was Grace's job to steady her during these times. Whenever Ada stepped onto a stage, Grace felt pride bloom within herself. She was an integral part of it all. Ada was a diva; she was needy, self-absorbed, obsessed with what others thought of her. And Ada was a genius; her music was the sharp shafts of light in which Grace could see herself.

It was the same in the way Ed was visible through his paintings. Some people might see one and walk on by, but others, like Grace, were caught, snagged, unable to look away.

She was fascinated by the way his mind worked. The way he would be transfixed by a fluttering shadow on a wall, a detail she wouldn't even notice but would later find he was using for a painting. The painting wasn't *about* the shadow he told her. It wasn't even a painting of a shadow. It was something about the way light fused around the edges of a shape. Ed spent a lot of time thinking about light. She realised now that when he seemed to have drifted off in thought he hadn't drifted off at all—he was literally looking at the wall, or the ground, or a tree, and noticing the gradual shifts in colour. And the sky? Ed could stare at the sky forever. He liked the British sky, he said. It didn't blind you when you watched the clouds shift. He adored clouds most of all. 'They tell you what's happened somewhere else, what's about to happen where you are.' And in London clouds were in plentiful supply.

He was in the habit of taking a picnic rug to a park, lying on his back and looking at the sky. He'd had a smartphone for a little while, but he got lost in scrolling. Hours and hours gone, he said. So he returned to an old Nokia. They'd seen Livia at a party recently and she laughed at him about it. Laughed and looked at Ed like she wanted to gobble him up. Grace hated that look.

Ed didn't seem to be the kind of person to get erratic, although he had told Grace that he'd experienced periods of immense darkness, times when nothing caught his imagination, when vivid colours had no effect on him. These stretches of time were made worse by the way he missed his usual self, the self that looked at the sky, trees, fields, anything, and saw infinite possibilities for paintings. During his bad periods seeing beauty made him sadder. He told Grace that continuing to paint even when he didn't want to was the only way to deal with it.

Those paintings while he was doing them, always seemed terrible. Afterwards, when he was feeling better, he usually saw that they were okay and he was able to keep going and bring out the painting that was waiting. That's how he talked about his work—he said that there was always the painting inside while he was working on it, he just had to find a way of letting it out. Of freeing it, he said.

All of this he had told Grace within months of knowing her. He trusted her. Grace saw him regularly, talked with him for ages on the phone about Ada, her work, the people she met and places she visited. Grace thought of him constantly and yet still managed to 'hold him at arm's bloody length', as Nish said.

'Like, do you ever talk to him about your actual feelings?' Nish asked. 'That's a thing people do: have feelings and chat about them. Ever start a sentence with "I feel"?'

'It's not like that, it's—'

'Practise with me. I'll start: I feel a bit sad today because, I don't know, fuck, I miss my mum chucking stuff at me in the kitchen. She's getting old and she's a right pain in the bum, but I love her. You go. C'mon: *Today I felt . . .*'

'Nish.'

'I got an invite today.'

'To what?'

'To Ravi's wedding. Today I felt like shite because I've been invited to the wedding of a bloke whom I happen to know is still in love with me but I fucked it up. Your turn.'

'Oh, Nish. I'm so sorry.'

'Good men don't come along every day. So either do something real, or leave the poor guy be.'

15

ED

EVEN BEFORE HE MET GRACE, ED WAS LONELY. THE WAY HE DISCOVERED it (if you could discover loneliness) was dumb: it was just a story on *BBC Breakfast*—which he only put on sometimes if he woke up feeling uneasy and, ha, very alone. They said there was a loneliness epidemic sweeping London. Ed heard it and thought: Oh, that's me. It was like when two days after a soccer match he'd been told his wrist was broken and he finally had a name to call the constant ache.

He didn't have anyone to share this new diagnosis with. Ha again.

Grace was driving him insane in the most exquisite of ways. His mates said she was toying with him. And Livia smelled blood and persisted with her circling, popping up randomly, always ready with snide remark and a suggestion in his ear.

Several times he'd been out with Grace and had everything he was going to say all worked out in his head: I like you but I want this to be more than it is; I can't hang around forever. But the truth was he probably could hang around forever and sometimes he wondered if he could find contentment in being hers without her ever being his.

So London remained lonely. Ed was in love with a woman who was very impressive and important and took him to gigs and had dinner with him but whom he hadn't even kissed.

The work he was producing was great.

No matter how hard Ed tried, he couldn't go on like this. And so, on a Wednesday when she had a free window between five and seven thirty, she arrived on the doorstep of his flat (nursing a large potted plant on her hip?) so he could make her a seafood spaghetti thing and deliver all the perfectly constructed sentences he had been rehearsing in his head.

He opened the door, and she beamed at him and thrust the pot plant in his direction.

'Care for a plant?'

'Um . . .'

'Tony's got a girl in redecorating the office. Apparently this particular variety of ficus is no longer cool, so I've taken it for rehoming.'

'You're rehoming it with me?'

'You seem hesitant. Should I check your living conditions first? Before I grant you custody?'

She was wearing a trench coat over a silky blue dress. The fabric had threads of gold through it and her heels were so high she was almost taller than him.

'Either way, can you please take it? It's heavy.'

So he did. And then he asked her in.

Grace had never been to his apartment. Until now he couldn't bring himself to say, 'Do you want to come to my place for dinner?' because that was what people said when they meant, 'Can you please sleep with me?' Obviously he did want to sleep with her, but the dinner thing was genuine. He worried that if he invited her over she might say no, that he had it all wrong, that's not what this thing was and that they were just friends. He would have made it awkward and weird. He would no longer be in her orbit; he would be flung out into space, or a black hole, and crushed into oblivion—or whatever it was that happened to things when they were flung into black holes.

But he'd taken the risk.

And she'd said she'd love him to make her dinner.

Now, Ed took the plant from her and set it in a corner near the window. It was perfect. If tonight went how he feared it was going to go, he'd have to get rid of it.

Grace shrugged off her coat and looked around his tiny home, which wasn't even a proper apartment, just a studio without what he needed, which was an actual studio. She peered at the pictures on the walls and the books on the wobbly shelf he'd found on the street and carried home. When she tugged at the spine of a book the whole shelf swayed. She froze.

'Anything you break you will have to buy,' Ed said. He impressed himself, the way he could pretend he was cool and didn't have an ocean of turmoil in his stomach.

'Deal,' she said. 'I like your place. You're very neat, aren't you?'

'Am I?'

'I think so.'

'Maybe I just spent two hours cleaning up.' It would be stupid to cook. He wouldn't be able to eat anything.

'Your books are in alphabetical order.'

Grace, her eyes on Ed's walls, stood on one leg and took her shoe off, then did the same with the other. He found this simple act, and her now bare feet on his rug, impossibly erotic. The plan was to pour her a glass of wine, make her dinner and then do the talk.

'Hey,' he said.

She looked at him over her shoulder.

'Can I talk to you for a sec?' He hadn't even got the glass out of the cupboard; nothing was sticking to plan.

Grace turned to face him and clasped her hands behind her back like a pupil at the principal's office. 'What have I done?'

'No, you haven't done anything. I . . .'

'Forgot to buy the food?'

'No.'

'Don't like the plant?'

'I like the plant. And . . . I like you even more, but I'm going home for a bit—Australia—and I don't know for how long. Or if I should come back.'

He could tell she read the question in him and that she knew exactly what the deciding factor was in his return or otherwise.

'When are you going?'

'I haven't booked yet.'

'Oh.'

Grace sat on the couch. She in fact sunk into it, like it was familiar and comfortable and she was in her very own home.

'Soon,' Ed said. 'The television reckons I'm lonely and . . . you're not helping. You're actually making it worse.'

Grace didn't say anything. She looked at the wall, or the pictures on the wall, and tucked a lock of hair behind her ear. Ed reflected on what he'd just said, specifically the accusatory nature of it.

'I'm sorry. I made it sound like it's your fault.'

'But it is my fault,' she said.

Ed didn't know what to say to that. Colour left Grace. She was looking at her shoes in the middle of his carpet. 'I really like you,' she said. She did not look at him. Ed wanted to thank her for liking him. He wanted to thank her for being in his house. He did neither. Rather, he waited for her to continue. *I really like you, but.*

Nothing more came.

Ed hadn't put the water on to boil. An uncut onion sat on the chopping board beside two green capsicums that he had bought from the farmers' market that morning, when he had been jangling equally with nerves and thrill.

Grace turned her lovely face to him. Her eyes were teary. 'I should go,' she said.

She carried her shoes in her hand when she left, like she didn't want to take up any more of his time by putting them on. Neither of them spoke, despite Ed wanting to beg her to stay. In the doorway she put her hand on his arm but she still wouldn't look at him.

And then she was gone.

The potted ficus stood in the corner by the window. He would have to leave instructions for the new tenant—whoever that turned out to be—to look after it.

16

GRACE

GRACE CONTINUED TO THINK OF ED CONSTANTLY ONCE HE WAS GONE. In the supermarket, on the bus, at gigs, at meetings. Not so much thinking of him, but more thinking about what she would tell him about her day. Trivial things, like an argument between the bus driver and an elderly woman over Oyster cards, or a client who refused to eat anything at a restaurant meeting because he had an ethical problem with everything on the menu, or how Ada desperately wanted to include details about her star sign in the liner notes of her next album and expected Grace to find an appropriate place for them.

Nish didn't react to Ed's departure in the way Grace expected. There were no exasperated sighs, no lectures.

'Do you think you're not worthy of him, or do you want to shag other people?'

'I don't want to shag other people.'

'Because that's what I wanted to do and it's not all it's cracked up to be.'

'I could have told you that.'

'Is it 'cause you don't want to leave me broken-hearted and alone? I mean, hoes before bros and all, but he's a lovely fella.'

'I know he is.'

'You're still a top chick. Even if you do look knackered eighty percent of the time. You are worthy of him. You deserve to be loved.'

Grace went into her room, closed the door and lay on the floor. The view out the window was of a lone tree branch and grey sky. Grace put her headphones on, but music was unbearable. She couldn't listen at Ada's gigs either, hiding backstage in the dressing room then lying about it and telling Ada that she had been brilliant onstage.

Five weeks after Ed left London he sent her a brief message about a new movie he'd seen. No, *Hello, how are you?* Or, *I hope you've been well.* Just, *Holy shit, that's two hours of my life I will never get back.* Grace had been with Ada's stylist, checking over a bunch of looks collated for an upcoming *Rolling Stone* feature. Ada had said she didn't care what she wore, but she would. She always did.

Grace saw the message and wondered where Ed was when he sent it. She couldn't get the picture clear in her head. Was he at home? Where even was home for him? Was he in Sydney? With friends? She hardly knew who his friends were. Was he out? It would have been late evening in Sydney. Ed didn't love being out at night. He was tucked away somewhere. Thinking. Watching the light. What was he painting? Was he working at all? He had grown bored with the colours of London. He wanted the sunlight. He wanted Grace. He couldn't have both.

Grace had assumed that he left the UK feeling only resentment for her. The stylist said something about an Alexander McQueen skirt. Grace excused herself.

In reply to his message, Grace told him that she had watched *Dirty Dancing* on a plane for the first time only the week before. *It's quite good,* she wrote. *I wish more people knew about it.*

Haha, he replied.

Grace pictured him smiling as he texted, sitting on the couch in a lounge room she imagined. Or not. Maybe he had instantly regretted messaging her in the first place. Maybe that would be the only reply she got.

I've never seen it. Is it just about sexy dancing?

It's: don't have unprotected sex with dickheads, take dance classes to get others out of trouble, have sex with Patrick Swayze, and don't sit in the corner because that's not where you belong if you are a good dancer.

Noted.

The stylist appeared. He was holding two pairs of heels and looking stressed.

I have to go and choose between two pairs of identical shoes for Ada.

I'll watch DD and let you know my thoughts.

Please do.

A few days later Grace texted Ed to tell him that the guy who ran her local off-licence had started a 'sale' section where he sold shockingly out-of-date food and how, for reasons unknown to her, she had purchased a packet of heavily discounted cheese Wotsits and found them to be a little spongy but not too bad. These exchanges of little substance became regular. She could track him somewhat, knowing when he found a mid-century armchair discarded on the side of the road. He was restoring it, guided by YouTube videos and the advice of an old bloke he met at the hardware store. Likewise, Ed knew when Grace had fallen asleep one morning on her way to work and ended up on the other side of London, minus her favourite coat. *What sort of coat was it?* he asked her.

A Burberry trench. It was very expensive.

Ah, he replied. *Hopefully it went to someone who really appreciates it.*

Ed was staying with a friend who lived in a place called Enfield in Sydney. He said lots of people got Enfield mixed up with Enmore and sometimes he didn't clarify, because Enmore would have been a far more interesting and generally cooler place to live. The apartment, coincidentally, was above a panel beater, and there was a long message thread in which he and Grace reflected on the experience of living, or in her case working, above a place that emitted so much noise and even more fumes. *Although, you're probably fine with the fumes,* she'd noted.

They're the only thing keeping me here, Ed wrote. *Smells like home.*

The apartment was at the intersection of two major arterial roads. One day Grace received a series of texts from Ed at what would have been one a.m. in Sydney. A motorcyclist had collided with a car earlier that night. The motorcyclist had been flung into the air and landed within metres of Ed's front door.

He answered Grace's phone call without ceremony, as if it had only been that morning since he'd last seen her.

'All these people came out of their houses and buildings and stood around the guy lying on the ground—the motorcyclist—but no one was talking to him or doing anything. I asked if someone had called an ambulance, and they had but everyone was just standing around. He was only a kid, twenty maybe. He was breathing but I didn't know if he was conscious; his eyes were mostly closed. He wasn't moving. There was glass everywhere, from the car's windscreen. I could hear him breathing. He was breathing. Everyone was just standing there.'

'What did you do?'

'I sat next to him on the road. Held his hand. Talked to him about whatever until the ambulance came. It took forever. There was blood all in his nose. And the sound of his breathing. Shit. But he was breathing. The ambos came and told everyone to clear away, so I did. I just thought, if that was my kid, I wouldn't want him lying there by himself like that, you know?'

It wasn't the thought of the boy on the road which was making Grace tear up—although that was awful; it was the thought of Ed, beautiful Ed, alone in the apartment talking to her, seventeen thousand kilometres away. She could picture him there, sitting in the armchair.

'Can I come and see you?' Grace asked.

'Sorry? I didn't hear you.'

'I said can I, or would you mind, if I came to see you?'

'In Sydney?'

'I can get a flight tomorrow morning. I have a few things I need to sort out, but I can do that this afternoon. I don't have to stay with you, I could get a hotel or something. I mean, you could stay in the hotel if you want. If you need to get away from the panel beater. I can push things around and stay for a week. If you have time, of course. I know you're probably working.'

'I have time.'

PART THREE

A Great and Impossible Task

17
GRACE

APRIL 2022

IT WAS ALMOST DARK BY THE TIME GRACE HAD DISPATCHED TRENT TO his pathetic van in the vet's car park. She allowed herself the brief moment of recalibration and returned to Grevillea Close. Dorothy must have been listening for the sound of Grace's car, because as soon as she came through the front door Grace's children were seated at the dining table, where May was already finding fault.

'Where are the plates with the orange flowers?' she asked, looking at the bone-white side plate her nuggets were served on, itself the size of a frozen pond.

'Granny decided they were out of fashion,' said Warren. 'Even though they were perfectly good plates. Over forty years old and still not a chip in them. They don't make things like that anymore. This one, and I won't tell you how much it cost, already has scratches on.'

'That's because you put them in the dishwasher!' said Dorothy.

'What's the point of a dishwasher if you can't put anything in it?'

'You can put things in it. Just not the Good Plates.'

'They're nice plates, Mum.'

'How much were they?' asked Henry.

May was frowning at her plate now and Grace knew what was coming next.

'Who wants wine?' Warren asked.

'I don't want this plate,' May said. 'I want a flower plate.'

'I'm afraid I don't have the flower plates anymore,' Dorothy said.

May pushed her white pond away, puckering the carefully ironed tablecloth. 'I want a flower plate!'

'You'll have what you're given, young lady,' said Warren, and both May and Grace looked at him in shock.

'What? She can't carry on like that at the dinner table.'

May's mouth dropped open and the sound she produced was like something from *Alien*. Where was Sigourney when you needed her?

'Dad, really not helpful.'

'She has to learn she can't dictate everything,' Warren said.

'I thought you were getting some help with this?' said Dorothy, raising her voice to be heard over the wail.

Grace stood up and went into the kitchen. She rummaged around in the cupboards until she found a purple plastic container and returned to the dining room.

'Granny,' Grace said to her mother, 'would May be able to borrow your very special purple box?'

Dorothy was quick on the uptake. 'Only if she is very careful,' she said, really taking her acting assignment quite seriously. 'It is my best one. Very special.'

May fell silent. Her expression was speculative. Warren opened his mouth to speak but Grace shot him a look dark enough to make him think twice. This was a spell that could be broken with the slightest slip-up. Even Henry looked nervous.

May gave a subtle nod and Grace dumped the nuggets in the container. Victory.

◎

After dinner, Grace helped Warren handwash her mother's precious plates.

'I just don't think May's temper should be setting the agenda. You should be.' He handed Grace a sudsy plate for her to dry.

'I do. I also choose my battles, and I really needed to be able to sit down for five minutes and eat. May doesn't need her granddad to be some kind of disciplinarian.'

'Is she the same with Ed?'

No. She wasn't. This was a special self that May reserved for Grace.

'She's like this with everyone.'

'Her little world's been turned upside down.'

Grace put the dried plate on the stack and took the next one from him. She could hear Dorothy playing UNO with the kids in the lounge room. She was challenging Henry on the pick-up-put-down rule. Big mistake.

'My life is upside down and inside out. But please, go ahead and give me all your tips on handling a five-year-old gone nuclear, if you've got so much experience. Which you don't, because you were always at work.'

Warren held up both hands—encased in pink polka-dot washing-up gloves—in surrender. Grace held out her hand for another plate, but they were all done and the water was already gurgling down the sink.

'I just worry so much about you,' Warren said.

'Thank you, but I'm handling everything.'

'There's no shame in asking for help.'

But there was. Because if she asked for help this time, everyone would remember the last time. And it would be her fault all over again.

◎

Grace was running the bath for May when Julie the vet rang. Slinky had survived surgery but a hind leg had been amputated. Julie said she wasn't sure if Slinky would survive the night but she was hopeful because Slinky was 'a fighter'. Grace agreed that, yes, Slinky was indeed a fighter. 'But how will she survive in general with only three legs?'

'Most dogs get along very well with just three.'

'I can't imagine a three-legged dachshund.'

Julie then asked if there were many stairs in the house and Grace told her there were. 'You can always have ramps installed,' Julie suggested. 'Or a stair lift for steeper sections.'

A world in which Grace would have to alter her house to accommodate a three-legged dachshund was not one that she could face right now, so she offered a cheery thanks and ended the conversation.

Henry and May received the news of Slinky's survival with unbridled joy that was demonstrated, much to Dorothy's displeasure, by jumping on the carefully made-up guest beds. Warren, having taken on Grace's instruction to please remain the fun granddad, joined in and due to the incongruous impossibility of him jumping on the bed also, the celebrations transformed into him tossing each of the kids repeatedly on the beds from ever increasing distances. Until May hit her head and things came to an abrupt halt. Never mind.

◎

Later, when the kids were in bed, Grace sat in the lounge room scrolling through Instagram while Dorothy knitted and Warren watched a documentary on Stasi spies. Grace used to be a reader but now, especially with Ed gone, she was too tired in the evenings. She'd (ironically) read an article in *The Atlantic* about how smartphones were retraining people's brains so that they couldn't concentrate on anything for more than thirty seconds before they needed new stimulus. Or something—it was difficult to concentrate. Grace wasn't sure if this was her situation or if she was just a single parent with two children under ten and a full-time job, who just needed a moment's fucking peace looking at pretty pictures of other people's homes. She wished she could do something useful instead, like knit a jumper, but she couldn't knit. Grace could have asked Dorothy to teach her, but she never had. Maybe she was just too tired.

Grace's phone pinged. A message.

Trent.

She killed the screen and put the phone in her pocket. Time to learn the secrets of the Stasi spies. It was interesting actually; lots of wigs involved. And she discovered just how much she recalled from a visit to the Stasi Museum in Berlin years ago. With Ed. He'd been fascinated by communist furniture design and they'd joked about redecorating their apartment in East German chic. Maybe her brain cells weren't as dead as *The Atlantic* would have her believe.

Ping!

'Goodness. It's a bit late for that,' Dorothy said, her needles clacking away. 'This is when people should be left alone to relax.'

'That's what your mother says every time someone messages her after seven thirty,' Warren said.

'You do know that people can't actually see what you're doing when they message you?' Grace said. 'They don't know they're interrupting your knitting. And if it bothers you that much, just turn your phone off.'

'But it might be an emergency. I can guarantee that the one time I turn my phone off there'll be a crisis and I'll be needed.'

'And I can guarantee that in a crisis you are the last person anyone would want involved,' Warren added.

'Do you see what I have to live with?' Dorothy said. 'No wonder I'm exhausted.'

She said something after that but Warren increased the volume of the television and drowned her out.

'Are your ears going?' Dorothy said. 'The neighbours will be complaining.'

'What?'

'I said the neighbours will be complaining!'

'Why?'

'Because it's so loud!'

'Well, I can't hear it with you nattering on and on,' Warren said.

Grace focused on ignoring her need to read Trent's message. She failed.

Any news on Slinky? :)

Slinky. Why should he get to call her dog by its name? As if he was so familiar with her. And a smiley face? What was that about?

Another ping.

I know you never want to talk to me again. Just let me know if she's okay and I'll leave you alone forever.

No abbreviations. Complete sentences. Her thumb hovered over the keypad as she contemplated replying.

Ping!

'Don't these friends of yours go to bed?' asked Dorothy.

'You're not in bed yet,' Grace said.

'I'll just put the subtitles on, shall I?' said Warren.

'Why are you watching this anyway?' asked Dorothy. 'What more could you possibly need to know about spies?'

◎

Dorothy and Warren's back deck was a minefield of gum nuts; they felt like Lego underfoot. Grace was tempted to go back inside and get her shoes, but Dorothy would have said, 'What were you doing out there?' and Grace didn't feel like answering that line of inquiry.

At least the cicadas had settled for the night. Ed once told her that they spent seven years underground before burrowing up and emerging from Warren's nice lawn to live a short but no doubt wondrous life. Grace thought it would be a useful thing to be able to hibernate unseen for seven years and emerge all fresh and new with beautiful wings. No one asking questions about where she'd been.

Now she looked over Trent's message and tried to think of an appropriate reply, if replying at all was even appropriate.

Sorry for messaging so late, he'd written. Always so bloody polite.

Ping!

And do you think I could get that t-shirt back? Sorry, but it's my favourite.

Fine, Grace would deign to reply.

Slinky's leg was amputated. I'll need to get ramps installed in the house because she won't be able to use stairs, which is dumb but I have no choice. Your t-shirt is covered in blood.

I'll wear it at Halloween. Glad she's okay.

So you still want the t-shirt?

Yes please.

Give me an address and I'll drop it off tomorrow.

O'Leary's, thirty minutes.

I'm not going there.

You're too good for O'Leary's now? Well la-di-da.

Honestly, what kind of man said la-di-da? Pathetic.

'Grace?' Dorothy stepped outside, hugging her fluffy bathrobe around herself. It was covered in big, brash love hearts; a Mother's Day gift chosen by May. Grace had been sure her mother would hide it in the back of the wardrobe and it would never see the light of day, but Dorothy wore it all the time. 'What are you doing out here?'

'I had to deal with some emails. And get away from the Stasi.'

'You know he's already seen that one a thousand times? Has it on DVD but wanted to watch it because it was on TV. Honestly! I'm making tea. Would you like one? And we really must talk about your blood pressure.'

Ping!

I can pick you up if you want. Risky leaving the Lotus in that car park.

◎

Dorothy had made Grace a cup of tea in a china cup with a ginger snap nestled on the saucer. Grace picked it up and took a bite.

'I'm going out.'

Dorothy looked at Grace as if she'd said she was sailing to the moon. 'What? Where?'

'Meeting some old friends.'

'You're not going out with that'—Grace could tell Dorothy was mentally reaching for a fitting noun—'boy?'

Evidently she hadn't found one.

'No.'

'I didn't know you were still in touch with him. Does Ed know—'

'I'm not still in touch with him. That's not what this is . . .' Grace paused, frustrated to find herself caught in one of Dorothy's riddles. 'The kids are asleep; you and Dad can go to bed. I'll see you in the morning.'

'Who are you catching up with then, if not him?'

'Oh, for eff's sake, Mum. I have his t-shirt and—'

Dorothy's mouth dropped open.

'I have his t-shirt because he wrapped the dog in it when she was hit by the car. He wants it back.'

'Oh.'

'Yes, *oh*. I'm not the deranged nymphomaniac you think I am. I wish I was—that would be more fun.'

'I don't think you're a . . . I'm just not sure you should be going out with him.'

'I'm forty-one years old, Mother.'

'I'm concerned for you, darling.'

'I'm meeting some friends. He will, unfortunately, be there. That's it. I am perfectly emotionally sound. Thank you for your concern.'

'I just . . . Well, it's obvious he's not a very trustworthy person.'

'That was twenty years ago.'

'You'd have to take anything he has to say with a grain of salt.'

'Obviously.'

'I think it would be best if you were to stay here.'

Dorothy was wringing her hands. Her concern was almost sweet.

'Mother, I am an adult. We were children. I'm giving him back his t-shirt. That is all. You don't need to worry about me.'

'Yes, but that's my job.'

◎

Outside, Grace stood on the grass verge, strategically choosing a spot that placed a shrub between herself and the front of her parents' house. She definitely did not want Warren to see her getting into a van with Trent, nor did she want Dorothy watching and analysing body language.

If Dorothy was watching right now she would know by the way Grace was constantly yawning that she was nervous. The nervousness was irritating. Grace pulled the t-shirt out of her bag. It only had one small smear of blood on it. It was a Radiohead t-shirt with the word *CREW* printed on the back. Well la-di-da. Congratulations, Trent. You carried an amp for Thom Yorke. Was that the most exciting thing he'd done with his life and his talent? Probably.

She folded the t-shirt up and placed it on top of the letterbox, began walking back up the driveway towards the house. Switched her phone off.

But now headlights swung into the driveway. 'Are you standing me up?' Trent called.

Grace went to his window. 'I'm not standing you up, because you have to be going on a date with someone to stand them up. We were never doing that; I was simply returning your t-shirt.'

'So you're going back inside to watch *Midsomer Murders* with Dorothy? *That* would be a good name for a show actually. Come and have a beer. Or a wine, or vodka, or whatever suits you. Lemonade? Fire engine? Grace?'

Grace glanced over her shoulder. The lounge room curtain twitched.

'One drink,' she said.

18

2009

WHEN ED FIRST TOLD GRACE THAT HIS PARENTS WERE VISITING LONDON she filed it away in her mental calendar like she did for work commitments. Only as the date neared did she see this wasn't an introduction that could make or break a client's dreams. Joan and Ian wouldn't be assessing someone else; they would be assessing *her*. And Ed's poorly hidden nervousness didn't help. There was a long drama about accommodation because according to Joan and Ian everything was either too expensive, or not nice enough, too far from public transport, or too close to a main road. It turned into a circus. At one point she offered to put them up in a fancy hotel Eastlake Management used for clients, but Ed looked at her in horror and said, 'Dad would rather die than accept charity.'

Joan and Ian insisted on meeting Ed and Grace for dinner the very same day that they landed in London, despite Ed's advice that they might want to give themselves a day in between to deal with jet lag.

'It's fine,' Joan said when she and Ian arrived at the bar. 'I slept four hours this afternoon. I'm fresh as a daisy.'

'Because your body thinks it's eight a.m.,' Ed said.

Joan ignored him and proceeded to enthuse about the nice and clean serviced apartment they had at the Farrington Holiday Inn. (Farrington, being nowhere near conveniently located.) 'Isn't it nice, Ian?' she said, searching for back-up, but Ian was taking in the view. Ed had chosen the bar on the top floor of the Tate Modern so his parents could do just that. Ian took in the view for about five seconds and then said, 'There's a lot of foreigners in London, isn't there.'

'Technically you are one,' said Ed. To which Joan responded with a nervous trilling sort of laugh. Ian huffed and asked Ed to get him a VB.

'They don't have VB, Dad. But I can get you a nice IPA.'

Ian muttered something about pommy beer and said he'd have to choose his own.

When they were gone Grace said to Joan that it was nice to finally meet her, Joan gave a strained sort of smile and said, 'Yes.' After which Grace attempted some benign chat about their flight, to which Joan responded with curt replies and then eventually, 'Well, I imagine you only fly first class.'

Grace was trying to find an answer when Joan continued. 'Ed tells me you work in the music industry,' she said.

'Yes, artist management mostly.'

'How interesting.' Joan sounded about as interested as if Grace had just told her she was the bin man. 'You must be very clever.'

Grace was unsure if Joan thought that was a good thing.

'How nice to be so successful at such a young age,' Joan added.

'There's been a lot of hard work but, um, yes. It has been good.'

'And how did you meet my Ed?'

Grace laughed. 'It's a funny story actually—I was locked in the men's toilets at a pub and he helped me get out.'

Grace didn't even make it to the end of her sentence before it became clear that Joan's idea of a funny story might be different from her own.

'Well,' Joan said after a long pause, 'he likes you very much. We thought he might stay in Australia. It really seemed like he had had enough of everything over here.'

It was also clear that Joan believed it was Grace whom Ed had had enough of.

'But'—Joan made an expressive sweep of her arms—'look where we are! He's happy. I've never seen him so wrapped up in a girl.'

Ed and Warren had taken their pommy beers over to the window, where Ed was pointing out various things.

'And I know that young people play all sorts of . . . well, I won't say games, but I do know that things aren't always clear and—'

'I'm not playing games.'

'I never said you were.'

Grace was going to say that Joan kind of did.

Joan held up a hand to stop her. 'But from where I'm sitting, I can see that he is very serious about you, and although you do have, as you say, a very successful career . . .'

'Ed has a very successful career of his own.'

'Yes, well, he's getting there. I'm asking that you don't mess him around. There. I've said it.'

Grace picked up her glass and took a long sip. She placed it down. She should look Joan in the eye and inform her that she didn't mess around with anyone and that her work was irrelevant when it came to Ed.

Grace looked at Joan. Joan raised her chin.

'I don't mess around with anyone,' Grace said with a marked lack of assertiveness. 'There was a university boyfriend and then no one. Until Ed. He's . . .' All the adjectives were trite, none of them worthy of the person Grace couldn't be without.

Ed and Warren were coming back. Ed smiled at Grace, and when he sat down he took her hand briefly and squeezed it. Joan looked away.

◎

It wasn't long after Joan and Ian's visit that Ed's move into Grace's apartment began: his toothbrush first and then, by degrees, the rest of him. By that time Nish had moved out of the Shoreditch apartment and was living with Ravi in Oxford, where he was doing his PhD. (It was a testament to Nish's will that his three-day wedding—with two hundred and fifty confirmed guests—had been cancelled.)

Grace told Ed that she wanted him to be there when she came home from work.

'Like, all the time,' she said. 'I miss you whenever you're not here.'

It was a Friday night. Hotter than was normal for London. They were in Grace's kitchen and she was wearing a summer dress that was probably too short for work but she had only realised this once she'd left the house that morning.

'Would I have a curfew?' Ed asked now. 'I have to be here when you get home? Am I ever allowed to leave?'

'Only at pre-approved times.'

'Oh, is that right?' His fingertips were at the hem of her dress, on her thighs.

Later, he asked how much the rent was and she told him not to worry about it, that he didn't have to pay rent.

'Of course I'll help you with the rent,' he said, rolling onto his side and looking at her.

'I don't pay rent,' she said.

'Did you buy this place?'

'Yes.'

'Then let me help with the mortgage.'

Grace sat up and pulled the sheet around her; the weather had changed and a cool breeze was coming through the window. She looked around on the carpet beside the bed for her dress. 'You don't have to do that.'

'Yes, I do.'

She spotted the dress and leaned over to reach it.

'If I'm going to move in, it has to be fair on you,' he said. 'How much is the mortgage per week?'

'I don't have a mortgage.'

'What do you mean?'

'I paid it off last year.'

'Okay. Wow.'

'So it's fine.'

'Ada's album?'

'Yes.'

Ed sat up. He rubbed both hands through his hair. 'Grace, I . . .'

She pulled the dress over her head.

'Can you just look at me for a minute?' he said. 'I can't just move into your apartment and not . . . contribute.'

She'd had a belt on but she couldn't find it.

'Grace.'

It was over near the doorway. There had been quite a slow and eventful progression from the kitchen to the bedroom.

'Grace.'

She stopped halfway across the room. 'Please leave it,' she said. 'I don't want this to be weird. Please just move in.'

But he had a look of exasperation and his thick hair was sticking out at crazy angles because of his worried hands. She could have joked about him paying her when he sold a million-dollar painting, but that would have drawn attention to what was already clear: even with a successful career as a painter, Ed would probably never make enough money to pay her for half the apartment.

'I earn a lot of money,' she said. 'It's just what it is. Please don't make me date some dickhead, start-up tech billionaire.'

Ed looked out the window.

'I don't want to have to date Zuckerburg.'

He was silent. But he grinned.

19

2011

IN MARCH 2011 GRACE BOUGHT HER FIRST CAR, A 1976 PORSCHE 911 Turbo. Ed teased her mercilessly for having a Porsche as her first car.

She also bought a house in Primrose Hill. With four bedrooms and two bathrooms, it felt like overkill (Grace could tell Ed felt the same, but he never said this aloud) until Dorothy rang and said she and Warren were 'just desperate' to come and see Grace in London. It had been two years since their last visit. They knew that Grace had made good business decisions because that was how she had described her career to them. They had seen Ada win a Grammy, a Brit Award. They knew that Grace was Ada's manager, but they hadn't yet seen the tangible evidence of their daughter's success. Warren would be proud. And Dorothy? Grace didn't know how she would react. Besides, it wasn't Grace that Dorothy was just desperate to see—it was Ed.

Right now, however, Dorothy would be fuming. Grace had blocked out her morning to pick up her parents from the airport. And yet here was Ada, at seven a.m., standing on Grace's doorstep in her gym gear with tears running down the perfectly applied foundation on her cheeks.

'Grace, I tried to call. I've been up all night—'

'My phone was on silent,' said Grace. 'Because it was night-time. Don't you have a training session with Karun right now?'

'I was on my way, but I just can't do it, Grace. Oh god.' Ada sniffed, dabbing under her eyes with the tip of her pinky, a delicate operation given the length of her false lashes and the length of her false fingernails.

'Can't do what? The session?'

'No! The album, Grace! I can't release it. It's a fucking embarrassment.'

Grace needed to be in a cab to Heathrow in ten minutes. She could picture Dorothy checking her watch, tapping her foot, shooting accusing glances at passers-by whom she was convinced would mug her. (Warren, on the other hand, would be a content observer.)

'We've been through this.' Patient voice, Grace. Gentle and patient. Any inkling that she was losing patience and Ada would storm off and be uncontactable for days. 'It's a brilliant album.'

'Sentimental and irrelevant, that's what they'll say.'

Ada had a tendency to vocalise every negative review she could imagine.

'And what would you say to that?' Grace asked. She really should let Ada inside, but then Ada would want tea and a hug and an hour's worth of comforting on the couch.

'It doesn't matter what I say!'

'We went through this with the last album. It always happens right before—'

'You have to call Tony. You have to pull it.'

In her mind, Grace shouted at Ada that it was a fifty-million-pound contract that one couldn't simply 'pull' because of last-minute jitters.

'You're scared because you're vulnerable. This album is really close to you, that's why it's so scary and that's why it's so brilliant.'

She could see Ada teetering on the edge of belief and disbelief. Behind Grace, in the house, Ed cleared his throat loudly.

'Is that Ed?' Ada asked.

'Ada, I'm sorry but I have to—'

'Is that you, Ed? How are you, babes?'

Ed now, in a t-shirt and pyjama bottoms, standing behind Grace in the doorway.

'Oh, hi, Ada,' he said. 'Thought you were the cab driver.'

A lie.

'Cab driver?' Ada asked. 'Grace are you going somewhere? I'm so sorry.'

'The airport,' Ed said.

'What? Why?'

'My parents are visiting,' Grace said.

'Oh! I forgot! And here's me keeping you. Don't take a cab. Come with me. I'll get Ted to swing by the airport. Will you contact Karun and tell him I'm going to miss the session? And you can call Tony from the car too.'

Grace's phone began to ring.

'Oh, that will be Karun now!' Ada said.

Ada was correct and Grace really did not have time for any of this.

'Where are they staying, your mum and dad?'

'Here.' And the kitchen was still a mess and the guest bed was yet to be made up.

'You should have said, babe! They could have had my Chelsea place!'

Ada skipped down the stairs to where the black Bentley was parked on the street and knocked on her driver's window. Grace and Ed watched her talking to him.

'Is this what you want?' Ed asked Grace.

'It's irrelevant.'

'Boundaries, Grace.'

'She's fragile. She's got Graham Norton tomorrow night.'

'That doesn't mean she can just . . .'

'And I'm late.'

◎

Ada's driver swung the Bentley into the pick-up lane outside the terminal.

'Do you want Ted to go in? You can take the sign, Ted.' Ada looked back to Grace. 'He'll take the sign. What're their names? Dorothy and Warren, is it?'

'No. Ted, it's fine. I'll go get them.'

'Send Ted! They'll love it. Get a right kick out of it.'

'Mum will think I'm rude for not getting out the car.'

A scenario which involved Dorothy and Ada not only meeting but sharing a car ride was one Grace hadn't allowed herself to envisage. Dorothy would say something insensitive and Ada would have a nervous breakdown. How would she make it up to Ada? Promise never to speak to Dorothy again?

Dorothy and Warren stood outside the same Waterstones where Grace had met Nish all those years ago. Dorothy's suitcase and matching carry-on were parked at her heel, her eyes darting about at passers-by, just as Grace had predicted. Warren was leafing through a magazine, whistling to himself.

'There you are!' Dorothy said when she saw Grace. 'I was about to call! You won't believe what happened. My bag was coming around on the carousel and two women—*women!*—pushed in front of me, knocked my bag clear off the carousel—'

Grace suspected Dorothy liked the word 'carousel'; anyone else would just say 'luggage thing'.

'—and, well, didn't I have something to say about that!'

'She sure did.' Warren had replaced the magazine in the rack beside him. He gave Grace a kiss on the cheek. 'They've got a good range of magazines here, love. Do you want anything?'

'I'm okay, Dad. Thanks.'

'Italian, I think they were,' Dorothy continued. 'Both with Gucci bags—real or not I couldn't tell, so you have to give them that. Of course they both pretended not to understand what I was saying. But they knew. Where are you parked?'

'Out here.'

'Not in the drop-off zone, I hope? I don't want you to get a fine for leaving the car unattended. But I do hope we won't have to walk far, as this suitcase is terribly heavy and the wheels have a mind of their own.'

'I have offered to carry it,' said Warren.

'Let me take it,' said Grace.

'Don't be silly. Goodness, is that your car? Your father said you'd bought an old car.'

'No, it's—'

'Is that Edward?'

'No one calls him Edward, Mum. And that's the driver.'

'The driver! A taxi? That doesn't look like a taxi.'

Ted got out of the car, took off his black hat and gave a slight bow. 'Good morning, ma'am. Sir.'

Dorothy looked back at Grace, wide-eyed. 'Goodness! What a fuss! Hello there.'

Warren shook Ted's hand and then Ted took Dorothy's bags and deposited them in the boot while Warren asked him questions about boot space and how expensive it was to insure a Bentley.

Ada, with a black baseball cap and sunglasses on, got out of the car. ''Allo, Dorothy. Warren. Glorious to meet you. Hop in.'

Warren sat in the front so that he could ask Ted more questions about the car as well as what it was like to drive in London, tolls, road conditions, the price of fuel and so on. Ted seemed to enjoy the attention. Meanwhile, in the back, Dorothy and Ada talked about shopping in London. Both of them seeming to have quite a lot of material on the matter. Grace spent the drive home looking out the window, ears attuned to every variation in Dorothy's tone and wishing she'd got another coffee at the airport.

◎

Ed came out to meet them as soon as the car pulled up outside the house. He kissed Dorothy on the cheek and she giggled. She never giggled.

Inside, Dorothy paused in the foyer, taking in the high ceiling with the beautiful cornices, the restored original chandelier, the polished parquet floor, the peacock-print wallpaper.

'Goodness. What a beautiful house. Grace, you never said it was so lovely. I thought London was too expensive for this type of thing. I thought you'd just bought a little place. I mean, I know you're doing well, but . . . is it yours?'

'Yes.' Grace wanted to say that she had been able to buy it outright, but Dorothy would think she was gloating or maybe showing off. She wouldn't say, 'That's wonderful,' or, 'I'm so happy for you.'

'I made up the spare bedroom,' Ed said, following Dorothy through the front door with her suitcase. 'You have to tell me if there's not enough blankets. And I'll show you how to use the radiator.'

Dorothy beamed. 'Goodness, you're useful! Isn't he useful?'

In the kitchen, Grace took three mugs from the cupboard and flicked on the kettle as Ed led Warren and Dorothy upstairs. Dorothy was asking what the neighbours were like. Were they very posh? Stuck-up? Warren was interested in council rates and how often they had to put the bins out. Grace's phone showed she'd missed four calls in the last ten minutes. She didn't know if her parents even wanted tea. Or what sort they would like. (Nish had recently become fanatical about tea, attempting to use it as a substitute for alcohol, and had bought Grace a wooden box with twenty varieties.) Grace stared at the box and all the little coloured packets. She really should be listening to her voicemails. There were no biscuits, Grace was sure she'd bought some because Dorothy and Warren always had a biscuit with their tea. Perhaps Ed had eaten them. Her phone pinged with three messages. But here were Dorothy, Warren and Ed.

'Tea?' Grace asked. 'And a biscuit if you've got one,' said Warren.

Grace put the box of teas on the bench in front of her parents. 'Take your pick.'

'What a variety!' said Warren. 'That's something I remember from last time. Such a variety of things in the UK.'

Dorothy was not looking at the impressive range of teas; she was looking at the three mugs on the counter beside the kettle.

'Are you not having a cup of tea?' she asked Grace.

'I'm sorry, I have to—'

Grace's phone began to ring. Dorothy gave her a look like she was daring Grace to answer it. The caller was Martin Shenk, a new exec at Atlantic. Grace had been trying to get hold of him for three days. She silenced the phone.

'Grace has to go to work,' Ed said, 'but I'll take you guys out. We can go for a bit of a walk, grab something to eat if you want?'

Dorothy leafed through the tea packets rather than looking at Grace. 'I thought you said you were taking leave?'

'I am, after today.'

'Well, I hope you are.'

'I am.'

'Well, that's good.'

And Dorothy watched on as Grace picked up her bag and jacket and walked out the door.

◎

By the time Grace left work that evening it was raining, a London drizzle that couldn't decide if it was a shower or not. She had no umbrella and was in such a rush to leave the office she had left her jacket behind. A last-minute phone conference had put her thirty-six minutes over schedule, and she'd spent every one of those minutes worrying about what variety of psychological trickery Dorothy was using on Ed in those exact moments. Grace had been careful to warn him about Dorothy's judgemental nature and extreme passive aggression. Warren was less of a worry—he'd declared how thrilled he was just to be there several times on the way home from the airport. 'What a blast!' he'd said, again and again. It was true that he would have been quite happy to drive around all day and just look out the window.

On her way home, Grace picked up the takeaway—rogan josh and chicken korma (as mild as possible, she had requested).

By the time she got to the front door her hair was wet and the plastic from the bag was cutting into her fingers.

Inside, Dorothy was perched on a kitchen stool, already in her pyjamas and a kimono robe she must have found in Grace's wardrobe.

'You're a drowned rat!' she exclaimed.

'It's raining,' said Grace.

'Such a shame. We had lovely weather today. Didn't we have lovely weather, Warren?'

Grace's father was in the living room. 'Lovely weather.'

'And you don't expect that in London, do you.'

'I guess not.' Grace disentangled her hand from the plastic bag and put the food on the counter. 'Where's Ed?'

'Upstairs. He's very worried about the blankets in our room. I told him not to worry, but he is because he said that it gets quite cool in the mornings. I thought you had a car. Why were you walking?'

Grace opened the dishwasher, but Ed had already emptied it. 'I don't like the traffic. I take the tube most days. And the restaurant's just around the corner.'

'But it's raining!'

Grace took plates from the cupboard.

'Can I help?' asked Dorothy.

'No, it's . . . There's nothing to do.'

'Grace.'

'Hmm?' One of the plates had a chip on the rim; she went back to the cupboard to swap it.

'He's just wonderful.'

Grace paused. 'Oh.'

Dorothy came and took the plate from her. 'I mean it. Do you understand?'

'Yes.'

'Good. What you have here is a good thing. He's a good man.'

'Why are you looking at me like that?'

'I'm not looking at you like anything!'

But it was a warning look Grace knew well: *Don't stuff this up.*

Warren came into the kitchen and sat on Dorothy's stool. 'Wow, that smells good. I tell you what, I'm absolutely buggered. We must have walked for hours. We got a great lunch in Bethel Green.'

'Bethnal Green?'

'I think so. Cafe under the arches of the railway line. Under the arches! I've never seen anything like it.'

'I can't believe he took you all the way there.'

'We took the sightseeing bus some of the way. It was good fun to sit up the top.' Dorothy gave Grace a pointed look. 'Of course, it wasn't raining then.'

'The bus I catch has a roof, Mum.'

'And Ed said the best thing for jet lag is to take a good long walk outside,' said Warren.'

'He's an expert,' Grace said and immediately wished she hadn't.

'Yes,' Dorothy said. 'He says he goes home to visit his mum and dad twice a year.'

'Hmm.'

'He said his mother had cancer. You never told me that.'

'She's better now.'

'Still. What a thing to go through. With her all the way on the other side of the world.'

Ed came downstairs and announced that he had found two cotton blankets that wouldn't be too heavy. 'You can use one or both, see how you go,' he said.

Dorothy beamed at him, then gave Grace a look that said, *Isn't he wonderful?* and also, *He visits his mother twice a year.*

As they moved to the dining table Grace said that she should probably get a better tablecloth, but Dorothy told her not to be silly and just sit down. 'You should have had a nice warm shower,' she said. 'You still look soaked through. Oh, and I tested the rice and it's still nice and hot.'

'What a relief,' said Grace.

Ed encouraged them to dig in.

'It's Indian,' Grace said.

'Yes, darling. Do you know we went to an Indian wedding last year? April, it must have been.'

'Yes, April,' said Warren.

'It was a teacher from Warren's school. Lovely girl. Oh, the food!'

'Fantastic,' said Warren.

'And you know, the spice isn't so bad once you get used to it.' She ate a mouthful of korma then said, 'This is very mild.'

'Very mild,' Warren agreed.

'Oh, well, I wasn't sure if you liked spicy food.'

'We do now. I did an Indian cooking course. Only four weeks, but gosh it was fun. How *is* Anishka?'

'Are you asking me that because we're eating Indian?'

'It just made me think of her—what's wrong with that?'

'She's having a baby,' Ed said.

'Is she?' Dorothy looked at Grace. 'You never told me! With that fellow?'

'Yes. Ravi.'

'Oh, how lovely for her. Isn't that just lovely?'

This would have been a perfect time for Dorothy to give Grace a look that said: *I hope you have a baby soon.* It was strange that she didn't.

◎

Dorothy and Warren were in bed half an hour after dinner was done.

Ed stacked the dishwasher, and Grace wiped the bench down with a cloth that they really should replace but she'd forgotten to buy another one. Dorothy would notice.

'Dorothy's amazing,' Ed said.

'What do you mean, she's amazing?'

'She's so interested in things. Everything. I mean, your dad is too; we talked a lot about the London transport system.'

'I bet you did.'

'But your mum, she's sharp, hey.'

'She is.'

'She's great.'

'See, I've never thought of her as great. That is not an adjective I would use.'

'She thinks a lot about things, and she wanted to know all about my work.'

'Oh. Sorry about that.'

'No, it's fine. She's like you.'

'Okay, now that's completely—I don't know what that is. I don't think that's accurate.'

'She's hilarious.'

'See, I don't think she means to be hilarious.'

'She does. She's dry as but, yeah, I think most of the time she's taking the piss.'

'No, that's her actual personality.'

'Well, I like her.'

'I think she's in love with you.'

20

GRACE HAD BEEN WORKING CRAZY HOURS FOR THE LAST FEW MONTHS, often out the door before Ed was up and not home until after eight, sometimes nine. Ed had said carefully that he felt like he never saw her, so they agreed to meet for lunch in Hyde Park when Grace had a long gap between meetings. Shoes off, they were stretched out in the sun, eating sandwiches and watching a small group of solemn people wearing black gathered at a nearby tree; one of them was attempting to furtively sprinkle the contents of an urn.

'I'm sure you need a permit for that,' Ed said.

'Probably a lot of paperwork.'

'Just chuck me in a cardboard box,' Ed said. 'Don't waste money on mahogany. Put me in the garden.' He lay back with his head on his jacket like it was a pillow.

'You'd definitely need a permit to put someone in a garden,' Grace said.

'Nah, who's going check? Just make a note of where you've put me, so you don't accidentally dig me up.'

'Cardboard boxes can be expensive,' Grace said.

'Fine, roll me up in some butcher's paper.'

'Like fish and chips.'

'That's perfect, because I do really enjoy fish and chips.'

'I just feel that Joan might want something a bit more . . .'

'Sturdy?'

'Hmm.'

'Ah, I won't die for a while, I don't reckon. She'll be gone by then.'

Grace kicked him. 'You can't say that! Jeez.'

'It's true, though.'

'Okay. Yes. Sure. But could you shout *me* a box?' said Grace. 'I'd like a box. Cardboard is fine but do a drawing on it or something.'

Grace waited for him to laugh but he didn't. 'That makes me feel a bit sick,' he said. 'Don't die, Grace. Promise me you won't die. Ever.'

'I'll try.'

'No more fast cars.'

'We'll see.'

He reached over and squeezed her hand. 'I bloody love you.'

'Good. I'm quite partial to you too.'

'So we should get married. I'd like to marry you.'

She laughed. Not the reaction she'd rehearsed. 'Would you?'

'Um. Yes. I've thought about it.'

'Just now?'

'Yeah, just had the idea.' Ed rolled onto his side, propped his head on his elbow. 'Grace Harlow, will you marry me?'

Down by the lake, two backpackers were looking at the swans. She thought of Trent. She remembered the Spaniard.

'Your silence is making me a bit nervous,' Ed said.

Grace reached over and touched the bristle of Ed's beard. 'Yes. I will absolutely marry you.'

◎

Grace chose to phone Dorothy from the back garden because that's where she felt the most calm. It was a long skinny slice of green with a paved area and a water feature that Grace always forgot to turn on. She wanted to get a timer for it, but Ed said they didn't need one. Grace had expected Dorothy to be elated by the news. And Dorothy did say she was pleased. So, so pleased. But after that there was a pause and Grace said, 'Do you think I'm doing the right thing?'

'Of course you are.'

'I think so too.'

'Ed must be pleased.'

'Yep. He is. We both are.'

'Good. That's good.' Another pause. 'I'll tell your father. He'll be thrilled. Or do you want to tell him?'

'Maybe I should. Is he there?'

'He's at the hardware store looking at a bike shed. It's a little shed that fits a bike. Only small but it has a lock on it.'

Grace wasn't expecting to be discussing bike sheds at this point and didn't want to pursue it, but neither did she want to ask Dorothy what was wrong. Clearly something was wrong.

'Does he have a bike?' Grace asked. 'Like a pushbike?'

'Yes. He bought one, oh, it must have been about three or four months ago. His friend Greg—he's from the Rotary Club, and I think he might be a freemason too, but that's beside the point. Anyway, Greg goes cycling quite often and I did say to your father that it would be good for him to do some sort of activity now that he doesn't play golf anymore.'

'He doesn't play golf anymore?'

'Well, no, because there was this one fellow in the little group who your dad just can't stand. And you know your dad, he gets along with anyone, but this man, I don't know. He must be a real pain in the backside because your father won't play golf with that group anymore.'

'Oh. Okay, well, when should I call him? Should I try in an hour? Or maybe in the morning—tonight your time?'

'That's a good idea.'

Pause. Don't do it, Grace. 'Are you all right, Mum?'

'Of course I'm all right!'

'Well, I'm glad you're pleased.'

'Of course I'm pleased!'

'Okay. Well, I'd better—'

'Where will you have the wedding?'

And there it was.

'We haven't really—'

'Because I don't know if Ian can fly at the moment. Or for a while. Since he had knee surgery.'

'When were you speaking to Ian?'

'I saw on Facebook that he'd had knee surgery; Joan put something up. Some terrible photo of his knee. The actual surgery! Can you believe that?'

'Ed hasn't said anything about him not being able to fly.'

'And, you know, there're some lovely venues in the mountains. Pamela's daughter, Sarah, got married in Katoomba . . .'

'I don't want to get married in Katoomba, Mum.'

'It wouldn't have to be Katoomba, and you don't need to decide now. I'm just saying there are a lot of options.'

'I think we'd prefer to get married in London. All our friends are here.'

Another, longer, pause.

'It's early days,' Dorothy said. 'There's plenty of time to decide. Okay, well, I'll get your father to call you.'

'I'll call him.'

'All right, darling. Talk soon.'

Grace stood up stood and went to the fountain. She flicked it on, even though there was no real point because she was going inside now anyway. The conversation was done.

21
DOROTHY

'I'D LIKE A LATTE,' DOROTHY TOLD THE BOY AT THE COUNTER.

She remembered a time when lattes were a new thing and came in a nice tall glass with a little handle. They used to have three layers: strong coffee down the bottom, a layer of milky coffee, and then a thin layer of foam on top. Like a layer cake except not as fattening—not if you had it with skim milk, anyway. Dorothy always had a third of a teaspoon of sugar and found the process of tipping the sachet in the side and then swirling all the layers together with a long spoon very satisfying. Almost as good as drinking the coffee itself. Take pleasure in the little things, she said to Grace. Another roll of the eyes. Gosh, what Dorothy would give to see her again soon, even if she did just roll her eyes the whole time.

What was one to do when those little things that gave joy were taken away? You couldn't get lattes like that anymore. The glasses were half the size and no one knew how to do the layers. Once she'd even tried asking for a proper latte, only to get a blank stare from the anaemic-looking girl behind the counter.

(Probably a vegan. Dorothy wanted to ask if she'd had her iron levels checked.)

Warren didn't miss those lattes. 'I don't care as long as there's a coffee bean involved somewhere along the line,' he would say on their coffee mornings. Almost every morning was a coffee morning for the two of them these days. Warren had bought her a coffee machine for her birthday so they wouldn't have to go out all the time. He didn't realise that going out was half the point. Perhaps if he had spent all the years at home that she had, he would. Besides which, she couldn't work out how to use the damned thing. Dottery Dorothy.

Warren wasn't with her this morning. He had a meeting at the aviation club, flying remote control planes about and pretending it was World War II. She was here alone with only this young man in ill-fitting trousers (surely his ankles were cold) who was taking her order. Dorothy hadn't met this one before. He'd given her a look when she came in, a *what are you doing in this cool cafe?* sort of look. (Although he probably didn't use the word 'cool'; he probably used something else, something cooler.) Dorothy was in this cafe because she appreciated the decor—so many plants! And the formica tables like the one she'd grown up with, with comfortable chairs at exactly the right height. And Rosie, who reminded her of Grace in the way she dressed and who knew exactly how Dorothy liked her coffee; Rosie, who was noticeably absent this morning.

'And could you please make sure it's nice and hot?' Dorothy said as the young man fiddled about with a notepad. It was unbelievable how many places couldn't even make a nice hot coffee these days.

The young man sighed.

'Is that a problem?'

'No problem at all,' he said in a way which communicated the opposite. Did he think she was stupid? Dottery Dorothy. But Dorothy didn't comment because she was a master of self-control.

Dorothy took her usual table next to the window and checked her voicemail in case Grace had called. She couldn't get the phone to show on its home screen when she had voice messages. It was like a mystery box. Dorothy dialled the voicemail but there were no new messages. She hadn't heard from Grace since Grace had announced she and Ed were getting married. It had been a whole week. The strangest thing for Dorothy—and she hadn't anticipated this about herself—was that she hadn't told a single person. Other than Warren, of course. 'You must pretend that you don't know,' she'd said to him. 'When Grace calls tonight you must act surprised.' Dorothy hadn't even told Pamela. Surely this was the first time she hadn't shared such a thing with her best friend in the world. Pamela's first question would be: where are they getting married? Dorothy had always imagined Grace getting married at that nice old sandstone church just off the highway. The one with the big tall gum trees all around it. Grace would stay over the night before with Dorothy and Warren; she would be able to get dressed for the wedding in her old room. It was the guest room now, but such a nice big room. Plenty of space. She could have some photos in the front garden, the white roses and Grace's white dress.

Dorothy had heard that a lot of women nowadays didn't even bother to spend the night before the wedding apart from their fiancé. A lot of them didn't wear white either.

Lately Dorothy had noticed a strange feeling inside herself. She wasn't certain that it was a feeling. Maybe it was a sensation. Maybe it was an emotion. If it was an emotion, she didn't know what emotion it was. She found herself crying sometimes: on her own in the car mostly, or sometimes first thing in the morning before she got up. Warren didn't know. Nobody knew. And what on earth would she say? *I feel strange and sometimes I cry?* Pamela was a crier. She'd cry at the drop of a hat. Prior to this year Dorothy couldn't remember the last time she'd cried. Her father's funeral, probably. But even then, she hadn't had this feeling, as though she was unspooling, threads of herself getting all knotted up.

The feeling, the sensation, or whatever it was, was there within her this morning. It was unexpected because she liked going to the cafe. But without Warren there, Dorothy had nothing to do except wait for her coffee. She refused to be one of those people who couldn't go five minutes without scrolling on their smartphone, but she had to admit that she did feel awkward with no one to talk to and would have appreciated something to do rather than just sit there feeling strange and out of place. She was the oldest person in the room. Why hadn't she thought to bring a book?

Another five minutes passed without her coffee arriving. Dorothy flagged down the young man as he was clearing plates from another table.

'I ordered a coffee?' she said, hoping he would pick up what she was putting down so she wouldn't have to add, 'Where the heck is it?'

'Yep,' he said, without even looking at her. 'And it's on its way.'

Another full five minutes passed before the young man finally delivered her coffee with an expression that suggested he was actually a slave kept there against his will.

Dorothy took a sip. It was lukewarm. If it had been lovely Rosie, Dorothy would have ignored the slip-up. But this young man hadn't earned such grace. Dorothy motioned to him and he sauntered back to the table.

'Yeah?'

'This is cold.'

Another sigh. 'No, it's exactly how it's supposed to be. We don't burn the milk here.'

'I asked for a hot coffee.'

Another sigh.

'You seem to have an issue with that,' Dorothy said. 'Which I find odd because you're not the one drinking it.'

'I don't have an issue, lady. If you don't like it go to McCafé or some shit.'

'Don't swear at me.'

'I didn't swear *at* you, I . . . whatever.' He snatched up the cup and took it away.

How dare he! Grace was the only one who was allowed to talk to her like that. Grace would know exactly what to say to this boy. There was another one of them behind the counter now, a girl who wasn't Rosie. The boy said something to her and she looked over at Dorothy and snickered. She clearly thought Dorothy was too old to hear her call Dorothy a stupid old bitch.

Dorothy stood up and approached the counter. 'I heard what you called me, young lady.'

The girl and the boy both started laughing.

Rage rose up in Dorothy from some long-forgotten reservoir and she picked up one of their stupid little glasses from where it was stacked on top of the coffee machine and hurled it at the wall. It exploded like a missile. Warren would be proud.

The room went quiet.

'Fucking hell!' said the boy.

'I didn't throw it *at* you!'

'Okaaaay,' said the girl. 'You need to leave now.'

Dorothy pointed a finger at the boy. 'You wouldn't have talked to my husband like that. You think it's okay to treat me like rubbish because I'm an older woman.'

And at that moment Rosie walked in the door, into the silence, where every eye was on the madwoman.

Dorothy saw the look on Rosie's face. Shock and confusion. And Dorothy saw herself the way every other person in the room must have.

22

GRACE

ADA HAD CHOSEN THE RESTAURANT. IT WAS ON THE CANAL SAINT-Martin, poorly lit and with an air of decaying grandeur which anywhere else in the world would be seedy but in Paris was cool. (Grace didn't know if cool people used the word 'cool' anymore. She was in the kind of profession where she should probably be across that kind of thing but lately had found herself caring less and less.) The lighting suited Ada—she was able to retain a level of anonymity. But it did make it difficult for Grace to read her face. This of course wasn't helped by the fake lashes and extreme eyeliner. Grace sometimes felt that if Ada truly didn't want to be recognised it would be a good idea to ditch both.

'Do you want to tell me what happened?' Grace asked.

'No,' said Ada.

'Let's rephrase: tell me what happened.'

Ada twisted black spaghetti around her fork and shovelled it into her mouth. Carbs. Things were bad if there were carbs happening.

'Because you know this isn't good,' Grace said. 'If you can give me something, anything, we can find a way to work it. You know the Variety performance is off the cards, right?'

'I don't want to do the bloody Variety performance.'

'Well, that's lucky.'

Ada raised a finger and a waiter arrived at the table. He looked like he was determined to be uninterested in the celebrity he was serving. Ada pointed at her empty wineglass. 'Sweetheart, I need another one of those. My friend here does too.'

'I don't,' said Grace.

The waiter said something in French and gesticulated in a way that suggested he was now no longer just uninterested but also pissed off.

'Seriously?' Grace said to him. 'You can understand everything she's saying. I'll have a sparkling water.'

He huffed and left, returning moments later with a full glass of wine and a bottle of San Pellegrino, muttering to himself.

'Thank you, darlin'.' Ada brushed a hand over his and he paused. She gave him a wink and his facade of indifference fell apart.

'Is that what happened?' Grace asked when he was gone.

Ada shrugged.

'Oh, drop it,' Grace told her. 'Charlie called *me* when he saw the story. Your husband called *me* distraught because he knew I wouldn't give him any bullshit. Stop the act or I'll leave right now and you can deal with it all on your own. Were you drunk? Because you looked pretty drunk in the pictures. Drunk we can work with. Maybe.'

'I wasn't drunk.'

'You gave the photographer the middle finger.'

'I wasn't drunk! I was on my own. I'd been on my own for two months.' Ada fiddled with her rings.

'If you don't tell me exactly what happened I can't help you,' Grace said.

'Two months with strangers. That's all. Just strangers.'

'I was there sometimes.'

'Yeah, but you're not family, are you? This is your job.'

'You know it's not like that.'

Ada waved Grace's words away. Tears were welling in her eyes. 'Charlie rang me that day because Skylar had lost a tooth and she thought a piece of her brain was attached to it. She wouldn't listen to him when he told her it wasn't a piece of her brain and she wasn't dying. She wanted to talk to me, but I was doing press. So she refused to go to sleep and was still up at midnight.'

Ada tapped her nails on her wineglass, faster and faster.

'Anyway, he rings and tells me all this and he's pissed at me,' she said. 'Because I wasn't there. Like I had a choice. We'd made the decision he would stay behind, wouldn't come on tour because we didn't want to mess up the girls' schooling and that. What was I supposed to do? I couldn't get on a plane and come home. I would have if I could. But I couldn't do anything and he was blaming me. Not *blaming* blaming me, but I could hear it in his voice.'

'Did you fight?'

'No. He was pissed off and I couldn't do anything so I just said sorry, sorry, sorry, even though I had nothing to be sorry for. Then I went back to the hotel and cried for an hour in the bath. After that I had to tidy myself up so I could FaceTime Skylar and Susie before they went to bed. After that I did a bit more crying and then Luiz took me to a party. You know I hate all that, but I was lonely and I wanted to forget everything.'

'So who is the guy?'

'Nothing happened.'

'He was kissing your neck.'

'No, he never kissed my neck. It was the camera angle. He was bloody fit; I would remember if he kissed my neck.'

'Okay. Well, that's our story. The camera angle, old friend, blah blah blah.'

'It's not a story, Grace. It's what happened.'

Grace tore a piece of bread and slathered it with salted butter, actual salt crystals embedded in the butter. The French were a superior species.

'I hate having my neck kissed,' Grace said.

'Ed never kisses your neck?'

'No. I think it makes me imagine a lizard. A monitor lizard. They're very big and very tonguey.'

'That's why I haven't toured Australia. That right there. A big tonguey lizard. No thank you.'

Grace watched as Ada took a large mouthful of wine.

'Nothing happened, Grace. We kissed once in the back of a cab then I asked him politely to fuck off and make his own way home. I don't even know his name.'

'It's Alejandro de Leon. He's sold his story to *People*. "Ada Black broke my heart".'

'You have to stop it.'

'I tried. It will go online tomorrow. You need to warn Charlie.'

'You have to talk to him. He trusts you. If you tell him it was nothing he'll believe you.'

'Was it nothing?'

Tap, tap, tap. 'He'll listen to you.'

'Ada?'

'He's everything, Gracie. He's my world. You know Susie calls him Dad now?'

Ada wiped her eyes. Across the room the waiter was watching everything. His phone would come out soon.

'Charlie knew this was the deal. I didn't suddenly spring this life on him overnight. This is who I am, this is what I do. And he likes the houses, he likes the jets and the holidays. He's happy to take all of that. What could I do? He was so pissed at me. He's never pissed at me, not like that. I've never felt so helpless, so useless. So lonely. I can't lose him. He'll believe you.'

'You want me to lie to Charlie for you?'

'You wouldn't be lying. You spoke to me and I said nothing happened.'

'But I don't believe you.'

'You don't know what it's like. You don't have kids. I'm sorry, but you can't judge me.'

'He would forgive you.'

Ada shook her head.

'He would. He loves you—truly, truly loves you.'

'So where's the angle for that? With the press? I'm the cheating mum.'

◎

Ada was still in tears when Grace bundled her into a taxi after dinner, bundled her in like you might a tired child. She closed the door and watched Ada be ferried away to her hotel, where hopefully she would go straight to bed.

Really, what Grace should have done was ride with her all the way back to the hotel and see her safely into her room. But Ada would want to talk more, she'd want to tell Grace how much she loved her, and honestly all Grace wanted was a glass of wine, on her own, in the nice dark restaurant.

The waiter, who was now very accommodating—'Would Mademoiselle like a complimentary dessert?' Yes, Mademoiselle would, thank you very much—filled her wineglass and Grace considered asking him if he would mind if she took off her heels and put her feet up on the table. He probably wouldn't. But she didn't ask; she checked her phone instead. And saw nine missed calls from Warren. Fuck. Her mum. Her mum was dead.

'Dad?'

'Oh! Love! You've called back.'

Warren had a habit of stating the perfectly obvious as a means of conversation.

'What's wrong?'

'Now, don't worry.'

'Is Mum okay? What's happened?'

Silence.

'Dad! You can't tell me not to worry and then go silent.'

'She's fine. She's just had a bit of a funny turn.'

'What does that mean?'

'She's gone into hospital.'

'Is it a heart attack?' Grace had always known it would have to be something huge to take her mother down. Either that or she'd live to a hundred and twenty.

Grace heard her father take a deep breath.

'A psychiatric hospital.'

'*What!* Why?'

'Something happened at a cafe. I wasn't there. She threw a glass at someone—got very worked up, apparently. I got a phone call from Rosie, a nice girl who works there, but the police had arrived when I showed up, and to be honest it was all a bit of a mess.'

'She's been arrested and put in a psych ward?'

Grace knew her mother was insane, but this was an unexpected development.

'Not arrested, no charges, thank goodness. But the community mental health people got involved and, well, she's in the locked ward at the hospital—'

'A locked ward? Bloody hell!' Grace imagined her mother pacing like a well-dressed caged tiger.

'They tend to worry about people who have been violent.'

'She's not violent!'

'Unfortunately the fellow she threw the glass at felt otherwise. It was either she went into the critical care unit at the hospital or she was arrested. But I'm going to get her out of there; we just need to have another assessment done. I've got her a spot in a private psychiatric hospital near Richmond. Lovely place, more like a resort really.' Warren chuckled. 'I wouldn't mind a stay there myself after all this is sorted out.'

23
DOROTHY

DR BROOKE HAD AN INTERESTING FACE, NEITHER HANDSOME NOR PLAIN, and wore an ill-advised beard. (It was patchy in places; perhaps that was what made his face interesting.) He wasn't very old—certainly not old enough to be telling Dorothy what to think. He wasn't a real doctor anyway, he was a psychologist, and he continually told Dorothy that he couldn't fix anything—which made her wonder what the point of him was—but he could give her the tools to help her manage things herself, he said. What things needed managing exactly, he didn't specify. Probably something to do with the cafe incident, which had been blown completely out of proportion. If only she'd stopped and thought about what she was doing before she did it, which was what she had always done—thought very carefully before acting. (It was what she always advised Grace to do.) Yet here she was, having broken her own rule. One slip-up and she was packed up and sent off to the funny farm like a dribbling imbecile. (Although it wasn't just one slip-up, was it? It was two now, if you counted that time in the car park. But Dorothy had banned herself from thinking about that day. It had been the worst day of her life.)

She could never remember the psychologist–doctor's name—something to do with water. Dr Flood? Dr Creek? Dr Drip? Details had become slippery since they started her on the tablets. It wasn't him who prescribed the tablets; he wasn't allowed to do that. (Again, what was the point of him?) It was the other one. The older one with the very trim moustache. Dr Veslovic. Now *there* was a handsome man. Quite dashing. The type who instilled confidence. If anyone else had prescribed medication she would have refused it.

Although he was dashing and capable of instilling confidence, Dr Veslovic wouldn't give Dorothy a straight answer when she asked how long she would be in this place. The indefinite nature of her stay was the one thing Dorothy objected to the most. Its length would be determined by the twice-weekly reviews carried out by Dr Veslovic, reviews which Dorothy felt she really should be present for. As she understood it, the non-doctor (Brooke—that was it) would meet with Dr Veslovic and discuss Dorothy's sessions, her progress or otherwise. This was a terrible idea as Brooke seemed to have no understanding of Dorothy or her life at all. She didn't want her fate decided by him; Dr Veslovic was receiving second-hand information via an unreliable source. Brooke was always saying, 'Tell me more,' which indicated a deficit of basic understanding. She told him she missed her daughters (a slip of the tongue). It was a fairly basic concept; missing someone is missing someone. And then of course he'd wanted to hear all about her relationship with Grace, as if that were relevant to the degree to which Dorothy missed her. Which it wasn't. A daughter is a daughter. It all made Dorothy suspect that he didn't have children. She hoped this was the case, or God help the woman who had given birth to them. (That wasn't right. Mothered them? Mothering was an entirely different sort of verb to fathering wasn't it? 'Fathered' somehow implied a singular act: 'He fathered two children.' Yet to say a woman 'mothered two children' implied that she fussed over some who weren't hers. It was almost derogatory, whereas 'fathering' indicated a noble act of conquest in which the mother was irrelevant. How ridiculous.)

Where was she?

That's right: God help the mother of Dr Creek's children. If he had any. Which she suspected he did not.

◎

When Grace was very young Dorothy had purchased a pass that allowed the two of them to visit the zoo anytime. It was a good way to get out and about. Grace had to be kept busy or else she would climb the walls. (Quite literally: Dorothy had found scuff marks under the window in Grace's room.)

It wasn't a big zoo, just a small one with native animals, but it was big enough to keep Grace occupied for a good stretch of time. The calming effect of looking at the animals came as a surprise to Dorothy. Grace would stand silently watching them, her little hands gripping the railing, bouncing up and down on her toes, and Dorothy found that she could stare for quite some time herself. She had never had much to do with animals. Pets brought odours and unnecessary stress. The Harlow family had owned a kitten for one night—a fluffy, treacle-coloured thing that Grace had wanted to name Lolly. Dorothy had settled it in the laundry with its little bed and a hot-water bottle before she'd gone to bed herself. But it had meowed the whole night, a tiny pitiful sound that managed to find its way through multiple walls and right into Dorothy's ears. She simply couldn't stand it. Grace had cried her head off when Dorothy sent Warren to return the kitten the next day. Dorothy tried to tell Grace that the kitten had missed its mother too much but this had no impact on Grace's wailing. Dorothy felt strangely jealous. She would have liked the opportunity to wail every now and again.

For reasons that Dorothy couldn't remember, this zoo acquired two bears: a mother named Polly and her cub. They were brown grizzly bears, the only ones in captivity (or otherwise; Dorothy assumed there weren't any roaming free) in Australia. Dorothy and Grace fell into the habit of eating their lunch (sandwiches that Dorothy brought from home; the kiosk food was so expensive!) on the bench seat opposite the bear enclosure. Dorothy came to admire Polly for the way she dealt with the cub. It would clamber all over her and yet Polly was so dignified, allowing it to do this and then batting it away gently when she'd had enough. The cub was undeterred, though, so sure of its mother's love that it would get to its feet and continue to trot along beside her, while this time keeping a respectful distance.

Sometimes Polly and her cub would sit with the sun on their back, the same sun that warmed Dorothy and Grace as they ate their sandwiches, and Polly the bear would watch *them*. She would look right at Dorothy, and Dorothy came to feel that they shared a mutual understanding of this great and impossible task they had both been assigned. Dorothy wondered if Polly was glad that her cub was safe from the outside world, or if she longed for it to experience freedom.

People often talked about their pets as companions. Dorothy would never try to keep a bear as a pet—how humiliating for it—but Polly was a companion in those days. Those stifling, chaotic, anxiety-filled days when Dorothy so desperately needed space from Grace and yet was terrified to let her out of her sight. There was the occasional time, at the bear enclosure, when Dorothy would think about the baby she had lost. She'd been sure it was a girl. But it was silly to think about it that way; it wasn't a baby, it was a collection of cells, cells in the wrong place at the wrong time. Not her fault at all, that's what the doctor said. An ectopic pregnancy was just not meant to be.

On that horrible day, after buying Grace's shoes and the scene with the youth in the car park, Dorothy had in fact been on time for her doctor's appointment. Only, as she'd been sitting in the waiting room, she'd come over with a very sick feeling. Beyond sick. And then a pain so profound that she had doubled over and cried out. In the end, after she was taken to hospital for emergency surgery, she was told by the surgeon that they 'had taken out everything'. All the plumbing, that's what he called it. He'd smiled and said that many women had full hysterectomies 'and went on to live perfectly happy lives'. What was a 'perfectly happy life' anyway? (Warren probably knew.) And why did this man get to be the one who assessed such a thing? His grammar was also terrible; the women didn't go on to live perfectly happy lives, plural. It was just the one life.

The sadness that Dorothy carried for months after her so-called failed pregnancy felt as though it filled the space, heavy and unyielding, where she should have been carrying her baby. She had failed at pregnancy. Perhaps God (because she did partially still believe) thought she was ungrateful for the daughter she had and so decided not to give her another. But that was silly. And so was the sadness; it wasn't even a baby, it was cells. Particles. Tiny, precious and impossible. Dorothy was the one who was broken, who had done something wrong to the baby without even knowing; what right did she have to sadness? A woman who worked with Warren had had a stillbirth. Now *that* was a proper tragedy, although no one acknowledged that either. The poor thing had returned to work as though nothing had happened. Another of Warren's colleague had whispered the news to Dorothy in passing, as if it were a shameful secret. In comparison to that, what was Dorothy so upset about?

24
GRACE

THE HOSPITAL DIDN'T LOOK LIKE A HOSPITAL; IT WAS A SERIES OF SINGLE-storey brick buildings surrounded by expansive gardens and, beyond these, dairy farms. Grace was glad there was a buffer between her mother and the farms; the last place Dorothy belonged was among livestock.

A young nurse met Grace at the door.

'What should I expect?' Grace asked her.

'She's a little prickly this morning.'

'That's normal for her.'

The nurse laughed in a polite way, which Grace found annoying—as if the nurse thought that Dorothy's personality might be the symptom of a disorder.

The nurse led Grace along a wide, carpeted corridor with sedate watercolours on the walls. They passed a room where people were watching morning television, or reading, or sitting and looking at nothing.

'She's been very reluctant to come out of her room and socialise,' the nurse said.

'She doesn't know anyone here.'

'Exactly. Many of our patients benefit from getting to know one another. She's also been refusing to join the group therapy sessions which are a mandatory part of our program.'

Grace couldn't imagine a situation more unsuitable for her mother than a group therapy session.

'Is it costing her privileges?' Grace joked.

The nurse frowned at this show of levity. 'But she has been running,' she added.

'Away?'

'Patients are encouraged to exercise regularly. Some use the gym or walk; we have a long walking track that surrounds the grounds. Dorothy's been running.'

◎

Dorothy was sitting in an armchair reading when the nurse showed Grace into her room. She looked more serene than Grace had ever seen her and when she saw Grace she smiled.

'Welcome to the funny farm.'

The nurse made a disapproving huff and left them alone. Grace closed the door and the nurse opened it again. 'It's fine to have the door closed, but with Dorothy's history—'

'I'm right here,' said Dorothy.

'With your history, Dorothy, I will need to come and check on you in ten minutes.'

Dorothy stood up and closed the door in the nurse's face.

'Do you know I'm not allowed to keep my running shoes in here? It's the laces that are the problem. No knitting needles either. I'm welcome to knit in the common area. I wouldn't give her the satisfaction; she's smug enough as it is. How are you? You look tired.'

'Thanks, Mum. I did just get off a twenty-eight-hour flight.'

'I told your father to tell you not to come.'

But Grace didn't believe her. She looked a little watery around the eyes.

'What happened?'

'Apparently I'm violent because I lost my temper. Careful—I might attack you at any moment.' Dorothy wasn't looking Grace in the eye when she said this; she was fiddling with her watch. 'So they've locked me up and your father has to tell all our friends that I'm unwell. That's the term they use nowadays. Unwell. Who in the world is "well"? Honestly! And I have to attend therapy groups with lunatics.'

'The nurse said you haven't been going.'

'Of course I haven't. I don't want to sit in a circle and talk about my feelings with strangers. Who would want to do that? I shouldn't have to; it's a violation of my right to privacy. And probably a cost-saving measure: get everybody in and out at once.'

'How *are* you feeling?'

'Frustrated. I want to go home. But when I get annoyed and complain about it or ask how long they're going to keep me here, they say I'm agitated and try to give me a pill to "settle me down". Like I'm a bear in a zoo who has to be shot with a tranquilliser gun.'

For some reason this analogy, which was the very same as the one that had occurred to Grace, brought Grace undone a little.

'Good grief. Why are you crying?'

'I'm worried about you!'

'You don't need to be. There's nothing wrong with me. I lost my temper because I was being treated like a stupid old woman. That's what they called me, you know.'

'Who?'

'In the cafe. They called me a stupid old bitch.'

Grace had never heard that word come from her mother's mouth. It made her feel sick to think Dorothy had heard someone say that about her. 'Oh, Mum. That's awful.'

'It is. It is awful. I was condescended to and called that terrible name, yet when I defended myself, well, I'm the crazy person who gets put away. I didn't throw anything *at* him. I just needed to make sure he was paying attention.'

The door opened and the nurse stuck her head in.

'Oh, go away,' Dorothy and Grace said in unison. Dorothy looked at Grace, amused.

'Honestly, this whole thing is ridiculous,' Dorothy said. 'I finally start speaking my mind and everyone thinks, "Oh, Dorothy must be mentally ill"!' The words were tumbling out of her now. 'All this talk about "boomer" women! Well, yes, I sacrificed a university education so I could stay home and iron my husband's underpants and fold fitted sheets—that's an unacknowledged skill by the way; if it were men who folded the fitted sheets, there'd be a national award for it. All those years I put myself second, so if I want my latte hot now, I'll darn well tell you. If I want to talk to the manager, I bloody well will. Because after fifty-five years of staying quiet and doing what I'm told, I've had it!'

Now, Dorothy looked a little shocked herself. She stood up and seemed to look around for something. Sat back down again. 'What?' she said. 'It's true.'

'Okay. Um. But . . . are you anxious? Dad said they think—'

'Of course I'm anxious! I'm alive! Life is awful sometimes.'

'Is it like that a lot, Mum? Awful?'

The guilt was shredding through Grace's insides, whether it belonged there or not. Whether it was justified or not.

'I don't know,' Dorothy said.

Now Dorothy began to cry and Grace didn't know what to do, so she tried to hug her.

Dorothy batted her away. 'Oh, I'm fine. Stop it. Don't be silly. It's fine.'

'I don't think it's fine, Mum.'

'It's nobody else's business! Any of it. All these people asking questions about me and the thing that happened.'

'The thing in the cafe?'

'No. Not that.'

'What thing?'

Dorothy sighed. 'It really is irrelevant.'

'Doesn't sound irrelevant.'

Dorothy was quiet. Grace saw a look of vulnerability pass across her face, but it vanished as quickly as it had arrived.

'It's time for me to go for a run,' she said.

◎

One month later, Grace and Ed had a short ceremony in the Royal Botanical Garden in Sydney, followed by a small reception, only thirty people. The reality was that Grace and Ed's life was in London, as were most of their closest friends. Nish came over from London, accepting Grace's offer to pay for her and Ravi's travel and accommodation. Ada would have loved, absolutely loved, to have been there, she said, but the media attention would have made things difficult and stolen the spotlight from Grace and Ed. They both would have been happy to have the spotlight stolen; neither of them enjoyed being the centre of attention. Max, a photographer mate of Ed's, took candid shots—except for a posed one of The Happy Couple and Their Parents, and one of Ed and Grace sitting on a park bench. Grace had a difficult time remaining serious enough for Max to take the kind of picture Joan and Dorothy thought they wanted; instead he captured a moment when Ed had kissed her on the cheek while Grace was laughing at the ridiculousness of it all. It ended up being her favourite photo.

Dorothy never explicitly thanked Grace for agreeing to have the wedding in Sydney—and certainly no mention was ever made of Dorothy's recent hospital stay, probably because no one knew—but when Ed and Grace were leaving the reception Dorothy pulled her daughter into a rare embrace and held on for longer than Grace could ever remember her mother hugging her before.

25

APRIL 2022

TRENT ARRIVED AT THE TABLE CARRYING A BEER AND A LARGE LURID-looking cocktail complete with a paper umbrella.

'I got you a party drink,' he said.

'From 1987? I asked for a gin.'

'Gin is a sad-person drink. You look like you could use a party.' He winked at her. 'My treat.'

'I don't remember the last time I was here. Oh, wait. Yes, I do. I'd just moved back in with my parents and I came to see a thrash metal band because Nish thought there might be hot guys here.' Grace sipped her drink and winced. It tasted like drain cleaner.

'Were there?'

'No. There wasn't a playground either. I guess they're going for a different clientele now.'

'Or the same clientele just got older and had kids,' said Trent.

'Did you?'

'Not yet.'

'Oh yeah, you're a man with an infinite body clock. Anything's possible. Does Shaleah want kids?'

Drain cleaner and pineapple juice. Possibly coconut body lotion.

'Grace.'

'I'm serious. Where is she right now, by the way? Is it past her bedtime?' Grace was being a bitch to someone she didn't even know. She sounded old and jealous.

'She's gone.'

'Gone where?'

'Home, maybe. I don't know. She just left.'

'Why?'

'Because I didn't say she was my girlfriend when I introduced you. Turns out it's a sore point.'

'Gosh, I wonder why.'

'Are you going to be mean the whole time?'

Grace was suddenly very tired and wondering what the hell she was doing there. She should leave. But it was only nine thirty. Dorothy and her judgement would still be wide awake.

A group of guys entered the pub, loud, self-consciously confident. Grace recognised one of them as a now very faded former rugby star from her school. He had not aged well—gone to seed, Dorothy would have said. Grace pivoted ever so slightly on her stool so she was facing away from them. She was grateful that Trent didn't seem to notice.

'So how are you?' Trent asked.

'I'm fine.'

'Are you?'

'I'm just very tired and my dog was hit by a car.'

'You must love that dog. I'm sorry she—'

'I don't care about the dog. That's not true. I do a bit. But if you call her my fur baby I will vomit right here on the table. I have an appropriate level of attachment to an animal that my kids love. So.'

'Well, for what it's worth, I'm glad you're doing well,' he said. 'Even if you hate your dog.'

'I am doing well. Thank you. I don't hate her. She's cute when she's asleep.'

'Where's home?'

'Are you going to stalk me?'

'Yes. Where do you live?'

'Where do *you* live?' she asked.

'I already told you. Why are you being cagey?'

'I'm not.'

'Yes, you are.'

'It doesn't matter where I live.'

'Riiiight.'

'Fine.' She looked at him. 'I live in Mosman.'

He burst out laughing. 'Ohhh. Well, that explains it. You're really winning at life.'

'I'm very good at my job.'

'I don't doubt it.'

'So?' she said. 'Do you have one? A job? Other than the band? I'm assuming you've got something that's paying the bills.'

'You're assuming the band doesn't pay the bills.'

'Well, I've never heard of it.'

'Ouch. You don't even know what it's called.'

'How I dread to think what it's called.'

'It's called The Swell.'

Grace had heard of The Swell; it was a name that was floating around. She couldn't remember the context.

'We're doing pretty good. We're with a label. It's small, sure, but it's not nothing. They used one of our songs on some TV hospital drama. I also manage a bar for a mate.'

'Ah.'

'You're so judgemental.'

'I'm not,' said Grace. 'I mean, I am, yes. But if that works, good for you.'

'Not everyone gets the big bucks.'

'I work really hard.'

'So do I.' He held her in his gaze.

She was glad he was making music. She kept this to herself.

'I read an article about you,' Trent said. Well, not about *you*—about Ada Black.'

'Did you google me?'

'Of course. You're pretty shadowy, though. No social media.'

'So you *are* stalking me.'

'Why wouldn't I?' He chuckled to himself and shook his head. 'You were the love of my life.'

'Oh, piss off. Don't do this. I don't want to do this.' Grace pushed the glass away. 'I'm out. Goodbye, Trent.'

'Don't go!' He grabbed her hand, laughing. 'No! Stay. Please stay. I'm sorry I killed the vibe. Truly.'

'Sorry you *killed the vibe*? What are you? Sixteen?'

'Stay. Stay and make fun of me. Please. You're really good at it. It's truly amazing to watch.' He dropped her hand. 'I just want to know you a bit. It's very unlikely I will ever see you again. Have mercy.'

She sat back down.

'So.' Trent cleared his throat and sat up straight, as if he were conducting a television interview. 'To continue: you can't do social media because you'll get stalked? Or harassed?'

'Both. People think I can make their dreams come true.'

'I saw something about you starting a record label.'

'I signed Ada when I worked for a small management company. We—me and Tony, the guy who owned the company—started a label of our own. Recorded her and a bunch of other artists. It got huge and in 2017 I sold most of my share to my co-founder for a fair bit of money. That's why I live where I do. Which is a beautiful place to live.'

'I'm sure it is. How much money?'

'A lot.'

'How much?'

'That's really rude to ask, you know.'

'I don't care. How much money?'

'You can google it. I'm sure Wikipedia will give you the inside info.'

'Enough that you don't have to work, like, ever again?'

'I like working. It's not just Ada; I get to work with a lot of talented people.'

'What do you do with all your riches?' Trent asked.

'Not much. It exists in a series of accounts, investments. I give a lot away. I tried to buy Mum and Dad a new house but they don't want one. They let me pay for a kitchen reno, though. I bought them both new cars.'

This would have been the time to say that Ed didn't want much to do with the money and found it embarrassing, but she didn't want Trent even knowing Ed's name.

'And if you don't grow up with money like that it's just weird,' Grace said. 'I mean, I come from a comfortable middle-class family, but this is something else completely. I'm not complaining; I've just never quite adjusted to it. The kids go to a public school because we didn't want them being in a crazy affluent world with yachts and stuff. Trouble is most of the kids at the public school near us have yachts anyway.'

'You're buying the next round of drinks.'

'Okay.'

'And can you get me a new van? Someone said I look like a kidnapper.'

'No. Buy your own van.'

26

2013

GRACE WAS IN A SO-CALLED CREATIVE DEVELOPMENT MEETING WITH a band called Disquiet. If they were going to pull together a decent debut album they needed to ditch tracks four, five and seven and come up with something new. Grace had negotiated an excellent deal with Universal for them. An excellent deal that would require three replacement tracks. Or at least two tracks rewritten to the point where they bore no resemblance to the originals. It was never an easy conversation to have. She wouldn't use the term 'shithouse' when referring to those particular tracks. Not once.

She had just finished her spiel—hitting hard on 'revisiting', 'potential' and 'capable'. She'd even replaced 'rework' with 'elevate'—a good strategy. The band sat opposite her. Two of them were blinking like baby animals seeing the sun for the first time. The frontman, Taylor Crowe (not his real name), was frowning and staring into the middle distance. The drummer was blank-faced, possibly stoned. They were all digesting. This was a good sign. Until Taylor, rather disappointingly, launched into an ill-fated defence of his shithouse songs. Grace faded out a little, her mind wandering over to notice that she was feeling a little off, a little dizzy, and then . . . how long? Six weeks? That wasn't a late period. That was a no-show.

Shit.

'What I'm trying to say,' Taylor whined, 'is that just because *they* don't get what we're trying to do here—'

Wow. He was still talking? Accept defeat, buddy. You're trying and failing.

Was she going to vomit? Was that pregnancy? Or just the fear that she might be pregnant? Did it matter? A vomit was a vomit. Why the hell did the interior designer take away the pot plants?

The only receptacle within reach was a bowl of croissants, which was a shame because she'd planned on having a *pain au chocolat* after the meeting. Never mind.

Taylor was quite sweet about it, saying, 'Fuck,' over and over again while snatching semi-used napkins from his bandmates. He handed them to Grace while she took a break from vomiting and poured a glass of water for her from the jug.

Grace left the meeting, locked her office door and pressed her forehead against the cold glass of the window. She watched a tourist boat cruising along the Thames, the sightseers bundled up in parkas and beanies (you'd have to be mad to do a boat cruise in January, Grace thought), standing on the deck and pointing to the wonders of London. Was her dizziness a pregnancy thing or just general panic? Why was she panicking? Through the haze of shock she found her phone on her desk and called Nish.

'Well, congratu-bloody-lations!' Nish said.

'I said I *think* I'm pregnant. I don't even know for sure.'

'Of course you are. What are you going to name it? Ravi and I couldn't agree on anything for ages. Too many options these days. I met a baby called Jupiter the other day. Fucking hell. Like, imagine if it turns out to be a bit fat. Biggest planet, Jupiter is.'

'I don't know what we're going to call it, Nish. It's a bit early—'

'Gosh, Ed's going to lose it, don't you think? He'll be well chuffed.'

'Should I go to a doctor or something? Home tests are unreliable, aren't they? I need to know for sure as soon as possible.' Grace was too busy for the doctor. She didn't have a regular one. If she was sick she dosed up on cold and flu tablets and worked through it.

'If you do two tests, mate, there's no denying you're preggers. But, yeah. See a doctor. Go to mine. I'll send you her number. Have you told Dorothy? God, I can just imagine. Has she been hounding you since the moment you met Ed?'

It occurred to Grace now that Dorothy had never asked her when she was going to have children. Not once. She must have thought Grace would be no good at it. Too busy or selfish or some other reason that she secretly judged Grace for.

Grace knew people who had tried to get pregnant for ages before actually becoming so. They called it Trying. 'We're trying,' they would say. Grace never wanted to utter those words and it was too soon anyway. She'd been off the pill for six weeks, nothing on the grand scale of Trying. It hadn't even been Ed's idea that she stop. It was hers. Grace had never wanted babies, not in the abstract sense. But she wanted Ed's child. Maybe he hadn't been the one to initiate the Trying because he didn't think she was motherhood material either. She decided she wouldn't tell him about the missing period until things were confirmed. No point getting his hopes up, if there were hopes. Or maybe she just dreaded the moment when he would pretend to be happy but inwardly think it was a disaster.

◎

That evening Grace walked into the house and was hit with the scent of Ed's cooking. It was Italian of some kind. Grace could specifically smell fresh basil. She dropped her bag on the floor and ran to the bathroom. She didn't make it and he was beside her then, with a cool face washer and a bucket. 'Is this what I think it is?' he asked. Grace shrugged: maybe, probably. She grabbed at the bucket.

He ran her a bath. It was the perfect thing to do and Grace wasn't sure how he knew that. She hadn't even known that. Ed sat beside her on the tiles. He couldn't stop smiling.

'Don't get too excited,' Grace said. 'It might not work out.'

'I can't help it.'

◎

Dr Cheng was wearing a beautiful mauve silk dress. She exuded an air of being capable and impatient with the incompetencies of others.

'I've come because I think I'm pregnant and I guess I'm supposed to book in somewhere or something.'

'Book in somewhere?' Dr Cheng asked.

'To have the baby.'

'I was just about to ask if this was a planned pregnancy.'

'Not planned but not deliberately avoided. We were taking a "let's see what happens when it happens" approach. I found out what happens.'

Dr Cheng's expression was blank.

'I was joking. I know what happens.'

Dr Cheng pushed her sleek hair behind her ear and clicked about on her computer. She started firing a series of intrusive questions at Grace. It was weird to sit down with a stranger and rattle off intimate details about herself.

'And are you on any medications at the moment?' Dr Cheng asked. 'Any psychiatric medications in particular?'

Was she insinuating that Grace should be on psychiatric medications? Was it something to do with Grace's flippant comment about 'finding out what happens'?

'God no.'

Dr Cheng frowned. 'It's nothing to be ashamed of. I need to check because it's not safe to fall pregnant on some medications.'

'I'm not ashamed. I'm just not on anything like that.'

'Any issues with substance abuse?'

And on it went. Grace feared she might be asked to consent to a cavity search at any moment.

Just when it seemed the questions were drying up Dr Cheng shot another one.

'And how are you feeling?'

'Nervous, to be honest. And a bit shocked.'

'I mean physically.'

'Oh. Nauseous and vomity. But fine. Good.'

◎

It was true that Grace should have called Dorothy at a time when they could have a proper conversation. Instead Grace chose to call her at seven in the morning London time, when she knew she had a meeting at eight, a meeting that would take her at least fifty minutes to get to. It was the time difference, she told herself. It made things difficult.

'Is now a good time?' Grace asked when Dorothy answered.

'Well, this is the time when you have chosen to call, so I suppose it's the only time.'

'Mum. Please don't.'

'Please don't what? I'm your mother and I never hear from you!'

'I talked to you last week.'

'No, it was the week *before* last. I was about to go into a yoga class. Remember? I missed the first ten minutes. The instructor—I'm not going to call her a yogi, it makes me think of an imbecile cartoon bear and that is a very unhelpful association when one is there to improve mindfulness—anyway, you should have seen the look she gave me. I had to explain that I'd had to take a call from my daughter in London and that you are always so busy looking after Ada Black. And *then*, well, I think she thought I must have dementia. She clearly didn't want to hear any more.'

'I don't imagine she would if she was in the middle of trying to teach a yoga class.'

'Well, anyway, I'm not sure I'm suited to yoga. Pamela said it helps with weight loss, but between you and me, she's been doing yoga for a year now and I honestly haven't seen any change in her.'

'It's not like you have to lose weight, Mum.'

'That's easy for you to say.'

'I can guarantee I weigh more than you and, honestly, who gives a shit?'

'There's no need to talk to me like that.'

'Okay, well, I rang to tell you something.'

'I don't suppose you're coming to visit?'

'Mum, I have so much—'

'Work. Yes, I know. We all do, Grace.'

'I'm having a baby.'

The phone went silent.

'Did you hear what I said?'

'No, I think it was breaking up.'

'I said I was pregnant. Am pregnant. Was, am and hopefully will continue to be for the next seven-ish months.'

'Are you sure?'

'I've had blood tests. So, yeah, pretty sure.'

'Oh, Grace.' Dorothy sounded breathless.

'Are you okay, Mum?'

'I'm just . . . Oh, Grace.'

She didn't sound right. A long pause and then, more collected now: 'Darling, that's just wonderful. I'm just so . . .'

'Do you need to sit down or something?'

'Yes, I do actually, but there's not many options, I'm afraid. I'm in the supermarket, you see.'

'You should have said! I would have called you back.'

'No, no, it's fine, it's fine. I'll just pay for the groceries and then—oh, Grace. I didn't think you would want children.'

'I never said I didn't want children.'

'Yes, but you never said you *did* want children and, oh . . . Is Ed pleased?'

'He's thrilled.'

'Of course he is. You're so lucky to have him. Well, this means you'll have to stop work.'

'Mum—'

'And you should come home. Oh, come home, Grace. If you're not working you can come home. Just for a little while. Bring the baby.'

'I haven't even thought that far ahead.'

'Darling, you can't stay there forever.'

'This is where I live. Are you okay?'

'Yes. But London isn't safe, you know . . . And, and, you know what happened there and—'

'That was eight years ago.'

'And it's a miracle it hasn't happened again. You know, Pamela's daughter Laura—you remember Laura—she left New York as soon as she could after September eleven.'

Dorothy was rushing her words. She wasn't calm, but she wasn't excited. This was something else.

'She was an exchange student,' Grace said.

'Darling, it doesn't matter what she was. These things don't discriminate!'

'Are you okay?'

'Of course! I'm thrilled!'

'I thought you would be pleased.'

'I am pleased—I'm thrilled!'

'Okay.'

'Okay. Grace?'

'What?'

'It's not . . . Darling, you have to tell your doctor something.'

The allotted conversation time was over, but Dorothy's tone was all wrong.

'Mum?'

'I had . . . Oh dear. You see, I didn't think I'd have to talk to you about this because I wasn't sure if you'd ever have time for children.'

'About what? Talk to me about what?'

'You must have an ultrasound right away. Now. Grace, straight away. Please.'

'Mum?'

'I had . . . Look. It might be, I mean, it could be . . . I had an ectopic pregnancy, Grace. You have to check; you have to make sure—'

It clicked, a sudden crisp moment of clarity within Grace.

'Mum, can you find somewhere to sit down? Just leave the groceries there.'

'You have to make sure . . .'

Grace was picturing her mother in the supermarket aisle, under the bright lights, eyes darting about in panic. It was all her imagination, because Grace had never seen her mother panic. 'Breathe. Mum, take some deep breaths in and out. It's okay.'

'You don't know that!'

'I'll make sure I tell the doctor.'

'Today.'

'I have an appointment on—'

'Today, Grace.'

'Okay, I'll go today. Are you okay? Why don't you call Dad? He can come and get you.'

'I don't know if . . . I don't know.'

'I'll call him. Right now. I'll call him and he can come and get you.'

'All right. Okay.'

'Go and find somewhere to sit.'

'They'll think I've stolen something.'

'They won't, and it doesn't matter anyway. Just take some deep breaths. I'll call Dad and then I'll call you right back and talk to you until he gets there.'

'All right. If that's okay with you. Do you have time?'

Dorothy's words made Grace's heart split straight down the middle.

'Of course I have time.'

27

NISH CUT A THICK WEDGE OF BRIE AND SLATHERED IT ON A CRACKER.

They were having high tea because, according to Nish, once the baby came it would be ages before Grace could be around fine bone china again.

'I mean, sure, have your tea set out before they can move around and grab things,' she said. 'But toddlers are fuckwits; they'll break everything they touch. You chucking much? God, with Ollie I was spewing my guts up. Remember? Fuck.'

'Every now and then. It's not too bad.'

Grace had not found space to tell Nish about her conversation with Dorothy.

'And the worst thing?' Nish said. 'I made a decision when I was thirty: I was, like, enough with the polyester, yeah? Like, buy organic whatever. Silk. Invest in silk. Don't buy half-price H&M shit, save your fucking money and buy a couple of nice silk shirts. Like our grandmothers, yeah?'

'I don't think my grandmother wore silk shirts. Polyester was invented for her generation. And Mum's mum died before—'

'Whatever, like Audrey Hepburn then. She'd wear silk. And we're supposed to be like her, yeah? *Breakfast at Tiffany's?*'

'Yep, thin but loving the pastries. Classy, but actually a hooker.'

'Exactly. So I was, like, I'm buying silk shirts and I'm hand-washing because dry-cleaning fills your clothes with toxins.'

'Sure.'

'And I buy, like, four silk shirts and, like, three dresses. Six months later, fucking pregnant. And *then* when you've had the baby your boobs are so bloody big they won't fit in. Or you're lactating all over the shop. Or, in the case of that Prada I got on The Outnet—highly discounted, mind . . .'

'Seventy percent off.'

'Yeah, and that's no small thing. And Ollie goes and chucks all over it, doesn't he? And it's like you're supposed to laugh it off. And if you don't, if you've waited your whole life to buy a bloody Prada dress and you're actually like proper upset, you shouldn't be because some women can't even have kids. So, like, suck it up.' Nish turned the cheese plate so the hard cheeses were closest to Grace. 'But I love Ollie!'

'I know.'

'And no one wants to hear this shit. The world is bored with the whole "mothership is hard" thing—'

'Mother*hood*.'

'Shit, what did I say?'

'Mothership.'

'Fuck me. Long night, that's all I can say. Ollie was up at four thirty. So, like, long day, then. I s'pose. Anyway, the world is over the "motherhood is hard and sometimes you cry and sometimes your Prada dress is covered in spew" thing. A Bridget Jones movie or, like, a show where Reese bloody Witherspoon struggles getting a pushchair up a hill and then it's like no one's interested anymore. "It's not a Pampers commercial, love. Move on."'

Grace leaned over to cut a sliver of cheddar. Aged, sure. But still just basic cheddar.

'So, when you due?' Nish asked. 'Did Cheng work it out? She couldn't work out mine because I couldn't remember when my last period was. Honestly, who even keeps track of that?'

'September.'

'After Ada's tour, yeah?'

'Yes. Paris, Berlin, Rome, Amsterdam. I'll be thirty-seven weeks by the end.'

'You're going to be tired slogging around at seven months pregnant.'

'I can always leave the tour early.'

'Ha! Good luck with that. As if Ada would allow it. You like Cheng?'

'I think so. She's very . . . I don't know the word. I mean, she's not very warm, is she? I think she thinks I'm stupid.'

'Doctors think everyone is stupid. But yeah, she is ice-cold. Proper hot, though. I actually developed quite a crush on her.'

'I get that.'

Grace tried not to focus on the circles like dark nimbus clouds under Nish's eyes.

'You're having it in hospital, yeah? Someone suggested I have mine at home and I was, like, but what about the fucking carpet? And our bathroom is way too small, can you imagine? You can't fit more than one person in there.'

'Yes, hospital. Cheng gave me the number of a few midwives. They all seem fine so I just kind of chose one at random.'

'You chose one at random?'

'What?'

Grace knew what; she knew she wasn't allowing the reality of having a baby to settle in. She'd booked the midwife with less consideration than she gave a hair appointment, because if she thought about giving birth the idea was terrifying. Which was dumb. She was too old to be scared of childbirth. That was a childish thing to worry about.

'I just hope you did your bloody research.'

'I did.'

'Sure you did. And how's Ed with it all? Ravi cried for forty-eight hours and then was fine.'

'Really?'

'Yeah, total crisis of confidence. The man has an PhD in engineering from Oxford but he didn't think he was capable of fatherhood. Well, he's not fine really. I think he's stressed—he's always at the bloody gym. It's getting a bit much actually. He's like proper ripped, but almost too much? Like bloody He-Man. But he doesn't wax his chest. Thank fuck for that. So? Ed?'

'He said that I'd be a great mum.'

'Oh, sweet.'

'Don't you think it's a bit of a weird thing to say? Like he was trying to reassure me—or maybe himself?'

'Um, no? You will be great. Well, most of the time. Show me a woman who's great at it all the time, especially at four-fucking-thirty a.m.'

Nish ate another macaron. Grace was still on her first tiny sandwich.

'Love, trust me, you'll be great. What did Dorothy say? I can only imagine.'

So Grace told her about the conversation with Dorothy.

'Fucking hell,' said Nish. 'That's intense. You had an ultrasound?'

'Yes. It's all fine.'

'That the first time you've done what Dorothy's told you to?'

'Could be.'

'Do you think that's why she went a bit, you know, loopy? That would fuck with your head. Like, if you were keen on another baby and then—you know.'

'Nish. That happened to Mum, and now she's the way she is with me and . . .'

'Yeah?'

'*Her* mother was bonkers apparently. Maybe the women in my family aren't meant to be mothers. I'm going to put on weight. That's the first thing I thought when I knew. That and I'm going to have to take time off. They're not natural mother things to think.'

'Bullshit. Think whatever you like. We're hardwired to believe thin is a life goal. And taking time off *is* terrifying, 'specially for someone with a corner office.'

'I don't think I'll be able to keep it.'

'Oh . . . Look, that's okay. I mean, talk to Ed obviously—'

'The corner office. I meant I won't be able to keep the corner office.'

'Well, thank god for that, because I already bought a little dress for it. Make sure it's a girl, yeah? Or let me know soon, I've got thirty days to return it.'

'I won't know in time for that, Nish.'

'Fine. Whatever.'

Grace looked up at the giant sparkling chandelier above them. She had to blink away tears. They might have been hormonal. They might have been for Dorothy.

Nish got up from her seat and came to sit beside Grace. She put her arm around her and pulled Grace close. 'You'll be fucking brilliant. And you know, even if you're not the kid will be fine. They're bloody resilient. That's what I tell myself, anyway.'

It was Ed who did all the calling around to find a prenatal class. The one they ended up at was run by a midwife called Val who wore a lot of cheesecloth and had a long salt-and-pepper plait which she flicked about at regular intervals. In the first class, when Grace was six months pregnant, Val encouraged everyone to remove their shoes and sit on a beanbag in a circle. Grace felt this was a cruel joke, the punchline arriving at the end when all the pregnant women attempted to extract themselves from their beanbag.

'I'm going to teach you how to empower yourself and your body for when that special, magical time comes and your baby is born,' cooed Val. 'What we're going to do here is arm you with knowledge so that you can make informed choices for you and your baby. And all choices should stem from the knowledge that your body is built for giving birth—it already knows what to do! You just have to know that it knows. Once you know it knows, that is the most important knowledge you can have.'

Val nodded as she spoke, looking each person in the eye as if checking for signs of dissent.

'The most important thing to know is that the best kind of intervention is no intervention! Okay? Your baby will come when it's ready. Your body will do what it needs to do. Women have been doing this for thousands of years. It's only recently we've been shoved into hospital and forced to give birth there instead of in the comfort of our own homes. I of course one hundred percent respect a woman's right to choose if she wants to have her baby in a hospital, but it isn't your only option and it may not be the best option. For you. You could say that walking into a hospital is the very first step in what we call the cascade of intervention.'

Grace had read about the cascade of intervention. It made her think of her pregnant body tumbling down a waterfall into a treacherous pit of panic and surgical gloves.

'Sometimes women are having regular contractions, they walk into hospital and bam!' Val clapped her hands. The woman opposite Grace flinched. 'The contractions stop! But if you've chosen to give birth in hospital, I one hundred percent respect that. One hundred percent. And sometimes women even have positive experiences birthing in hospital. Sometimes they really do! And good on them! But I do have lots of information here on home birthing for you to have a look at. I find that many women come in here booked into a hospital, but once they learn more about their body's natural superpowers they cancel that booking and embrace those true powers.'

During the break, when it finally came, Grace and Ed sat outside on a bench and dipped Jammie Dodgers into the herbal tea Val had thrust upon everyone. (No caffeine, ladies!) A tiny leaf from the jacaranda above dropped into Grace's tea and she wondered if she should try to scoop it out of the boiling water with her finger. She was too afraid to ask Val for a fresh cup.

Ed leaned close to her and lowered his voice. 'Did you already know about your superpowers? Can't believe you've kept them from me all this time. What else can you do?'

'I don't know. Val will probably tell me. And the breastfeeding spiel's going to blow us away, I reckon.'

'I look forward to it.'

'Nish said the woman who ran hers had a knitted boob.'

'Just the one?'

'No, not her actual boob. Like a demo boob.'

'I hope Val has a knitted boob.'

'Same.'

'Hey, are you okay with doing the hospital thing? What did Cheng say?'

'She didn't mention my powers.' Grace tried to fish the leaf out of her tea with the biscuit. It was futile. 'It will be fine. Nish went to hospital. The obstetrician said they have exercise balls and baths and all that at the hospital. And I'd worry. If something goes wrong. I like doctors. Nish told me this might happen. People have strong views. It's okay.'

◎

The house was in darkness. Grace dropped her keys in the little bowl on the sideboard, slipped off her heels and placed them on the shoe rack. It was then that she saw Ed's boots on the floor. She'd assumed that he was out, maybe at the studio. She went through to the living room, flicked on the light, and when she saw him sitting on the sofa she almost fell over with fright. Or not fell over so much as had a slight loss of bladder control—pelvic floor exercises hadn't been on the agenda as much as they should have been. (Nish had said she should try to remember to do them at every tube stop. Grace had failed to remember this.)

'Sorry.' Ed rubbed his face with both hands. He looked desolate.

'What's wrong?'

'It's cancer. Mum's results . . . The cancer's back.'

'Oh, Ed.' She went and sat beside him. He was rocking back and forth, just a little, barely noticeable.

'Did she call?' It was a useless thing to say but it was something.

'Dad did. He was crying.'

'Oh, Ed.'

She sat with him for a moment, then got up and walked in the direction of the kitchen.

'We're out of tissues,' Ed said. 'And I forgot to get something for dinner.'

'It's okay. It's fine. We'll get takeaway.'

'I'm not really hungry.'

'Okay.' She sat beside him again.

'How was your day?' he asked.

But she leaned into him and he grabbed onto her hand.

'What did the doctors say? Do you know?'

'It's worse than last time. The doctor was pretty blunt. She's already in hospital. I mean, they'll operate, but . . .'

The two of them sat there and looked at the sky outside the window. It was windy and the branches of the neighbour's tree had grown too far over the fence; the leaves were scudding on the windowpane like fingertips.

'I'll need to go home,' Ed said.

'I should come with you.'

'Ada's going on tour next week.'

Ada had told Grace—over and over and over again—that she couldn't do the tour without her. Only the night before, Ada had called just as Grace was about to get in the shower. Ed was in the bedroom and he'd called out, 'It's Ada.' And Grace just knew. After that it was forty minutes of Grace convincing Ada that she could do it, that Grace would be with her for every step.

'I'll come back for the tour. Maybe.'

'But I don't know how long she has or what's happening.'

'Let's just go back to Australia and see where things go from there.' Grace knew she sounded very calm and reasonable, like it was nothing at all for her to put her work on hold and fly across the world.

'I've already looked at flights,' Ed said.

'I just need to talk to Tony.'

'Sooner is better than later.'

She rubbed the back of his hand with her thumb. 'Yep.'

◎

Ed was awake beside her; she was sure of it because of his breathing. He would have known that she was awake too. They didn't talk. She didn't say how scared she was that they would fly back to Australia only to have the whole thing drag out for months and end up stuck there. Because what could she say? *I'm worried your mum won't get better fast enough? I'm worried your mum won't die fast enough?*

PART FOUR

Furniture is Not Something I'm Worried About

28
GRACE

APRIL 2022

GRACE TOLD TRENT STORIES OF DRUNK MUSICIANS SHE'D HAD TO HAUL offstage or talk down from rooftops, PR messes she'd had to clean up, nightmare egos she'd wrangled. Trent listened with a giddy look on his face, like he couldn't believe the stories, or couldn't believe what she'd been up to, or couldn't believe she was here sitting opposite him. Perhaps all three. It was that look of utter wonder and glee, and because it felt nice she let herself revel in it. It was a feeling that had been absent since Ed left.

Grace went to get more drinks, and when she came back to the table her phone buzzed with a text.

'Is that Ada Black?'

'Ada doesn't so much text as leave me long—I mean *really* long—voice messages about the universe and love and life balance and chakras and god knows what. Or she'll email but put the entire message in the subject line. I've never seen one shorter than fifteen words. Often they're so long they get cut off and I have to call her and say, "Can you please email like a normal person?" Of course, I don't use those exact words.'

He laughed.

'At the moment she's obsessed with grounding and is always asking when was the last time I stood barefoot in dirt.'

'Can I see an email?'

The text was from Dorothy. Grace turned her phone to silent.

'No.'

'That was Dorothy, wasn't it?'

'She's checking I'm not drunk in a ditch somewhere.'

'God, she hasn't changed much, has she? I can't imagine her with a phone. Shit. How do you breathe?'

Grace texted Dorothy back. *Drunk in ditch. Don't wait up.* She flashed Trent the screen and he cracked up.

'I'll be in big trouble now,' Grace said and took a large mouthful of gin.

'Can I please listen to Ada Black's voice messages? Please, please, Grace.'

She found a message from long ago and handed the phone over. He pressed the phone to his ear, his eyes growing wider and wider as he listened.

Grace watched him and remembered how she had loved Trent's childhood self, the boy she saw in the photographs on his dad's walls: the grinning ten-year old, the gawky teenager. She loved him for the things he collected, the things he was afraid of. Back then, when they were together, she had wanted to gather all of him—the child, the gawky teen, the young man not fully formed—and hug him deep inside herself. The small schoolyard injustices tore at her, the pain and confusion of his mother's death. The things he recounted became her own in the way they built the person who she loved.

She had loved the way he sat in a chair; how he tilted his head slightly to the left when driving; the way he draped his wrist over the wheel; the shape of his neck and shoulders seen from behind. His sigh. And the way he looked at her, like he didn't quite comprehend how she could be his. After it was over she would catch herself wondering about Future Trent. He would always be imaginary, never realised. A figment of speculation, intangible and huge.

Future Trent was no longer intangible. It felt strange to have it confirmed that he had been a real person, that she had felt what she'd felt and it wasn't childish or silly. She had loved him. No wonder it crumbled her the way it had all those years ago. There was a certain validation here in the way they spoke to each other—as if no time had passed.

Trent finished listening to Ada's message and handed Grace her phone back.

'I still have your beetles,' Grace said.

The glass in Trent's hand wobbled, a slight tremor. When he finally did say something it was so soft that she couldn't hear him.

'I didn't catch that,' she said.

'You kept them?'

'I told you I would.'

'Where are they?'

'They're in a small box at the back of . . .'

'What?'

It felt like she was giving something away, something about the feelings she had held onto. About what they had been together.

'The back of my drawer.'

The same drawer where she kept bits of her grandmother's jewellery that didn't suit her but were too precious to throw out, some of her kids' drawings, a favourite t-shirt of Henry's that was now too small, the tie Ed wore at their wedding.

'After all this time? I thought you must have thrown them out.'

'I'm not good at throwing things away.'

He understood her meaning.

'If you give me your postal address I can send them to you.'

'Thank you. I appreciate that. I thought I'd never see them again.'

Grace couldn't think of anything to say.

Trent sipped his beer and then rubbed his palms on the tops of his thighs, up and down, up and down. 'Sorry, I didn't mean for it to get this intense,' he said.

'Nothing's changed there then.'

He smiled ruefully. 'Touché, Grace Harlow. Touché.'

'What's your music like?'

'You know that's a weird question.' He chuckled. 'What's being a mum like?'

'Complicated.'

'I bet you're a great mum.'

'My kids are still alive. So.'

It was the classic parenting joke.

Trent laughed. 'Kids are resilient anyway, right?'

'That's what they say.'

'This is your cue to say, "I bet you're a great musician."'

'Are you?'

'What am I supposed to say to that? Yes? I try hard?'

'I'm trying to get a sense of how someone so talented could end up . . .'

He was waiting.

'I don't know.' Lie.

'Do you do this with everyone?'

'Do what?'

'Scrutinise them,' he said.

'I'm not scrutinising.'

'You're preparing to. I can tell you're gathering ammunition because you still get that same look in your eye. It's a very unsettling, gleamy type of look that is very—I will say it—it is very sexy and it is also very scary.'

'Stop trying to distract me with flattery.'

He laughed to himself. 'Fuck, you used to make me nervous when you were at gigs. You made everyone nervous.'

'Ah. So it's my fault you never found fame.'

'Wow. Okay. Thank you for finally delivering your assessment. Never found fame. No, I definitely did not. I wouldn't normally stick around for this kind of assassination but I've waited a long time. I think making music for no other reason than that's what you're born to do takes guts. Actually I know it does because I'm the one who has to put up with everyone else's judgement about how I live my life.'

'I just wish . . .' What she wished for him gave away how much she cared and had always cared, so Grace stopped.

'Our society has created this goal of stability,' Trent said. 'Get a steady job that numbs the mind, get married, procreate. I don't want a boring life. I want to do as much of the thing that brings me joy as possible, and that thing is making music. I haven't compromised. Ever. And I'm not ashamed of it.'

'I have a boring life because I got married and have kids?'

'Okay, forget the thing about marriage and kids. And trust me, no one thinks you live a boring life. I just mean, unless you're a musician or an artist or whatever, you don't know what it's like to lay yourself bare for people to devour or spit out. I wish more people understood what that takes. No one would think twice if

I was, I dunno, some single guy at the front of a headliner. The financial gain would bring me respect.'

'Tell me again that I don't know what it's like to be devoured at spat out?'

'Okay. Sure. That was the wrong—'

'Yes, it was. On many levels. And even if you made a stack of cash and everyone thought you were a musical genius, you'd still be lonely.'

'I'm not lonely.'

'You forgot about your girlfriend.'

'I . . . whatever. I'm fine.'

Grace laughed. 'Yeah. Both of us are fine.'

'Are you lonely?'

'I'm not going to talk about that with you.'

'But you're not okay.'

29

2013

JOAN HAD THE DISCONCERTING LOOK OF SOMEONE WHO WAS completely healthy. Ian, on the other hand, looked brittle and exhausted. It would be a double mastectomy, Joan announced. She said there had been a 'bit of spread' of the cancer and she'd be starting chemo straight away. 'I've beat the bastard before,' declared Joan. 'I'll beat it again.' Ian seemed less certain.

◎

In the following days Grace felt like an appendage. She'd forgotten how much sitting around was involved in hospital visits. Some of the time Joan talked, some of the time she was content just to have Ed next to her. Ed was the same. The inaction was excruciating enough without the added factor of being a pregnant person confined to a plastic chair. Grace's feet were still swollen from the plane and the headaches were worse. She felt awkward in the silences when clearly no one else did, and shackled, the time zone preventing her from doing her job. The only thing she could do was read emails which had already been taken care of by her assistant. Grace's assistant wasn't flawless. He could easily miss something important. He hadn't as yet. But he could. Joan made some comments about Grace being 'busy, busy!' and because Joan was likely to be dying Grace had felt terrible and rude and unable to stop checking her phone again for new emails that would not be appearing because everyone in the UK was asleep.

After two days of this, Ed gently told Grace that she didn't need to come to the hospital. 'Go up the mountains and spend some time with your mum,' he said. 'You look tired. Just have a bit of a break.'

Dorothy was predictably thrilled at this prospect and didn't hesitate to collect Grace and bring her home. They were barely in the door before Dorothy whisked Grace and Warren off for lunch at a deli-cafe that had failed to change its menu or decor in the entire twenty-five years it had been there. Grace ate a frittata-focaccia and listened while Dorothy updated her on everything that had happened to anyone in the Blue Mountains who Grace had ever met. It seemed that every one of Dorothy's friends had children and grandchildren who notably had not relocated overseas.

'Do you think you'll be staying here a while?' Dorothy asked. 'I imagine Ed wants to stay as long as he can to support Joan.'

'Ada's tour starts in just over a week,' Grace said. 'I'm supposed to be with her for that. But Ed . . .'

'He's taking things hard,' Dorothy sympathised very sympathetically. 'He and Joan are close.'

'Well, not that close, but yes. It's hard.'

'And you want to do what's best for him.'

'Yes.'

'And the baby.'

'The baby is fine, Mum.'

'I know, but international travel and a busy schedule aren't good for anyone. I don't know how you do it. You must be exhausted.'

'I'm fine.'

'You do look tired,' piped up Warren. This was unexpected. 'I'm sorry, love,' he continued. 'But you do.'

'I'm a long way from home and still dealing with jet lag,' Grace pointed out.

'You don't think of here as home?' asked Dorothy.

'Mum.'

'You can stay with us while Ed does all the visiting at the hospital,' said Dorothy, adding, 'I just want what's best for you. And Ed. And the baby.'

'I think what would be best right now is that you maybe stop with all the . . . the . . .' Grace couldn't find the right word.

Her parents smiled with concern. Both of them. On the same concerned team.

Despite Warren's protest, Grace insisted on paying for lunch. Her parents waited outside the cafe while Grace stood in line at the counter. One moment she was looking at the slabs of mud cake in the cabinet, the next she felt a wave of such light-headedness that she had to grab (embarrassingly) the shoulder of the man in front of her in attempt to stop herself from passing out. The attempt largely failed and it was the man who was then grabbing on to Grace to stop her falling. And while it was all happening, it wasn't fear for her health or the baby's that Grace thought of—it was the fact that this was exactly the sort of thing Dorothy and Warren were worried about.

◎

The obstetrician was older, male and claimed to have a lot of experience. Val would probably disapprove of him, but he was the only one who could fit Grace in. He said Grace shouldn't be flying to Europe. She shouldn't be flying home. She shouldn't be going anywhere until the baby was born. He said she was exhausted and her blood pressure was 'all over the shop'.

'Is it pre-eclampsia?' Grace asked.

'No, it's not.'

'Then I'll be fine.'

Ed sighed. 'Grace.'

'If you want to do what's best for your baby and for yourself, you need to stay put,' the doctor said. 'Rest. I wouldn't advise any of my patients to do a long-haul flight at your stage anyway. I'm surprised your doctor in London told you it would be okay.'

Ed was looking at Grace now with something like suspicion.

'The airline said—' Grace began.

'The airline isn't delivering your baby,' the doctor said. 'Do yourself and your poor husband a favour and take it easy.'

In the hire car (a ridiculous people mover; there had been a mix-up with the booking) Grace pressed her cheek against the cool glass of her window and watched Sydney slide by. Ed had hardly said anything; when Grace did glance over at him she saw his blank expression.

'Are you okay?' Grace asked.

'You need to listen to him, Grace. For once in your life just take someone's bloody advice.'

◎

Grace called Ada on what would have been a rest day between shows. Despite being in bed in a plush hotel room, the Ada Grace received was full-strength. 'They know I'm allergic to strawberries,'

Ada said. 'And yet here, in front of me, I have a fruit platter and guess what is front and centre? That hair and make-up girl you found is very clever, but bright red welts might be beyond even her capabilities.'

'You could just avoid them.'

'I don't know what else they've touched! And if I send a fruit platter the size of a small nation back I'm going to look like a brat.'

Grace knew that Ada was fine with behaving like a diva, it was the perception that she might actually be one that bothered her.

'This whole circus falls apart without you,' Ada continued, now chewing audibly on something. 'When's your flight back?'

'I can't fly back . . .'

No response.

'Ada?'

Nothing.

'I said I can't fly back; the obstetrician says it's not safe.'

'Are you having me on?'

'No.'

'What obstetrician? What are his qualifications? Can you even trust him? A lot of those doctors are old men who don't think women are capable of anything, least of all pushing out a baby. They're all stuck in 1956. You need a second opinion.'

'I don't. I need to stay here until—'

The obstetrician had told Grace it wasn't a good idea to do a long-haul flight until the baby's immune system had developed. Three months, two at a minimum.

'—until after the baby is born.'

'That's not for ages! What do you expect me to do? They're already trying to kill me with fucking strawberries!'

'No one is trying to kill you. I have no control over this.'

'You're abandoning me.'

'I'm not, I'm trying to look after my baby.'

'Find a new obstetrician—I'll pay for them to accompany you on the flight back. We'll charter a flight.'

Grace wasn't sure if she had ever said no to Ada before. She imagined the poor housekeeper who might soon have to clean up a fruit platter thrown to the floor. If Grace was to take up Ada's offer, Ed wouldn't throw fruit or have a tantrum; he would package up his anger at Grace and hold it inside, and the air between him and Grace would turn cold.

'I don't care what it costs,' Ada said.

Grace felt the baby move within her; she knew its movements now like one knew the tides. Her baby didn't jerk and kick out like Dorothy said Grace had. Instead Grace's baby seemed to make slow, languid readjustments of position, as if stretching.

'No,' Grace said. 'I'm not coming back. I'll find someone to fill in.'

The line cut out.

'Joan's very unwell, thanks for asking,' Grace said into the dead phone.

What had she been expecting? Concern? Care? Grace wondered if she had really believed that Ada would tell her to rest and not worry about a thing, encourage Grace to prioritise herself. Ada would never do that. She prioritised her art and that, Grace knew, was how she justified the majority of her behaviour. The difficulty with this was that the art was so brilliant it was hard to argue.

To be anything other than professional in this circumstance would be emotionally catastrophic, Grace knew; she needed to respond in a calculated, practical, rational way, devoid of the gnawing feeling of hurt. *You've abandoned me*. She spent the following days finding someone to handle Ada. At least it gave her something to do. Once that task was ticked off, Grace found a new one: searching for somewhere to live until she could return home. Staying with Dorothy in the mountains while Ed slept on a fold-out bed at his parents' was a less than ideal arrangement and one that wouldn't work once the baby arrived.

The real estate agent agreed. 'You poor thing,' she said to Grace over the phone. From the profile picture on the website, Grace knew that Rhonda was in her fifties. Her tone was warm, like a counsellor. She lapped up all the details Grace poured out. Too many details. 'Wrenched from your home when you are so vulnerable!' Rhonda said. 'We must find you a nest, sweetheart.'

◎

Ed didn't understand why the nest Grace and Rhonda chose had to be on such a grand scale. As soon as Grace drove them over the Harbour Bridge he turned sceptical.

'Don't you bloody dare,' he said.

'Just have a look. Rhonda is really lovely. She's been so helpful.'

'It's her job to be lovely and helpful. She has a bloodhound's nose for money.'

Grace didn't argue that Rhonda was more of a labrador than a bloodhound. Ed had been so irritable lately, probably on account of the fold-out bed and, more likely, his critically ill mother.

'The only people who live in Mosman are brain surgeons and women with face lifts,' Ed said.

'Men have face lifts too. Remember Reginald across the street? His eyebrows were practically on the back of his head.'

Ed didn't reply at first. Then: 'Did I tell you he tried to kiss me?'

This was a good sign.

'God, Ed. Only every day. Get over it.'

But once they were through the house's grand automatic gates and in the enormous foyer Ed's cynicism returned. He stared up at the ornate designer ceiling lamp and said, 'That thing's going to get full of gnats.'

Grace felt he was looking for excuses; Ed had never expressed concern about light fittings before, gnat-filled or otherwise. She flicked the light switch on and twinkling shards of light danced on the walls.

'It's a bit like being underwater,' she said.

'Sure,' said Ed, unamused. 'But we don't need five bedrooms. We're not having quince.'

'Quintuplets?' Grace said. 'Quince are a fruit.'

'A three-bedder will do us.'

'You can't get three-bedroom houses here. And not for a short-term contract. And definitely not with a studio out the back. You'll be able to paint. You miss painting in Australia.'

'We don't have to live *here*.'

'It's beautiful.'

'Yeah, but . . .'

'It's close to the obstetrician and fifteen minutes from your dad's.'

Ed had no retort, but his mood didn't lift as Grace and Rhonda led him through the vast kitchen/living/dining. 'Did these people forget to put the walls in?' he asked.

Maybe it would have been okay if Rhonda hadn't used the word 'palatial' three times.

'Who needs three ovens?' Ed asked.

'It's an aesthetic choice,' Rhonda said. 'Creates a more balanced composition.'

'Composition?'

'Visually.'

Ed hooted with laughter. Rhonda found this confusing but carried on with the tour nevertheless.

Ed also had some thoughts about the necessity (or lack thereof) of a television that lowered itself through the ceiling when you clapped twice. 'This is more like a theme park, Grace.'

'Look at that view, Ed.'

'I can see the view.'

'We can walk to the beach, it's just down the hill. If we're going to have to stay, we should make it worthwhile. It'll be like a holiday. And this is fully furnished. We won't have to worry about that.' Grace had in fact been disappointed that she would be deprived of the task of acquiring furniture.

'Furniture is not something I'm worried about. Who's going to look after the pool? I'm not hiring someone. That's a bridge too far.'

'Ha, I see what you did there.'

'I'm not joking.'

He followed her outside, along the flagstone path, past the infinity pool and beyond a large hedge. When he saw the studio he stopped walking.

'Oh.'

'It's got a wood burner inside. And the doors fold open; this whole wall opens up. Eleven-foot ceilings. Skylights, Ed. Have a look in there, the light is incredible.'

It was the light that did it. Always the light.

◎

Grace tried to keep busy. She swam as much as possible, took pregnancy yoga classes, and on a particularly boring day she road-tested seven different prams. She even went for occasional lunches with Dorothy. (Grace had found a gorgeous old Porsche 911 which made driving anywhere, even on the M4, glorious.) Tony had told Grace he would let her know if he needed anything from her. Apparently he needed nothing; Lila, the replacement Grace found, was doing an excellent job of mopping Ada up. It was all good as long as Grace continued to avoid any media coverage of Ada and her tour. All totally fine and she would be back home in London in no time. When Grace told Nish that she hadn't been able to find a private midwife for the birth and was worried about her baby being delivered by a stranger, Nish reassured her that there were women who gave birth in deserts, so Grace would be fine on the North bloody Shore. The obstetrician repeated this sentiment, albeit in fewer words. The rest had done wonders for her, he said. Grace would be good as gold.

As Grace's due date neared, she found herself talking to the baby more often, usually when she was in the car. She told it all about London. She thought about how after the baby was born it would be able to recognise music she was listening to and imagined a toddler who liked dancing to Talking Heads (Grace's current obsession, she suspected because it was unlike anything to do with her work). Whenever Grace felt despair at being on the wrong side of the globe she would picture herself and Ed at the airport, their perfect little baby in a capsule, the three of them boarding a plane. Heading home.

◎

The baby didn't come. The obstetrician wanted Grace to have an induction but she couldn't get Val's rant about intervention out of her head. The obstetrician was going interstate. If she waited he might not be back for the birth. But she held out. Until he phoned Grace on day nine and said she couldn't hold out any longer. This baby needed to be born.

Grace was allocated a midwife called Jan, shunted into the birthing suite and given an intravenous concoction to induce labour. Jan was dismissive and spoke to Grace like she was a child, not someone giving birth to one. Or attempting to, anyway. And whenever Jan came into the room she would announce herself by asking, 'Any movement at the station?' like a headmistress with a Banjo Paterson obsession. Grace didn't appreciate her body being likened to a mustering yard and unborn child to a colt; it didn't help with the visualisation techniques she was already struggling to employ. And wasn't it Jan's job to track the progress? Grace had no idea what was going on other than unimaginable pain. Actually 'pain' was too short and neat a word to describe the contractions. Agony was too ornate. There needed to be a long, complex and awful word. Possibly there was one in German. Grace vowed to find out so she had it ready when people asked how the birth was.

'Come on, get up and on your feet,' ordered Jan. Her name tag had smiley stickers on it. 'Walk around the room! The only way your baby's going to come is if you put in some work of your own!'

After barking instructions Jan would then (thankfully) disappear for long intervals. Sometimes over an hour. It didn't seem right, but Grace didn't want her around anyway. In the birthing class there had been no training in how to deal with this. They'd covered visualisation and aromatherapy but not the management of a patronising and aggressive midwife. Grace hoped that maybe Ed would step in and tell Jan to adjust her attitude, but he didn't.

Hour fifteen rolled around with still barely any movement at the station, despite Grace feeling like she was being sawed in half at five-minute intervals. Then seven-minute intervals. It wasn't supposed to happen in that order, it was supposed to get shorter and shorter, then pop! Here's your beautiful baby!

Ed had lost the ability to be patient and calm like Grace needed him to be. And worse, he was trying to hide it. He was talking to her in a voice she wasn't familiar with. (She'd know it later when he'd use it with the kids. *It's okay, there's no monsters in the dark. Thunder is just a sound the clouds make. Lightning won't hit the house. Everything is going to be okay.*)

◎

An alarm of some sort sounded. It slid and pulsed right through Grace's body. There was yelling in the corridor. Some other people came into the room. Grace forgot who they were as soon as she was told. Someone said something about blood pressure and then there were the words 'baby' and 'distress'. All the light seemed to drain from the room. Grace was swirling. Her body liquid, swirling around and around a plughole. She reached out for Ed. 'Pull me out! Pull me out!' But she couldn't find him. And she couldn't feel her own hands.

30

ED

HE HAD TO STOP THINKING OF HER AS GRACE. AS HIS GRACE. SHE HAD to just be a woman in a room with him who was in a tremendous amount of pain. Because if he looked at her and saw Grace he froze, couldn't think, stood like a pillar in an inconvenient spot in the middle of the room while the useful people got on with their jobs. So when he reflected on it later (which he did, because that's what he always seemed to do: reflect; never move forward; dwell) he realised that he'd switched to thinking of her as a nice woman whom he happened to stumble upon while she was giving birth. (Or trying to. There was more trying than he'd anticipated. There had been a lot of talk during the prenatal classes about 'natural processes', like giving birth was something that happened to someone rather than something someone did.) So now here he was in a hospital room with this nice woman who was in a lot of pain.

It seemed as if whenever a woman was giving birth in a movie there was always a moment when she turned on her partner in venomous rage. *You did this to me! This is your fault!* Grace didn't do that; instead she looked at him with pleading intensity. *Please help me. Please help me.* It was horrible because he'd never felt so useless in his life. And that was the point of men, wasn't it? To be useful? Fetching paper cups of ice chips for her to suck felt like the most frivolous thing in the world. Music had been a big part of their birth plan. He'd brought along the portable speaker in her birthing kit. She'd listened to two songs (Brian Eno—so odd) before she'd decided that music reminded her of work. And for some reason this really distressed her.

When she got the pleading look in her eyes he stopped thinking of her as Grace. He stopped looking at her face. This was selfish, he knew. But all he could do was hold her hands and stare at them. Luckily she wasn't wearing her wedding ring or any other wife-signalling things on her hands.

'Ed, something's wrong. Something's wrong.'

'It's okay. You're doing well.'

'Please help me. Please. Make it stop.' She began to cry. Not cry, sob. Jan was MIA again and had been for a long time. Grace clutched at Ed's hand. 'Please make it stop.'

'I'll get help.'

With what? He pressed the green call button. No one came. He pressed it again.

Grace started screaming.

'What's all this then?' said Jan as she bustled in. There was a chocolate sprinkle stuck to her lower lip. It wobbled and fell on her bosom when she talked.

He wasn't a violent person. Never hit a person or a thing in his life. But he wanted to walk over and slap the woman's face. Instead he said, 'Can you stop being such a bitch and help my wife?'

'Excuse me! There is no need—'

'It's been fifteen hours.'

Jan checked her watch as if she didn't believe him. 'Sir, we've been very busy and—'

'My name's Ed. I told you that this morning.'

'Ed, we've had a number of emergencies. This isn't an unusual labour! She's doing well!' Jan smiled at Grace. It wasn't convincing. 'Let's just check that cervix again!'

Jan's face disappeared from Ed's view into the space between Grace's knees.

Grace howled with agony.

'How long has she been ten centimetres?' Jan asked. Chirpy and panicked at once.

'I don't fucking know!' said Ed. 'I'm not the one who's supposed to be checking!'

'Let's just . . . let's just . . .' Jan was rattling around with a monitor. Then she hit the red button on the wall and fled. Ed heard her yelling something in the corridor.

31
GRACE

GRACE DIDN'T WANT ED TO SEND OUT A MESSAGE. SHE'D SEEN PLENTY of those messages. It was customary to say, *Mum and bub both doing well*. Or, *We're tired but thrilled*. Grace wasn't tired. Tired didn't begin to cover it. Tired was what you felt after a big week at work, or a few all-nighters in a row, or perhaps even after a trip to the shops. Grace wasn't tired, she was obliterated, as if her body had been dismantled molecule by molecule, blasted apart like a firework.

Ed was tired and she envied him.

The baby was fine and she envied him beyond words.

When Grace finally allowed herself to be discharged (*Please don't make me do this on my own; can't you see I'm incapable?*) and arrived back at the house, it felt like an alien landscape, similar to the house she knew but somehow different, like she'd stepped into an alternative reality and the other Grace, the normal one, was still living her old life concurrently in another dimension. What was Normal Grace doing? Was she driving to a meeting? Was she on a long-haul flight where the biggest problem she faced was the impossibility of going to the loo without waking her sleeping neighbour? Or was she doing something else entirely? Listing to music with Trent Keaton in a world where she knew she wasn't meant to have children and she hadn't inflicted herself on a perfect, precious, fragile baby.

The presents kept on coming.

Blue wrapping paper. Blue ribbons. Cards with joyful messages.

A near-death experience is such a weird thing to celebrate.

Grace couldn't look at the gifts, couldn't open them. Ed did all of that. Grace couldn't even handle seeing a scrap of wrapping paper in the bin. She was crazy and later, when she finally found the strength to push the pram, she felt so sure everyone would be able to tell she was crazy that she couldn't look anyone in the eye.

Everything made her anxious: the baby was too hot, too cold; the kitchen bin needed to be emptied; Ed needed to make a list of things to buy at the shops; there was poo stuck to the change mat and she couldn't get it off, the baby would surely ingest it and die; she was running out of clean undies; she hadn't had time to brush her teeth; the baby was crying; why wouldn't he settle? And the constant jokes from well-meaning community health nurses: if only babies came with an instruction booklet! Ha-ha-HA! A happy mum is a happy baby!

Be happy, Grace. Be happy, be happy, be happy. Can't you see you're damaging him?

Nobody likes a crazy lady. And once, when Grace was walking along the street and she saw a woman walking in dizzy circles and talking to herself outside Woolworths, Grace had a compulsion to go and talk to her. As if she'd slipped over a line between 'normal' and those other people we don't understand and are afraid of. Strangely, Grace had stopped being afraid of anything—other than herself.

◎

Nish arrived, looking fabulous in a palm-tree-print jumpsuit and platform espadrilles. You wouldn't know that she'd just got off a long-haul flight.

'Thought I'd go a tropical vibe, yeah? Even had a vodka pineapple juice on the plane.'

Oh, to be in London. There was nowhere else Grace wanted like she wanted London. Ada had played Wembley the week before. She'd tried to call Grace before she went onstage. Grace had seen her number on the screen, known exactly where Ada was, the thousands waiting for her, the heat of the spotlights showing the dust of powder over Ada's cheeks. Grace put the phone in the drawer and walked out of the room.

'Honestly, I never thought I'd say this but that plane trip was a bloody dream,' Nish continued. 'Twenty-eight hours without having to lift a bloody finger. Just me sat in front of a screen while a nice lady brings me food and wine. Amazing. I tell you what, kids change your perspective on everything.'

Grace's eyes welled up.

'Oh, babe,' Nish said soothingly. 'Come 'ere.' She wrapped her coconut-scented arms around Grace and Grace sobbed into her shoulder. She wanted to smell of coconut and wear a fabulous jumpsuit.

'I'm here. We'll sort it all out, yeah? Now, where's that beautiful baby of yours?'

After Grace told Ada she would have to stay in Australia, Ada had organised an interior decorator to replicate every furnishing and detail Grace had prepared for the baby's room in London. Ada had done it in secret, she and Ed concocting the plan together.

Grace hated it; the room taunted her every time she walked in.

Now, Nish stood at the window with the sun on her back, holding Grace's baby close to her chest, bobbing up and down while he fussed and squirmed. Grace felt sick in the stomach when he was like that, but Nish was aglow with the treat of it, breathing in the scent of his little head and whispering to him. Grace had never envied anyone like she did Nish right then. To have a magical moment with the baby. Grace couldn't remember what peace felt like: to stand in the sun and close her eyes, just to feel the warmth on her skin and think of nothing else. She was sure she could never be that way again. The baby was here to stay, motherhood was here to stay, there would be endless worries from now on, endless buzz inside her head with no rest from it at all.

◎

Nish poured a glass of wine and held it out to Grace. 'You bottle-feeding or is Henry on the boob?'

'Boob.'

'Oh.' Nish took a swig of wine. 'Shame. I mean it's fine, but I'd rather have wine.'

'You didn't bottle-feed.'

'Not for want of bloody trying. You know Ollie used to munch on my boobs like he was chewing a steak? Good god, the pain. And he was always hungry. Fucking exhausting.'

'Did you feel like shit? Like, all the time? I go to sleep at night and . . .' Grace trailed off.

Nish leaned forward and took her hand.

'And what, babe?'

'I hope I don't wake up.'

Grace could tell from Nish's silence that she'd never felt that.

'I know how hard it is,' Nish said. 'Honestly, I really know everything you're going through. It's fucking mental.' She sipped her wine and looked around the room. 'This place is bonkers. Like a palace built by *Vogue Living* minions. If I had a pool like that I'd never get out.'

'Mm.'

'Henry always sleep like this? He's been out for two hours.'

'Yeah. Sometimes.'

'Count yourself lucky, babe. Ollie would do twenty-five minutes max during the day. The midwives are all, like, "Make sure you rest while he rests! Have a cup of tea, put your feet up!" Fucking hell, by the time I took out the tea bag he was up again, trying to get at me boobs. Ada sends her love, by the way. Made sure to tell me how lost she is without you.'

'I'm a bit lost without her.'

'You could always come back.'

'Not with him. I'm a mess. My head is useless.'

'You mean Henry?'

'Mm.'

'Look, don't take this the wrong way, yeah? I get it, I really do. But fuck, Grace, look around you. Look at what you *have*. Perfect baby, perfect house, perfect husband. I went on this retreat run by some guru, lots of Buddhist shit. So helpful. She was an amazing lady, right bonkers but really fucking inspirational. Battled cancer, all that. Anyway, she was, like, "You got to let go of your ego," and you know, that's so helpful.'

'You think I have a problem with my ego?'

'I just mean that we got all these ideas about what we need and they're all bullshit. Look at what you have. She told a story about a goat and I wish I could remember what it was because it made shit really clear, but the gist was gratitude. Something about the goat stuck on a hill but surrounded by grass.'

'Goats climb mountains for fun. They don't get stuck.'

'Fucking hell, Grace. Maybe it was a llama. Irrelevant. What I mean is, you have everything you need. More than. Look, I wasn't going to bring this up, but Ravi and me, we've been trying for another kid for ages. Nothing. Nada. Looks like it will need to be IVF, which we'd need to take out a fucking big loan for. So, you know, you're lucky.'

It was happening again. That feeling that nothing around Grace was real. The light was all wrong. Nish. The furniture. Like she was in a simulation of her life but not her actual life. Like if she touched the wall her hand would go straight through as if the wall was a hologram, a trick of the light. It occurred to her that she could touch the wall, reassure herself that it was real. The house was real. She was her actual self. But what if her hand did go straight through? The thought made her panic. Why hadn't the baby woken up? Was he dead? Was he real?

'Grace? Babe? You okay?'

'Hmm?'

◎

If Grace had been able to articulate how she felt at the time she would have said that the thing she missed most about her work, about Ada, was the sense of being indispensable, being needed, being the one who gets someone brilliant off the floor, pushes them out into the light. There was an end goal and Grace knew how to get there. She knew that if she was beside Ada, Ada would be able to her job, she would deliver every time. Grace knew how to pull her together and form the Ada who could make a stadium of people collectively hold their breath when she opened her mouth to sing.

With the baby, Grace didn't know what the end goal was. A full tummy? Sleeping through the night? And when she made it through one day, unsure the whole time if she was doing it correctly, it just started all over again the next day. She was swimming without any land in sight. Ed kept on telling her what a great job she was doing. She didn't want to be doing a good job; she wanted to reach the end goal. But there wasn't one. Not that she could figure out, anyway.

◎

'So many women experience this,' the counsellor said. 'It's more common than you think!'

She sounded almost thrilled about the fact that countless mothers were living in a mental hellscape. Her name was Rowena and she had an asymmetrical haircut that Grace found distracting. The couch where Grace sat had piles of throw cushions on it. Too many. For some reason this made Grace anxious.

'You can cuddle one if you want,' Rowena said. 'Some people find that calming.'

She must have noticed Grace looking at them. Grace felt like she'd rather tear one apart with her teeth but did not think Rowena would be so accommodating of that.

Rowena's office was on Military Road, above a hairdresser. When she and Ed walked past the window, Grace noticed the women inside having their hair styled. They were sipping champagne. It reminded Grace of when she'd had her first tattoo done. The guy who did it offered Grace a shot of tequila and Grace had accepted. It was ten o'clock in the morning. That was forever ago, before Ed, when she was still heartbroken and embarrassed about how long she'd felt that way.

It had been difficult to get a parking spot on Military Road. Ed had been stressed and the baby started to cry while he was trying to do a reverse park. Grace wanted to tell him just to drive them all home. She wasn't worth the fuss.

'It's so important you know that everything you say in this space is completely confidential,' Rowena was saying. 'This is a safe space.'

Was it? There was a large marble vase on the table which one could easily smash the window with. But Grace needed an answer. She needed to open her mouth and let the words out so that maybe the question would stop whirring around in her head. It whipped around in there like a fly in a bottle, smacking up against the sides, the sound growing louder and louder. All night. Rowena with her weird hair and terrible cushions was ready to listen.

'Do you think there's any way . . .' Grace tried. 'Can you put a baby . . .'

Damn it. Speak, woman. You fucking moron. Everyone else can do this thing, everyone else can look after a baby, what the fuck is wrong with you? The tears came. Like the stupid fly in her head was trying to get out via her eyeballs. The desire to grab that marble vase and smash the window was so intense she had to close her eyes, pretend she was somewhere else. Where was she? She was in the car, Trent's Beemer. She was driving and he was laughing. What at? She couldn't remember.

In the next room the baby began to cry.

'Grace, can you tell me what's going on for you right now? What's the thought in your head?'

Grace couldn't speak.

'Don't worry about Henry; Ed's looking after him. I can ask if he'll take him for a walk. Would that be helpful? Just so we can speak a bit longer?'

Speak a bit longer? Grace had barely said anything.

Rowena stood up and went to the door. She opened it a fraction and when she did the baby's howling flooded into the room. Rowena said something to Ed and after that she closed the door and sat back down, smiled at Grace as if everything was fine and normal.

It was the community health nurse who gave Ed Rowena's contact details. She had visited to weigh the baby a few days after Nish left. Grace hadn't been able to stop crying the whole time she was there. The nurse had spoken quietly to Ed in the other room and given him a pamphlet that explained what to do if a new mother went mental.

'Ed's taking him for a little walk,' Rowena said. 'There's no rush.'

But there was, because Ed was gone and she didn't know how much time she had.

'Is it possible to . . . Is it too late to . . .'

'To what Grace? I'm listening. I'm here.'

'To put the baby up for adoption? Do you think? I want it to be looked after, but . . .'

Silence. Did Grace stand up? She must have because she was holding the vase now and it had been on the table and she wouldn't have been able to reach it if she was still sitting. The marble was cool against her palm.

The vase was heavy.

A hand now: warm, gentle, over Grace's. Taking the vase.

'It's okay, Grace. You're safe. Your baby is safe. I know you want your baby to be safe.'

Grace opened her eyes. Rowena was not laughing. She was not smiling. Nor was she alarmed or panicking. She hadn't phoned the police. Rowena was calm. And she didn't appear to be shocked.

'That's what makes you a good mother,' Rowena said. 'Anything else your brain is telling you is a lie.'

When Henry was seven weeks old, Joan came to visit, bringing with her a box of pastries and good intentions.

Grace had no appetite. She'd never been so thin. It wasn't helped by the fact that she'd lost all the baby weight during labour. Her body had burned all its reserves for energy; she hadn't known that was possible.

Grace politely declined the offer of an almond croissant. Joan tutted. 'Darling, you should have one. It's fine. You look fantastic! I don't know where the baby weight has gone!'

So, because Grace had no fight left in her, she put the pastry on her plate and looked at it. Any step beyond that was impossible.

'I know you've been feeling out of sorts,' Joan said. 'Trust me, it's so important to do little things for yourself. A happy mother means a happy baby!'

No pressure then.

'So I brought you a little gift. I talked about it with Ed, and he said he can look after Henry while you're gone.'

For a brief moment Grace was elated. Gone? Gone where? She would love to be gone. Maybe Joan had sensed Grace's desperation and booked her a ticket back to London. Just for a little while, until she got her mind back and could be the person she needed to be. She could stay with Nish. A cicada burrowed underground until it emerged with new wings.

Joan pressed a mauve envelope into Grace's hand with a very, very understanding smile.

It was a voucher for a spa treatment in Manly.

'Kelsey will look after you. She's my girl.'

Of course. A facial. A treatment. That's what Grace needed.

'Kelsey will fix you up and you'll be good as new.'

Grace laughed. 'I didn't know there was anything wrong with my face. But thank you!' (Turned out Grace had a bit of fight left in her after all.)

Joan's expression changed from one of shock to one of pity.

'Darling, the tragedy here, the real tragedy, is that you don't have the capacity right now to see how lucky you are to have a beautiful, healthy baby. It's not your fault; you just can't see that right now. But once you do, everything will improve. A little Me Time will—'

'I don't want Me Time.'

Joan flinched.

'Grace.' Ed now, holding the baby, jiggling him up and down. She didn't like the way Ed was doing that. He wasn't supporting the baby's head properly. It didn't seem safe. But Grace couldn't say anything. Because what right did she have? Ed was being wonderful. Just wonderful, as Joan loved to tell people. Adorable! Wonderful and adorable.

'Mum's just trying to help.'

'Thanks so much for your help, Joan.'

'Grace.'

'It's okay,' Joan assured Ed. 'I'm glad you feel you can be honest, darling. I think the problem is you're so used to having everything, aren't you? So used to being in control! To dictating what happens in your day. And now all that is gone.'

'Yep. I was too successful before. It's actually a problem I created.'

'I didn't mean that, Gracie.'

Grace stood up. 'Don't call me that.'

'Darling, I—'

Ed and Joan were looking at her. Did Ed wonder who had taken his wife away and replaced her with this unhinged, unmotherly maniac?

The baby started crying. It made Grace feel sick all though her body. The most horrible, dizzying sickness. Please stop, please stop, please stop. I'm sorry, I'm sorry, I'm sorry.

◎

Ed was loading the dishwasher. The baby was asleep.

'She means well,' said Ed.

Joan was gone, leaving in a cloud of lavender and sympathetic smiles.

'And I'm sorry,' Ed said. 'I know you're tired, but that was just rude.'

He had his back to her, putting the glasses in the cupboard, lining them up according to size and shape, just the way he liked them. Grace suspected he wouldn't have been able to say what he really felt if he was looking her in the face.

'I'll try and work on my manners.'

Ed turned around and threw his hands up in exasperation. 'This isn't her fault! I know what you're thinking.'

'I doubt that.'

'You're thinking this wouldn't have happened if we had stayed in London.'

Grace would have liked to disagree but she was incapable of lying to him. She always had been.

'She was dying, Grace.'

'I know.'

Ed turned back to the cupboard. 'For what it's worth, I think this might have happened even if we hadn't moved.'

'What is *this*? You mean me losing my mind and ruining your dreams of perfect fatherhood? I'm not the smiling wife you ordered?'

He turned quickly, raised a mug like he was going to hurl it across the room. Instead he breathed in slowly. Put the mug gently onto the benchtop.

'You are my dream, Grace. You still are.' He spoke with quiet force. 'I've done everything I can to show you that. It will never change. Ever.'

Then he turned away from her and walked out of the kitchen.

The baby started to cry. Grace felt her boobs tingle. She couldn't move.

32

GRACE HAD NO INTENTION OF DRIVING TO MANLY SO SOME STRANGER called Kelsey could put goo all over her face. (Kelsey would no doubt have singsong things to say about Grace being a new mum. God, Grace was a bitch. Kelsey was probably a really lovely person.) But she said goodbye to Ed and got in the car, and when she started the engine she felt it reverberate through her whole body, that growl. Like the car was her only friend and it was asking where she wanted to go.

So Grace took it onto the freeway, heading north for a bit. A dickhead in a Hilux came and sat on her tail, flashed his fucking headlights, so she roared off—she must have hit one-forty (a leisurely stroll for the Porsche—leaving him in her wake). When he was out of sight she slid into the left lane and waited for him. The dickhead finally caught up and Grace slipped into the right-hand lane onto his tail. She really went for it then, flashing the headlights, swerving from side to side like she was warming her tyres at Monza. She caught his eye in the rear-view mirror, saw his fury and raised her middle finger. But he just shook his head and pulled left to let her by. She thought he might tail her again, but he didn't. She was the Crazy Bitch.

◎

Not long after the Hilux incident Grace's phone began to ring. Ed. Grace took the next exit, two hours north of Sydney now, drove over the motorway, took the southbound on-ramp and congratulated herself for turning around in a responsible manner rather than just doing a U-turn across six lanes. Back to Sydney. Back to Ed. Back to the baby and her mind that refused to do what she needed it to.

But when she approached the turn-off to Mosman she couldn't do it.

She kept right on driving over the Harbour Bridge. The water shimmered below her, a big world full of creatures alive and doing what they needed to do to stay that way. Grace asked Siri to phone the Park Hyatt.

'What's the best room you have available tonight?' she asked the woman who answered.

'The roof-top suite is available, ma'am.'

'Okay, I'll take that. I'll be there in fifteen minutes. Please have some champagne and some . . . I don't know—do you have nice cake?'

'We have a Belgian chocolate torte, ma'am?'

'Excellent. I'll have four slices. With berries. Can you get berries?'

'Of course, ma'am.'

'Thank you.'

Grace recited her credit card number.

'I'd like a swim in your pool, but I don't have any swimmers. Can you get me some? Whatever's easy. Size six.'

'Absolutely, ma'am.'

'Thank you so much.'

'Thank *you*, ma'am. We look forward to hosting you.'

◎

After the bath, but before she smashed her phone, Grace sent a text to Dorothy:

Tell Ed I'm okay. Nothing terrible has happened.

◎

Dorothy was sitting on the sofa leafing through one of Ed's art books when Grace walked through her front door two days later. Dorothy raised her chin, wordless, eyes fixed on Grace's, and she gave Grace a small nod. An acknowledgement, perhaps. Approval of her return. *You've done the right thing.* It wasn't something she gave very often.

'Ed's out of his mind,' she said.

Grace's instinct was to apologise. But Dorothy didn't seem to be looking for an apology.

'Are you okay?' she asked.

'I don't know.'

Dorothy stood up, adjusted the perfectly rolled cuffs of her tailored white shirt. She was wearing ankle-skimming black pants and a chunky gold necklace. Grace thought she must be okay because she'd noted that she liked Dorothy's outfit. It was a long time since Grace could remember liking anything at all.

'Where have you been?'

It wasn't accusatory, more curious.

'The Park Hyatt. I had some chocolate cake and a long bath.'

The corner of Dorothy's mouth twitched a little. More approval. This was nothing like what Grace had expected of her. Ever.

'Do you feel better?'

'Not really.'

'But you've come home.'

'Yes.'

Ed was in the room then. He'd been carrying a basket of washing and it fell to the floor with a thunk when he saw Grace, tipping on its side and spilling several tiny onesies. A thumb-sized sock. The sight of it made Grace feel sick with guilt. The crackle of the baby's corresponding cry sounded over the baby monitor. She'd only had to walk back into the house and the crying started.

'I'm sorry,' Grace said. And he knew she was talking about waking the baby.

'It's okay, he's been down nearly . . .'

'Two hours,' Dorothy supplied.

Ed rushed towards Grace, wrapping her in his arms and burying his face in her hair.

'Are you okay?' His voice was breaking over the words. 'Are you okay? I thought I'd lost you.'

◎

Ed had taken Henry into his bedroom to give him a bottle. 'I discovered that if he's in a dark room he's not as distracted and drinks more,' he explained. The milk Grace had expressed before she vanished had run out, of course. Ed had called Dorothy and she came straight away, bringing formula. Months later Grace asked him why he hadn't called his own mother. 'I didn't want her judging you,' Ed said. 'And Nish was on the other side of the world. Dorothy was the next best thing.'

Now, Dorothy sat beside Grace on the couch, ankles crossed, hands folded in her lap like the queen. She had the forthright practical disposition to go with it.

'What's wrong with me?' Grace asked. It wasn't a rhetorical question; she needed an answer. The feeling coursing through Grace was heavier than anything she'd ever felt; it was the thick, heavy ooze of shame.

'You're going to say I don't know what I'm talking about,' Dorothy replied. 'But I do, because you and I are alike, Grace. I know you don't like to hear that, but it's true.'

Grace looked away, out the window, up at the ceiling.

'I understand how you feel.' Dorothy said the words in a firm, measured voice. As if giving evidence in court—gosh, she'd be so good at that. 'We're both driven in a way most people don't even get a taste of. I know what it's like—half an hour with nothing to do and your brain starts gnawing away at itself like a kelpie locked in an apartment. There's nothing wrong with you, you're just not where you feel you're meant to be.'

'Where are *you* meant to be?' Grace asked her.

'Parliament, I think. But I suspect it's too late for that.'

'Is this how you felt when I was a baby?'

'No. I'd been taught from a young age that I belonged in the home raising children; I never knew anything different.'

'So it's my fault for having a career?'

'Don't you ever let anyone tell you this is your fault.'

Grace closed her eyes and leaned her head on Dorothy's bony shoulder. She felt her mother stiffen a little, caught off guard by the rare physical contact. Grace thought Dorothy might pull away, but instead she placed a cool hand on Grace's forehead and smoothed her hair from her eyes.

'Why did you come home?' Dorothy asked.

'I wanted to watch TV and eat pizza with Ed. It's what we used to do when I had a crap day at work. And . . . I want another chance to get it right.'

'Darling, I hate to tell you this, but there is no way of getting this right. All you can do is love Henry and keep the wolves from the door. I suspect you'll be very good at that. And one day he'll lean his head on your shoulder and you'll be able to tell him that everything will be okay. And you'll know that it's true.'

◎

Grace sat on the edge of the bed. Nothing seemed familiar—not the carpet under her bare feet, nor the slice of sunshine on the wardrobe doors, nor the colour of the ocean outside the window. The only thing that gave her a vague sense of being anchored in this world was the framed wedding photo on Ed's bedside table: Ed in the grey tweed three-piece suit; Grace in her wedding dress, a pink peony chosen by Ed in her hair. In the photograph they were sitting on a park bench. She was laughing and he was looking at her in adoration.

Dorothy was gone now, saying quiet words to Ed before she left: 'Find her a good doctor, not some shiny know-it-all. Preferably a woman.' And Ed was downstairs in the kitchen making dinner, although Grace couldn't imagine eating. The baby was with him, probably strapped into the front pack (Swedish ergonomic design!) and Grace heard the baby begin to grizzle. Ed must have tried to hold out as long as possible before he brought him up to Grace, by which time the baby was squawking. Grace felt the prickle of heat in her boobs and the sweat on her lower back.

Ed knocked softly before he came into the room. 'Do you want to feed him? Otherwise I can just give him a bottle. He's really used to it now.'

'No. This is better for him.'

The midwives, accompanied by posters all over the maternity ward, had made that abundantly clear months ago. And then, of course, there was the video they'd watched in birthing class which outlined every benefit of breastfeeding, how it was the absolute best thing, how any substitute was inferior no matter what lies the multinational conglomerate companies that marketed formula peddled. (Grace wondered whether she'd failed birth class. Probably.)

So Ed arranged the pillows and Grace propped herself up while she fed the baby.

'Thank you,' Ed whispered.

'It's fine.'

'I mean for coming home.'

He took her hand and she squeezed it as tightly as she could. He would hold her there; he would stop her from drifting off into the dark stratosphere of her mind.

◎

Rowena found Grace a psychiatrist. Dr Trish Rousband was a cold woman, she didn't offer words of comfort, but she did provide Grace with a clear outline of the steps she would take in treating her, and when she did this there was no trepidation in her voice, no doubt. She was a woman who was sure of herself. This was something Grace found more comforting than the kind words Dr Rousband could have spoken to her. When she handed Grace a prescription for antidepressants and an antipsychotic (which was something Grace had never imagined she would need in her life; did this make her a psycho?), she looked her in the eye and said, 'You need to find something you can do that gets you out of your head. Something sensory that quietens you. Yoga, or walking, or listening to music. Something that's not going to frighten your husband.'

When Grace got home she told Ed what the doctor had said. He went into the bedroom and when he came back out he had Grace's headphones in his hand. 'Lie on the ground,' he said. 'Look at the sky.'

And when she did lie on the ground Grace felt a little less like the world was spinning too fast, a little less like she might be flung into space. Into nothing. The grass, the earth below it, the plant roots, the bedrock, the sand turned to stone after thousands of years—all of it was holding her weight.

Grace slept. She fell into the earth and the music enveloped her. She only stirred when Ed gathered her up in his arms and carried her into the house.

◎

It was a few weeks later, a Tuesday—Grace always remembered that—around six, the time of morning when the light seems to find the ocean before it finds the sky. The sound of Henry found her ear and it wasn't like all the other times. It was a different type of sound, a different tone, a different undulation of sound waves through the atmosphere. Ed didn't stir. Grace sat up, pushed the warmth of the blanket away. The rug was cold on the soles of her feet. But it wasn't like the other times.

She went to Henry's room. He was on his back in his cot and, having freed his arms of his wrap he was beating them up and down, stretched out at his sides like wings, making a sound like he was singing, just quietly, just to himself. He saw Grace, his big eyes seeing hers, and his smile—toothless, wide—was glorious. The light found the sky.

◎

As Grace began to heal, she and Ed never discussed staying in Australia; it wasn't a decision they made, it was just that neither of them suggested going back to London. Grace felt her mind slowly recovering, almost regrowing into this new life, like foliage after a fire. The medication helped. There were bad days, they just grew further and further apart as Henry grew more and more into himself. And rather than feeling like she was scattered all over the place, Grace felt the three of them—Ed, Henry and herself—come together. The lease on the house came to an end so Grace made the owners an offer they couldn't refuse; it had unexpectedly begun to feel like home.

She did wonder if she was afraid to go back to London, afraid to pick up her life where she had left off and discover that she was irrevocably altered by what she had gone through. That she couldn't do it anymore. That she'd lost her edge. Tony—being someone who loved her, someone who valued her, and perhaps the first person to see Grace's potential—told her not to rush. Grace could stay across the large-scale workings of the business from Australia to keep her head in the game.

In the weeks after Henry was born Ada had tried frequently to contact Grace, probably full of apologies, congratulations, requests. Almost once a day for a while, until Ed asked her to stop. Now that she was better, it would make sense for Grace to reach out to Ada and clear the air, only Grace never did. Maybe it was hurt and anger over Ada's tantrum. Or maybe, as Nish pointed out, Grace was grieving a life she felt she had lost and Ada was a painful reminder. But how could you call it grief or loss when you looked at the little person Grace had gained? Observed him pattering around the garden collecting worms in a bucket? Watched him bounce up and down in his highchair saying, 'Oh, oh, oh,' when 'Single Ladies' came on the radio? Or returning from the beach with a hat full of shells to be lined up on the kitchen table and under no circumstances be touched by anyone else, shells that he would sing little songs to and cover with a pillow-case when they were 'tired'?

And the truth was Ada didn't owe Grace an apology. She owed Grace nothing other than financial renumeration. Theirs was a business partnership. This was a cold but true assessment. Cut-throat. The kind of judgement that made Grace successful in the first place. Grace gave Ada's full-time care over to Lila, the woman who had taken Grace's role when she had been unable to return to London.

Grace asked Tony not to tell her how Ada reacted to this. She didn't want to know.

33

2015

THE SHOPPING TROLLEY HAD A FUNNY WHEEL AND GRACE HAD TO WALK it sideways across the car park, using all her weight to stop it swinging into the back of the Porsche. The car already had a nasty scratch on the rear bumper from where Dorothy had had a 'bit of a tangle' with a bollard during a playgroup excursion to Inflatable World. That was the day when Dorothy claimed she had forgotten to bring her own child seat and couldn't be bothered switching Grace's into the back of her car. Grace didn't believe her for a second; Dorothy never forgot anything. More likely Dorothy wanted another go in the Porsche after first driving it the week before, an experience she said she found quite thrilling.

('Closet petrol head?' Grace had joked.

'Don't be silly,' Dorothy said. 'I'm far too worried about climate change.')

The thrill of Dorothy's second drive had been short-lived, however, once she came into contact with the bollard. Ed was trying to use it as an excuse to sell the thing so that Grace could get something more practical, something better suited to a car seat, something with actual safety features.

However, today the rear of the Porsche was spared thanks to Grace's quick last-minute intervention which saw the trolley pull up just in time with only millimetres to spare.

'Crashed!' squealed Henry with delight.

'I didn't. Look—it's not even touching the car.'

'Crashed!'

'No. Not crashed.'

'Crashed!'

It was then that she saw he had been shoplifting again, a silver box of whitening toothpaste clutched in his little fist. The previous incidents had mostly taken place in department stores, where Henry was partial to nabbing a single shoe. The first time it happened Grace hadn't discovered the stolen item until at least fifteen minutes later, when she was putting Henry in the car. On that and following occasions she'd gone sheepishly back into the store and everyone had had a good chuckle about how adorable Henry was. This time, after a marathon supermarket expedition, halfway through which Henry had clearly done something spectacular in his nappy, it was far less adorable, more inconvenient and possibly incriminating.

'Henry, you can't take things from the shop.'

'Henny wants things from shop.'

'No. We have to take it back.' Grace extracted the box of toothpaste from his sticky grip. Henry screamed and kicked his fierce little legs. A woman in immaculate athleisure-wear glanced over, not bothering to hide her disapproval. There was no way Grace could get the fully loaded trolley with its funny wheel all the way back across the car park. She opened the boot and the trolley slid away, only slightly, only thirty centimetres before she realised and grabbed it, but Henry believed he was moments from death and the screaming intensified.

Fuck the toothpaste. She gave it back to him and put him in the car along with a packet of tiny teddies. Which was when her phone rang. And she couldn't find it, of course. She'd stopped using a nappy bag as soon as Henry was past the stage of three changes every hour and had started throwing all her stuff into a leather tote. More stylish, less practical. The phone stopped ringing by the time she found it. Private number. Probably spam.

It started ringing again.

'Hello?'

''Allo, darlin'.'

'This isn't your number,' was all Grace could say.

'No, babe,' said Ada. 'Thought I might be able to catch you out. Seems you've ghosted me, which is deserved. I was a right bitch. Can't believe what I did to you. Every day I've thought about it. All I've wanted is to say I'm sorry. That's it. I'm so sorry, babe.'

Grace let it sink in. She remembered Ada in the French restaurant after the cheating scandal, nervous fingernails on the wineglass—*tap, tap, tap*. 'Biggest mistake I ever made,' Ada said now, 'what I did to you. Dropped you cold. And over the phone when you was so vulnerable.'

'Where are you?' Grace asked.

'At the zoo, if you can believe it.'

'At night? It must be two in the morning or something?'

'I'm down the road. Taronga. I'm eating a fucking awful sandwich and Skylar is having a face-off with a chimpanzee. I don't care for primates; they know more than they let on.'

Grace asked Ada what did she mean, that she was at the zoo down the road eating a sandwich, and Ada said, 'I mean I'm at the zoo down the road from you eating a sandwich.'

Henry had gobbled all the tiny teddies. 'All gone! Teddies gone!'

'You should bring him along,' Ada said. 'He and Skylar can squeal at the chimpanzees together. Although she should know better by now.'

'He's tired. He needs a nap.'

'Then come to the hotel for a drink or dinner or whatever you can manage. I'll wait. God knows how many times you've had to wait for me.'

After the call, Grace stared at the phone in her hand as if it might give her guidance on how to proceed. She should call back and say no, that she was done, she was happy in her new life with Ed and their beautiful little boy, she was happy and fulfilled reading *Where Is the Green Sheep?* twelve times a day and scraping squashed sultanas off the floor. She had quit Ada. She had quit the chaos and the thrill, the goosebumps on her skin when the lights dimmed and the music swelled.

Henry fixed her in his gaze, his dark eyebrows (like little caterpillars) furrowed. A glob of snot had formed under his gorgeous nose.

'Issue,' he said.

'You need a tissue?'

He gave his signature solemn nod. Grace rummaged through her bag once more. Not a tissue or a baby wipe to be found. Nothing useful in her pockets either. The tissue issue was intensifying rapidly.

'Issue!'

Grace pulled at the silky lining of her jacket and somehow managed to use it to wipe Henry's nose. 'Better?'

He smiled. 'Bedder.'

◎

Ada was staying at a hotel just north of Circular Quay. Her room was on the top floor with flawless views of the harbour and the bridge. Grace didn't understand the nervousness she felt as she stood outside Ada's door. It was a tightness in her chest, an inexplicable fear of something—she didn't know what. Getting dressed to go out had felt like putting on the costume of a character she used to play effortlessly, but now the costume didn't fit. It had felt strange to leave the house with nothing but her wallet, phone and keys—no nappies, drink bottle, snacks, tiny jumper in case of rain, hat in case of sun, sunscreen, Matchbox car or baby wipes—and she couldn't shake the feeling that she had left something important behind and would be caught out by an unexpected poo or similar. ('Henry's or yours?' Nish asked later.)

But Ada opened the door and, when she saw her, Grace's eyes welled up.

'Oh, babe,' said Ada. 'I can't tell you how good it is to see you.'

Ada had ordered prawns and champagne. She and Grace sat on the balcony and watched the water as it shimmered in the late afternoon light. Back at home, Ed was probably beginning to prepare Henry's dinner. Grace couldn't remember the last time she'd eaten later than six. For that matter, she couldn't remember the last time she'd eaten.

'Sometimes I miss those days when it were just me and Susie and she was little and we'd play dolls for ages. It was so simple then, yeah? Now it's all go, go, go all the time. But look . . .' Ada swept her hand across the view. 'Not a bad living. No complaints.'

'How are you?' Grace asked.

'I'm not the same without you, but that's no big secret.'

'You're doing pretty well by yourself. I saw the pictures from Glastonbury.'

'So you have been paying attention!'

'I pay attention.'

'You know Lila wants me to get back-up dancers? Me? I was like, babe, not happening. But she's still on about it. I had to call Tony and ask him to get her to calm the fuck down.'

'I can't see you with back-up dancers.'

'Thank you.'

'The album's good.'

'You've heard it?

'Really good. You do know that?'

'It's all right.'

'It's good, Ada.'

'Well, thank you. I think I got the tone right. The flavour. It's not all overproduced and processed and all that. They actually listened to me.'

'See? You're fine without me.'

'I had to cancel three shows. Completely lost my nerve.'

'Nobody's perfect.'

'That's good news because I certainly ain't.'

They sat in the quiet for a few moments. And then, 'How's Ed?'

'Ed's good. Really good.'

'Ah. I see.'

'He's followed me around a lot, Ada. It's his turn to do his thing.'

◎

When Grace got home Henry was still up, sitting in front of the television while Ed cleaned the kitchen. Ed said he thought Grace might want to say goodnight. He asked her how it was seeing Ada and Grace said it was lovely. It was quiet for a little while; Grace swept the mess up from under the highchair.

Then Ed said, 'Do you want to move back to London?'

Grace stopped what she was doing. 'Do you want to move back?'

Ed didn't answer. He pulled the sink strainer out and rinsed it under the tap.

Grace took the plastic bowl from the tray of Henry's highchair and put it in the dishwasher.

'I think that makes the plastic disintegrate,' Ed said.

'It's BPA-free.'

'Yeah, but plastic will break down at high temperatures.'

Grace handed him the bowl and he put the plug in the sink, began to fill it with hot water.

'All your friends are in London,' he said.

'You have friends there too.'

'I know.'

'I mean, we hardly ever see your parents anyway.'

'Well . . .' he began. But he stopped.

'What?'

'I'm not saying it's your fault.'

'How is it my fault?'

'I'm not saying it is. But I think Mum thinks . . . Well, ever since . . .'

Grace knew he was talking about when she had run away to a hotel. It was a subject they had silently agreed never to talk about again.

'And what about your parents?' he asked.

'I can't stay here for Dorothy.'

'Henry will miss them.'

'They can visit whenever they want,' Grace said. 'They're both retired, for god's sake. It's not like they don't have time.'

'So you do want to go back?'

'I don't have infinite time to go AWOL.'

'You're not. You're still involved.'

But they both knew it wasn't the same.

'I have to ask myself what the plan is,' she said. 'We've been rolling along without a plan.'

'Rolling along is good.'

It's boring, she wanted to say. Boring and terrifying.

'What do you want to do?' Ed asked.

Grace took a damp cloth and attempted to wipe sticky rice from the highchair. It was in all the creases of the seat, as were other varieties of unidentifiable grot.

'It's a bit manipulative,' Ed said. 'Ada turning up here.'

'I hadn't answered any of her calls or messages or anything.'

'I know, but to fly all the way over here. She is capable of doing her job without you. Obviously.'

'She cancelled three shows.'

'That's not your responsibility.'

'It kind of is. Would you want to move back?' Grace asked. 'Be honest.'

'I like the work I'm doing here. Gustus is still happy to rep me from London so it's not like I have to be there. And it would be tricky with Henry if we were both working full-time without your mum to help out.'

'I was only ever going to have twelve months off.'

'I know. But it's been good for him. It's been good for both of you.'

'I'm allowed to go back to work.'

'You said be honest. Going back to work is one thing, but Ada is on a different continent.'

Grace rinsed the cloth and washed the rice from her hands. On the television, Igglepiggle was getting into his rowboat and soon the credits would roll. Henry was rubbing at his ears.

'I don't have to move back permanently. I could fly back there and be with Ada for tours and maybe sometimes for meetings or recording. Dorothy could always help out here when I'm gone, which really won't have to be that often.'

'I need to think about this,' said Ed.

'Of course.'

'I wish she hadn't ambushed you. Us.'

'I don't think she meant to do that.'

But Ed gave her a look, disagreeing.

◎

At the airport the first time Grace went back to London, Henry sat in his little stroller, holding an apple juice popper and watching his parents with big, curious eyes. Ed wrapped his arms around Grace and kissed her on the forehead. Henry had two band-aids on his elbow from when he'd tripped over at the park the day before. It had only been a scrape, but he had demanded two band-aids. 'Is a two bad one,' he'd said to Grace, his brow furrowed.

'It's not too bad,' she replied.

'Is two bad,' he countered. So two band-aids it was.

Grace knew that he would resist having the band-aids pulled off and it would take several baths before they were soft and peeling enough to come away easily. The thing to do would be to distract him with the Igglepiggle boat Dorothy had bought him then whip them off without warning. The element of surprise was always more difficult with two band-aids.

But Ed knew all of that. There was no need for Grace to tell him.

Ed released her from his hug. 'Okay, well,' he said.

'Okay.'

'We'll see you in a few weeks.'

'Yes.'

'Say bye to Mum. Henry?'

Henry had removed the straw from his popper and was now holding the carton upside down and shaking it. Drops were landing all over his clothes. Ed took the popper off him, which Henry objected to very strongly.

'We don't shake it upside down,' Ed said.

Henry insisted that we do; we do shake it upside down.

Grace wanted to enter into the argument but she also didn't want Henry to be angry with her before she left him for three weeks.

'Henry say goodbye to Mum?' she said, crouching down in front of the stroller. He was straining forward in the harness in an attempt to regain control of the popper. 'Henry? Henry, look at me.'

'You should just go,' said Ed.

'Henry?'

'It's okay,' said Ed.

'It's not.' She wiped at the tears under her eyes. 'Henry, I'm going on the aeroplane. It's time to say goodbye.'

Her son was all red in the face now, with tiny curls formed at his damp temples from the exertion of his battle.

'Can he just have the popper so I can say goodbye to him? It's pretty much empty.'

'We can't give in to this.'

Grace took a deep breath, as if she were going underwater for a long time. She took Henry's chubby little hands and kissed them, but he writhed out of her grip.

'Okay. Okay.'

Grace stood up and Ed handed over her carry-on and the empty popper. He took the handles of the stroller and flipped the brake with the toe of his shoe.

'We'll go,' he said. 'Love you.'

'Love you too.'

Ed turned the stroller and walked away, with Henry straining towards Grace, desperate for the popper. She turned away and headed for the check-in desk, binning the juice box on her way. Henry had begun to screech in protest; Grace could hear it fading as the distance between them grew and Ed went through the terminal doors.

◎

Ada had a four-bedroom penthouse apartment in the clock tower of St Pancras Chambers. To anyone in Sydney it sounded ridiculous, like living at Central Railway Station, with the endless rumble of trains and engulfing exhaust fumes. In reality the building swept in a grand curve along Euston Road, a Gothic confection of salmon pink brick and sandstone, complete with spires and a convenient two-and-a-half-hour commute to Paris. The apartment itself comprised three mezzanine levels, threaded with spiral staircases and huge timber buttresses like the ribs of a whale. The living room, over which the upper levels looked, had ten-metre-high ceilings, Ada enthused, leading Grace through the entry foyer. 'Lila found it for me, if you can believe it. Honest to god, I said I want to be able to get to Paris easy and she goes and finds me this. I can literally see the Eurostar. And the girls love it. Skylar said it's like living in Hogwarts, but with nicer bathrooms.'

At Ada's insistence, Grace had booked herself a room in the hotel that took up the majority of the building. 'We'll be so close,' Ada said. 'Really convenient but not in each other's pockets.' Grace was to have dinner with Ada, Charlie and the girls before turning in and attempting to recover from her journey. The schedule for the following three weeks was full of press, ten performances across the UK and planning for a North American tour.

At Lila's encouragement, Ada had been taking cooking lessons with a Japanese chef as a means of relaxation. 'She says I got to find something that has nothing to do with performance or nothing,' Ada said, chopping vegetables at a speed Grace found both impressive and alarming. 'And I am literally nourishing my family and, honest to god, it is exactly what I need to do. She has been good, Lila, don't get me wrong—but it's not what you and me have, is it? Charlie says you bring out the best in me, don't you, babe?'

'Yeah, babe,' said Charlie from the couch, where he was sipping a beer and watching *Britain's Got Talent* with Skylar and Susie. Susie was thirteen now, with her mother's fine features and sass. Grace couldn't imagine Henry at thirteen.

On the television a trio of acrobats had been given a mediocre score and now one of them was sobbing.

'It's you and me where the magic happens, Grace. And I can't tell you how much it means to have you here.' Ada scraped the vegetables into the wok, where they hissed in squealed. It would be Wednesday morning in Australia. Henry would be eating eggs and toast soldiers. Ed wasn't great at getting the tops off the eggs and Henry would always say, 'Mummy do it!' The popper drama would be forgotten by now. Either that or 'Henry have popper?' would be the first thing he said to Grace when she got off the plane.

◎

Grace was too tired to enjoy the food and had to summon all her energy to be enthusiastic and complimentary when Ada repeatedly asked for her opinion during the meal. She was desperate for sleep and was in her pyjamas within moments of arriving in her room. Grace was brushing her teeth when her phone rang. It would be Ed, she was sure of it. A quick check-in before she went to bed. He would know the exact time in London and would have allowed time for her dinner with Ada before calling. Grace spat out the toothpaste and rinsed her mouth while the phone buzzed. She grabbed it and saw that it wasn't Ed at all, it was Lila.

'Hiya,' Lila said. 'Flight all right? So I wanted to grab you before you went to bed to let you know I've got Ada in for a wardrobe consult at seven tomorrow.'

'Oh, that's new.'

'Yep, I think she's put on a few pounds and I'm worried that our options aren't options anymore.' Lila went on to say that Mei, Ada's stylist, was in the loop on it all, but nothing had been mentioned to Ada. 'I figure you're the best person to talk her through it, yeah? It's above my pay grade now that she's yours again. And honestly, last time we had a similar conversation she completely flew off the handle.'

'What was the similar conversation?'

'Oh, you know, I said we might have to up the training sessions before Europe. Just to get a little off the waist.'

'Ada's waist?'

'Well, not mine.'

'She looks good to me.'

'Yeah, but we got that *Harper's* cover in August. I'm regretting the cooking lessons.'

'She looks good to me.'

'Sure, well, like I said, above my pay grade now.'

'Okay, goodnight.'

Ed had tried to call her while she was talking to Lila. Grace was so tired now that she felt as though her skull was expanding and contracting with each breath.

He didn't answer on her first attempt but he called her back straight away after that.

'Hey, I can't find Henry's red gumboots.'

'They should be in the cupboard by the front door.'

'They're not.'

'Then I don't know, Ed.'

'Right.'

'The flight was okay,' Grace said. She could hear Henry in the background.

'What's that?'

'I said—'

'No, I was talking to Henry.' Ed's voice, fainter now, not speaking to her. 'We'll leave in a minute. We need to find your boots.'

'I should probably let you go,' Grace said.

'Yeah, okay. Love you.'

'Love you too.'

◎

After setting up their lives in Australia, Grace and Ed had kept the London house and leased it out. Once Grace's transcontinental life established its rhythm she used the house as her base in London. It was a helpful set piece once she found the old muscle within herself that was able to divide Grace into two parts: the

Grace in London and the Grace in Australia. When she was in the London house she could almost believe that Ed was the only one missing from her life, like Henry was a fragment of a dream. It wasn't always sustainable: a glimpse of a curly-haired toddler, a child crying on the bus or, once, a forlorn Igglepiggle toy lying on the pavement outside a cafe would leave Grace with a feeling of dislocation, like a part of her wasn't where it should be. She allowed herself short, scheduled times to cry and it was fine as long as there was enough time to pull herself back together to resume as London Grace.

One evening, as she was parking in her driveway in Primrose Hill, Grace saw that the kitchen light was on. Before she even reached the front steps she sensed the alteration in the atmosphere.

Ed opened the door. He was holding Henry, who, on seeing Grace, broke into a wide smile.

In the kitchen, with Henry's sleeping head snuggled against her chest and his chubby arms griping her neck, Grace tried to recalibrate. Ed asked her something about food—had she eaten? And for a moment she didn't know. It was okay, he said. There was leftover Turkish that he had bought for his and Henry's dinner. It was from the place Grace and he had always gone to. 'You should have seen their faces when I brought Henry in,' Ed said. 'Asya covered him in kisses. She wouldn't let me pay for the food.'

Grace didn't need food. She recalled now that she had eaten at Ada's. Ed said that he hadn't really planned the visit. It wasn't until Grace had been in London for two weeks that he had the idea of surprising her.

'I didn't want you to worry about logistics or how Henry would go on the plane. And you don't need to change anything. I spoke to Tony; he's made sure that you have the rest of the week off.'

'But Ada has a radio thing tomorrow morning.'

'It's okay. Tony's squared it with that other woman who was looking after her . . .'

'Lila.'

'Yeah, Lila has it sorted for the rest of the week. You can meet Ada in Frankfurt on Sunday. I'll stay here with Henry and catch up with some people, and we'll be here when you get back. We'll have four days together and then I'll take Henry home. You can do the next three weeks with Ada and come home afterwards.'

'Does Ada know about this?'

'Lila has it, Grace.'

Grace, one-handed, found her phone in her bag.

'Grace,' said Ed.

'Can you take him for a sec?'

Ed reached for their son. He wouldn't look at her now. 'I thought you'd be happy to see us.'

'I am, but I'm still working. I just have to check in with Ada and then . . . then I'm all yours.'

'Tony has it covered.'

'She's going to turn up tomorrow and freak out. It's live radio.'

Ed held the sleeping Henry. 'For fuck's sake,' he said, almost inaudibly.

'What am I supposed to do?'

'You're supposed to take the week off.'

Henry roused; his brow crumpled in warning of the meltdown that would soon be upon them. Ed lowered his voice to a whisper. 'We've travelled across the world to be here with you.'

'I didn't know.'

'It was a surprise.'

'And I'm surprised.'

Ed turned away from her, heading for the stairs.

'Wait. I'm sorry. I won't call her.'

He paused.

'I won't call her.'

She met him at the bottom of the stairs. Kissed him on the lips over Henry's sleeping head. 'I'm so happy to see you,' she whispered. 'I won't call her.'

◎

They did all the London things that Ed admitted he missed: parks, galleries, museums. They took Henry on the London Eye, to the city farm to look at the enormous pigs, rode the bus, the tube and the ferry. They ate pastries in the park and went to their favourite cafes, the ones Grace avoided when she was in London now.

When Ed and Henry were gone again, Grace felt like she had to mop up all the new memories and put them somewhere they couldn't taunt her.

34

ED

GRACE DIDN'T UNDERSTAND WHAT IT WAS LIKE TAKING A THREE-YEAR-OLD on a flight to the other side of the world. The million little logistical problems amounted to a challenge so great that it was inexplicable; there was no way of accurately communicating what it was like. The simple act of using the bathroom on an aeroplane became complex and its success entirely dependent on Henry's willingness or otherwise to wait with the flight attendant while Ed went. You just couldn't fit an adult and a child in a plane bathroom. Ed had planned to do all sorts of things while Henry slept: eat, pee, sleep. But Henry didn't sleep, so he became overtired, wouldn't eat and definitely wouldn't wait with a stranger while Ed took a desperately needed pee. So Ed didn't pee during the first fifteen-hour leg. When Henry did finally fall asleep it was ten minutes before landing and he woke up as soon as Ed lifted him out of the seat. Woke and, due to the not-eating and catastrophic overtiredness, proceeded to vomit down Ed's back.

The other passengers thought a dad taking his son on a solo journey was adorable up until that point.

He couldn't push a stroller and a suitcase, so Ed had packed three weeks' worth of clothing for himself and Henry into the backpack he had used on a tour of Spain and Portugal a decade ago. Thank god Henry's clothes were small. There was probably some rich-person thing he could have done, like organised someone to wheel his suitcase through the airport for him or something like that. A porter? Was that what they were called? How frigging embarrassing. Ed wouldn't know where to start with that stuff. The business-class tickets were out of character enough as it was. Maybe if he'd gone first class, which they could very much afford, someone would have explained all the wealthy-person options he had. But first class was an obscene amount of money. Most rich people probably didn't even pay attention to the numbers in front of them, they just got whatever it was that they wanted: first-class tickets, three-hundred-year-old bottles of wine, caviar or whatever. Monogrammed luggage. He couldn't do that; he couldn't stop looking at price tags and thinking, That's three months' rent for someone.

So he didn't bother trying to explain to Grace how difficult it had been getting to London. She would have thought he was stupid for not finding out how to make it easier. And anyway, she didn't even ask how the flight was.

Ed hadn't been prepared for her reaction when she saw them, and later, when he thought about it on the flight home, he wondered what it was he'd been expecting. Tears? Would she burst into sobs and hold on to his neck and tell him how much she missed him; how wonderful it was that he was there; how it was the only thing she wanted? No. He knew her well enough to know she was too cool for any of that. Uncontrolled emotion wasn't Grace's thing. When she opened the door and saw him standing in her house her reaction was confusion and probably even slight irritation—he wasn't where he was supposed to be.

Ed had been unsettled himself to see how different she was from the Grace he'd said goodbye to back in Australia. The Grace who'd arrived home from work to their London house was one he hadn't seen for a long time; she was so sleek. She'd filled the wardrobe there with beautiful clothes, shoes, handbags. No point dragging clothes back and forth when she travelled, she said. He hadn't realised the extent to which she had gone in setting herself up over there. He had never seen the dress she was wearing that night when he arrived. It didn't matter. It really didn't. But there was such an otherness to her. Even her accent sounded more British.

The time they spent in London together was great. It was. They had fun; she'd loved taking Henry to the parks and on the red buses. She had to buy some casual clothes, though, as everything in her London wardrobe was workwear or evening stuff for special events. She couldn't wear silk tops around a toddler, she said.

It seemed to Ed that it wasn't just a job that Grace was doing over there; she had an entire parallel life.

35

FOUR WEEKS LATER, GRACE WAS BACK IN LONDON—IN THE MIDDLE OF a meeting between Ada and a potential new producer—when Ed rang. She hadn't even noticed the missed call until she was in the cab afterwards. It wasn't the scheduled time for a call. He'd left a message simply asking her to call him. It made her worry.

Ed's phone only rang once before he answered.

'Grace!'

'Ed? What's wrong?'

'Nothing! Hi!'

This wasn't normal.

'Hi. What's going on? Is it Henry?'

'I'm a finalist, Grace. I know you're probably busy, but I wanted to tell you as soon as I could. I can't believe it.'

'Oh, that's great! A finalist for what?'

A fraction of a pause. 'For the Wynne Prize. I entered a while ago.'

'I'm sorry. I forgot. I was just at a breakfast and I've got a thousand things going through my—'

'Sorry for interrupting.'

'No! Don't apologise.' She knew she sounded strangely formal. 'I'm glad you called. That's amazing.'

'It's the big one—they award it alongside the Archibald.'

'Yes, I know. I remember. It's great. I'm proud of you.'

She wasn't sure if she sounded patronising.

'Thanks. I'm pretty chuffed.'

'You should be.'

'There's just a few things I want to talk to you about and I want to get the ball moving before you come back.'

The ball moving? Grace wasn't sure she'd ever heard Ed use that phrase, or anything like it.

'What things?'

'Just logistics stuff. I know you don't have time right now.'

'No, I do.'

'I've got to get Henry in the bath—I just rang to tell you in person. About the prize.'

'I'll call you in the morning your time? Like seven? Oh no, it's preschool, isn't it. What about nine? After you drop him off?'

'That's eleven at night for you, Grace.'

'It's fine. I haven't been sleeping great anyway, so.'

But he messaged her that night telling her there was no reason for her to call. He would talk to her when she got home. *Get some sleep. Love you.*

◎

On the evening Grace got home, Ed told her that because of the Wynne a Sydney gallerist wanted to represent him. They were sitting outside; Grace had her feet in the pool. She'd been looking forward to seeing Henry but her flight had been delayed and he was already asleep.

It was an important gallery, Ed told her. A big deal. This person wanted Ed to work towards a solo exhibition.

'I think I'm going to need to get a nanny,' Ed said. 'Henry's at child care two days a week but it's not going to be enough time for me to work. And I'd rather have someone here so he can have days at home. It's too much for Dorothy to take on.'

'I'm here for the next three weeks, and after that it's only eight days in Tokyo,' Grace said. 'Then I'll be back.'

'Yeah, but you're still working when you're here. It'll just be more stable for him to have someone more consistent—'

'Than his mother?'

'That's not what I'm saying. I'm saying that I need to work too, and what's best for him is consistency so he's not being shunted all over the place.'

'I wouldn't be shunting him anywhere.'

'Shit, Grace.' He was tired. He only swore when he was tired. 'This isn't about you. This is about Henry and . . . and my work.'

'You've just caught me off guard.'

'I wouldn't have dropped it on you like this—I mean, it's not a big deal, but I get that it might be for you. And I would have talked to you about it earlier, but it's hard. To get the timing right. You know.'

'I was happy to wait up that night.'

'You would have been tired, and I know you might have been stressed about it, or . . . I know it's a big deal.'

'You said it wasn't a big deal.'

'Clearly it is.'

◎

He had set up a series of interviews with nannies from an agency. The first two applicants were fine but Henry seemed hesitant to talk or interact with them and maybe that was normal, maybe he would be like that with anyone. Ed felt that it wouldn't hurt to keep looking. 'He's super clingy at the moment anyway,' Ed said, and it was true: Henry had been insisting on Ed for bedtime stories, Ed for bath time, Ed for everything. This made things difficult given that the plan was for Grace to do the majority of parenting during her Sydney stretch so that Ed could work. There had been several mornings when Henry cried so much at Ed's departure that the stuttery spasms of breath, like hiccups, carried on for ten minutes after the crying itself stopped. A routine of Daddy Going to Work Now was implemented where Ed would pack his lunch and everything he needed for the day and leave via the front door while Henry and Grace waved goodbye (Grace did most of the waving). An integral element of this charade was the step which involved Ed then creeping down the side of the house and into his studio so that he wouldn't be seen and Henry would believe that his father was inaccessible for the entire day.

Lotte arrived for her interview ten minutes early, and when Ed opened the door Grace overheard Lotte apologise for being ahead of schedule and offer to remain on the front porch until the allotted time. Ed said it was totally fine for her to come in, no trouble at all.

'I have a habit of being too early,' Lotte explained as she came into the kitchen. 'A family I met a couple of weeks ago asked that I wait outside, so I thought that is maybe the correct thing to do.'

'Whoa. No, we would not make you wait outside,' Ed said.

Lotte smiled brightly when she saw Grace. Grace wanted to ask why Lotte hadn't taken the other job, whether it was because she had been asked to wait outside or it hadn't been offered to her.

'I'm so excited to meet you all!' Lotte said.

Grace wondered whether a nannying interview could warrant the level of excitement Lotte was displaying.

Henry, who was in the living room undertaking a serious mission involving wooden blocks and his Tonka truck, looked over to the chirpy young woman with curiosity.

'And this must be Henry!' Lotte said. 'May I?'

Grace hesitated. Ed said, 'Of course!'

Lotte kneeled down beside Henry. 'Wow, you have a lot of blocks here,' she said. 'May I build a tower for you? I love to build towers. And then, if you want, you can knock it down with your truck?'

Henry looked to his dad for reassurance. Ed nodded. Henry pushed some blocks in Lotte's direction.

'I can build a tower?' she asked.

Henry gave a nod. 'That yours blocks.'

'Oh, thank you! That is so kind!'

'Good sharing, Henry,' said Ed, and the tiny Belgian elf girl began to build a tower. She had this whole thing in the bag. A total interview pro.

Later, when—much to Henry's dismay—she had left, Ed smiled at Grace. 'That's the one, yeah?'

'I haven't looked at her résumé yet.'

'I looked over it; it's all totally fine. She has a work visa and already worked for a family in France.'

'Can you forward it to me?'

'I already did.'

'I think it got lost in work emails.'

Ed let out a breath that was almost a sigh and opened his laptop.

'What?' Grace said.

'Nothing. There, I've sent it again. We don't have to make this harder than it needs to be. Henry likes her, I like her.'

'I can have an opinion about who is going to be looking after our child.'

Ed snapped the laptop shut. 'What's your opinion then? Why wouldn't I hire her?'

'Why wouldn't *we* hire her,' Grace corrected. The problem—which she didn't have a way to say—was that Lotte was pretty and perky and nineteen and would be spending more time with Ed than Grace would. ('He would never,' Nish would say later. 'Like, Ed is the last guy on earth who would do that.' And it was true. But still.)

'I just need some time to think,' Grace said.

'Sure. Okay. But this is your choice.' He meant her work arrangement. 'And I totally support you, but you have to let me do what I need to do to make it work for me. My work is important too.'

'I know it is. I would never say it wasn't.'

'Okay then.'

'Okay.'

He was walking away now, going to get Henry who was ready for his nap.

'Ed?'

'Yeah?'

'Just stop for a sec.'

He turned to look at Grace.

'I am really, really happy that this has happened for you. You deserve it. So much.'

'Dad!'

Ed hesitated on the steps between the kitchen and the lounge room.

'Dad! Dad, Dad, Dad!'

'I mean it.'

'Thank you.'

'I love you.'

'I love you too.'

'Dad, Dad, Dad!'

That evening they had dinner outside on the deck. Grace made a ramen soup that Ada had taught her, and for once Henry wanted to sit on Grace's lap while she ate. Henry had his own bowl of noodles which he ate with his fingers, tilting his little head back and opening his mouth as wide as he could to drop the noodles in. Grace worried about them going straight down his throat. Ed said it would be fine.

'I looked at Lotte's résumé,' Grace said. 'We should hire her.'

'Okay, great. I think so too.'

36
GRACE

2016

'GRACIE? YOU ALL RIGHT IN THERE?'

The East Common office. Tony knocking on Grace's door.

'Marketing strat meet. Your girl says you know about it. I would have sent her in after you but she's mucking about with fruit in the boardroom. Apt bloody title that is, I tell you.'

'Okay!' Grace tried to sound perky and indeed okay.

It had started in the car on the way in. The driver pulled up at a red light and although the lurch wasn't severe, it was enough to bring her breakfast smoothie back up her throat. She'd had nothing to spew into other than her handbag, the contents of which she'd had to fish out and rinse in the bathroom, drying each individual item under the hand dryer, one foot against the door to stop anyone walking in on her.

Unlike the last time, the vomit wasn't the first sign. The first sign was a physical exhaustion which Grace had attempted to persuade herself was jet lag, general fatigue, lack of red meat in her diet.

Grace was now bagging the spewed-in handbag in a bin liner. Attempting to tie a knot effective enough to stop the acrid scent escaping.

'Can I come in then?'

'Sure!'

Grace dumped the knotted bag in the bin.

'That social media lad you hired just rolled in wearing a hat.' Tony strolled into Grace's office. 'A straw hat like those Eton tossers wear to a boat tournament or whatever they call it. Rowboat race. Do we need to review?'

'Based on a hat?'

'If Flip sees him he might punch him in the face. Whoa, you look like shit.'

'Thank you. He's not on Flip.'

'I should bloody hope not—he talks like Prince Philip. What's wrong with you?'

Grace burst into tears, and because Tony wasn't a hugger he cancelled the meeting instead. Cancelled the meeting and yelled at Raoul about his choice of hat. It was something Grace would have to patch up later.

She and Ed had been so careful. It was all Grace could think, over and over, on the flight back to Australia a few days later: we were so careful, we were so careful. Until she remembered that about a month ago she'd had food poisoning. Two days afterwards Grace had been on her way out to a fancy dinner thing and Ed, dishevelled and with flecks of paint in his hair, wandered into their room when she was getting dressed. He hadn't said anything, only tilted his head to the side while he looked at her in the black silk slip dress. It was fortunate that Henry was fully occupied downstairs watching *Toy Story*.

Grace had had nightmares about falling pregnant a second time. Proper nightmares in which she yelled out and cried and woke herself up. She couldn't go through it again; she didn't have time to lose her mind. It was Nish who suggested that maybe it would be okay. 'Eighty percent of your brain cells are new now,' Nish said. 'I read about how cells regenerate every five years or something so you basically become a new person.'

'I don't think that's true.'

But when Grace was home, sitting on the toilet lid while Henry had a bath, watching as he built little bubble mounds along the edge and gave them all names, Grace wondered if this was her chance. A second chance. A chance to get it right. All the times she had held him as a baby and felt nothing; those lost, wasted times never to be recaptured. Never to be done over. Now, when Grace saw new mothers gazing with adoration at their newborns it undid something inside her, so that she felt pain might flood out. This was a chance to carry the tiny precious impossible thing within her, when all she had to do to keep the little one safe was breathe and put one foot in front of the other.

Besides, as Grace walked the streets of London that spring, she could feel the girl already asserting herself within, coiled energy. *I'm here, lady. Get ready.*

May was a force.

This time would be different. And it was, she made it so. Grace divorced herself of emotion as she stepped back from her senior operations management role to minimise her travel time. All she had to do was focus on her family. And Ada.

37

2020

DOROTHY. ON THE PHONE WHEN GRACE WAS TRYING TO MAKE DINNER.

'Are you watching the news?'

'No. I'm trying to make dinner.'

'I thought you might be. Well, this terrible bat disease is spreading. There are cases here now. Did you see that?'

'No, I'm making dinner.'

'I just thought that you might have seen it on Facebook or something.'

'You shouldn't get your news from Facebook.'

'I didn't. I'm getting it from the television and I'm very concerned.'

'Can I call you later?'

'Aren't you supposed to be going back to the UK soon? I think you should reconsider. Pamela said they might close the borders. You might not be able to get back into the country.'

'Mum, they're never going to stop citizens coming back. They just won't.'

'I wouldn't be so sure. They've done it in other places. If they close the borders you won't be able to get back to Ed and the children in god knows how long. Could be years.'

'You're being very dramatic.'

'You have to call the airline and see what they say.'

'I'm not sure Qantas, or Pamela, is in charge of border control, Mum. I need to drain the pasta. Bye.'

A week later Grace was in the baggage check-in line. Only two people on the desk. The borders wouldn't be closed. That was a ridiculous idea. Yes, the US had done it, but they were nuts. Or just in possession of valuable information about what this virus was going to do next, as if it were a Hollywood madman holding the world and all its airlines and travel plans hostage. No. The US was in reality under the control of a madman and by no means to be used as a barometer for anything.

The woman behind the counter was smiling at Grace; it was her turn.

Grace apologised and turned away, exiting the queue. Dorothy would be unbearably smug when she found out.

◎

The worldwide lockdowns that ensued felt like a line of dominoes: the first one was pushed and the long line of others followed in collapse. China, Italy, France, Spain, the UK. On and on it went through March. Tony was on the phone; Ada was on the phone. Grace was soon spending large portions of every evening in frantic Zoom meetings with Tony trying to work out how to deal with the multiple artists who were already on tour, having venue after venue close down. Then there were the ones who were scheduled to drop albums, the ones scheduled to go on tour, the media commitments, the studios that were booked and musicians who couldn't get to them. She attempted to adjust her circadian rhythm so she could work through the night.

Grace constantly scoured the updates about various border closures and shifting travel laws in the UK, trying to get some idea of how and when she could get to London to help Tony put out the fires that were springing up everywhere. If Ed happened to walk past she would snap her laptop shut so he wouldn't know.

When Sydney went into its first lockdown Grace felt as if she were trapped in a garbage compressor, the walls slowly closing in on her. Soon there would be no room for her to breathe.

She tried to set the kids up at home as well as possible. She ordered a large set of rock-climbing holds to affix to the wall outside, so that the kids would have the necessary equipment for when they began literally climbing the walls. (Grace made sure to never mention to Nish the vast array of outdoor recreational facilities her kids had access to during lockdown. Even still, Nish regularly made a point of saying to Grace that being confined to an enormous five-bedroom home with a heated swimming pool and media room hardly qualified as being in 'lockdown'. 'Cry me a fucking river,' were her exact words.)

The alternative timeline, the one that existed in a parallel universe without Covid, was always in Grace's mind. Beyond that she imagined all the events—the strategising, the marketing campaigns, the HR manoeuvres—that she was no longer a part of since the downsizing of her role. She imagined them while doing routine things: helping May into socks and gumboots for a puddle search, Grace would feel the softness of her daughter's exquisite little feet, listen to her singing 'Puddle feet, puddle feet, where are ew?' (a song May had invented so she could be like Aunty Ada) and wonder if it would be worth trading these small moments for the experience of being back among it all in London. Absolutely not, she assured herself. On the occasions when May would refuse to put on socks before gumboots and scream in frustration when her little feet would inevitably get stuck in them, Grace's feelings were more complicated.

One night, while she was brushing her teeth, Ed leaned on the bathroom wall with his hands in his pockets and watched her. 'Waa?' she asked through a mouthful of toothpaste.

'I'm a terrible person,' he said.

She spat and rinsed. 'Oh yeah?'

'Because there's a pandemic, but I'm thrilled that you are here with me all the time.'

'Is that so?'

He raised an eyebrow. Mischievous grin.

'The kids asleep?' she asked.

'Absolutely.'

During the moments that followed this exchange, Grace didn't think of her hypothetical life once.

And then it was over and Ed was asleep. Grace couldn't allow herself to drift off. She had a call with Ada scheduled in fifteen minutes.

38

SINGAPORE, 2021

WHEN GRACE WAS AWOKEN BY THE KNOCK ON HER DOOR, SHE THOUGHT she was lying in bed beside Ed. She waited for him to stir the way he always did at the slightest sound from Henry or May in the night. He didn't stir because he wasn't there. And this night-time request wasn't his responsibility anyway.

'Grace? Are you awake?'

Yes. Yes, she was now awake thanks to Ada's persistence. Weren't these rooms supposed to be sound-proof? Grace was sure she had read something like that when she made the booking. Sound-proof was perfect for Ada when she was on edge and needed her sleep. Perfect for Grace when she needed to deny that she had heard Ada trying to wake her up in the night.

'Grace? Please. Please. I don't know what to do.'

Didn't know what to do about what? The blister on her heel that was keeping her awake? The lack of fresh green juices on the room service menu?

Grace opened the door and found Ada wild-eyed and hugging a Gucci silk robe around herself. Ada burst into tears. Precisely timed for full impact.

'I don't know what to do.'

'Hmm?'

Ada held the glowing screen of her mobile up for Grace to see. It showed a paparazzi shot of Ada emerging from St Pancras Chambers, glowering into the camera with a particularly disdainful expression.

'That's me going to Tesco's, got nothing to do with anything. Nothing. They just chose that shot 'cause I look like a right cow.'

'Can we talk about this in the morning?'

'Read the headline!'

Love Rat Ada Breaks Hubby's Heart.

'Okay. We've talked about this before. People are going to keep coming up with this crap. It's what they do for a living. This is the same old shit.'

Ada sniffed and dabbed the tip of her pinky under her eye. 'Scroll down.'

Beneath the headline and the photograph was another grainy image of Ada locked in a kiss with a man who was not her husband.

'Ada. For frig's sake—'

'You know who sent it to me?'

'No. I do not know who sent it to you.'

'Susie. So she's about as pissed off with me as you can imagine.'

'When did this happen?'

'A week ago. That *Vanity Fair* party I didn't want to go to. I told you this tour was too long. This is what happens when I'm tired and lonely.'

'You've been bleeding money in Covid. We had no choice about the tour—'

'I told you and you didn't listen, did you. Now my family is fallin' apart like nobody's business.'

'We'll discuss it in the morning.'

'Don't talk to me like that! Like I'm a kid! I told you the tour was too long.'

'Ada, this is not my fault. You fucked up. Not me. I'm not here to hold your hand every second so you don't make stupid choices.'

'What the fuck *are* you here for then?'

'I'm not talking about this now.'

Ada was pointing a finger at Grace, mascara running down her cheeks. 'Yes, we are talking about this now because Charlie has already texted me to say he's not meeting us in LA. He's having the locks changed instead.'

Grace was annoyed about the mascara. She had told the make-up girl to remove every skerrick before Ada went back to the hotel. Grace would need to have a word with her in the morning—nice girl but a bit thick. Evidently.

'So you need to call him right now,' Ada said.

'No. I'm going to bed.' Grace closed the door in Ada's face.

Ada was pounding on the door. Grace put in her earplugs but they failed to drown out the hysterical woman. She went to the door and opened it.

'Don't you dare close the door in my face!' Ada squealed. 'I'm paying you three million just for Singapore. Don't you dare!'

'Let me go to bed or I quit. Here and now, I'm done.'

Ada's anger vanished and her eyes widened in genuine panic. 'No, no, Grace. You can't. No!'

'Then let me go to sleep. Call your husband yourself.'

The next day. A fitting for the MTV Awards in two weeks' time. Because of Ada's tight tour schedule, a Japanese designer had been selected, someone who was doing extraordinary things with pleated sleeves. (Gucci had offered to fly a team into Singapore for a fitting, but Ada said anyone could wear Gucci.) Getting Ada out of bed was a challenge and, yes, Ada cried throughout the very late breakfast and also in the car to the designer's studio. But she was still functioning enough to do what needed to be done.

Ed's name lit up on Grace's phone.

'Mum's got Covid,' Ed said. 'She got conjunctivitis and had to go to a pharmacy. That's where we think she got it. I'm pissed off with Dad—he should have gone for her.'

Although Joan had been free of cancer for years, the doctors felt her past illness had made her more vulnerable. So far it was only a runny nose and scratchy throat, Ed told Grace, just as Ian had told him. She was to monitor herself for worsening symptoms at home.

'Try not to worry,' Grace said, a useless thing to say.

'I wish you were here.' It wasn't only his dad Ed was pissed off with, Grace could tell.

'I didn't know this would happen.'

'Nobody knows when this shit happens. That's why I wish you hadn't gone over there in the first place.'

Grace left Ada with the seamstress and walked into an adjoining room. 'I won't go to the awards,' she said. 'I'll come home.'

'You'll have to be in hotel quarantine for two weeks.'

'At least I'll be in the country.'

She heard Ed's sigh over the phone. 'I'll call you later.'

◎

In a cab now, and Dorothy on the phone. 'I just don't understand any of it,' she said. 'Joan is in excellent shape. She had an exercise bike set up at home! And a doctor on television said he saw a young man fit as a fiddle pass away. What exactly are we supposed to take from that? Am I to stop running?'

'Please don't stop running!' Warren shouted in the background.

'Honestly, the sooner everyone stops banging on with their theories and actually finds a cure the better.'

'I think theorising is a vital step in finding that cure, Mum.'

'Well, they need to get on with it because my roots are showing; I've never needed to see a hairdresser so desperately in my life. Pamela thinks that if everyone increases their vitamin C intake we'll be right as rain. Although that's probably the Valium talking. I wouldn't mention it to Joan.'

There was no time to mention anything to Joan, even if Grace hadn't been on the other side of the world. Twelve hours later Ed messaged Grace to say that Joan had gone to hospital. Just as a precaution.

Grace booked a flight leaving for Sydney at the same time as Ada's flight to LA. She didn't tell her till they were at the airport, a surprise ripping off of the band-aid.

'You can't leave me like this,' said Ada, wide-eyed. 'I'm falling apart. How can you ambush me with this now? I'm supposed to get on a stage tomorrow night!'

'Lila will take care of you.'

It was like dropping a child off at day care; Grace had to turn around and walk away without looking back.

The next day, Grace was walking through the arrivals terminal in Sydney when she saw the headline on morning television: *Ada Black Onstage Meltdown.* The footage—taken on somebody's mobile phone—showed Ada mumbling into the microphone and then swearing, really letting loose at the crowd, calling them all sorts of things, most of which were bleeped out for the broadcast. The tirade only ended when several security guards escorted Ada from the stage.

◎

Grace was in the quarantine hotel when Joan died.

She imagined what Ed looked like as he told her this, his voice cracking with grief over the phone line. There would be a crumpling of his frame. He would be too agitated with it to sit down. Maybe he paused as he tried to pace through the terrible words. Maybe he held on to the doorframe when he should have been able to hold on to her.

He hadn't been able to say goodbye to his mother; only Ian had been allowed in to visit her. This woman, the one who had birthed the person Grace loved most in the world, had died without her children present. Even Joan, who didn't appear to be afraid of anything, ever, would have been terrified.

Grace couldn't pinpoint exactly when she had last seen her own mother in person.

PART FIVE

I'm Going to Cause You Chaos, I'm Going to Rule Your Heart

39

GRACE

LATE MARCH 2022

A WEEK BEFORE GRACE WAS DUE TO TAKE THE KIDS TO VISIT HER PARENTS, and a week after she'd made her impromptu Lotus acquisition, Grace opened her front door to find Dorothy on her doorstep. She was holding a large garment bag.

'What are you doing here?' Grace said.

'Good afternoon to you too! Are you going to let me in?' Dorothy asked.

'What are you doing here?'

Dorothy was wearing a floral dress and eggshell blue trench coat. Her hair was freshly coiffed. 'I was in the city and thought I'd drop by.'

'Why were you in the city?'

'Are you going to let me in?'

Grace had been working at the kitchen bench, emails mostly. She had an office space upstairs, it had a big window looking out over the harbour. She could even see the bridge. Living alone in a place like this was like going to the movies on your own, watching a funny scene and turning to laugh with the person next to you, only to be reminded that you were on your own, that there was no one to share it with. And Grace sure as hell didn't deserve to have it all to herself. So Grace worked at the kitchen bench instead, hunched on a stool. She bought a fit ball to try to help with her posture, but she never used it.

During the weeks when Grace didn't have the kids she didn't tidy up. She sat surrounded by her children's empty cereal bowls, crumbs, smears of Vegemite on the Caesarstone. A reminder that she wouldn't be on her own too long. They would be tumbling back into the house that afternoon, full of requests and grievances, sticky hands (May) and thoughtful reflections on a week with their dad (Henry). It was Grace's plan to tidy all of it up before Ed dropped them home.

Grace didn't want to let Dorothy in. One of Dorothy's favourite sayings was that the state of a person's home reflected their state of mind. Grace had a number of issues with this assertion, none of which she felt like discussing. But Dorothy had travelled three hours to be here. She was also Grace's mother.

'Would you like me to take off my shoes?' Dorothy said, eyeing the pile of shoes in the foyer, none of which were on the shoe rack.

'No. Whatever. I don't mind.'

'I think I'll leave them on.'

'Why were you in the city?'

Dorothy followed Grace into the house.

'I had an appointment,' she said.

'What appointment?'

'Aren't you the busy bee today?'

'Mum, why would you need an appointment in Sydney?'

'It's nothing.'

'Are you okay?' Grace asked.

'Fine.'

Through the entrance hall and into the living/kitchen/dining. Dorothy stopped dead in her tracks. 'Good grief. I thought you had a nanny. Doesn't she clean? Is she ill?'

'Yes.'

'Are the children not with Ed this week?'

Grace was a terrible liar, but she had no way of explaining why she was prepared to live in squalor while her children were away. 'There was a change of plans and, well, this morning's been hectic, Zoom meetings back to back . . . How do you know whose week it is? Or is meant to be?'

'I talk to Ed!' Dorothy said.

'Do you want a cup of tea? Coffee?'

Dorothy's eyes were still on the carnage in the kitchen. 'No. I had a coffee in town.'

'What was the appointment, Mum? Was it a doctor?'

'Of sorts.'

'Are you okay?'

'I told you, I'm fine! I had an appointment and I thought I'd pop in and drop this off.'

She held up the garment bag. It was for a dress. Long. Dorothy went into the living room and laid the garment bag on the couch. She then cast her eyes around the room: toys on the floor, articles of the kids' clothing still in the spot where they had first been discarded.

'Shall we sit outside?' she suggested. 'It's such a lovely day.'

'What is that?' Grace asked, gesturing to the bag.

'I was doing a bit of a clean-out. It was in your old wardrobe.'

'I'm coming to stay in a week. Why not give it to me then?'

'This way you don't have to squeeze it into the car. And I was passing through.'

Grace recognised the bag now. 'Wow. This might be the most manipulative thing you've ever done.'

'Oh, shush. I don't have an ulterior motive. I've been very clear in what I think; I hardly need to resort to devious strategies. It was in the wardrobe and I need the space for my coats. I'll have a glass of water, if you don't mind, I'm quite parched.'

Outside, Ed's studio was locked, curtains drawn the way they had been for the last two months.

'Wherever does he paint now?' Dorothy asked.

'He rents a studio in Alexandria.'

'Surely he could still use his studio! He loves it. Such a shame to have to *rent*.'

'He doesn't want to use his studio.'

Dorothy stopped walking and turned to face Grace. 'Is this still a break? You both told me it was a break and, while I don't understand how it is possible to take a break from a marriage, I am rather holding on to the hope of its impermanence.'

'I don't want to talk about this.'

'Fine. Gosh, your tomato vine's going great guns, isn't it?'

Dorothy perched on a chair and put on a pair of oversized dark sunglasses. She was Anna Wintour at a runway show.

'I like those,' said Grace.

'Thank you! They're Dolce and Gabbana! Your father says I look like Andy Warhol. I don't think he knows what Andy Warhol looks like.'

'Why were you seeing a doctor?'

'I've decided to have some things done.'

'What does that mean?'

Dorothy took off her sunglasses and placed them in her lap. She put her fingers to her temples and lifted the skin, widening her eyes.

'A little lift. Just a little.'

'You're joking.'

'I'm not joking and one day you will understand.'

◎

Later, when Dorothy and her face lift plans had departed and Grace was again alone in the silent house, she stood and looked down on the dress bag. It was like a heavy ghost taking a nap on her couch. The Ghost of Weddings Past. Grace had never felt as beautiful as she had when she wore that dress. Was she supposed to feel ashamed of that? Ashamed of the pleasure she took in feeling beautiful that day? If you're not allowed to feel beautiful on your wedding day, when were you allowed to feel beautiful? There were so many rules about what you were and weren't supposed to feel as a woman it was difficult to keep track.

Upstairs in the bedroom Grace unzipped the bag and took out the dress. It wasn't silk—although she had been able to afford silk by the time she got married—but it was a very good polyester imitation. Dorothy had insisted on paying for it and really Grace didn't care as much about what it was made out of as she did how it looked. And it looked gorgeous. Floor-length and bias cut with various panels in the skirt, like a twenties ballgown. Cap sleeves of filigree lace embellished with crystals, like icicles falling from her shoulders.

'You look like Daisy from *Gatsby*,' Ed had told her.

'Is that a good thing?'

'It is as long as I don't get shot at the end.'

'Spoiler alert.'

Grace undressed. It was a shame she was wearing a sports bra but she couldn't be arsed changing it. It wasn't like anyone was going to see her. She gathered up the silky fabric and pulled on the dress. It was tricky to get it over her shoulders (had she missed another zipper somewhere?) but, with a bit of wriggling and gentle tugging, eventually she was in. She shimmied the dress down her torso and let the fabric fall from her hips. It was tighter, pulling awkwardly around her bum in a way she definitely didn't remember. And her boobs were different now, bigger. (Not necessarily better.) But it was fine in the waist. Totally fine. She took in her reflection in the full-length mirror. Her sports bra wasn't doing her any favours but she still looked good.

So it was time to take it off. Wasn't it? What else was she supposed to do? Post a picture on Instagram? *Still got it!* Maybe she could just sit and have a cup of tea. Grace checked her watch. Four twenty-five.

Shit.

◎

It wouldn't come off.

She had it up over her torso, bending over and trying to narrow her shoulders like she was preparing to dive into a pool, the dress half off, falling over her head and pooling on the carpet. It was stuck somewhere between her shoulders and her boobs. She tugged, gently, gently. She really did not want to rip a seam. This was ridiculous. She was ridiculous. And now for reasons which probably would have been obvious to anyone she was crying. Trapped inside the Ghost of Weddings Past and blubbering like an idiot.

She heard the front door open. May and Henry in the foyer, dumping their bags, kicking off shoes. 'Mum?'

She always met them at the door. Ed never came in; sometimes he wouldn't even make eye contact.

'Mum?'

'Mum?'

'Grace?'

Okay. So. This was very bad. She straightened up. But now the dress wouldn't come back down over her chest. She couldn't get out, she couldn't get in.

'Grace?!'

'Where's Mum?' Henry asked his dad. He sounded scared.

'MUM!!!!' May screamed.

'May, stop,' Ed said. 'That's way too much.'

'We need to find her!'

'Grace?'

Grace opened the bedroom door a crack. 'Ed?'

'Mum!'

'No! Please, May. Stay down there. I'm fine. Just stay down there. Ed? Can you come up here?'

The front door closed. Ed was on the stairs. The familiar rhythm of his footsteps now at the bedroom door.

'Grace?'

The concern in his voice made the tears worse.

'Don't come in yet!'

'Right. What is happening here?'

'I'm stuck. I need help.'

'You're stuck?'

'Please don't say anything.'

'What would I say? Why aren't I allowed to talk?'

'Come in, but I don't want to talk about it.'

She opened the door and turned away. 'I wanted to see if it still fitted. I can't get it off. This is not a scheme. I am genuinely stuck. As you can see.'

'Am I allowed to talk?'

'No. I'm going to bend over and try to pull it over my head. I need you to try to slide it over my shoulders.'

So he did. And the whole time he didn't say a word.

She was freed. Standing there in her sports bra and the undies she really should have chucked out a long time ago. Ed was holding the dress. He looked away and handed it to her.

'Different experience from last time,' he said.

40

ED

THE KITCHEN WAS A BOMB SITE. GRACE MUST HAVE GONE AWAY FOR the week and hadn't tidied up before she left. Amid the chaos, May and Henry were raiding the pantry in search of snacks. Ed knew he should tell the kids not to open the Twisties and instead have a piece of fruit, but he'd just helped Grace out of her wedding dress and right now he couldn't think of what he might say.

Ed knew more about Grace than he knew about anyone else. He knew she hated green tea. She liked Earl Grey, the bag left in, a touch of milk. He knew she liked her toast lightly toasted. (Any more and she would try to sneak it into the bin without him seeing. He usually saw.) Bright sunlight made her sneeze. She always woke up snotty in April and May, but never in spring. She always ignored the dosage instructions for paracetamol, said it was more of a guide. (It wasn't.) She hated having her feet touched or her neck kissed. She got terrible dermatitis behind her ears if she didn't dry them properly after a shower. She liked to shower morning and night. Even though money was not an issue she hated spending it on socks or bath towels. She had a terrible weakness for houseplants, but he was the one who watered them. And the cars. Shit, all the cars. It was bizarre. Her old '68 Lotus was the favourite of all the cars she'd ever owned. An absolute death trap. He'd been relieved when someone rear-ended it at a roundabout and that was the end of that. Written off. She'd searched for months for another one and eventually found a replacement but it had black leather upholstery and she preferred tan. Also a sticky clutch. She tried to get along with it for three months, but the spark wasn't there, apparently, so she sold it to an old guy called George whom she met at the park. Gave it to him for ten grand because he really liked Lotuses, she said, but he wouldn't take it for free. She believed that all people should have access to the things that brought them joy.

This was the tiniest fraction of what he knew about her.

Yet he didn't know where she'd been that week. And with who.

Seeing her in that dress had broken him apart.

The kids had run outside now, Slinky scampering after them, yapping with glee. Ed called after them to say goodbye, but they kept running, the dog's barking drowning out Ed's voice. He let them go. He had to get some things from the garage anyway. He would slip out afterwards and save himself, Henry and May the ordeal of goodbye. Henry would stand silently looking at the floor, and when Ed told Henry he loved him, Henry would nod and mutter that he loved Ed too, as if it required all his energy to hold it together and he had nothing left. Ed knew his son's internal world so well that he could paint it. May, on the other hand, would grip Ed's arm, pulling at him with all her might, determination ablaze in her eyes. That look. God, that look. When Ed first held his newborn daughter May had locked her eyes onto his in a way which wasn't supposed to be possible with newborns. A look so familiar to him. A look he had been enchanted by ever since the night Grace got herself stuck in a pub toilet.

I'm going to cause you chaos. I'm going to rule your heart.

Ed had a friend, Omar, who was a sculptor. He did fugly porcelain human forms and busts in garish colours. He made a lot of money with them, and while they weren't the kind of thing Ed was into, he could see how good they were, he could see why Omar was so successful. The trouble with Omar was that when he was happy and content, usually because he was in a stable relationship, his work wasn't as good.

Grace had talked about a similar thing with her musicians. That had been back in London, before Henry. After Henry was born, in those hazy months when the jubilation of his son's birth was complicated by the terror of Grace's unravelling, Ed had worked so, so much. It helped Grace to know that he wasn't far away, just out in his studio in the garden. Or at least he had thought it helped Grace. She never said; she hadn't spoken to him much at all during that time. If he was just out the back in his studio he could always wander inside every now and again to check on Grace and Henry. 'Check for what?' Ravi had asked him over the phone. Check they were okay, he supposed. Although it was clear as soon as Henry was born that Grace wasn't okay. It got to the point where he dreaded leaving the studio and going into the house.

But the paintings he did at the time were good. He'd never had so much confidence in his work, ever. Now, since he had left her, life was so much worse. Everything he did—getting out of bed, buying groceries, moving through his stupid empty apartment—felt like swimming in dark water. The only thing that felt right was painting.

◎

The sleeping bags were not on the bottom garage shelf where they should have been. Nor were the bedrolls, the cooker or the tent.

Grace's voice startled him.

'What are you looking for?'

'Everything. Nothing's where it should be.'

'I haven't moved it.'

Ed didn't respond.

'Where are you camping?' She was nervous. He was so attuned to her he could almost match his heart rate with hers.

'Nowhere if I can't find the gear.'

Grace pulled the ladder down from the ceiling and climbed up into the roof cavity. She was wearing a skirt. He looked away from her legs.

'It's up here!' she said. 'We moved it before all the rain. You were worried . . .'

About the garage flooding. He remembered now.

Grace came halfway down the ladder and passed him the bag with the tent inside. 'Careful, it's heavy,' she said.

'I can grab the rest,' he said. Grace came down. He expected her to go back into the house but she stood there in her skirt and bare legs, watching him.

'So where are you going?'

'Euroka Clearing. There'll be lots of kangaroos.'

'Oh, nice. Here . . .' She held out her hands and took the sleeping bags from him.

'Is it still okay if I get the kids Sunday night? I'll wait until after dinner. You don't mind only having one night at your mum's with them?'

'Ed, Dorothy just delivered my wedding dress. She is in full flight. One night is my limit.'

Grace walked out to Ed's car and tossed the sleeping bags in the back. She waited while he rearranged them.

'Okay, well . . . See you next Sunday.'

She was still standing there after he closed the boot. 'Ed, can we just . . . This is horrible.'

He felt like someone had him by the throat, squeezing his larynx. 'I can't talk about this right now.'

'I'd like to.'

'I know it's horrible,' he said. 'But . . .'

She looked so sad. Beyond sad.

He tried to look her right in the eye as he spoke. 'But I was already lonely even before I left . . .'

You, he wanted to say.

'All this . . .' Ed made a big gesture with his hands, encircling the house and Grace. 'I've been miserable for a long time, waiting for you to—'

'I love you,' she said.

'Do you?'

'Ed.'

'Have some mercy, for god's sake. Just leave me be. I'll see you Sunday night.'

He got in the car. Closed the door. Backed out of the driveway, the automatic gate sliding open on cue. It was only as he was driving away, leaving her in the rear-view, that he let the pain leave his body and cried like a child.

41
GRACE

APRIL 2022

GRACE COULD SEE THE INTENSITY GROWING WITHIN TRENT. HE HAD A beautiful face, even more so now he was older. When she saw Ed's face for the first time, it was Trent's face she compared it with. The door of the toilet stall had opened, and she'd been underwhelmed after all that time they'd spent chatting. What a stupid, shallow thing to feel. How immature she'd been. Ignoring this initial reaction, listening to Nish's voice of reason by allowing herself to open up to Ed, had been one of the best decisions she'd ever made. Whenever she signed a young musician, she wondered about Trent—it was a reflex she couldn't shake. Many musicians can write one good song. Many could write five. Had those songs of his, which she hadn't heard in years, been as good as she remembered? Years in the industry had taught Grace that good wasn't enough. Good would perhaps reap a few thousand streams, but it wouldn't sell out a tour. To really get somewhere required flawless excellence. Was that what Trent had? Or was it a beautiful face and the ability to take a girl (any girl), say the right things, look her in the eye like she was the only woman alive and sweep her off her feet?

'Why aren't you okay?' Trent held her in his soft gaze.

It was very late now; Grace felt like she was fading out and back into the low light of the room. 'Poor sad little rich girl,' she said. 'That's the story, right? Ever notice how there's no poor little rich boy cliché?'

'Ha. No. Why are you sad?'

'I'm not sad.'

'I don't want to be creepy when I ask you this, I'm genuinely interested: is there a Mr Grace?'

'There was.'

'I'm sorry. I'm genuinely sorry. That sucks.'

'You're using the word "genuinely" a lot.'

'It does make me sound creepy, doesn't it?'

Across the room, the faded rugby star was jabbing at a pokie machine while his friends, beers in hand, guffawed.

'Yes.'

'How long were you together?' Trent asked.

The rugby star was making a show of slapping the side of the machine in frustration. His wedding ring glinted in the light. He probably had children asleep somewhere, put to bed by his wife—whoever she was.

'I'd rather not say. Longer than you and Shaleah.'

He laughed. 'That's not hard.' And then, quietly, staring into his beer. 'Tell me he didn't stand you up at the airport. Rookie error, that one.'

Grace hadn't talked to anyone about what had happened between her and Ed. She had no one to tell. Grace opened her mouth because she was beginning to feel that if she didn't talk soon to someone, anyone, she would implode.

'I nearly got married,' Trent said, cutting her off. 'Her name was Melinda. She was great. We . . . She was great. I didn't get married because I didn't feel the way I felt with you. And yes, say we were just kids or whatever. But I didn't realise how extraordinary you were and I'm sad to hear that you were with someone who didn't see that either.'

He was wrong. Ed had thought she was extraordinary. Once.

'I think I wanted to see you tonight because I need you to validate the years I've spent trying to make music that counts,' he said. 'And to tell you that I know now how full of my own shit I was back then. I didn't realise that what we had doesn't come along again. That people chase that magic their entire lives.'

Grace's career had put her in the same room as people her teenage self would never have dreamed she would meet. It was thrilling until it became normal, once she understood that she had earned her right to be there. She was doing a job and doing it extremely well. After a few years she got used to most of the celebrities and didn't think there could be anyone who could truly make her giddy. Sure, there were encounters that were surreal, interactions that she would remember forever, but she no longer felt in awe or unable to be herself rather than a dazed fan. Until one night, when she had been at a Rock and Roll Hall of Fame induction. She could no longer remember who was being inducted, but it didn't matter because at a table nearby sat one of the legendary Canyon artists she'd yabbered on to her friends about when she was a teenager. Graham Nash. He was old now, of course. In his seventies. To Grace his age was irrelevant. What mattered was the way she had felt when she first heard a song of his—'Better Days'. Seventeen years old, sitting in front of the record player Dorothy had tried to replace with a CD system, Grace had listened to the opening bars: a simple piano chord sequence with Nash's vocals.

Fine. Nothing remarkable.

Then, within a perfect, breathless beat, the bass, drums and guitar kicked in.

The sound was warm honey, golden syrup. Light in an amber glass. When she heard it Grace knew that she could love any man who could conceive of that exquisite moment and bring it into the world—she could love that person forever. She never acknowledged it to herself, but it was what she had felt when she looked at Ed's painting for the first time. It was colour and shape that he had pulled out from within him and laid bare.

Trent leaned closer across the table. 'The magic of us was right there in front of me and I was too stupid to know,' he said. 'It's why I've written about love over and over.'

All the ice in Suki's Sunrise had melted. The faded rugby star and his bloated mates had gone. Trent and Grace were the only ones left other than the morose kid stacking schooners from the dishwasher. He couldn't have been more than twenty.

'I should go,' said Grace. 'I should have gone hours ago.'

◎

Trent started the ignition. He fiddled around with his phone and 'Go Your Own Way' soon flooded through the speakers. Mick Fleetwood's drums kicked in and Trent turned to face Grace with a wicked grin. He bobbed his head to the beat. 'It's your legacy to me,' he shouted over the music. He put his hand to his heart. 'The Mac. So good. It keeps me going, I tell you.'

On the drive back, Trent negotiated the bends at a very responsible speed and Grace watched the black sky through the windshield. The track finished and a song by a different band came on. She knew it. The band had put out an excellent debut album. Their new track was going to drop in the following month and Grace knew it was awful and the cause of much stress for Tony. For now, though, they were a promising new act. Fresh and clear-eyed.

Trent pulled into Dorothy and Warren's driveway. Dorothy had left the porch light on.

'Thanks for letting me spend time with you,' Trent said.

The look on his face gave Grace the panicked thought that he might try to kiss her. He took his right hand from the steering wheel. Paused. Grace felt around for the doorhandle.

'I hope everything works out,' he said instead. 'I know that sounds a bit lame.' He rubbed his palm on his thighs.

'It does. But thank you.'

'You're so welcome.'

Grace got out of the car. Before she walked away she opened the van door again and Trent's face lit up.

'You know that song, "Go Your Own Way", it's not about freedom. Everyone thinks it's about doing what you want and being yourself, but if you listen to the lyrics, really listen, you'll hear that it's not.'

◎

Dorothy was awake. She was lying on the couch with her feet up and a cushion under her head, reading. Grace had never seen her do something so relaxed as putting her feet on the couch. When Dorothy looked up, Grace thought she saw alarm in her expression.

'Are you okay?' was Dorothy's first question.

'Fine.'

Dorothy sat up. With her make-up off and her hair messy from the pillow she looked something Grace never thought her mother would be: old.

'Oh, that's a relief,' Dorothy said. 'Well, I don't mind if you want to talk about it. Or about Ed. You still haven't told me what happened. I just don't understand. It must have been something awful . . .'

'Do you remember when Nish came to visit?'

'Yes, I remember.' Dorothy gave Grace a look. 'Without Ravi.'

'Yes.'

'Ed wouldn't. No, I won't believe it.' Then she put a hand to her mouth. 'Good god, not you and Ravi!'

'No! Ew. I mean, he's lovely, but no. Not any of that.'

'What then? Grace?'

So Grace told her mother about what had happened at the beach.

42

FEBRUARY 2022

ONCE AUSTRALIA REOPENED FOR INTERNATIONAL TRAVEL, NISH HAD asked Grace if she would be able to help her with airfares so she could bring the kids to Australia. 'I don't like to ask,' Nish said, 'but it goes without saying that I've got no fucking money after everything. The company Ravi worked for had all its finances tied up in cruise line shares or some shit, so he was out of work for months. He can't come with. No holiday leave. But me mum is desperate to see the kids.'

Nish wanted to take her kids to the beach, almost as soon as they arrived. The weather wasn't ideal—overcast and windy—but Nish was determined to give her kids the full Australian experience. 'Everything I used to do,' she said.

'Except the acid?'

'That was once, Grace.'

And apparently the short walk from Grace's house to Taylors Bay wasn't the Full Australian Experience. Nish wanted them to be able to swim at a 'real beach, not just some North Shore paddling pool'. It had to be iconic, she insisted, and preferably south so that they could drive over the Harbour Bridge. They'd bundled the kids and the beach paraphernalia into the Land Rover (which had seven seats, thankfully) and battled traffic across Sydney to Bronte Beach. Unfortunately Nish's kids were locked in a battle over an iPad and didn't even notice when they went over the bridge.

Ed drove around and around looking for a parking spot.

'What are all these people doing here?' Nish said. 'Don't they have jobs to go to?'

She had two boys, both of them completely off the wall, neither of them with any understanding of the words 'no', 'stop it', 'please' or 'thank you'. Grace wished they could have the opportunity to spend time with Dorothy.

'They're just boys,' Nish had said during the barbecue the night before when, after being denied a swim in the pool due to the cold and the wind, eleven-year-old Ollie had slipped outside, dragged a chair over to the pool gate, climbed up and opened it himself. His three-year-old brother was an inch from the water's edge before anyone noticed. Grace didn't feel gender was sufficient explanation for this or for when, later, Ollie let himself into the garage, found a hammer and chased Henry and May around the yard with it. Ed had had to lock the garage to keep the child out. He locked the studio too—although, Ed said, if the kid did end up taking a few sips of turps he might settle down a bit.

Now the boys were yelling and whacking each other with pool noodles as Ed attempted a reverse park. (No, he didn't want Grace to do it for him.) He asked for quiet twice before bellowing at them to, 'Shut the eff up!' May and Henry were both awed by the never-before-seen demonstration of aggression from their gentle father. He must have been very tired. (Probably something to do with the five a.m. wake-up when Sebby located the TV remote—and its volume function. 'I really wish this house had more walls,' Ed had said.)

Grace glanced in the rear-view mirror and saw Nish with a dead sort of expression on her face, gazing out the window like she hadn't even noticed. The lines around her eyes were deeper than when Grace had seen her last. It had been an age. She'd arrived the day before in her vibrant Nish way: full of hugs and smiles and sharp jokes. And wine, so much duty-free wine. Grace had tried to carve out some quiet moments with her after all the kids had gone to bed; she knew Nish had been doing work consulting with a refugee organisation in Lebanon, which was probably emotionally exhausting. When the quiet time came, and Grace asked Nish how she was doing, Nish launched into a funny story about how she'd turned up to a crisis meeting wearing her skirt inside out and hadn't even noticed until the end of the day.

Finally, after what Grace had to admit was a flawless reverse parking demonstration, they were all out of the car. Nish's hat caught in the wind and she struggled to put her sunglasses on while saving the hat—and Sebby, who had almost launched himself onto the busy road. 'Be careful,' Nish said through clenched teeth.

'Here,' Grace said, hoisting Sebby onto her hip. 'I'll take him.'

'Thank fuck for that,' Nish said.

Ed picked up the esky Nish had packed then looked at Grace, wide-eyed. 'I reckon you've got the lighter load,' he whispered.

Despite the wind, the beach was crowded and they had to trudge all the way to the far end, well beyond the flags, to find enough space for the seven of them. Soon, though, they had their own patch of sand. The kids were digging tunnels (May and Henry) and terrorising strangers (Sebby and Ollie). The sun emerged from behind the clouds. For a little while at least it could be described as pleasant.

'God, I've missed this,' said Nish as she poured another glass of prosecco.

'You never went to the beach,' said Grace.

'I know, but the idea of it. Always an option, wasn't it. On a hot day you would think, yeah, I could go a swim. Not in London. Want another?'

The half a glass Grace had drunk felt like it was already swilling around in her head. She couldn't drink on an empty stomach. Nish had gone to the shops for supplies before they left home, saying that she would take care of all the food and drinks for the day. As it turned out she felt a few boxes of sultanas for the kids, some dips, crackers and four bottles of wine for the grown-ups would be sufficient.

Sebby and Ollie grew bored with throwing pebbles at seagulls and strangers and now wanted to swim. The southerly started up again and the ocean, already awash with white water, started to turn from vaguely inviting to definitely foreboding. Ollie was pulling on Nish's arm. 'I want to go in! I want to go in!'

Henry watched on, brow furrowed. Who were these feral children with such a flagrant disregard for safety?

Nish ignored Ollie (Dr Rosie would have been impressed), sipped her wine and shouted conversation (largely one-sided) over the wind and whining.

May started pulling at Grace's arm now. 'I'm hungry! I'm hungry!'

'Maybe food will help?' suggested Grace.

'I'll get fish and chips,' said Ed, already on his feet.

'I'll come help you carry it,' said Grace. 'Will you watch the kids, Nish?'

'Of course,' Nish said.

Grace hesitated but May, placated by the prospect of chips, was digging in the sand again and Henry, darling child, was wrapped in his towel reading a book.

'Don't let them in the water,' Ed said. 'That rip's huge.'

'Of course I won't let them in the bloody water.'

As it turned out, everyone at the beach thought food would help, and Grace and Ed stood in line for ten minutes before they made it to the counter. The wind intensified and Ed wrapped his arms around Grace.

'I don't remember her being this . . .' He trailed off.

'Hmm?'

'Intense.'

'She's always been intense.'

'She's drinking a lot. A *lot*, a lot.'

'Her work is difficult right now, I think. And I'd drink too with kids like that.'

'You're a terrible person.'

'I know.'

When Ed and Grace returned with the food, Henry was helping May with her sandcastle. Sebby was back to throwing rocks. And Nish was leaning back in her chair, hat over her face.

'Food,' announced Ed.

Henry and May scrambled over.

'Nish? Food.'

Nish stirred, eventually emerging from under her hat. 'Did you get squid?'

'You didn't say you wanted any,' said Ed.

'I assumed you'd get some.'

'You could always go grab it yourself,' Ed muttered.

'Where's Ollie?' Grace asked.

'What?'

Grace looked up and down the beach. Nish was loading a napkin with fish cocktails.

'I can't see Ollie.'

Nish looked around.

Ed shook his head and focused on getting food for his own kids.

'Fuck, where is he?' Nish said. 'Ollie! Ollie!'

Sebby ran over, inadvertently kicking sand all over the chips. Ed was doing an excellent job of keeping his irritation contained.

'Ollie!' Nish got to her feet. She headed to the shoreline. *'Ollie!'*

It was then that Grace saw the little boy, out beyond the whitewater, his head disappearing and reappearing as the waves rolled.

Nish started screaming.

Two lifeguards began sprinting down the beach; another, out in the water, was approaching on a jet ski. Ed pulled his t-shirt off over his head. 'Quicker to go in at the rocks,' he said.

Grace grabbed hold of his arm. 'No. Ed, you'll kill yourself.'

'I've got it.'

'Please. I'm asking you not to go in. Please.'

He was sprinting away from her now, the lifeguards following. Grace watched as her husband bolted over the rocks; he must have been looking for somewhere to go in. The waves were towering, thundering down. Exploding. Grace ran along the shoreline after Ed. Screamed at him not to go in. But he was. Splashing and hauling himself through the water. So this was how it would happen—this was how she would lose him.

The waves kept on interrupting her line of sight. One minute she could see Ed and the boy, the next moment a wave would rise up blocking her view. They rose and fell, rose and fell. She was aware of May next to her, screaming. And Henry, silent. Grace couldn't see Ed anymore, couldn't see either of them. The jet ski announced itself with a grinding shriek and Grace watched it jumping over the waves. Another lifeguard was onboard, pulling Ollie to safety. Where was Ed?

There was a dinghy out in the water now. One of those red inflatable things. For Grace, everything fell silent as she watched. The waves kept rolling, again and again. She couldn't see Ed.

It was a long time before the dinghy headed back towards the shore, scudding and leaping over the enormous waves. Grace didn't even know they had Ed until she saw the lifeguards hauling him out and laying him on the sand.

She had no conscious recollection of sprinting over to him, but now she was on her knees in the sand beside him while one lifeguard rolled Ed onto his side. He was dead, Grace was sure of it. He was lost to her. What would she trade? If that was what was required to save Ed's life, to have him back with her, what would she trade? The kids? If there was a God (she presumed that's who she was negotiating with) would He/She/They accept that she wasn't willing to trade her children's lives for her husband's? Could she still get him back? Anything else. She'd give up her parents, her home, sunshine, water, music, laughter. All of that just to have Ed be okay.

Yes.

All of that.

All of that for Ed.

He started coughing, spluttering.

Alive.

◎

Nish was sitting in the back of an ambulance with Sebby on her lap. Ollie—wrapped in a silvery foil blanket—sat beside her, swinging his legs back and forth.

'They're going to take Ollie to hospital to check his lungs,' Nish said to Grace. 'He seems fine, but it's best to be safe.'

'Yep,' Grace said. 'Best to be safe.' She had come over to see if Nish wanted her to take Sebby. She found herself searching Nish's face for any sign of contrition.

'Ed okay?' Nish asked.

'He's okay.'

'You okay?'

'I'm fine . . . The kids are fine. You're clearly fine. Everyone is just fine. I'll talk to you later.'

Grace turned to walk back to where Ed was sitting, a towel over his shoulders, May and Henry on either side of him. A lifeguard was crouched down talking to Ed. May's little hand rested on her dad's back. Patting, comforting, like she did to her toys.

'What does that mean, *I'm clearly fine?*' Nish had followed Grace; now she stepped into her path. 'Huh? What the fuck does that mean?'

'Forget it.'

'You don't look like *you* want to forget it.'

'You were supposed to be looking after the kids.'

'I told them not to go in the water!'

'My husband nearly drowned.'

'My kid nearly drowned!'

'You've had a whole bottle of wine,' Grace whispered. 'You weren't even watching them.'

'I'm fucking jet-lagged! We don't all fly first class.'

'I offered—'

'Oh, fuck off.'

Grace refused to be pulled into Nish's vitriol. She took a deep breath. 'I think we all need space. I'll book you a room at a hotel.'

Nish grabbed Grace by the arm before she could walk away. 'I'll book my own hotel.' Nish was too loud; a group of teenagers nearby were staring. 'You think you can manage me? Put me in a little hotel room and call by when you need a laugh? Or entertainment? Or someone to cry to about your so-called stressful life? You have absolutely no idea what my life is like. No clue what anyone with a real actual important job goes through.'

'Nothing gives you the right to get so pissed that your son can wander into the ocean.'

'Do you know what I was doing last week?' Nish hissed. 'Trying to organise somewhere to bury the people who died from Covid at refugee camps in Lebanon. So parents won't have to burn the bodies of their children in a fucking pile. What do you do? Book massages for Ada Black. Good job. Don't you dare talk to me about looking after *my* kids,' Nish said. 'I do just fine. We don't all need staff to do it for us.'

Grace felt as though she had been shoved in the chest; she couldn't steady herself or recalibrate.

'You can't stand being around your family for more than five minutes,' Nish continued. 'You love being needed by a spoilt celebrity but don't give a shit about anyone else.'

It was then that Grace noticed Ed, who had come over to the ambulance to check on Ollie. He was listening to Nish's every word and saying nothing to defend Grace.

'What?' said Nish. 'It's true.'

'I think we should go,' Ed said to Grace. 'Don't make it worse than it already is.'

'How am I making it worse? She—' Grace stopped short. She knew how petulant she sounded.

Ed took her by the hand and led her away.

43

ED SAID THAT HIS WHOLE BODY WAS SORE, PROBABLY FROM THE PHYSICAL exertion involved in trying to stay alive. Grace drove the four of them home, numb, drained and replaying the events of the day and her argument with Nish over and over in her head.

'Where's Aunty Nish?' May asked.

'Are they coming back to our house?' Henry asked.

'Is the big boy going to die?'

'Ollie is not going to die. The doctors are double-checking him to be safe.'

May was satisfied with this answer and asked if there were any chips left.

'The birds ate all the chips,' Ed said.

'Are they coming back to our house?' asked Henry again.

'The birds aren't coming to our house,' Ed said.

Henry was unamused. 'Mum?'

'I don't think so. They might go and stay in a hotel for a little while.'

'Why?'

'Does their hotel have a pool?' May asked. 'Ollie shouldn't go in the pool.'

'Ollie won't go in the pool.'

'When will we see them again?' Henry asked.

'Can I just drive, please? I can't answer all the questions and deal with the traffic.'

Ed put a soft hand on her shoulder. Shushing her. 'Let Mum focus on the road,' he said. Calm. Always calm. Always reasonable. Until he went into the water after someone else's child.

Grace felt she was more in shock than Ed was. After dinner they were watching a comedy panel show and Ed had laughed at a joke that wasn't even funny. Perhaps a near drowning wasn't as much of a shock to the person who had been near-drowning. Perhaps they saw it coming. Grace assumed shock was the thing she was feeling—something residual from the panic at the beach. Disorientation. Anger? At who? Only Nish?

Grace was so tired she felt like her body was walking around on its own without herself inside it. She spent almost an hour lying beside her daughter waiting for her to go to sleep without any success. Ed took over. May was asleep within ten minutes.

Afterwards he was in the kitchen helping her tidy up even though she had insisted that there was no need.

'Have you spoken to Nish again?' Ed asked. Ever the peacemaker.

'No.'

'She could have come back here, Grace. It would have been okay.'

'You think I made the wrong decision?'

'I just—'

'Did you miss the bit when she got off her face and her kid, and by extension you, nearly drowned?'

'I didn't nearly—'

'You did. They had to pull you out of the water.'

'Yeah, but they were there in time. I took on a bit of water, that's all.'

'Why are you downplaying this?'

'She screwed up. Yes, in a big way, but I'm okay. We're all okay.'

'You nearly drowned.'

'Oh, Grace,' he said, in that way that he had: gentle, reassuring.

'You nearly died.'

'But I didn't.'

'I asked you not to go in,' said Grace. Anyone else would have cut in to defend themselves at that moment, but because Ed was Ed he didn't. He was too patient.

'It wasn't our kid,' Grace said. 'It wasn't May or Henry. You went in there without even thinking. The lifeguards got to him before you did.'

He took a moment. 'I couldn't just stand there while he drowned.'

'I asked you not to,' she repeated. 'I was so scared. May and Henry were terrified.'

He was watching her and something was happening inside him. She could tell from the way he shifted his weight from left to right. He was about to speak, but he stopped himself. Shook his head. Stepped away from her.

'I'm going to bed.'

'What were you going to say?'

'Nothing. I'm going to bed. You can't be angry with me about this, Grace. It's not fair. Not when you—'

'Do you actually believe what Nish said? She was trying to hurt me; you know she talks crap when she's angry.'

'That's not what I'm talking about.'

'Then what are you talking about?'

He walked out of the kitchen. Grace followed him to the foot of the stairs.

'I'm going to bed,' he said over his shoulder.

'Are you talking about . . .' Grace wanted to believe that he was talking about her going off to work all the time. But she knew that wasn't it. He meant the thing they never talked about.

'Ed?'

He said nothing more. He disappeared up the stairs. Grace stood on the bottom step unable to move. She heard the shower start.

Grace waited in the bedroom. She sat on the edge of the bed and listened to the water running until it stopped.

He came into the room eventually. Wordless. Changing into a t-shirt.

'Did you mean when I left when Henry was a baby?' she said.

'I shouldn't have said anything. I apologise.'

Grace felt like a cold light had been switched on, everything illuminated, grotesque, unflattering.

'You got to go home after the birth.' Grace's voice was a whisper. It was all she had left. 'You had three nights sleeping in your own bed to recover.'

'Please, Grace. Enough. I said I was sorry.'

He didn't sound sorry.

'The baby slept for two hours after he was born,' Grace said. 'And after that, he was awake, hungry, but the milk hadn't come in. So he cried and cried.'

'Grace.'

'I asked when I could have a rest and the midwife laughed. She actually laughed and made a joke. As if it was somehow funny that I *nearly died* and then wouldn't get a night off to recover for eighteen years. The baby's healthy, that's the main thing. Everyone said that. The baby is fine, so Mum can stop being such a needy, flaky bitch and get on with it.'

Ed sat up. 'Nobody said that.'

'They didn't have to. Joan called me six times a day claiming she was supporting me when really she was just checking I hadn't smothered the baby.'

Grace regretted it the moment she said it—not because it wasn't true, but because she saw how it cut into him.

'Grace.'

'I went away for two nights. Two. I made sure you knew I was okay.'

'Fine. You want me to talk about it? It was the most terrifying forty-eight hours of my entire life. I'm not sure you realise that. I'm not sure you think about what anything is like for me. Ever. Or care. Last year you couldn't wait to get out of the country—as soon as you were allowed on a plane you were out of here. And I'm always waiting, perpetually waiting, without knowing anything about what you do or who you're with when you're away.'

'I'm not even going to dignify that with a response.'

'Well, you don't seem to miss me. Ever since you left us that day I've been dreading the day you'll do it again and not come back.'

'I would never do that.'

'But you did. Don't you get that? Nish is right: you love being needed as long as you don't have to give anything *real* back. Anything that you can't control you run from. I'm done with it.'

He left after that. Walked out, closing the door quietly behind him so he wouldn't wake the kids.

44

DURING THE SLEEPLESS NIGHT THAT FOLLOWED, GRACE THOUGHT SHE heard Ed's footsteps on the stairs several times, but he never returned to her side. She tried to imagine what might happen between them next so she could prepare. Nothing came to her.

In the morning May asked where Ed was and Grace told her he was sleeping, not to be disturbed. Henry didn't have any questions. Not a single one. His eyes barely left the pages of his book as he ate breakfast. He didn't need to say that he knew everything was wrong.

Grace did all the morning things in an absent-minded haze, slow and muddled. She waited for Ed to walk in. He didn't.

All the blinds of his studio were drawn. This was a small comfort—he hadn't *left* left, he'd slept in his studio. She hovered outside the door, raised a hand to knock and thought about how she never knocked when she came in, she was always welcome to be wherever he was. She could just say, 'Hello?' as she opened the door. That would be friendly. She didn't feel friendly. She didn't knock either. The door opened anyway.

'I need to go and get some stuff from inside,' he said, avoiding her eyes.

'Okay.'

Neither of them moved. She thought he might apologise; he was always the first. 'Can you take the kids to the park or something?' he said.

'Why?'

'I don't want them to see me leaving with my stuff. I'm going to Dad's.'

No.

No.

No.

This would be the time for her to speak, say anything at all to halt the thing that was rolling towards her.

'I've had time to think,' he said. 'And I think . . . What I think is . . .' Grace could see Henry in the way he was trying to put his words together carefully. 'What I think is that I need to be away from you for a while.'

Grace's hurt flared white-hot.

'Because of what happened nine years ago?'

Ed closed his eyes momentarily and took a breath.

'No, not because of that—because of everything in the nine years since.'

'You get to paint because of me. You don't have to scrape and—'

'You think I couldn't make a career without you? Wow. Thanks, Grace.'

'You know what I mean.'

'Yeah, I think I do.'

'You get to live in one of the most beautiful places in the country, you get a beautiful studio, and you still find ways to be unhappy with it. As if you're compromising so I can work like any man would.'

'So you're saying I'm a sexist prick because I miss my wife. Is that really who you think I am?'

In that small moment Grace didn't know what she thought he was. But the moment passed. He was Ed. He was her Ed.

He was looking at her like she was a stranger.

◎

Ed took his things; not much, but enough. A few days later he came back while Grace was out and took more. He left a note about his plans to rent an apartment. And a studio somewhere. Grace felt as if her entire world with him had been revealed as a flimsy film set. Push on a wall and it fell over. Everything just a trick.

A chaotic week passed. Lotte couldn't step in to fill every gap. Grace was supposed to be in Bruges with Ada only another week later. She couldn't make all the puzzle pieces of an existence without Ed fit together.

Grace didn't tell Ada herself that she wouldn't be coming. She left Tony a message saying there was a family emergency and he'd need to find someone to fill the gap for Ada. When Ada tried to call, Grace let it go to voicemail.

The person Grace desperately needed to speak to about what had happened with Ed, if it could be the way it used to be, was Nish.

45

APRIL 2022

DOROTHY LISTENED WHILE GRACE RECOUNTED EVERYTHING THAT HAD happened between herself, Ed and Nish. At some point she had given Grace a tissue. Grace twisted and twisted it until it was all tiny little pieces.

'Don't be the woman who's better at her job than she is at being a wife and a mother,' Grace said.

Dorothy said nothing and Grace wondered if she agreed that Grace was a terrible wife and a worse mother.

'We can't fix it,' Grace said. 'How do we fix it?'

Dorothy shook her head. Her eyes, usually bright, inquisitive, darting, were dull.

'I've always thought that being a mother is purely trying and praying,' Dorothy said. 'You try and try and try, and pray that you get something right.' Dorothy waved her hands around, as if trying to find words. 'Yes, there are things I missed out on in life. But raising you? That wasn't a mistake. Look at you.' Although

Dorothy wasn't smiling, Grace was sure she was doing her best to say that she was proud of her.

'Thank you.'

'You can't have everything. Nobody can. You can only make sure that you love what you've got.'

'I've built so much, Mum. I've loved so much of it.'

They sat in silence. Grace expected Dorothy to say that she should be getting to bed.

'Do you still see the colours?' Dorothy asked.

'What?'

'When you hear songs. When you were little you told me that "Purple Haze" was the wrong name for the Jimi Hendrix song because it was actually lime green. You were so odd like that. I didn't know what to make of it and I've wondered if it happens still.'

'Sometimes. Not really.'

'That's a shame.'

◎

Morning. Grace thought her mother might sleep in, but Dorothy had already set the dining table and was fluttering about in the kitchen. Warren was waiting at his usual seat, reading glasses on the tip of his nose, perusing the local paper. 'She's decided everyone will want omelettes,' he said.

Dorothy arrived with a plate for Grace.

'I thought it would be nice to breakfast in here,' she said. Dorothy's prolific use of the word 'breakfast' as a verb was a recent development. As if she were the lady of a grand manor in a nineteenth-century novel or, with enough small adjustments of this nature, she could transform herself into the Queen.

Grace took the seat that had always been hers. She could see Henry and May in the lounge room, mesmerised by the television.

'I put *The Sound of Music* on for them,' Dorothy said. 'They said they'd never seen it! Henry said he only watches YouTube!'

'I do keep an eye on it. He doesn't just watch whatever he wants.'

This wasn't entirely true.

'Yes, but not to have seen *The Sound of Music*,' she tutted, pouring tea into a china cup and pushing the saucer across to Grace.

'One of the great injustices of their existence,' Warren muttered.

Dorothy rolled her eyes.

'I'd like it noted that I told her not to wait up for you,' continued Warren. 'And I was ignored.'

'Oh, for goodness sake. I was reading.'

'Ask her what she's reading.'

'Stop it. Honestly. It's for book club.'

'*War and Peace*. How long have you been reading it?' Warren didn't wait for an answer. 'They meet once a year at the bowling club. Last year Pamela had to be rolled into a taxi afterwards.'

'She was light-headed! She'd just had her booster! And it was only two bottles of chardonnay between the four of us. How many times—'

'I asked her which character she identifies with,' Warren said. 'Do you know what she said?'

'Warren, that is enough,' said Dorothy.

'Napoleon,' said Warren.

'What I meant was I feel that Tolstoy—'

'Look how much she loves throwing Tolstoy into a conversation.'

Dorothy raised her voice to drown him out. 'I feel that Tolstoy was taking the mickey a bit. Making fun of Napoleon.'

'And you identify with that, do you?' asked Warren. 'Funny thing is,' he said to Grace, 'I can believe she would invade another country if she had the chance.'

'What country, Mum?'

Dorothy was trying to frown and bristle. She picked up her tea, paused before taking a sip. 'I've always liked New Zealand,' she said.

Warren stood up from the table, folded the newspaper and tucked it under his arm. He gave his wife a kiss on the top of her head as he left the table. 'That's my girl.'

'You better not take that into the toilet with you,' Dorothy called after him.

'I'll be careful not to drop it in.'

'Oh, my goodness, Warren.'

'Oh, my goodness, Dorothy.'

Grace's phone rang. Furry Friends Animal Hospital.

Julie the vet was in fine spirits. She had wonderful news! Slinky had not only survived the night but was feeling so well that she was awake and barking her head off.

'She's very vocal, isn't she?' said Julie. 'I think she's just so happy to be alive. She'll be unsteady on her feet for a good while, so you'll have to carry her around a lot. And you can buy her a little pram to get her out and about.'

Grace ended the call with as much enthusiasm as she could muster. Of course she would carry Slinky wherever Slinky needed to go! Prams for dogs! What a great idea!

'Do you have coffee?' Grace asked Dorothy.

'No, we go out for coffee.'

'Every day?'

'Every bloody day,' shouted Warren from the hallway.

'I've worked very hard my whole life,' Dorothy said. 'I shouldn't have to make my own coffee.'

Grace needed caffeine. The kids were happy in front of the TV and Dorothy said she didn't mind at all if Grace took herself out for a coffee as long as she brought one back for her.

Grace got into the Lotus and checked her phone for a message from Ed. She was always checking for a message from Ed when there never was one. The knock on the car window startled her. Grace looked up and there was Trent. Sheepish-looking. Crumpled-looking. Like he'd had roughly the same amount of sleep as Grace had. She wound down the window.

'I need to say something,' he said.

'Have you been there all night?'

His van was parked up the street.

'I didn't trust myself to keep driving. Too tired, too many beers. And I wanted to catch you because—'

'No.'

'You don't know what I'm going to say!'

'Yes, I do and the answer's no. I'm not in love with you.'

Trent shook his head. 'Please. This is important. I want you to know that I waited a long time for you to call. A very long time. A year. That's a long time when you're twenty-one. But I also knew why you didn't call and I want to thank you, because you not doing that, well, I think it changed me. I became less of an arsehole.'

'What are you talking? Why would *I* have called *you*?'

'I asked Dorothy to tell you that I knew I'd made a dickhead mistake,' Trent said. 'I came here the next day looking for you. I asked her to get you to call me and let me know where you were in Europe and I would come and meet you.'

Trent's words, fluttering darting things, swooped into Grace, dismantling a song she'd thought she knew by heart.

'Could we just—' But he stopped, reading the look on her face. 'Are you okay?' Comprehension dawned. 'Did Dorothy not tell you?' he asked.

'I need you to leave. Please.'

'I can't believe she never told you I came here! What a bitch. You thought I'd just dumped you and you never heard from me again?'

Grace realised that the reason Dorothy hadn't wanted Grace to go out with Trent the night before wasn't because she didn't trust Grace's judgement; she was afraid that if Grace found out what she had done twenty years ago, their relationship would be ruined. Maybe it would have been. If Grace had found that out in the year after she arrived in London, she would have screamed and shouted at Dorothy. She would have flown back home for Trent. Given up everything for him. No Tony. No career. No Ada. No Ed.

'Don't call my mother a bitch. You did dump me. You left me at the airport with my bags all packed, ready for the exciting future you had all mapped out. And you never showed up.'

'I told her to tell you I'd come looking for you!'

'You thought I wouldn't get on the plane without you?'

'I felt so much love for you. I know it's crazy, but I still do! I told her to—'

'Love isn't a feeling, Trent. It's a verb.'

Grace could tell he didn't know what a verb was. She was too tired to explain it to him as he was now: a forty-two-year-old man who had spent the last twenty years of his life clinging to a juvenile, romanticised theory of love to justify his wasted talent and to fuel what Grace would bet were mediocre songs.

And now—oh, wow, he was actually going to do it—Trent held out a card with a QR code.

'There's a link to my music. Will you have a listen?'

'You want me to give you a record deal?'

'I just—'

'You owe Shaleah an apology.'

Grace put the window up and backed out of the driveway. Left him standing there in his vintage ripped denim and Pixies t-shirt, his breeze-whipped morning hair aglow in the morning sun. Like a matinee Kurt Cobain tribute act.

46

ADA

THE LAST PERSON ADA EXPECTED A PHONE CALL FROM WAS DOROTHY. It was mid-morning—so it must have been late at night in Australia—and Ada was alone in her lavish St Pancras apartment. Before she met Grace she would never have dreamed of living anywhere like it. Back then, she'd been terrified to get on a stage and always spewed her guts up beforehand. She worried that the people up the front would notice the stink of her breath while she sang. She would do everything she could—mouthwash, gum, those weird mouth sprays old blokes use—to rid her mouth of the residual vomit stench, but she was certain it remained. On the night she first saw Grace, sixteen years ago at Drop, Ada hadn't been able to eat anything since breakfast, so bad were her nerves. It was a surprise how much came up when—just before she was due onstage—she heaved over the grotty toilet bowl.

Drop wasn't a great venue. The bar staff were tossers, and the acoustics were rubbish because it didn't matter when half the acts were screeching desperados. Cut-price Sex Pistols or, worse, someone claiming to have something to do with jazz.

(No one should have anything to do with jazz if they didn't know a thing beyond Miles Davis.) However, it was small, and because Ada had played there once she seemed to be able to do it again, whereas anywhere else she was always pulling out at the last minute and nobody would book her anymore. Drop always booked her and it always sold out, putting something in her pocket, however paltry. It also wasn't far from her ma's; Ada could drop Susie off, do the gig, and crash there afterwards. It was possible she'd have to live there permanent if something didn't change soon. The money from Sammy had been trickling away. It had seemed a sizeable payout at the time, the compo. The company he worked for must have seen her as this young girl who'd get excited over a few thousand quid in her piggy bank. And she was, that was the shame of it. Well, not excited. It is not exciting when the father of your little one gets crushed doing his bloody job. It's eviscerating. That was the only word she could find that came within a shadow of doing justice to the pain of it. Before, when Sammy was around, Ada used to sing about whatever rubbish popped into her head. Stupid love songs. She wrote the words on the bus after work. They meant nothing. But after Sammy died? That was when it happened. That was when she changed and the songs began to mean something. It was the only good thing to come of his death. And yeah, she would trade it to have him back.

That night at Drop, Ada had come onstage and almost didn't even open her mouth because of the stench in her nostrils. They'd all smell it, the entire front row. The lads were doing their best to cover for her; they kept the beat rolling over the gap where her voice should be. It was the thought of Susie that made her sing, the thought of her and Susie in her ma's poky sodding flat. Ada closed her eyes, because sometimes that helped. She sang and she was doing all right for two songs, but then she got the wobbles, feeling dizzy 'cause she wasn't taking in enough breath. She opened her eyes and saw a girl up front, a cool-looking chick, swaying to the beat and bawling her eyes out, like the music meant something real to her. It made Ada keep singing.

◎

Grace had the look of someone who could make things happen. Sharp, like. But she was nervous when she met Ada that day in the park. Speaking very quick, like she was worried Ada might run away. And Ada almost did, until she remembered the way this girl had cried to the sound of Ada's music. It was the best decision of her life to trust Grace. All the drama Ada created: mess with the press, the fuck-ups with Charlie, the gigs she'd bombed—Grace had handled all of it. She would swoop in and put all the pieces back in place. Ada often felt like Frankenstein's monster—bits and pieces of herself cobbled together. It was Grace who would look at her and tell her she was beautiful.

Ada owed her everything.

She used to think that it was the men absent from her life who made her the way she was: her dead boyfriend; the father who left before she was born; Charlie, who she'd driven away time and time again. But more likely it was the women who believed in her when she was crippled by doubt. It was her mother, who stood by her when she had Susie at seventeen; it was her little girls; it was Grace, always there for her, night and day. Crossing seas for Ada. Leaving behind the man who loved her for Ada.

Ada didn't even realise she had Dorothy's number in her phone until the screen lit up with her name. Ada must have given it to her all those years ago when they'd gone high street shopping together. Harrods, H&M, Topshop, Cos. Dorothy loved H&M;

she'd tried on a thousand hats and modelled each one for Ada. God, she was a laugh. When Ada told Grace how much fun they'd had Grace had said, 'She's never like that with me.' Now, when the phone rang, Ada panicked. Something awful must have happened. And the panic got even worse when she actually answered, because Dorothy was panicking too.

'Oh, thank goodness,' Dorothy said. After that she said many things very quickly, most of which Ada couldn't understand, and Ada had to ask her outright if Grace was dead.

'No,' said Dorothy. 'But things are terrible for her. And I just can't think what to do about it.' Dorothy told Ada that Ed had left and Grace couldn't do anything to make it right. 'Because you can't, can you? You can't do anything right when you're a woman needed by everyone,' Dorothy said. 'The only thing worse than that is to be needed by no one. You might think that sounds liberating, but it's not.'

◎

After the conversation, Ada sat back and pondered if life with back-up dancers really would be all that bad.

47

GRACE

ED HAD PICKED THE KIDS UP FROM DOROTHY AND WARREN'S AT EXACTLY the time he said he would, Sunday night after dinner. No one else would have noticed the way Grace was waiting for him. Even hours before, she had been listening for the sound of his truck. For the entire time that they'd been together, the sound of him arriving home had given her warmth. *Ed's here.* But since February, the anticipation had made her feel queasy. He would see the Lotus in the driveway and think of it as proof that she didn't need him, she only needed the trimmings of her work. That, and he'd worry about the safety rating.

When he arrived, Ed said nothing about the car. Instead he put on a convincing act for the kids and Grace's parents, hanging on to every word as the kids gave a thorough recount of Slinky's ordeal. When Henry told Ed how a guy called Trent had driven them because Grace had fainted and hit her head, Ed shot Grace a brief look of concern.

'I'm fine,' she said.

Thankfully, the kids rolled on, past the details of the man who had driven them, on to questions about camping. Ed picked up the part of excited dad flawlessly: marshmallows, kayaks, of course they would make a fire. Of course he had already set up the tent. Of course they could stay up late. But they would have to be up early in the morning to see the kangaroos. Kangaroos! Grace watched it all and saw how the performance wearied him. She noticed the length of every beat before he responded to the questions, and the way he moved, too quick, too eager to put on the happy show. Tiny things nobody else would see. She saw him.

While the kids were saying their goodbyes to Dorothy and Warren (a long process due to Warren's instigation of a tickle fight), Grace helped Ed take the bags outside to the muddy Land Rover. She set them on the driveway and waited as Ed arranged the back of the truck. The tag of his jumper was sticking out and, without thinking, Grace tucked it in as he turned to her. Ed paused. Grace was standing very close to him. He didn't move away.

'You hit your head?'

'I was tired and in a bit of shock after Slinky.'

'Are you sure you're okay? You should get it checked out.'

'Maybe. Probably.'

'Definitely. You care about Slinky?' He was teasing her.

'We're very attached now.'

'Bonded through shared trauma?' he asked.

'Yes. Although I'm disappointed they didn't remove her voice box during surgery.'

Ed laughed. Grace held on to the sound and the sight of him there, so close to her.

◎

Grace drove home in silence. When she pulled up in front of her home, she saw that none of the lights were on. The timer hadn't done its job. It was the kind of thing Ed looked after and Grace had no idea how to check if it was working. Grace sat in the car. She wound down the window. Outside, the April air remained absurdly warm and, despite the change in season, the cicadas were still chirping, wringing as much life as possible out of their final days. Grace started the car again and reversed out of the gates.

◎

Even though the harbour tunnel would have been more direct, Grace took the bridge. She wanted the feeling of the dark water under her, she wanted the lights glancing off the windshield. Ed had chosen Alexandria because it had the studio space he needed and it wasn't too far for when he came to collect the kids. He was ever practical. It had once been a mattress factory, the place where his studio was: cavernous, with a high, raked ceiling. Grace had never been there before. She parked the car and walked the length of the building's facade until she found the right door. No keyhole; a code lock instead.

Ed had a terrible memory for passwords, pin numbers, anything like that. Grace punched in Henry's birth date. No luck. She tried May's.

Bingo.

The woody scent of oil paint met Grace. A warm, golden sort of smell. After feeling blindly around on the wall, Grace found a switch and the space flooded with white light. Tubes of paint in caulking guns. More tubes, unopened in their boxes. Old tins crammed with brushes, large bottles of turps and smaller ones of linseed oil. Jars half full of mysterious liquids, lids screwed on tight. Palette knives. Sponges. An old bucket full of rags. In the centre of the room was one painting, large and in the proportion that Ed always called square-adjacent. It was so big that it needed two easels to hold it. The canvas was covered with a loose sheet which was propped a little away from the canvas's surface so it wouldn't stick to the wet paint. Grace recognised the sheet; it was an old king-size one from their bed, relegated to the home studio long ago.

Grace walked around the canvas and found that on the other side was another, smaller easel. Beside it a little table cluttered with tubes of acrylic paints, a tin of pastel crayons, a shoebox of coloured pencils. May's pencils. A stack of papers of various sizes was weighed down with a rock. Grace picked up the rock and held it in her palm. She remembered the time she had talked to Henry on the phone just after he started school. He told her about a rock he had found. 'It's shaped like Darth Vader's helmet,' he had told her. 'It broke in half but Dad is going to glue it back together.' He had too. Grace had returned home from Austria, or wherever the hell she'd been, and Henry had showed her the rock, already repaired by Ed.

Grace looked through the paintings and drawings, spreading them out over the floor. They were all May's. So many that all the walls could have been papered with their beautiful chaos.

The armchair Ed had always had in his studio, the one shipped all the way from London, sat facing the big sheet-covered canvas. On it was a sketchbook. Grace knew she shouldn't, but she needed to feel Ed. She opened the book. There were drawings of May and Henry. Wobbly and awkward at first, but better and more confident as the pages turned. And finally, a sketch of someone else. The drawing was very pared back, only a few careful pencil marks. It was a sketch of Grace.

She went to the painting and pulled up the edge of the sheet. Carefully, she unveiled the canvas.

Grace sat down in the armchair and took the painting in. She let the abstraction swallow her up. The colour, the texture. It was dark. So dark, but there, in the bottom right-hand corner, was a thread of light.

Grace breathed the painting in. She listened to its song.

ACKNOWLEDGEMENTS

NOVEL WRITING INVOLVES WORKING WITH MANY FICTIONAL PEOPLE, but there are lots of real people behind the scenes who help turn a story into a book. Thank you to my extraordinary super-agent Grace Heifetz at Left Bank Literary for reading many redrafts and championing this story from the very beginning. Thanks to Cate Paterson for seeing the potential in *Better Days* and embracing it with enthusiasm. Thanks also to my copyeditor Ali Lavau and her extraordinary eye for detail. I have tried to keep everything within the story as close as possible to real life, however I did take some liberties: cicadas don't chirp in April, and Wayne Thiebald's *Lemon Meringue Pie* was not on loan to the Tate Modern in 2008.

Thank you to my readers: Katie, Celli, Carla, Lauren, Bec and Steph for their early feedback and encouragement. Thanks to Celli for many things, including her East London knowledge (any mistakes are my own), her shoutline used on the cover and especially the anecdote about toddler snot. Thanks to Steph for allowing Henry to have Willis's eyebrows. I must also thank my sons: Eli for his shoplifting tendencies as a toddler, and Ayrton for allowing me to use his anecdote about the Darth Vader rock.

Most of all, thank you to Nathan for the love amid the chaos.